THE MAURYAN

A management graduate, Komal Bhanver began her career in the information technology industry. After working for almost a decade, she decided to take a sabbatical to raise her children. Post that, she has worked in the education sector as the director of PeopleFirst. She is the co-founder of The Next Milestone Technologies, an organization with a vision to enhance employability. The author in her awakened quite accidently but, to her delight, she immensely enjoyed the process of weaving stories. She lives in Mumbai with her husband, two children and a pet Labrador.

THE MAURYAN

THE LEGEND OF ASHOKA

KOMAL BHANVER

hachette
INDIA

First published in India in 2017 by Hachette India
(Registered name: Hachette Book Publishing India Pvt. Ltd)
An Hachette UK company
www.hachetteindia.com

SRD

ISBN 978-93-5195-053-0

Hachette Book Publishing India Pvt. Ltd
4th & 5th Floors, Corporate Centre,
Plot No. 94, Sector 44, Gurgaon – 122003, India

Typeset in Palatino Linotype by SÜRYA, New Delhi

Printed and bound in India by
Manipal Technologies Limited, Manipal

MIX
Paper | Supporting responsible forestry
FSC™ C043100
www.fsc.org

With the blessings of our parents,
Laju and Ram Shahdadpuri;
Lilly and Manmohan Singh Bhanver.

I dedicate this book to my husband, Jagmohan, and our many evenings of reading sessions.
Without his encouragement, the journey and adventures of *The Mauryan* would never have begun.

Prologue

Ashoka trudged on aimlessly, his senses deadened. From a deep corner of his mind, a voice was telling him that his throat was parched. His mouth felt like he had swallowed the embers from a raging fire. The voice inside his head pleaded to be heard while there was still life within him. But the voice could not break through the haze of agony that enveloped him. At last, when he dropped down to his knees in sheer fatigue, the wailing within his mind became audible; it occurred to him that he hadn't had even a sip of water in the past several *horas*.

He looked around, not really knowing what it was that he was searching for. There were only ominous shadows whose presence in his path was ubiquitous. He racked his brains to recollect why he was here. But all explanations eluded him. It was an eerie feeling to be walking aimlessly. In the past, there had always been a purpose to his actions.

Ashoka looked up towards the sky, hoping it would offer him a clue. *Even the sky is heartless today*, he reflected bitterly.

Is it morning already? he wondered as he saw specks of light seeping through the thick foliage of giant trees. His warrior instincts never deserted him. They were always there, even if only at a subconscious level.

He tried to moisten his mouth with his own saliva. But his tongue felt leathery inside the dry cavity. The feeling of thirst seemed to overpower every other sensation all at once.

Water! I need water, he thought desperately as the voice within his head turned into a scream of agony. His warrior instincts told him a shutdown was imminent. Systematically and surely, all his bodily functions would soon stop. The blood flowing through his veins had already slowed down, as had his heartbeat.

A thorny shrub jabbed his arms. But he scarcely noticed. His legs felt as if he were dragging an elephant tied to a rope behind him. Finally, darkness descended like a dark cloak, enveloping him within its fold.

Ashoka spat the dirt out of his mouth as he used the last vestiges of his strength to drag himself up from the ground. With an explosion of extraordinary willpower, he walked ahead one step at a time.

As a sudden blaze of bright light struck from overhead, Ashoka covered his eyes involuntarily. The forest was behind him now. His survival instincts surfaced as he heard the gentle ripple of water somewhere close by. The inviting vision of fresh water spurred him on.

The water was hidden from sight by a pile of large rocks. Gritting his teeth, he forced himself to climb over their craggy surface. As he reached the top, he felt the hot rays of the sun falling on his back more cruelly than ever before. *It must be well past noon,* he considered, squinting his eyes.

Yes! He sighed in relief as the pristine waters of the stream gushed before his eyes. Ashoka rolled rather than climbed down the rocks. Summoning all his strength, he ran towards the water. Lying down on his stomach, he dunked his head in the icy cold stream taking in huge gulps of water.

His thirst now quenched, he became aware of a reflection in the water. But it was not his own image that he saw mirrored there. It was her! She was laughing at him, jesting with him like she always did. Her hair blew across her beautiful face and he could see her lovely forehead, with her favourite red bindi in the centre. For an inexplicable reason, Ashoka's eyes were drawn to the scarlet coloured bindi that seemed to glow unnaturally. And then, before his very eyes, the scarlet dot on her forehead started to grow bigger…and bigger. The image stopped laughing, as if aware that the time for jesting was over. As Ashoka looked on horrified, the scarlet dot in the center of her forehead burst and ripples of blood spread over the surface of the water.

'No…*no*!' Ashoka screamed. *This can't be!* He raged in frustration as he frantically plunged his hands into the water to hold the woman's face. But her face had been completely obliterated by the wave of scarlet floating on the surface. Ashoka pulled his hands out of the water – they were red… with her blood.

'No!' he screamed again as he slumped to the ground.

1

The *chautha prahar* of the day had just commenced. But the unseasonal storm raging over the Mauryan kingdom cast a pall of darkness on the city.

As if in defiance of the dark and dreary exterior, the palace was brightly lit. The torches adorning the walls lent the rooms a warm golden glow. The multi-storeyed royal building was made of the finest wood, and the walls, polished to perfection, shone in a dull gold hue.

Inside, in a private discussion hall, Bindusara was conducting a meeting with Senapati Ajaya and Mahamantri Radheya. This was a 20-pillared room – a smaller version of the 100-pillared hall used for public court proceedings. The carvings on the walls captured the stately life led by the royal family.

In sharp contrast to the elaborate surroundings, Bindusara, the great emperor of the Mauryan empire, was dressed simply. His jet-black, well-oiled hair fell flat on his forehead, the long spiked ends almost touching his shoulders. His *uttariya* was a plain piece of linen, flung casually across his broad shoulders. The thin muslin of the *antariya,* the garment covering the lower part of his body, barely concealed his athletic legs. The only embellishment that gave away his status was the ruby-inlaid *kantha,* a flat, short necklace that he wore on his otherwise bare chest.

He scratched his chin thoughtfully. 'I think it is time we expanded the empire in the south.' The reflection of the flames of a lamp danced in his small brown eyes as he observed the reactions of his mahamantri and senapati.

Mahamantri Radheya exchanged a quick look with Senapati Ajaya. The Mauryan forces had not waged a war in several years. It hadn't been necessary. The two men wondered what had happened to warrant a war now.

'Sometimes it is necessary to wage war in order to maintain peace,' Bindusara said quietly. Radheya and Ajaya were used to Bindusara's cryptic statements – more often than not, the emperor left it to them to figure out the meaning of his words.

It took the young and pleasant-faced Radheya a couple of *kashtas* to realize what Bindusara meant. He nodded slowly. 'Yes, it is time.'

Bindusara reclined on the silk cushions, knowing he could depend on his astute mahamantri. Radheya looked in his direction, seeking permission to speak. Bindusara nodded.

'The old Raja Mahajan of Mahishur is no more. His twin sons Kavin and Aagney are fighting for the throne. Young blood is frequently like an astra fired aimlessly, causing more damage than good. It is imperative that we take Mahishur under the Mauryan empire before their dispute spreads to other nations and finally lands at our doorstep. Today, the two may be fighting for Mahishur. But tomorrow. . .who has seen tomorrow? They may set eyes on our border states,' said Radheya.

Ajaya nodded in agreement. Sitting ramrod straight – the posture of a man who had spent his entire adult life fighting battles for his country – he ran his fingers over his peppery hair, his expression thoughtful. Now in his mid-forties, he still had the vigour of a man half his age.

'Our spies tell us that Mahishur's senapati and their chief minister are in favour of Aagney as the new king,' Radheya added as an afterthought.

Ajaya finally spoke. 'We have had a long era of peace.

Intense training, however, has ensured that our soldiers have not grown lazy. We are ready for war. The rift between the brothers will work in our favour. We can propose to make Kavin the governor of Mahishur, provided he helps us gain control of the city.'

Bindusara did not comment immediately. He shot a glance at Radheya, who looked pensive. 'What's on your mind?' Bindusara asked the mahamantri.

'I think that a person who can betray his own brother can betray you too, Raje. I would never be comfortable backing such a person as the governor.'

'What you say is true,' admitted Ajaya. 'But this is the easiest way to win the war against Mahishur. We can make Kavin the governor but keep him under surveillance until we are assured of his loyalty.'

Radheya nodded silently, still unconvinced.

Senapati Ajaya took Radheya's silence as acquiescence and continued. 'Mahishur has a large army. To meet the might of their forces, we will need to take a significant chunk of our army with us.' He turned towards Bindusara. 'And we will need to leave a large enough force here, in order to quell any rebellion in your absence.'

'What do our spies tell us about Mahishur?' Bindusara asked in his resonant voice.

'Mahishur is incredibly well protected,' replied Ajaya. 'I will go over the details and share the strategy with you shortly.'

'Very well,' conceded Bindusara who usually listened to his close aides before taking a decision. 'We will meet after seven sunsets to discuss the details.'

The two men bowed and left the hall. Bindusara sat motionless, his face reflective as he examined Radheya's viewpoint. He knew Radheya would always be true to the Mauryan empire. His loyalty was first to the empire and then to Bindusara. 'The eternal giver' was how Bindusara thought of him. Despite his youth and relative lack of experience, Radheya never shied away from expressing a point of view completely opposite to that of the emperor's. That was what endeared him to Bindusara.

The first rays of dawn lent the sky an orange hue. Bindusara effortlessly mounted his stallion and started at a canter. The early morning air invigorated him. Once in a while, he gave in to the luxury of riding where he pleased, without a destination in mind. Now, his alert eyes took in everything as he rode through the streets of his beloved Pataliputra. The capital of the Mauryan empire was a large fortified city that was virtually impregnable. A wide moat, 150 *dandas* in breadth, spanned the perimeter of the city, making it effectively impossible to breach security. The moat acted as a defensive measure against invasions, and also served as a sewage disposal mechanism for the city. The city had 570 towers, and a large number of soldiers were required to guard these, even during times of peace. There were four gates, dedicated to Yama, Indra, Kshatriya and Brahma. These gates were used for different purposes.

Bindusara galloped ahead, leaving his bodyguards covered in a cloud of dust as they tried in vain to keep the emperor in sight. The guards at the Kshatriya gate stepped aside to let him pass. The thick forest whizzed past and Bindusara soon chanced upon a clearing, on which he espied a small hut. An uncanny feeling compelled him to slow down. He caught sight of a figure just outside the hut, sitting under a banyan tree. It was a hermit – he sat cross-legged, deep in meditation.

In that moment Bindusara envied the hermit his aura of peace and serenity. He had a handsome countenance and appeared to Bindusara to be too young to lead such an austere life. *What could possibly have prompted this young man to forsake the pleasures of youth?* Bindusara wondered. Not wanting to disturb the ascetic, he turned his horse around and left abruptly.

Unknown to Bindusara, the hermit had sensed his presence long before he entered the clearing. Years of penance had sharpened the hermit's awareness. As he now watched the king ride away, his mind inexplicably went back to a strange episode he had witnessed a few years ago, before he came to live in this forest clearing by the city.

He was then living alone in the forest with only wild animals for company. In a cave, not far from where the hermit stayed, a small pride of lions had made their home. The lions frequently crossed the hermit's path, but strangely they never bothered him. The aura emanating from the hermit possibly let the beasts know they had nothing to fear from him. The pride comprised a large male lion and two lionesses. One of the lionesses had a cub. The cub appeared strong and intelligent, and it was apparent he would grow up into a strong and healthy adult. The hermit observed that the lion was exceedingly possessive and fond of the cub.

In time, the other lioness conceived too. When it was time to deliver, she came near the hermit's clearing and quietly gave birth to a cub behind the privacy of the bushes. The hermit was the first human to lay eyes on this cub. He saw that the cub was a pitiful creature, with eyes tightly shut and limbs that looked lifeless. But he was breathing. This seemed to be enough for the lioness.

The hermit was amazed to see how gentle the lioness was with her weak cub. She seemed to feel that she and her cub were safe in the vicinity of the hermit's dwelling. She had not yet taken the cub to meet the father. At the end of one week, the cub finally opened his eyes, and gently prodded by his mother, took his first steps. His gait was unsteady.

'He will surely not survive for long…unless he has the will to do so,' thought the hermit sadly. The lioness seemed to read the hermit's mind and she now prodded the young cub more firmly. The cub took another few steps and then sat down, tired. He looked up at his mother, blinking in the harsh sun. They appeared to communicate

without speaking. After several unsuccessful attempts, the cub made a stupendous effort to drag himself up, and walked around with a little more attitude.

The next sunset, the lioness took him to meet the father. The lion showed no interest in the cub. He rejected him outright and walked away. The older, healthier cub from the other lioness looked at his stepbrother with interest. The little one bore the scrutiny with ease. Finally, the older cub came nearer and knocked him down in a display of strength. The new-born cub appeared not to mind. He thought it was a game.

Fascinated, the hermit keenly observed the pride over the next year. He noticed that when food was scarce, the younger cub's mother relinquished her share in favour of the little one, who rapidly flourished under her care. The lion never let the younger cub climb over him and play with his mane, and frequently yanked him away impatiently. The lioness, however, took the cub with her on hunts and soon he was steady enough.

The two cubs grew bigger and displayed fierce rivalry. They constantly challenged each other to races across the hills. The older cub always won by a wide margin and seemed to mock the younger one. The younger one seemed not to mind at all. The hermit noticed that the winning margin seemed to reduce each sunset. Then came the day when the hermit saw them scampering up the hill with the younger one surely and steadily gaining on the older one and finally taking the lead. The lion looked on, unmoving, at both his sons.

The hermit smiled as they disappeared across the horizon. That was the last he saw of them, for the very next sunset he moved to another place, in his incessant search for truth.

The ascetic shook his head, wondering why this memory had flashed unbidden into his mind at the sight of the emperor. But he knew they were linked somehow.

'Time will tell...for time is the keeper of all secrets,' he thought to himself and smiled.

Seven sunsets had swiftly passed since Bindusara had called the meeting in his palace. Senapati Ajaya had given considerable thought to the strategy for war. Mahamantri Radheya and he now waited in the discussion hall for Bindusara. Ajaya glanced out at the palace gardens that boasted of 20 man-made pools harbouring exotic fishes. Flora from the world over found place in this haven of beauty and luxury.

It was late afternoon when the emperor joined them. He looked rested after his customary siesta. Bindusara gazed expectantly at them and finally focused his attention on Ajaya.

Taking the cue, Ajaya quickly shared his strategy. 'We will require a quarter of our army for this war. This would mean taking along with us 200,000 *pada* soldiers, 15,000 *turanga,* 500 *rathas* and 2,000 war *gaja*. This force will suffice to rout the Mahishur army if we launch a direct attack. The fort of Mahishur is surrounded on all sides by the Chamundi forest which offers it natural protection. However, the same forest that protects them can also provide us cover for a stealthy attack.'

'How long will it take us to march to the fort?' inquired Bindusara.

'Normally it shouldn't take more than 35 sunsets.' Ajaya considered his words before continuing. 'However, weighed down with the non-fighting men such as cooks, cleaners and tent pitchers, not to mention their extra baggage, we will most likely make it there in 45 sunsets.'

Bindusara pondered this information, without responding.

'I am hoping we can persuade Kavin to betray his twin in order to ascend to power,' added Ajaya quietly.

'The question is – what will we do with him even if he can be persuaded to betray his own brother. I continue to have serious reservations about letting him govern Mahishur,' said Radheya in a grave tone.

'Ah, Radheya. The best of people are swayed by the greed for power. We will have to live with such people on our rosters,' said Bindusara.

Radheya wasn't ready to give in. 'I still do not recommend such an approach. If we can take the fort of Mahishur by the sheer strength of our army, why should we stoop to a compromise?'

Bindusara looked at Radheya fondly. 'I will try to avoid any unnecessary settlement. But if the upside is too big to ignore, I might do it.'

Ajaya cleared his throat as he spread out the stitched-up palm leaves in front of him. His attention to detail was apparent in the way he had etched his plans in different colours of ink with copious notes and symbols.

'I have two plans in mind. Plan *prathma* is as follows. Mahishur has two gates diametrically opposite each other.' Bindusara and Mahamantri Radheya peered at the plan. Ajaya had labelled the gates as Uttara and Dakshin. 'We also know that Mahishur is protected on all sides by the Chamundi forest. However, this works like a double-edged sword. We will camp close to the Uttara gate. Our forces will be split, with half of them travelling by night to reach the Dakshin gate. By dawn we will launch an attack simultaneously, on both sides. Of course, we will comb the forest to dig out their spies, before launching into the plan. This will ensure that their spy network is unable to give them an advance warning. The Mahishur force within the fort will not be able to track our movements as the same forest that protects them will also give us cover. Mahishur will be forced to divide their forces to defend themselves at both the gates. Our larger army will easily rout them.'

He took a deep breath and continued. 'Plan *dwitiya* is an extension of the first plan. Half of our force will travel by night towards the Dakshin gate. This information will be deliberately fed to Mahishur through their spies. While they deploy a significant chunk of their force at the Dakshin gate, our forces will quickly backtrack and we will launch an attack of gargantuan proportions at the Uttara gate. It will be easy for us to enter the fort from this gate, and once inside we can easily rout the enemy.'

Bindusara was thoughtful. 'Do we have any tribals in our army?' he asked.

'No. It is difficult to train...' Ajaya started to reply before he was interrupted by the emperor.

'Then recruit the tribals. Our army will require them for this mission,' Bindusara said.

'And...' Senapati Ajaya asked hesitantly, expecting Bindusara to elaborate.

Just then a guard walked in. He waited deferentially for permission to speak.

'Raje, Queen Subhadrangi's chief aide requests an audience with you.'

Bindusara looked peeved at the interruption. Nevertheless, it was rare that anyone from his younger queen's entourage sought his audience. In this case, however, he had an inkling about the reason behind the interruption.

'Send her in,' he ordered, his tone betraying his excitement.

A young, pleasant-faced woman entered the chambers demurely. It was Daya, Queen Subhadrangi's chief aide and confidante. She bowed low to Bindusara before speaking. 'Raje, the queen is at the threshold of her labour and will deliver any moment.'

For once, Bindusara did not bother to formally conclude a meeting. He all but rushed out of the room in his excitement, making it difficult for Daya to keep pace with his long strides.

There was a hush about the palace on that fated day as Bindusara walked towards Subhadrangi's chambers. Subhadrangi was in delirium. The midwife's forehead was soaked in perspiration. It was a tough delivery. But the younger queen of Bindusara bore the pain with grace.

Bindusara waited in the outer chambers, till such time that

the delivery was over. His thoughts went unbidden to the day when Subhadrangi's father, a distinguished Brahmin, had asked for a private audience with him.

'O Raje,' the Brahmin told Bindusara, 'it is my daughter Subhadrangi's destiny to give birth to an emperor such as the world has not seen till now. I therefore offer her hand in marriage to you.'

The Raja of Magadha was amused but not convinced. The Brahmin was persuasive. 'O Raje, my daughter embodies the sweetness of honey and the pristine beauty of the mountains. You would not be doing me a favour by marrying her.'

Bindusara's curiosity was aroused. He asked to meet her.

'My daughter is not an object that you can assess,' retorted the Brahmin haughtily. 'At the most I will allow you to see her reflection. Noon tomorrow is auspicious.'

Bindusara decided to keep the visit clandestine. The next day, accompanied by his most trusted spy, he walked the lively streets of Pataliputra to the Brahmin's house. Dressed as commoners, they were indistinguishable from the rest of the crowd.

At the gate, Bindusara hesitated. He wondered whether he was making a fool of himself. 'It's too late to turn back now,' he decided. He told his companion to wait outside and entered the Brahmin's house with a sense of anticipation.

The Brahmin greeted the emperor formally. He beckoned to his wife to wash the emperor's feet. After Bindusara was comfortably settled, kshira *and* vataka *were served. Sensing Bindusara's growing impatience, the Brahmin asked the emperor to take a walk in the garden. As the Brahmin had promised, a full-length polished slab made of iron ore was placed in a corner of the garden, reflecting the afternoon light in its full glory. As Bindusara's eyes adjusted to the bright light, he grew conscious of a woman's reflection. It was a lithe figure, almost fragile.*

Bindusara's breath caught in his throat. Nothing he had seen before had prepared him for the beauty of Subhadrangi. She stood uncertainly, wearing a simple cotton antariya *around her waist.*

The decorative belt, mekhala, *was replete with fresh flowers. A plain* uttariya *was draped modestly over her upper body. The only ornaments Subhadrangi wore were flower armlets. Her complexion was a mixture of earth and honey. Bindusara's heart ached with desire at the sight of her doe-like light brown eyes and full lips.*

He wanted to turn and look at Subhadrangi in flesh and blood, but decided against it, lest he offend the Brahmin. He spent a couple of minutes gazing at her and then turned to the father.

Bindusara told the Brahmin that the royal priest would meet him to fix an auspicious date. For a brief instant, it crossed his mind that his existing wife, Agramahisi Rakshita, would not be too happy about his marriage to Subhadrangi. He shrugged – he had ways of dealing with that.

Bindusara walked back to the palace, scarcely conscious of his aide walking silently by his side. This was one day when the emperor did not notice the streets of his beloved Pataliputra. His mind was elsewhere, in a garden with a woman he had barely met.

The day Bindusara had waited for so desperately had finally arrived. The Brahmin had foretold that Subhadrangi was destined to give birth to an emperor even greater than he. Bindusara was impatient to look at the future ruler of his empire – the land that stretched from Magadha in the east to Takshashila in the west, with Ujjaini in the south.

Daya came running out. 'It's a boy!' she shouted in excitement.

'I know that. When can I hold him?' Bindusara asked impatiently.

The pathetic cries of the newborn grew louder as the midwife emerged with a bundle wrapped in red velvet.

Bindusara stared at his son, speechless. The baby's body seemed to be disproportionately tiny in comparison to the mass of thick brown curls on his head. He flailed his limbs in panic, as if missing the comfort of the womb he had just left. *This ugly weakling cannot be destined to be a future emperor,* Bindusara declared to himself with silent disappointment.

The baby suddenly became quiet, almost as if he understood the significance of the moment.

Bindusara abruptly turned around and left, his disgust showing. Daya saw him walking towards the far end of the long corridor. She knew he was headed to his Agramahisi Rakshita and their two-year-old son Susima.

Subhadrangi had a visitor that evening. It was Jayaraman, the royal astrologer, who had come to bless the new prince as per custom. Subhadrangi had named him Ashoka. It meant 'freedom from sorrow'. Those were the emotions she had felt when she held him for the first time. A freedom from sorrow, loneliness and endless empty sunsets.

Ashoka was handed over to Jayaraman. He blessed Subhadrangi first as she touched his feet. Then, studying the baby's tiny palms, he observed him carefully. Jayaraman frowned as he made calculations based on the date and time of Ashoka's birth. Jayaraman knew that in rare cases, very little could be predicted. This was the first case that had confounded him. His years of studying the shastra had been rendered useless.

'A mix of blood and water,' he said softly, staring at Subhadrangi. 'Daughter, I see a destiny I cannot understand. His destiny is in his own hands. Make what you will of it.'

'I don't understand...what do you mean?' His cryptic words made Subhadrangi anxious. Sensing this, he strove to lighten the mood. He did not want to explain to Subhadrangi that Ashoka's stars foretold two paths. One was full of despair and bloodshed and the other a path of righteousness and virtue...or both.

'Am I not going to be offered *madhuparka*? What shall I tell your father when he asks me about you? You should smile more often,' he added, patting her head affectionately.

Jayaraman left soon after. His parting words rang in Subhadrangi's ears. 'Remember my child, it is not often that God gives a person the opportunity to shape someone's destiny. You are the instrument he has chosen for Ashoka.'

Rakshita surreptitiously peeped through the slits in the curtains of her chambers as Bindusara sparred with a huge opponent in his private arena in the palace. Perspiration flowed down his bare chest. A few drops trickled down his eyes, blurring his vision till he impatiently wiped them off. The queen stared at him, mesmerized. He was thrashing his much younger opponent, who seemed to be at the end of his final reserves of strength. In a final, desperate effort he attempted a powerful thrust at Bindusara's chest. It was a classic move and it nearly worked. At the last moment, Bindusara deftly stepped aside, and without breaking his stride, he employed a complex manoeuvre to yank his opponent's sword away. The young man's sword clattered to the ground. Exhausted, he bowed to Bindusara and left the arena.

Bindusara gazed respectfully at his own sword. It had been given to him by his father; the great Chandragupta Maurya – founder of the Mauryan empire. The sword had a peacock carved on the hilt, and its blade shone with the intensity of the fire it had been hardened in. Bindusara adoringly touched the flat edge of the blade to his forehead. 'One day, I will hand you to my successor,' he murmured. Then, feeling someone's gaze on him, he turned to look towards the palace.

Rakshita guiltily hid her face behind a pillar as though she had been caught in an act she was not supposed to indulge in. She sighed wistfully. Bindusara would be away for many *ayanas. I will miss you,* she thought.

Despite her great love for Bindusara, the seeds of bitterness forever lurked in a corner of her mind. He had married another woman and given her too the status of a queen. At times, the pain gnawed at her so much that she felt she was being consumed from within by an army of angry ants.

Bindusara walked into Subhadrangi's private chambers. Tomorrow, when the first rays of the sun caressed his beloved Pataliputra, the march would commence. He wanted to bid goodbye to his younger queen. Standing silently, he took in the scene that greeted him. Subhadrangi radiated a combination of child-like innocence and motherly warmth as she lounged on the large bed. Her arm was draped possessively over the baby. The infant was a picture of serenity – as though he knew he was well protected. Mother and son seemed complete in each other's company.

Bindusara abruptly turned around and left. His departure was as unobtrusive as his entry had been.

2

War preparations had commenced. Most of Pataliputra seemed caught up in the arrangements. Mahamantri Radheya had taken on the task of managing the administration affairs of the kingdom in the emperor's absence. Senapati Ajaya monitored everything with the eyes of a hawk, with the heads of various divisions – infantry, cavalry, war chariots, elephants, supplies, transport and so on, keeping him updated on the progress. Weapons were required and a large number of iron smiths had been hired. They worked through the day and the better part of the night, fashioning spears, swords and giant balls – the latter would prove deadly when propelled from catapults. Each soldier had to have a spare set of leather armour and arm bucklers. Leather workers were happy as the administration paid them handsomely. Large quantities of food, required for the journey, was being organized. Some non-perishable items such as pulses, wheat grain and rice would be carried at the start of the journey, with more being procured on the way.

War elephants were rigorously trained as they would play an important role in the event of a head-on combat. Horses were taken for obstacle course exercises every day. The wheels of the chariots were oiled for maximum speed. Special chariots like the *rathamusala* were built. The *rathamusala* had blades jutting out of the hub of the wheels and a wooden compartment where archers could hide and spew a shower of arrows. Soldiers, who in times of peace led an easy life, were speedily getting battle ready.

The *bherigosha,* the war trumpet, sounded at dawn. Young Poulak jumped out of bed and bathed with water from the well behind his house. He was one of the marksmen trained to operate from the deadly *rathamusala* chariot. It was no small feat – he was the youngest to achieve this coveted position, at the age of thirteen. He said his prayers and went to bid goodbye to his widowed mother.

'Mother, I have come for your blessings,' he said, bowing to her.

'Son, you will always have my blessings, wherever you may be. But is it necessary to serve Magadha in this manner?' she looked at Poulak contemplatively. 'You remind me of how your father was. He died serving this country. And what did we get in return?' she snapped, her eyes flashing with suppressed anger.

'We got a handsome pension, Mother,' Poulak said a trifle impatiently. 'A soldier's destiny can lead him into the jaws of death. I accepted this fate the day I chose to be a Kshatriya.'

His mother heard in her son's words the echo of his father's voice before he had gone to his death. She sighed resignedly. 'Go then. Do what you must!'

'Not this way,' Poulak said, smiling at her. He lifted her in his strong arms, giving her a giant hug. 'Now I can go,' he said softly, drinking in the sight of his mother one last time before he left for battle.

The whole of Pataliputra was out on the streets to bid farewell to their brave soldiers. The cavalry were the first to emerge from the barracks. Most of the warriors had visited the royal priests at dawn to seek their blessings. The soldiers sat straight on their gleaming horses. All of them wore black turbans and had a red tilak on their foreheads, their leather armour fitting them like a second skin and securely fastened with bucklers. Each soldier's saddle held both his spear and sword. The soldiers started at a slow trot and gradually picked up speed.

The cavalry was followed by the *gaja*. The elephants evoked a loud cheer from the onlookers. The massive beasts were in their war armour, their trunks covered with a metallic mesh. The mahouts held a short stick with a metal hooked end to guide the elephants.

Bindusara sat resplendent on one of the elephants. His special golden armour was almost blinding in the morning sunlight.Beneath the glitter of the gold it had interlocking iron, steel and leather of the best quality. Devoid of all ornaments except a large black diamond pin on the traditional turban, he looked majestic and fearsome at the same time. The thick turban concealed a metallic skull cap. The crowd roared as he came in sight. He waved back, smiling indulgently at them as though they were his children. In Bindusara's absence from the city on '*Lakshya* Mahishur', Radheya would be in charge of the administrative affairs.

Next in line were the chariots, who in turn were followed by the infantry. The foot soldiers were well built and in superb form after their rigorous training. The last to exit was a convoy laden with supplies. The bullock carts that made up the convoy moved slowly and were accompanied by civilian helpers.

The 200,000 soldiers marched in perfect formation. The leader of each contingent had a map that let them know where they should halt at the end of the sunset. By dusk, they reached the outskirts of a village, and set up camp.

By the second day, the mammoth Mauryan army had picked up it's pace. They passed through numerous villages and jungles. The Mauryan empire was vast. However, Bindusara's governance had ensured the construction of proper roads so that mobility was never an impediment. After the signal was given to stop at the end of the seventh sunset, Bindusara instructed Ajaya and the rest of his commanders to plan a sunset's training exercise for the soldiers. The halt would rejuvenate the soldiers after the relentless march and this place offered a vast stretch of open ground that was perfect for training for various manoeuvres.

After a quick bath, the emperor went on a round to inspect the exercises. At the archery section, he was happy to observe that majority of the arrows were well-nigh at the centre of the target. Bindusara's attention was drawn to an archer who was being urged by his companions to shoot his arrow blindfolded. The target was a mango high up on a tree which was at a considerable distance. It looked like an impossible task, even to Bindusara. He looked on expectantly as the young soldier calmly took aim. With practised ease, he let loose his arrow. The arrow barely grazed the mango, and for a second, Bindusara thought the soldier had missed his mark. In the next instant, the mango fell to the ground, accompanied by a loud cheer from the other soldiers. The young man whipped off his blindfold and smiled at his companions, blushing slightly at their uninhibited praise.

'What is that soldier's name?' Bindusara asked the *nayaka* overseeing the exercise.

'Poulak, Raje. He is part of the *rathamusala* team.'

Bindusara nodded approvingly and rode away.

On the way back to his tent, he took a detour to the *gaja* section. Agni, his personal war elephant, trumpeted loyally when it spotted its master. The mahout in charge of Agni tapped it softly to quieten the elephant. Agni angrily shook its head and stood up on its hind legs. The mahout flicked it again, harder this time. Bindusara who knew Agni's nature well, dismounted and walked up to it.

'Hush, calm down, young one. Nobody understands you as well as I do. We are a team, you and I,' crooned Bindusara. This seemed to soothe the elephant. Bindusara caressed its trunk briefly before bidding it goodbye.

The break had been good for the soldiers. They were in high spirits and ready for another round of marching. It was another 10 sunsets before they finally halted near a lake to set up camp. In any other circumstance, it would have been a long unforgiving march for the soldiers. This was difficult. Bindusara expected Mahishur to know about his arrival. He knew his show of nonchalance would strike terror in their hearts. Everyone, including the beasts, had a well-deserved wash. The soldiers shared an easy camaraderie, and those amongst them who were good singers sang until late at night, entertaining their companions.

After the long halt, the Maurayan army resumed its march towards Mahishur. Finally, they reached the famous Chamundi forest – the jungle that offered natural protection to the city of Mahishur. It was dusk by the time they had settled down. Ajaya had already sent his spies to comb the forest for any lookouts from Mahishur, as they were now barely six *horas* walking distance from the main city. The spies would report early next morning with their findings. There was no singing that night. The easy banter was a thing of the past with all the men keyed up for the impending battle.

The camp has retired early tonight, Ajaya noted with satisfaction. The sentries patrolled the camp with synchronized frequency.

Ajaya was up at the first light of dawn, awaiting the return of his spies. He was joined in his tent by Balki, his first commander. Within a few minutes, two of the spies entered. They shook their heads in response to Ajaya's questioning look. 'Not a soul, sir. We didn't come across any lookout from Mahishur.'

Within the next *hora*, the rest of the spies returned. Twenty-nine of them had been sent to scout for enemy lookouts. None of them had seen anyone.

'It's unnatural that none of our spies bumped into any "friends",' Balki commented thoughtfully. One of the spies spoke, 'Sir, it is as if they don't care that we are preparing to attack them. The forest is completely devoid of Mahishur men.'

'I think it is a planned strategy to throw us off track,' volunteered another spy.

'Anything of consequence?' prodded Balki. He was met with total silence.

'Hmm…go and get some rest,' Balki said gently, dismissing the spies.

Balki and Ajaya exchanged puzzled looks. 'I think Mahishur is playing some game we have not fathomed yet. It is impossible that our spies did not spot a single Mahishur soldier in the forest, so close to the city,' Balki murmured with a frown.

'Unless it has been done by design!' Ajaya said softly. 'The question is why they would do this…' He spoke as if to himself. It did not help that Bindusara had not disclosed which plan of attack he preferred. Nebulous situations always irked him. He shook his head. 'Let us wait and see. In the meantime, send another group of spies to see if they can spot any action.'

Balki left to carry out Ajaya's instructions. Ajaya remained sitting, motionless, his seasoned mind telling him that the enemy was planning a move he would have to comprehend before it was too late.

By afternoon, the fresh lot of Mauryan spies sent a message that three men on horseback, in civilian clothes, were headed towards the camp. The riders appeared to know their way well. As soon as they arrived at the Mauryan camp, they were surrounded by sentries.

The captain of the guards approached them. 'What do you want?' he asked sternly.

'We want to meet your king,' one of them replied in a deep, calm voice.

'Introduce yourselves first. If there is merit in your purpose, we will inform the emperor. Else,' he said, giving them a meaningful look, 'you will be taken prisoner.'

The tallest amongst the riders spoke. 'I am Kavin, the Prince of Mahishur and son of the late Raja Mahajan. I have come here alone, apart from my two personal bodyguards. You and your emperor would be branded cowards if you were to hold me captive in this situation.'

The captain was taken aback. Signalling to the sentries to keep the riders under watch, he walked briskly towards Bindusara's tent. He returned almost immediately, an inscrutable expression on his face. He instructed the guards to take the swords of the Mahishur men, and then had them searched thoroughly. Convinced they were not carrying any hidden weapons, he led them to the threshold of Bindusara's tent.

Bindusara sat comfortably on a makeshift divan. Ajaya and Balki stood on either side of their king. Bowing in Bindusara's direction, the prince respectfully folded his hands.

'I am Kavin, the Prince of Mahishur and son of the late Raja Mahajan. I have a proposal to make to the great Raja Bindusara.'

'How old are you, son?' Bindusara asked, his expression conveying a modicum of curious amusement. 'Do you have the authority to make proposals?'

Ajaya observed the tall and lean youth with interest. His

eyes were light brown and shone with intelligence. His self-assured countenance betrayed no sign of awe in Bindusara's presence.

'My words carry the authority of the people of Mahishur,' Kavin replied in a slow, calm tone.

'What about your brother Aagney? We have heard that your Commander-in-Chief and ministers are in his favour,' retorted Bindusara, closely watching Kavin's expression. Kavin did not reply immediately, and Ajaya intervened before the situation took an uncomfortable turn.

'Now that you are here, tell us what is on your mind,' prompted Ajaya.

Kavin took a deep breath. 'I will help you win this battle if you guarantee my ascension to the throne of Mahishur.' He noticed the barely concealed look of contempt on Ajaya's face. 'I am not betraying my country for personal gains,' he said defiantly, gritting his teeth in suppressed fury. 'My brother is not fit to rule. Mahishur would be steeped in decadence if he ever became king. I would rather be judged by generations to come as the man who traded with the enemy, than see the throne go to my brother and have him plunge our land into misery.'

'Why should we trust you?' questioned Ajaya, still not certain he could respect a man who was selling out to the invaders of his nation.

'Because this is the easiest way you can gain victory over Mahishur. The army of Mahishur may be small, but the battle will be bloody,' stated Kavin dryly.

'What kind of help will we get?' questioned Balki, who had been silent until now.

'I will provide you information that will be invaluable if you want to be victorious,' Kavin answered evasively.

Bindusara got up abruptly. 'How about some refreshments?' he said, ending the meeting. 'We don't let visitors leave unless they have eaten. It is a Mauryan custom,' Bindusara gave an avuncular smile.

Kavin shrugged indifferently. Ajaya looked on as he extended the long, slender fingers of his left hand to take an apple. On a sudden impulse, he decided to have a word with his spies.

An entire week had elapsed since Kavin had first met Bindusara and his key commanders. Since then, they had had three more meetings. In their second meeting, Bindusara informed Kavin that after much deliberation, they had decided to accept the young prince's offer. He would be made governor of Mahishur once it was under Mauryan rule. Once he had Bindusara's word, Kavin began the process of sharing critical information with the Mauryan king and his commanders. Vital statistics regarding the size of the Mahishur army, the various entry gates, the number of sentries posted at each location and innumerable other facts were conveyed that would ensure a swift and bloodless victory.

Poulak hid behind a thick bush. He was puzzled by the orders he had been given. *My job is to follow orders, not question them,* he told himself.

He observed the trio on horseback emerge out of the forest. Poulak took careful aim and the arrow found its mark cleanly, piercing the heart of the bodyguard on the left. Before the other two riders realized what was happening, the bodyguard on Kavin's right was shot through the eye. Kavin's horse was surrounded by the camp guards, and his sword was confiscated. A hefty sentry grabbed the reins of the horse and led Kavin into the camp.

Kavin was taken to Bindusara's tent where Ajaya and Balki were also present. Bindusara noted that Kavin was trying desperately to maintain his composure.

Balki called out to Kavin. 'You look hungry. Catch…' He threw an apple at the young man. Kavin reflexively caught the apple with his left hand. There was complete silence in the room, and Kavin realized all eyes were on him.

'Did you really think you could get away with this, *Aagney*?' Bindusara said softly. 'Even identical twins have differences, you know. I think you underestimated our spy network.'

The young man looked at Bindusara, his expression reflecting his complete surprise. 'How did you…' he began. Bindusara interrupted him.

'Your twin brother Kavin would have caught the apple with his right hand,' Bindusara said matter-of-factly. 'Is the throne more important to you than your own brother?' he asked in a quiet tone.

'Kavin is not fit to rule over Mahishur,' Aagney said between clenched teeth. 'I would be disloyal to Mahishur if I allowed that to happen. I am the rightful heir to my father's throne.'

'Exactly what was your plan? To shove a lot of useless information down our throats and extract our plans in return?' Ajaya snapped.

Aagney stared back defiantly at Ajaya.

'What do we do with him?' Ajaya asked, looking in Bindusara's direction.

'I don't care if you kill me. I would gladly give my life for Mahishur,' Aagney said coldly.

Bindusara stared hard at the young man destiny had thrown his way. Finally, he looked at the guards helming Aagney on either side. 'Leave us alone,' he said. The guards hesitated for a brief second before exiting the royal tent.

'I admire your courage, young man. You are fortunate I am not in the habit of killing my enemies when they are at a disadvantage,' Bindusara said quietly. 'Go and prepare for battle. But remember, I may not be as merciful when we meet on the battlefield.'

Aagney looked at Bindusara with clear eyes. 'So be it.'

He bowed to Bindusara, and without giving the others a glance, abruptly turned and walked out. Seeing him come out, the guards rushed inside Bindusara's tent to see if there was any trouble. Balki signalled to them, confirming that everything was in order.

'Why did you let him go?' a bewildered Ajaya asked Bindusara. 'We could have won Mahishur in an instant.'

'He is courageous and passionate about his country. He deserves a fair fight,' Bindusara replied thoughtfully.

Ajaya and Balki nodded and took their leave. The battle for Mahishur would be fought the next day and they had a long night of hard work ahead of them.

Bindusara stood by himself, lost in thought. *Did I do the right thing by letting him go?* he asked himself. Time would answer all his questions.

3

Bindusara stared at the model representation of the fort of Mahishur. Ajaya had done a fantastic job of replicating the actual fort, with its various entrance gates placed at appropriate points.

'What do we know about the security at the fort's entrance?' Bindusara inquired, running his fingers through his shoulder-length hair – something he did whenever in deep thought.

Balki's reply was quick. 'According to our spies, the city wall is heavily patrolled with one platoon approximately 120 *kashtas* from the next.'

'Did we recruit the tribals?' Bindusara asked abruptly.

'Yes we did.' Ajaya nodded, remembering Bindusara's strange instruction of hiring tribals, given to him at Pataliputra. He had done so, reluctantly. A vague sense of discomfort plagued him regarding their ability to follow the discipline of the army.

'The tribals are good climbers and archers,' Bindusara said. He was being deliberately laconic but the scant words were enough for a war veteran like Ajaya to realize his true purport. Ajaya felt a bead of perspiration trickle down his forehead.

'Here is my plan,' Bindusara said, bending over the model of the Mahishur fort. 'Let us call this Plan *tritiya*. As the patrolling guards are 120 *kashtas* apart, a handpicked team of tribals can scale the fort walls and get in undetected. Their task will be twofold – to create confusion once they are inside and to unlock the Dakshin gate for us. In the meantime, we will make an open assault at the Uttara gate.' Bindusara paused meaningfully. 'The threefold attack will result in mayhem. You know what to do next.'

He has done it again…the master strategist, thought Ajaya. He mentally kicked himself for not thinking of this strategy himself. Ajaya was jolted out of his reverie by Balki's high-pitched voice.

'I need to check out something important,' Balki was saying excitedly. 'May I be excused?' he requested, urgency in his voice.

Ajaya nodded, wondering what had suddenly got into his commander. He knew Balki well enough to guess that whatever it was, it would be something that would help them in the war with Mahishur.

There was palpable activity within the Mauryan camp. Approximately half the soldiers readied themselves for the midnight march through the forest. Mandar, a tribal, was sharpening his arrows when his friend Alok rushed inside the tent.

'Mandar, Commander Balki is calling us for a brief. It must be something important,' he said breathlessly.

'Why, what do they want us for?' Mandar retorted nonchalantly.

Alok gave him a puzzled look. 'It is time to prove that we are as worthy as the trained soldiers of the Mauryan army,' he said eagerly, awaiting his older friend's reaction.

Mandar shrugged carelessly. He had decided to join the Mauryan forces only because they paid well. The last drought had rendered his tribe completely poverty stricken. At the age of 14, he was the oldest and the most responsible member of his family. He had taken it upon himself to raise the money to buy seeds for the next crop. Fortuitously, the army had been looking to hire tribals just then. Most of the boys in his tribe revered him and decided to follow him there, taking a calculated risk, since, in the absence of the warrior boys, their tribe would be relatively unprotected.

Given the nature of the mission, Mandar had insisted on taking the boys of his own tribe. They understood each other and could act in coordination. They moved through the dense forest at a frenetic pace. They had to reach the fort walls of Mahishur well before dawn. That would give them enough time to do what Balki had asked of them. If they were successful in their mission, the Mauryan army would enter the city of Mahishur by dawn, with minimum casualties. If they failed...Mandar, who was leading the squad, did not want to think of the consequences.

It is preposterous, he thought grimly. *In fact, it is downright suicidal. I wonder how many of us will survive this mission.* Mandar surreptitiously glanced sideways. He knew all his men well, and most of them had grown up together. He knew the death of even one of these men would weigh on his conscience forever. He glanced at Alok, the heartbreakingly young tribal who had never been privy to violence until now. *God, don't let anything happen to him,* he prayed.

None of the Mauryans, including the tribals, had ever seen the fort walls and Mandar fervently hoped they would be easy to scale. It was frustrating to make their way through the dense undergrowth in near total darkness. But it would have been suicidal to light lamps, as that would alert the Mahishurian lookouts. And it wasn't just the Mahishurian soldiers they had to worry about. Marching without a lamp to light their way left them vulnerable to the danger of wild beasts and snakes, both of which were rampant in the forest. The only saving grace was that there were some secrets only the tribals knew. One of these was a special ointment, which when smeared over the body emitted vapours that served to drive away most wild creatures.

They finally reached the edge of the forest cover from where the fort walls were in plain view. Mandar held up his hand as a signal to wait and watch. It was a full-moon night and the patrols on the fort's roof were in plain view.

'Commander Balki was right,' Mandar said softly. 'The guards are actually 120 *kashtas* apart before they meet. That is a reasonable period of time to scale it.' *But how?* he thought to himself.

Mandar nodded in Alok's direction. The young soldier instinctively understood what he was required to do. Grinning in anticipation, he waited for the coast to clear. Then he took a deep breath and ran with all the speed he could muster, towards the walls. He peered closely at the mass of fortification facing him. The wall was at least four *dandas* in height.

From a distance, Mandar saw Alok feeling the wall for possible crevices and nooks that could be useful while scaling the formidable structure. Time was running out for the young soldier. Just when Mandar thought Alok might be spotted, he turned around and darted back to where the rest of the tribals waited.

'The walls have been coated with a special lacquer that renders it too slippery for a climber to gain a foothold,' Alok said between pants. There was no grin on his face now, as he realized the enormity of the task ahead of them.

Mandar digested the bad news with an expressionless face. 'All right then, you know what to do,' he whispered to Alok.

Alok interlocked his fingers. The signal was enough for the rest of the group. They waited silently for the next opportune moment. The moment the guards were out of sight, the entire cohort sprinted to the edge of the wall. Mandar observed with satisfaction as his men climbed over each other to create a human ladder. Two of the browniest men stood below and lent their shoulders for others to climb on. The nimble and sure-footed tribals were quick to complete their task.

Mandar was the last to climb up and reach the top of the human ladder that covered half the height of the wall. Now came the tricky part. He had to throw an anchor across the top so that they could climb the rest of the way. It had been difficult enough to haul the heavy anchor with him. He was also mindful that the men at the bottom of the pyramid would be at the threshold of their endurance by now.

In a single fluid move, he threw the anchor in a wide arc. This was his only chance. He knew if the anchor failed to secure a hold in the first attempt, it might not only fall back on them, but also alert the Mahishurian sentries. He prayed fervently that the noise would be minimal. It was a perfect throw. There was an almost imperceptible thud as the anchor hugged the top edge of the wall. He tugged at it, gently at first and then with all his might.

It seems to be secure, Mandar thought, sighing in relief. He pulled himself up rapidly. Another two men followed him up the rope. They were now on the walkway of the fort rampart.

Mandar mentally calculated how much time had elapsed since the departure of the last patrol. Their time was almost up and the next patrol would arrive any moment. Mandar gave the rope two tight tugs. It signalled to the others to halt their climb and stay stock-still. Without wasting any time, Mandar and the other two darted into the shadows. They made it just in time, and Mandar sucked in his breath sharply as the patrol passed within inches of where they were hiding.

As soon as the patrol was out of sight, Mandar dashed back to the wall and used the standard tribal signal – a bird call repeated thrice in quick succession. In the unlikely event that one of the patrols heard it, they would think it was one of the several nocturnal birds calling out. But the tribals knew it was Mandar signalling to them from the other side. The men who had been holding on to the rope for dear life now hauled themselves up and jumped with practised ease on to the other side.

Mandar counted the men who were gathered next to him. All his men had made it. He grinned, his white teeth shining in the dark. The tribals felt a rush of adrenaline as they skulked in the shadows, waiting to waylay the next patrol.

Mandar rested on his haunches, letting Alok lead the ambush. The key was ensnaring the enemy without alerting other Mahishurian soldiers who might be nearby. The tribals carried short swords, the tips of which were smeared with deadly poison. A mere scratch would suffice to paralyse the opponent within a few seconds. While the Mauryan army prohibited the use of poison as an unfair means of war, the tribals had their own dictates, and they lived and fought by those rules.

Alok put a hand to his lips. He had heard the patrol approaching. The moment they were within striking distance, the tribals surged ahead. Mandar saw Alok clamp the mouth of one of the Mahishurian guards. The young man seemed to hesitate for a moment, and Mandar recognized the same signs of aversion towards violence in Alok that he had himself faced during his first kill. In that brief moment of uncertainty, the Mahishurian guard unsheathed his sword in an attempt to assault Alok. But the long sword of the Mahishurian soldier was not built for close encounters. Mandar saw Alok's wavering disappear as his instinct for survival kicked in. Before his antagonist realized what had happened, Alok thrust his short sword deep in the man's groin, giving him a quick death.

Mandar watched detachedly as the other tribals made a swift end of the remaining patrolmen.

The tribals quickly undressed the dead soldiers and donned their clothes over their own. Care had been taken to attack the Mahishurian soldiers in the lower part of the abdomen, so that the tears in the uniform or blood could be concealed under the sash tied to the waist that formed part of the outfit. The leather armour with the Mahishur seal on it would enable them to pass for Mahishur men. The tribals had not worn any headgear and after the tribals put on the Mahishur headgear, it would have been difficult even for the most perspicacious person to make out the difference. As an added precaution, they covered their faces, with only their eyes visible.

The tribal warriors now needed a quick exit down into the interiors of the city. The next patrol were sure to get suspicious when no one passed them at the designated time. Mandar spotted the steps that would take them down to the bottom of the fort. The band of 21 dashed down the steps, lest they be spotted by someone of authority. They had not bargained for the possibility that they would be greeted by a group of Mahishurian guards right at the bottom of the stairs.

The leader of the Mahishurian group glared at them. 'What are you doing here? Aren't you supposed to be guarding the fort?' he said gruffly. The man had a white spot right in the centre of his forehead. Mandar frantically racked his brains to come up with a suitable explanation. Fortuitously, at that very moment, another officer approached in haste.

'Quick…all teams are required to report to their commanders. The Mauryans have attacked the Uttara gate!' He was gone before anyone could utter a word.

Mandar let out a slow breath. The man had just provided him with a way to explain their presence to the Mahishurian officer. 'We were asked to join the rest of the battalion. We were on our way down when you stopped us,' he said, trying to sound earnest.

There was something about Mandar's accent that did not strike the right chord with the man. 'Show me your face, soldier,' he barked suspiciously.

A din of panic could be heard rising at a distance. An unexpectedly loud explosion made the air around them rife with tension. The leader of the Mahishurian group gazed uncomfortably in the direction of the blast.

'Hurry up, soldier. I have to leave,' he growled, unsheathing his sword. Mandar's forehead was wet with perspiration under the helmet. *I hope Alok and the rest of the men are ready with their swords, if it comes to a fight,* he thought desperately. He placed his hands on either side of the headgear, and in a deliberately slow motion, uncovered his head.

The Mahishur soldier stared hard at him. 'I don't know you,' he growled.

Mandar decided this was not the time to be courteous. The fear of compromising the operation lent his response a streak of urgency. 'You don't have to know everyone!' he retorted. 'Besides, you are holding me up and preventing me from doing my duty.'

There was another loud explosion, even more deafening than the first. The Mahishur officer hesitated for a moment, unsure what to do. 'I will give you a course in etiquette once this is over,' he said threateningly. Giving Mandar a final glare, he rushed off with his men.

'That man will kick himself tonight when this is over,' Alok said softly, looking at Mandar. Even though they were at a great distance from where the fighting was in progress, the pandemonium was tangible. *It looks like the Mauryan army has launched a full-blown attack at the Uttara gate,* Mandar thought with satisfaction.

With their entry inside the fort walls, the tribals had completed the first part of their task successfully. The second part would be equally tricky. They had to somehow unlock the Dakshin gate so that the rest of the mammoth Mauryan

army could enter the fort. Mandar looked around, gauging the time it would take to open this particular gate.

Poulak awaited a signal from Commander Balki. The first glimmer of daylight had just begun to colour the sky with an orange hue. Balki was second in command to Senapati Ajaya and a formidable warrior. It was he who was leading the full-scale assault at the Uttara gate.

Poulak saw Balki fisting his right hand and slapping it hard against the palm of his other hand. He knew this was the signal to the battering rams to start their charge. The Mauryan battering rams were logs of gigantic proportions sharpened at the edges to break open even the strongest enemy fortification. The massive logs were normally carried on multi-wheel carriages specially designed for this purpose. In this case, however, the Mauryans had been unable to drag the carriages through the dense forest. Consequently, they had to make do with medium-sized logs that could be physically carried by the infantry. Even so, the strongest men had been chosen for this task as it was a supreme test of strength as well as endurance.

Poulak watched in fascination as the men carrying the battering rams emitted blood-curdling yells as they charged at the Uttara gate. The Mauryan elephants stood by impatiently. The thunderous drumming coupled with the crashes of the battering rams on the surface of the gate drove the pachyderms to a fever pitch of excitement.

The Mauryans had, however, underestimated the resilience of Mahishur. Their answer to the Mauryan battering rams was to send a flurry of arrows fired from a height giving additional momentum to the sharp instruments of death. The cotton-covered oil-dipped arrow tips had been set alight and they lit up the sky more effectively than the fledgling sun at this *hora*. Many men were impaled where they stood as the arrows lodged themselves into their heads or torsos. And while they stood thus incapacitated, the surging fire from the deadly missiles burnt their limbs away, while they were still alive to feel the unbearable agony. The stench of burning flesh pervaded the air.

Commander Balki quickly planned his onslaught. He held his palm horizontal, thereby signalling to the soldiers standing on the side to step in with their shields. They carried huge shields, larger than what the foot soldiers typically used. Chandragupta Maurya, Bindusara's father had introduced this in the Mauryan army after observing its successful deployment by the Greeks. The soldiers held the shields over their heads, protecting the men deploying the battering ram as well as themselves. The shields were coated with a material that made them withstand heat and fire. Their efficacy was put to the test as the soldiers of Mahishur despatched their second batch of fire arrows. Unlike the first assault, the arrows now landed atop the massive shields. While some of them lodged thinly in the shields, the majority fell away harmlessly.

The gates to the fort were built of enduring *sangwan* wood, and did not succumb to the onslaught easily. At Balki's signal, another set of men stepped in to relieve their comrades who were by now at the threshold of their endurance. As the gates showed no visible signs of yielding, Balki deduced that they were fortified by sheets of iron on the other side. Veteran that he was, he quickly adapted his strategy.

The way was cleared for the elephants to be brought to the forefront. Already agitated by the loud noises around them, the beasts were driven to a frenzy by an even louder beating of the drums. The foot soldiers secured the knobs of the gargantuan gates with rope. The other end of the ropes was wound tightly around the legs of the elephants, as they stood facing away from the gates. Huge crowbars were also dug into the sides of the gate. Each crowbar was placed against a hinge of the gate, with the other end secured around a leg of an elephant with a rope. The mahouts drove the elephants, prodding them with their hooked rods. The beasts roared in anger.

Balki mentally evaluated the extent of their rage. Satisfied that the time was right, he gave the signal to the mahouts who dug the sharp rods into the animals'side. The elephants surged ahead. The more they endeavoured to move forward, the more the ropes tied around their legs cut through their skin. This gave rise to more fury and the elephants used all their might to run ahead.

Balki smiled as he saw the gates beginning to come apart. Finally, there was a ripping noise as the wood splintered and scattered in a thousand pieces. The iron sheets behind the wood, however, were still intact – but only for a brief moment. As the crowbars turned, the hinges came undone and the gates tottered with nothing to hold them in place. Like giants who had suddenly fallen unconscious, the massive gates came crashing down, threatening to bury everything in their way. For a few seconds, all else was eclipsed by clouds of reddish dust and debris.

Aagney stood stock-still on the other side of the crashing gates. He wondered whether their preparations had been enough. At the commander's orders, they had stocked up on weapons and armour. To increase the number of soldiers, they had reduced the age for entry into the army. However, the strife between the brothers had resulted in demotivating many sections. The question was, would they hold up against the superior Mauryan army?

As the clouds of red dust swirled around him, he had an epiphany. It dawned on him with sudden clarity that the attack on Mahishur could have been avoided if his brother Kavin and he had stood together as one.

How could I have forgotten that we are one? We grew up under the watchful eye of the same loving mother and doting father. We helped each other take our first steps, shared meals under the same trees. As he stood there, he reflected on how ironic it was that such peaceful memories should come flooding back to him in the midst of war and destruction.

Is my hunger for the throne so great that I can imprison my own bother, my other half? Aagney castigated himself. It was as if he was able to perceive everything clearly for the first time in his life, as if years of fog had suddenly cleared.

He made his decision. 'Hold the gate,' Aagney instructed his commander. 'I will be back.' Without waiting for a reply, he mounted his horse, galloping away towards the royal palace.

The Mahishur commander stared at the retreating figure of his prince, speechless. *What could be more important than protecting the gate right now?* he thought, shaking his head disapprovingly. He did not have time to dwell on the subject as the first wave of Mauryan riders swept into the city.

In another part of the city, Aagney and Kavin emerged from the royal palace together. They were identical in every respect except that Aagney carried his sword in his left hand, while Kavin wielded his with his right hand. They stared at each other as they stood at the threshold of the palace. Years of resentment and differences in opinion hung like a heavy invisible wall between them. Yet, they knew this could well be the last time they saw each other.

Oh Shiva! What have I done? Aagney thought to himself, as he moved forward to embrace his brother.

Kavin stood unmoving, unsure how to respond to the brother who had had him imprisoned two sunsets ago. He had hated Aagney when he was locked up in prison; he wanted to despise him even now. But to his astonishment, he felt himself returning his brother's warm embrace.

And in that moment of unrestrained affection, the wall that had crept up between the two brothers melted. There was no more anger, no more resentment. There was just a poignant and hollow feeling of what could have been and may never be. They shook hands as they used to when they were younger and preparing for a round of sword practice. Only this time, it was not a practice session they were gearing up for. It was war – with an enemy who had never been defeated since Bindusara's father had become the first emperor of the Mauryans.

'I need to head back to the Uttara gate,' Aagney said. 'Why don't you proceed to the Dakshin side?' he suggested.

Kavin gave him a meaningful smile. 'I can handle the fighting, brother. Let *me* go to the Uttara gate.'

Aagney hesitated. He had told the commander he would be back soon. Still, he didn't want Kavin to think he didn't trust him to handle the situation. And the commander wouldn't be able to make out the difference between the two brothers in any case.

'Okay.' Aagney sighed. 'You go to the Uttara gate.' As an afterthought he said quietly, 'Take care of yourself, brother.'

'Strength and honour.' Kavin said softly, voicing the Mahishur war chant.

'Strength and honour.' echoed Aagney, his voice firm and calm.

Kavin spurred his horse in the direction of the Uttara gate. The noise of the fighting was deafening even at this distance. Aagney sat on his horse for a while, watching his brother disappear in the distance. Then he goaded his horse towards the other end of the fort.

Poulak saw the formidable Uttara gate crash to the ground, raising a cloud of angry red dust that threatened to choke all those present in the vicinity. He unwittingly raised his hands to his face as he waited for the dust to subside.

'We are almost there,' he whispered soothingly to his bow. To Poulak, his bow was not a mere tool. It was a trusted companion that had been with him for several years and had won him countless accolades. His hands caressed the length of the bowstring. His touch was firm, yet light. The string was made of animal sinew, one of the toughest materials available for this purpose.

Poulak was sitting with five others in the *rathamusala*. The razor-sharp blades fitted to its wheels could literally cut their way through enemy territory. Poulak preferred to use the long bow as he could place it firmly in the crook of his big toe. The bow had a large draw-length that enabled him to use his longest arrows.

For the hundredth time that day, Poulak checked the contents of his quiver. He wanted to make sure he had the specific arrows he would require for the day. The arrowheads gleamed as the sun's rays fell upon them. The deadliest amongst the lot stood out, with its arrowhead made of yellow metal. This was the Agnibaan. It comprised a complex blend of various metals, mixed with defined measures of charcoal, oil wax and turpentine. Once the Agnibaan lodged inside the target, it would burst into flames and cause a conflagration from the inside out.

The *rathamusala* had openings just wide enough to fire arrows from. The archers within the chariot were well protected. The person driving the chariot was the only one who was exposed to danger from the enemy. But he was covered from head to toe in heavy, impenetrable armour. If per chance he was to be killed, a second man was always ready to take over. The chariot drivers were guarded by a group of soldiers whose sole objective was to ensure the former's safety.

From where he was standing, Poulak was able to gaze through the minute openings built into the sides of the chariot. The wreckage from the gates had been cleared up by the Mauryan elephants to make way for the infantry and other divisions to enter the city. Poulak saw Commander Balki issuing rapid instructions in the secret Kshatriya code. With a jerk, the *rathamusala* surged ahead. Poulak steadied himself – it was time for him to play his part in the battle.

His heightened sense of awareness made it seem as though things were happening in slow motion. But the *rathamusala* chariot was moving like a hurricane through the huge pillars where the Uttara gates had once stood. A large group of Mahishurian foot soldiers stood between the *rathamusala* and the city. The dense formation of Mahishurian soldiers resembled a human wall that seemed impossible to penetrate. Attired in brown, the Mahishur men looked like incarnations of asuras.

But even they were no match for the formidable *rathamusala*. The spiked wheels of the chariot sliced through human flesh and strewed it in different directions. Within no time, there was a ghastly smattering of blood and severed limbs that flew into the air and rained down on those hapless soldiers who had somehow survived the onslaught from the *rathamusala*. The dreadful sight of their companions' maimed bodies destroyed most of the Mahishurians' confidence. What was left of their morale was decimated by the steady shower of arrows fired with deadly accuracy by Poulak and his team from the *rathamusala*.

Like most warriors, Poulak too maintained a count of how many enemy soldiers he took down. He had just finished his thirtieth kill that day when a particular warrior on the Mahishur side caught his eye. The warrior wore armour that was far more elaborate than that of the others. Poulak stiffened as he recognized the royal emblem of Mahishur resplendent on the brilliantly shining armour. *It's the prince…or rather, one of them*, he thought, his mind racing. He muttered a brief prayer to Shiva and pulled the Agnibaan out of the quiver. This particular arrow was almost twice the size of the regular arrows – the arrowhead too was immense.

Poulak reverentially placed the Agnibaan on his bow. His shoulder muscles strained as he drew back the string to its limits. In that instant, his eyes locked with that of the prince. Somehow, the prince had sensed Poulak's presence even though the latter was hidden inside the chariot. Poulak saw a flash of understanding dawn in the prince's eyes as he perceived death just around the corner. Poulak released his breath and the Agnibaan in the same moment. The deadly arrow flew through one of the openings in the *rathamusala*.

Blood gushed like a fountain as the arrow pierced the left eye of the Mahishur prince. The Mahishur soldiers watched in horror as their prince fell to the ground. The dust had not yet settled from his fall, when his entire body exploded in a ball of fire. The embers of human dust swirled around the Mahishur men as they continued to gaze at what had been the vivacious Prince of Mahishur only moments ago.

The shock of witnessing the gruesome death of one of their princes made the men temporarily forget that they still had to defend their motherland. They were roused out of their stupor by the voice of their commander.

'ON THE BLOOD OF OUR PRINCE…FIGHT!' goaded the Mahishur commander as he launched himself at the Mauryans who had followed in the wake of the *rathamusala*.

Mandar surreptitiously led his band of twenty tribal warriors across the city. A large force of Mahishur soldiers were rapidly marching towards the Uttara gate where the major assault was underway. The civilian population of the city had been moved to basements and large trenches built expressly for such an eventuality.

Being a tribal, Mandar had spent most of his childhood moving from one place to the other. The tribals had never stayed within the confines of a city. The only friends they had were the other tribal families who travelled together, once every few years. As such, Mandar found it impossible to fathom the mindset of the Mahishur people that drove them to protect their city and country, even at the cost of their own lives. The same mindset made it difficult for him to understand the Mauryans' eagerness to wage war in order to expand their territories. It all felt surreal – as if he was witnessing everything around him from a distance. He felt strangely devoid of any emotion.

Mandar caught himself hesitating, wondering which alley he and his team ought to take. Being caught now meant certain death. *Is this risk worth it? What are we tribals doing in this senseless war? To satisfy one man's ambition of expanding his empire!* These thoughts came unbidden to him, increasing his agitation. But Mandar was a man of his word. The tribals and he had committed to unlock the Dakshin gate from within. A large part of the Mauryan forces waiting outside the city walls were relying on them.

Filled with resolve now, Mandar led his men purposefully towards their destination. The tribals could have easily passed as Mahishur soldiers but for their footwear. The Mauryan sandals were crafted with light coloured leather, unlike the Mahishur ones which had a darker tan. Mandar was quick to notice this and he stopped to dip his sandals in a spot of clayey mud. His companions realized what he was doing and followed suit. Convinced that they had removed the single giveaway sign, the group took rapid steps towards the Dakshin gate.

Alok gasped in awe as he saw the magnificent gates loom before them. The craftsmanship was exquisite. A narrow bend of steps were built adjacent to the walls on either side of the gates. Platoons of archers were positioned at various points on these stairs. They were firing arrows through the openings in the walls, and Mandar could only guess at the damage they would be inflicting on the Mauryans stationed outside. *We need to get these gates open quickly,* he thought savagely, desperately searching for a solution.

Mandar's attention was drawn by Alok trying to tell him something. Alok pointed towards a complex piece of machinery placed a slight distance from the gates. Mandar's eyes lit up with excitement. It was the machine that operated the opening and closure of the gate. Normally such machines were kept in enclosed towers at a reasonable height from the ground, and Mandar had wondered how they would locate it. The Mahishurians had committed the grave error of placing the machine in an accessible spot. *I guess they never thought they would be attacked like this,* Mandar reasoned.

A squad of 20 soldiers guarded the machinery. Mandar felt within the pocket of his dhoti and found what he was looking for. He mentally lauded Commander Balki's foresight. The packet he had given him would prove invaluable at the moment. He carefully extracted the packet from his pocket. Holding it firmly in his hands, he shook it violently before hurling it towards the soldiers guarding the machine.

One of the guards stared at the innocuous-looking packet that had fallen at his feet. Then he stared suspiciously at Mandar, trying to make out his features under the huge headgear. Mandar looked from the soldier to the packet that lay harmlessly on the ground. A bead of perspiration trickled down his forehead as he surmised that the stratagem had failed. The guard staring at Mandar seemed to make up his mind and bent down to pick up the fallen packet. All of a sudden, there was a hissing sound and the packet exploded, filling the air with dense smoke. Mandar sighed in relief and sent up a silent prayer to Shiva.

'Now!' he commanded his men, as he ran nimbly towards the machine, followed closely by Alok. Within a few seconds, Mandar had found the lever and tugged it with all the force he could summon. There was a gentle hum as the well-oiled bolts locking the gate began to move. The Mahishurian archers perched on the walls adjoining the Dakshin gate looked on in horror as the massive gates opened to let in the vast Mauryan forces.

The Mauryan soldiers stormed into the fort like the waters of a dam thrown open. Fuming at the death of their companions at the hands of the Mahishurian archers, they first attacked the bow-wielding soldiers who hadn't yet come down the walls. Next, they spent their unbridled fury on the other hapless Mahishur soldiers in the vicinity. It was a systematic massacre. Within a short time, all that was left of the Mahishur force guarding the gates were shreds of flesh and tattered limbs soaked in their own blood.

Mandar forced himself to shake off the feeling of revulsion that gripped him at the ghastly sight. He signalled his men to follow him as he began to retrace his steps.

Alok was the first to catch up with him. 'Where are we going?' he yelled at Mandar.

'The same place we came from,' replied Mandar with a sense of urgency in his voice. 'Our mission here is accomplished. There is nothing more left for us to do.'

Alok stared at Mandar, his expression inscrutable.

'What is it?' Mandar snapped uncharacteristically.

Alok seemed to hesitate. 'Let us fight besides our fellow Mauryans,' he finally whispered.

Mandar threw back his head and laughed bitterly. He looked Alok in the eye. 'Can't you see?' he hissed. 'We are tribals. That makes us expendable for the Mauryans. This is why they sent us on this suicidal mission,' he said quietly, the anger within him replaced by infinite regret at the step brotherly treatment constantly meted out to them by their own countrymen. The others looked on silently. Mandar's words were a reflection of their own inner turmoil.

Alok was not dissuaded. 'I think it is we who doubt them. Didn't we lead an untroubled life before the war? Did the emperor slight us in any way?'

'In many ways,' Mandar lashed out, his anger raising its head again. 'They charge taxes from us…for what? They treat us as outsiders in our own country. No tribal has ever been recruited into the army. Even now, they came to us only because they didn't want to send their own precious men on a suicidal mission.'

'That is not true,' Alok replied calmly. 'They treat us as outsiders because we choose to live by ourselves. They haven't inducted us in their army because we have been too proud to offer them our services until now. They approached us for this mission because they did not believe there is a single soldier in the Mauryan army who could achieve what we did today.'

Mandar stood silently. Something in what Alok said rang true. At that moment, their attention was distracted by the familiar sound of a loud drum. They recognized it as the rhythm reserved specially to announce of the arrival of the emperor. Bindusara had personally entered the fray.

'Come on, brother,' coaxed Alok. 'Let's fight alongside the emperor.'

Alok offered his hand to Mandar. After a moment's hesitation, Mandar gripped it hard. He took off the Mahishur headgear and armour he had been wearing as a disguise. Alok and the others followed suit, finally revealing themselves as the tribal warriors they were.

'Let us show our emperor how a tribal warrior fights,' Mandar said softly. The group cheered loudly as they rushed out to join the Mauryan forces.

Bindusara sat resplendent on the back of Agni. The royal elephant's long, gleaming tusks were covered by a sheath soaked in poison. Agni was like a messenger of death on the battlefield, destroying anything that came in its way. Sitting at that height, Bindusara showered torrents of arrows on the enemy. Senapati Ajaya was in his chariot, close behind Bindusara. Their majestic display of prowess and courage inspired the rest of the Mauryan army to fight even more valiantly.

Bindusara's eyes scanned the waves of soldiers for the one person that he was looking for. There he was, seated on his own elephant. Aagney's elephant looked simple without any of the adornments like that of Agni. The prince was surrounded by archers on all sides, keeping a close watch to thwart any attack on him. He himself looked steadily at Bindusara, his arrow pulled back, ready to let loose any moment. The poisoned arrow was aimed at his forehead. Bindusara smiled. He always enjoyed fighting the skilled and courageous.

Mandar suddenly found himself facing a man he recognized immediately. The other man recognized him in the same instant. It was the same Mahishur officer who had stopped Mandar and his men earlier. He raised his long sword menacingly. 'You won't get away now,' he growled, and before Mandar could react, the adversary swung his long sword straight at his abdomen.

Mandar felt Alok's weight on his shoulder as the young tribal pushed him aside. Mandar staggered but quickly regained his balance. The blade had missed him, owing to Alok's timely intervention.

Mandar took out his sword and turned to face the Mahishur officer. He gasped – Alok was impaled on the sword of his adversary. The boy fell to the ground, his lifeless eyes staring at Mandar, demanding vengeance. Mandar felt a wave of helplessness sweep over him as he took in the sight of his dead friend. The feral howl that escaped his mouth was a mix of agony and rage.

With a strength he did not know he possessed, Mandar hurled himself at his opponent. He did not feel the edge of the blade that grazed his shoulder. As the Mahishur officer struggled to regain his balance, Mandar brought his sword down hard and neatly sliced off his adversary's sword-wielding arm at the shoulder. The enemy's severed limb had not yet touched the ground when Mandar decapitated him.

Weeping inconsolably, Mandar dragged Alok's body to a nearby house. He gently placed the brave soldier's body on the ground, and chanted a brief prayer in his native tongue, exhorting their clan's holy spirit to transport Alok's soul to heaven. *I will fight alongside the Mauryan emperor for as long as I live, my friend,* he silently swore as he got up to rejoin the battle raging outside.

The setting of the sun brought an end to the bloody battle of Mahishur. The surviving Prince of Mahishur, Aagney, had been taken prisoner, and the commander of the Mahishur army had been killed in battle.

The dead warriors from both the armies were cremated together in a large open ground. Bindusara believed that in death, there were only heroes, no enemies. The haze of smoke from the mass cremation darkened the evening sky. The ashes of the Mahishur warriors would later be gathered and immersed into the Cauvery river as per their custom. Those of the Mauryan soldiers would be taken to their beloved Pataliputra and dispersed in the holy waters of the Ganga.

Away from the cremation of the Mahishur and Mauryan warriors, a small group of 20 tribals stood staring blankly at the flames emanating from Alok's pyre. Mandar had performed the duties of a clansman by lighting his friend's pyre. The group was pulled out of their reverie by the sound of several approaching footsteps. Mandar turned around to see a large number of Mauryan soldiers gathering around Alok's pyre, to pay their respects to the young warrior. Commander Balki and Senapati Ajaya were amongst those who had arrived to honour the brave tribal. Balki put his hand on Mandar's shoulder – the closest indication of camaraderie a warrior could provide.

Mandar finally understood what Alok had tried to explain to him earlier that day. He raised his head proudly as the thought came to him. *I too am a Mauryan.*

Aagney was ushered into Bindusara's tent. The former prince's hands were bound and there was not a spot on his body that was free of cuts and bruises received during the battle, yet he walked in with an air of defiance. Ajaya motioned to the guards to untie him.

'We meet again,' Bindusara said softly. Aagney gave him a steady stare, not bothering to reply.

Bindusara held out a glass, 'Drink it,' he said gently. 'It will make you feel better.'

Aagney made no move to accept the drink.

Bindusara shrugged. 'You are seething inside – and rightly so. Wars never have a happy ending', he said quietly. 'Would you believe me if I said that this war had more to do with preserving peace than anything else?'

Aagney's face registered incredulity. He wondered what the Mauryan conqueror meant by that.

Bindusara spoke in a mild tone. 'I am not required to give you an explanation, but I owe it to your father. We had a great understanding, you know.'

Aagney now stared at Bindusara with undisguised curiosity.

The Mauryan emperor sighed. 'If you and your brother had not been fighting for the throne, there would have been no danger to the peace in this land. I would not have had to intervene.' He paused. 'This war would never have happened.'

Aagney's face crumpled. The death of hundreds of his soldiers and his brother weighed heavy on his conscience. *I killed them, I killed my brother*, he mentally castigated himself, revolted at the ramifications of his overriding ambition.

Bindusara's words brought him back to the moment. 'The law demands that you be taken prisoner. However…'

I am already a prisoner. My soul will never be free after what I have done, Aagney was thinking.

'However, I can accord you a royal pardon once Mahishur is made a vassal of the Mauryan empire, with you governing it on my behalf.'

Your pardon won't be enough to make me pardon myself, Aagney's inner voice screamed inside his head.

Bindusara waited patiently for a reply. He knew he didn't need Aagney's acceptance to make Mahishur subservient to the Mauryan kingdom. But he admired the young man's spirit and wanted to give him a chance to save himself. Aagney was aware that Bindusara was trying to save him. But he also knew what Bindusara hadn't yet guessed – that he was beyond redemption.

'Give me an honourable death...a soldier's death,' Aagney whispered hoarsely, his eyes pleading with Bindusara for the first time.

Bindusara recognized the deeply haunted look in Aagney's eyes. He had seen the same look in the eyes of men who had lost all hope in life. He understood.

'Allow him to have his wish,' Bindusara said, looking in Ajaya's direction. 'Let him have his sword in his hand when the Mauryan arrows fly in his direction,' Bindusara said quietly.

Aagney smiled for the first time since the battle had ended. Bindusara had instructed the Mauryan senapati to give him a death reserved for the bravest of warriors. His soul would finally be free – soon.

He bowed to Bindusara and was escorted out by the guards.

Bindusara knew Aagney had not bowed to the man who had conquered him, but to one who had shown him compassion in his final moments.

4

Subhadrangi gazed adoringly through the window at Ashoka. The three-year-old and his friend Mali were displaying their prowess at swinging on the aerial prop roots of a large banyan tree. For some unfathomable reason, Subhadrangi's recent past flashed before her eyes...

The idea of marrying Bindusara had been both exciting and scary. Having lived the simple life of a Brahmin's daughter, the very notion of being the emperor's wife terrified her. Yet, some irrational sense told her that Bindusara would protect her as her father had, and love her as any other husband would. Subhadrangi was infatuated by his good looks and enigmatic personality. At 40, he was 22 years older than her. Yet, the stringent physical training he pushed himself to undergo every day made him look far younger than his age. Broad-shouldered and ivory-complexioned, he looked like a veritable god to Subhadrangi. His small beady eyes shone with unbridled intensity.

At her father's insistence, the wedding ceremony was held in a temple on the outskirts of Pataliputra. A hundred learned Brahmins from the city came to bless the couple, given that Subhadrangi was one of their own. She looked resplendent, attired in red and gold, and Bindusara was fascinated by her youth and innocent beauty.

Unknown to Subhadrangi, he had had an acrimonious discussion with Rakshita, the chief queen. Rakshita had not taken well to the impending wedding. Bindusara rationalized that a raja had many duties. Rakshita looked incredulous at this answer but decided to keep quiet. Bindusara however knew her well enough to understand that the matter had not ended.

A sunset after the wedding, Subhadrangi was getting ready after her bath when she was summoned by Agramahisi Rakshita. Daya, her new companion, cheerfully hummed a tune while adjusting her robes. The carefree tune was in stark contrast to the turmoil in Subhadrangi's mind. She felt completely unprepared to play the role of a young queen. A strong sense of foreboding enveloped her as she sensed that the light heartedness of her childhood sunsets was all but over.

'Oh Daya, how can you be so cheerful?' Subhadrangi sighed. 'I am not looking forward to meeting the agramahisi.'

Daya gave her a puzzled look. 'Why is that?' she asked, genuinely confused.

'I don't know the ways of royalty,' Subhadrangi said morosely. 'I am sure to make a fool of myself in front of the agramahasi.'

'It didn't matter to the raja that you are not of royal blood. Why does it bother you?'

'Oh, you won't understand,' said Subhadrangi in a dismal voice. 'I feel so out of place here.'

The silence loomed heavy in the room and it was at that moment that Daya knew for certain that Subhadrangi had not married Bindusara with the intent of becoming a queen. She mentally castigated herself for having participated earlier in malicious gossip about the new queen. Aloud she said, 'Don't worry! From now on I will do my best to keep you out of trouble. And don't underestimate my abilities.' Her eyes twinkling, she continued. 'I may be even younger than you. But I have been around the palace much longer.'

Subhadrangi smiled for the first time that morning.

Agramahisi Rakshita's chambers were as stately and elegant as she herself was. Patterns of green and gold woven around polished wood adorned her personal section of the large palace – an area where she reigned supreme. She came from one of the oldest royal families of the time. Even though kings were known to have many wives, Bindusara treaded carefully where she was concerned. Rakshita was a tall woman. Her glowing body was well toned and the sari draped loosely around her body did little to hide the seductive curves underneath. The jet-black hair was neatly combed into a bun held in place by an elephant-tooth comb. However, all her physical attractions failed to diminish the intelligence that lay behind the Queen's unearthly beauty.

A distinct scent of sweet rose incense pervaded the queen's personal chambers. Rakshita was sipping cool chaas *when the chambermaid announced Subhadrangi's arrival. The young queen tentatively entered Rakshita's inner chambers. Even though Daya's presence by her side comforted her, Subhadrangi was uncertain how to conduct herself in front of the senior queen.*

Then she recalled her father's words. 'A man is known by his deeds, not by his birth.' She felt imbued with a sudden surge of confidence. In a society that allowed a person's caste to dictate their life, her father's thoughts were revolutionary.

Subhadrangi touched Rakshita's feet and said softly, 'Please don't grudge my presence. We are all ruled by our destiny. I would like to be friends with you.'

Rakshita was taken aback. She had expected insolence from the new bride and was prepared for it. Subhadrangi's deference and grace came as a surprise.

'Friends, we can never be. You may as well accept that. Stay out of my way and I might be able to tolerate your presence in the palace.' To make things very clear, she leaned closer and whispered, 'You should also know that my son Susima is being groomed as the emperor of the Mauryan empire.'

Rakshita paused long enough for this to sink in before continuing. 'By the way, I have organized a feast in your honour.'

Subhadrangi looked at the queen, unable to believe that Rakshita could be so scornful one moment and welcoming the next. The grateful smile that was beginning to form on her lips died as soon as she heard Rakshita's next words.

'You will be serving the choicest meat delicacies to the royal guests,' Rakshita said in a sweet voice, the tone unable to mask the impact she knew her words would have on Subhadrangi.

Subhdrangi's stomach churned at the thought of meat. As a Brahmin, she felt it was the ultimate sin to kill other living beings.

'I…I will do that,' she managed to murmur in a shaky voice. But she found she was speaking to herself. Rakshita had already turned her back on the young bride and dismissed her as one would a lowly mendicant.

In the subsequent months Subhadrangi was denigrated by Rakshita on various occasions. Characteristically, she bore it in silence. Whenever Bindusara visited her, she never mentioned the snubs. Daya was the only one allowed to share her sorrow.

However, water usually overflows when a vessel is full to the brim. This was Subhadrangi's state of mind when Bindusara came to her one sunset. He found her usual effervescence lacking. She did make a genuine attempt to laugh at his jokes, but he could see through her. The laughter seemed hollow today.

'You are not happy,' he said softly. It was not a question – it was a statement born out of certainty.

Subhadrangi bit her lip, 'Do you think a bird would be happy in a cage, even if the cage is a golden one?'

Her words stung him to the core. He was quick to retort. 'Your father came to me with the marriage proposal, remember?'

For once, Subhadrangi was neither afraid nor submissive. I have to do this, she told herself. Aloud, she said, 'I want a palace of my own. I don't want to be anywhere near the agramahisi.'

Bindusara saw his timid child-like bride transform into a confident young woman before his very eyes. A part of him liked the change. However, the rest of him felt strangely betrayed – he had the feeling that her new life and having to deal with Rakshita had somehow advanced her maturity, stolen the innocence he had fallen in love with at first sight – the innocence and vulnerability he had never experienced with Rakshita. He felt a faint stirring of resentment. The time with her had been somehow corrupted and it bothered him that he didn't understand this change.

'So be it,' he said finally as he got up to leave. For a brief instant, he considered saying something that might possibly make the moment easier. But years of pride and of being obeyed without question were too strong in him. He nodded at her curtly and left without another word.

It took a couple of sunsets before Bindusara's agitation settled down sufficiently for him to do what needed to be done. He summoned the royal architect. 'You will design a marble palace in the middle of Lake Pyasi for my younger queen,' he commanded in a sonorous tone. 'It should be self-contained and have sprawling gardens. Access to it should be only by boat. Make sure the palace has all the facilities required by a young prince of the Mauryan empire.'

The architect, who had heard about the prediction of Subhadrangi giving birth to a future King of Kings, was only too happy to be a part of it.

'Raje, it shall be done. When the palace is completed, people from all over the Mauryan empire will come to admire it for the architectural wonder that it will be.'

Ashoka was barely a year old when Subhadrangi moved into the Lotus Lake Palace. The royal architect had lived up to his promise. The palace was an architectural wonder. It stood on an island at the centre of the lake, the entrance facing the sun, its rays flooding it with golden light. Each chamber had its own private pool that snaked its way to a larger one in a huge courtyard. The reflection of the sun travelled from one end of the large pool to the other over the course of the day so that it was possible to tell the time just by looking at it. The outer walls of the chambers had inlaid mirror work so that beautiful patterns adorned the opposite walls by virtue of its reflection. It was a marvellous play of light that never failed to enrapture the queen.

Subhadrangi sighed, gazing lovingly at Ashoka. 'This is our home, son. You and I are going to spend many happy horas *here. Others may not see your father's physical attributes and his royal bearing in you today. But you will be a man of deeds – somebody whose actions will speak louder than any royal posturing could ever do.' She paused before murmuring softly in his ears, 'And I will make you such a man!'*

A pair of intelligent-looking eyes stared back at her. He is so much like you Bindusara, *she thought to herself as she saw her husband's small beady eyes in their son's face.* Why can't you see it? *She sighed sadly, wondering whether Bindusara would ever grow to love their child as he doted on Susima. The toddler seemed to understand every word his mother spoke. His frail brown hands clutched at her* antariya.

Ashoka began to grow into a bright, happy child. Daya's son Mali was his constant companion. Younger than Ashoka, Mali was inseparable from the prince.

Between the long horas *spent being taught by Subhadrangi and playing with Mali, Ashoka displayed uncanny progress. He was an inquisitive child willing to devour learning through every pore of his being. Subhadrangi helped stimulate his desire to learn whatever he could, from wherever he could. It was as if she had decided to prove the world and Bindusara wrong.* My son is not the weakling you have declared him to be, *she thought calmly, her stoic upbringing enabling her to put all her energies into positive action rather than brooding over what she had seen on Bindusara's face.*

The sunsets passed swiftly, and soon Ashoka was a wiry three-year-old.

One sunset, Bindusara paid his customary visit to Subhadrangi's palace. He sucked in his breath as she looked up from what she was reading, her kohl-lined eyes reflecting her pleasure at seeing him. As always, her beauty mesmerized him.

He smiled at her. 'What are you reading?' he asked gently, even as she showed him the cover of the manuscript. The palm leaves of the manuscript flipped in the wind as Bindusara tried to make sense of what he had just seen. 'You are reading the *Arthashastra*!' He couldn't keep the surprise and confusion out of his voice. The *Arthashastra* was the undisputed text on matters of administration and economics. It was not a book to be taken lightly and very few, even among generals and kings, were able to follow what the great Chanakya had written in his masterpiece.

Subhadrangi was not surprised by Bindusara's bemusement. The *Arthashastra* was not a book fancied by queens. She smiled, 'Why not? I am the mother of a future emperor. I want Ashoka to learn how a raja should rule.' Seeing Bindusara look sceptical, she took his hand gently. 'I want him to be a great and just emperor – like his father.'

Bindusara sighed inwardly. *How do I explain to her that*

unlike his stepbrother Susima, Ashoka does not have the royal bearing of an emperor – that I see nothing of me in him, he thought. He clutched at his forehead. 'I have a headache. Can you rub some sandalwood paste on it?'

Subhadrangi was taken aback. Bindusara's change of subject and obvious reluctance to discuss Ashoka showed her afresh the disdain he felt for his younger son. She nodded absently and went to get the paste that usually helped calm Bindusara's frayed nerves and relieve his headache.

Bindusara loved Subhadrangi with a fervour he had not known existed within him, until he had met her. While Rakshita had no competitor when it came to seduction, he actually enjoyed the placid moments of conversation he had with Subhadrangi. And her innocent vulnerability did more to ignite his manhood than any art of seduction Rakshita could practise. In fact, as long as they could avoid the topic of Ashoka and the prediction – which now seemed completely implausible – they got along wonderfully. Over the past few months, Bindusara had frequently asked Subhadrangi to organize feasts for royal visitors at the Lake Palace. And no one who had been touched by her hospitality went away without wondering how the rough-hewn Bindusara had secured a bride as gentle and guileless as Subhadrangi.

Bindusara's thoughts turned to his older son, Susima – his pride. This was one thing Rakshita had given him that Subhadrangi had failed to provide. An heir who exhibited all the trappings of a future emperor – handsome like Bindusara himself and regal in his bearing and attitude. It was true that Susima was a trifle arrogant and fraternized only with children of royalty. But wasn't this too an indication of his princely demeanour? Ashoka's apparent inadequacy convinced Bindusara of Susima's eligibility more than anything Susima himself could have done.

Bindusara's reverie was rudely broken as Ashoka scampered up to him and tugged at his robe. Bindusara brushed him aside, barely noticing him. 'Not now. I am busy,' he growled, getting irritated as Ashoka continued to clutch at his clothes.

It was fortunate that Mali appeared just in time to rescue Ashoka from Bindusara's growing exasperation. 'Atoka, Atoka,' lisped Mali. 'Let us feed the tadpoles.'

Ashoka grinned and raced Mali to the pond. Bindusara looked on thoughtfully.

Suddenly Susima's shunning of commoners' children did not seem such a big issue to Bindusara. If anything, it actually seemed like the right thing to do.

Subhadrangi sat pensively. Ashoka was late for his evening lessons. And Daya had no idea where Mali was either. *The two of them must be out looking for tadpoles*, she thought to herself. But unlike other sunsets, the thought of her son's innocent pursuits did not make her smile. She had still not got over Bindusara's abrupt departure earlier in the day. She had returned with the sandalwood paste to rub on his forehead, but the emperor had already left without so much as a goodbye.

She heard Ashoka and Mali's voices before they came into sight. Ashoka was walking with a swagger, trying to copy his father's stately walk. Mali followed giggling, trying to imitate his slightly older friend. As they came nearer, Subhadrangi noticed telltale signs of mithai around their mouths. 'Have you been gorging on sweets again?' she asked softly, but there was veiled irritation beneath the soft tone. The boys had been told not to eat sweets as their teeth were faring badly owing to overindulgence in the sugary items doled out by the royal cook.

Ashoka realized his mother was not in a playful mood right then. 'No, Mother, we haven't!' he said quickly, attempting to dodge past her.

The slap resounded like a clap of thunder as it landed

squarely on his left cheek. Absolute silence filled the room, so much so that everyone in it could hear the other people's breathing.

Mali looked like he wanted to say something, but Subhadrangi's expression told him this was not the right time to open his mouth. Seeing her attention focused on Ashoka, he quietly tiptoed out of the room. Ashoka looked at his mother. He knew intuitively that he had done some grievous wrong for Subhadrangi to have slapped him.

'Are you going to lie to your mother now?' Subhadrangi asked softly. Each syllable she uttered felt like a series of slaps to Ashoka. He willed himself to hold back the tears that threatened to flow any moment. He had failed his mother by lying to her; he couldn't let her down further by displaying another weakness. 'I will never lie to you again, Mother.'

The words were spoken with a certitude that was not lost on Subhadrangi. She hugged him close. 'I love you, Ashoka, but I cannot, will not, bear any vices in you.'

As Ashoka grew older, Subhadrangi felt it was important for him to spend time with his brother. Ashoka and Mali were encouraged to visit the main palace so that they could play with Susima and his friends. But Ashoka often found himself at the receiving end of Susima's jokes. Susima had given him the nickname of Kalu as an overt reference to Ashoka's dark complexion.

Ashoka accepted all the jibes good-naturedly. 'Come, I will give you a hug and turn you black too. Nobody will know the difference then,' he laughed.

The boys were no longer mere children. They were all aged between seven and nine years. It was time for them to start their formal education. Ashoka was to be accompanied by Mali, his ever-present companion – it was at Subhadrangi's behest that he was to be taught alongside Ashoka. Susima had Devendra by his side. The latter was a distant cousin of Susima's from his mother's family. The four of them were to be trained by the man who had had the rare honour of being taught by the great Chanakya himself.

Chanakya, the author of *Arthashastra,* was revered by the Mauryans as much as the first Mauryan emperor Chandragupta, Bindusara's father. It was Chanakya, who with his astute guidance had helped Chandragupta Maurya overthrow the Nanda dynasty. The Mauryan empire was established jointly by Chanakya and Chandragupta Maurya.

Ashoka had grown up on tales told by Subhadrangi of how Chankaya had moulded Ashoka's grandfather from a village lad to become one of the greatest emperors in the land. Legend had it that in one of his wanderings, Chanakya observed a young boy playing with his friends. Dressed in tattered clothes, the youth was pretending to be a king. Chanakaya was impressed with the boy's obvious leadership qualities and took him to Takshashila to groom him.

Chanakya's interest in the boy was not entirely selfless. He wanted to use the youth to take revenge on the corrupt Raja Dhana Nanda, the ruler at that time. Dhana Nanda was known for his bad governance. Chanakya confronted him only to be insulted. He then swore to free the land from his shackles and create a just state. In the boy, he found a way of bringing his dream to life. Under his tutelage, the youth grew to excel in every subject possible, mastering the Vedas with the same ease as he did the tactics of war. Chanakya and the young man trained by him faced numerous defeats at the hands of the Nanda king. Finally, in a master stroke, the young man defeated the Nandas and founded his own empire.

This youth was Chandragupta Maurya, father of Bindusara, grandfather of Ashoka and Susima – but, above all, known to the world as the student of Chanakya.

After Chandragupta Maurya ascended the throne and founded the Mauryan empire, he persuaded his former acharya to stay on as his *agramatya.*

Chanakya was an enigmatic man. His ways were strange, especially those that dealt with ensuring the safety of his protégé, Chandragupta. These were the sunsets when assassins tried different ways to kill kings, the most common method being poisoning. To circumvent this possibility, the shrewd Chanakya started giving Chandragupta small doses of poison mixed in his food to help make him immune to its destructive effects. One fateful day, Chandragupta's wife unwittingly partook of some of his food. She was nine months pregnant at that time. The poison made her violently ill. When Chanakya realized what had happened, he cut open her belly to save the baby and named him 'Bindusara' as he was touched by a *bindu* of poison.

Chanakya had been defeated in political debate only once in his life. The man who vanquished the master of masters was none other than one of his own students. His name was Akila and he had once saved Bindusara's life in a conspiracy led by Kalinga, the neighbouring state. Henceforth, he had been appointed the security advisor to Bindusara. It was this illustrious personage whom Bindusara had now persuaded to teach his sons.

5

The long-awaited day had finally arrived. It was the fifth *hora* of the day. The darkness had not yet given way to light and the boys were up. Yearning for their warm beds, they found themselves instead in the spartan training room where Acharya Akila had summoned them. The boys waited with bated breath for the great master to arrive. There wasn't one of them who wasn't in awe of the acharya.

The wiry and lean Akila strode into the chambers. At 40,

he still retained a youthful look. His shoulder-length jet-black hair was combed back. Small piercing eyes scrutinized the boys, who held their breath in anticipation.

'I will teach you military strategy, international relations, economics and fiscal policy, among other subjects,' Akila started without preamble. 'Bakura will assist me in your physical training.' He indicated the tall, well-built man who had followed him into the room.

Akila paused, studying the impact his words had had so far on the boys. 'People say I have eyes at the back of my head. I hope you will remember this.' Then, turning towards Mali, he said with emphasis, 'You are here only because the raja wished it so. Make sure you prove yourself worthy of his trust.'

Mali looked towards Ashoka for moral support, but Ashoka was intent on holding the acharya's gaze, studying the master as the acharya observed them. Susima and Devendra suppressed a snicker at what they thought was the acharya's way of putting Mali in his place. Neither of them understood the acharya had simply made a matter-of-fact statement to Mali.

'Let us go out and enjoy the pleasures of nature.' Akila turned around abruptly and walked out of the room. The boys scrambled to keep pace with his long strides.

Akila halted when they reached the mango grove. He pointed to a ripe mango hanging on a tree. 'This mango will fall to the ground any moment now,' he said softly. 'Make a ladder,' he ordered. The boys looked on, confused.

Akila sighed. 'Stand so that the tallest person has his feet on the ground. The next person will climb on this person's shoulder, and continue till the shortest boy is at the top. The one at the top will be responsible for catching the mango as it falls.'

He looked at them to see if they had understood the instructions. 'The mango cannot be plucked. It has to fall on its own. And bear in mind, if any one of you totters to the ground, everybody loses!'

Mali gulped. He was the shortest. He didn't get time to think as Devendra climbed over Susima's shoulders, and Ashoka nimbly followed him. His legs shaking, Mali gingerly made his way to the top, unwittingly hitting Susima on his head with the heel of his foot. Susima growled in anger but stifled a retort. However, at the end of a few minutes, he could control himself no longer. 'How much do you guys eat,' he muttered. 'And don't you ever wash your feet, Devendra? The stink is unbearable,' he whispered, grimacing.

Ashoka concentrated on balancing himself. It wasn't easy with Mali's knees shaking continuously. Two *horas* passed, agonizingly slow. Mali's arms ached with the effort of keeping them stretched out to catch the mango.

Akila looked on, waiting to observe a sign of weakness in any of the boys. But none of them was willing to be the first to give up. By afternoon, the sun was searing hot and the boys were exhausted.

Akila smiled to himself. He knew it would happen any moment now. All of a sudden, Devendra wavered. He made a half-hearted attempt to balance himself and tottered to the ground. Ashoka and Mali came toppling down on Susima.

Like a deck of cards they all lay scattered on the ground, too exhausted to move. Lying down was a luxury none of them was keen on relinquishing right now.

Akila's calm and nonchalant voice broke through the haze of their exhaustion-induced delirium. 'We meet in the teaching room in half a *hora*.'

Ashoka groaned. *This is going to be tougher that I expected,* he thought. He saw Mali valiantly trying to drag himself off the ground. The usually immaculate Susima still lay unmoving, a ridiculous expression on his face. Devendra too appeared lost to the world. *I wonder if they even heard the acharya's command,* he thought to himself.

Ten minutes later, the boys sat slumped in the teaching room. Akila grinned at them.

'I see we have a lot of work to do,' he began. 'What did you learn from your task, if you did learn anything at all, that is?' he added acidly.

The boys were silent. Akila turned to Susima, the oldest amongst them. 'Why don't you answer, Prince? Let us see if you are worthy of Magadha,' he said in a half-mocking tone.

Susima, caught off-guard, stammered, 'A...acharya, in my opinion, you were testing our endurance skills. The exercise also stressed the importance of teamwork,' he said, glaring surreptitiously at Devendra, who smiled sheepishly.

'Does anybody want to add anything?' Akila said without commenting on Susima's analysis.

'The weakest link in the chain can disrupt the entire operation,' Ashoka said softly. 'It must be replaced with immediate effect – otherwise, the goal may not be achieved.' Devendra gave Ashoka a hostile glare, which the latter ignored.

Akila gazed expressionlessly at Ashoka. 'I am glad that there is something apart from cow dung in your heads,' he said, addressing the class as a whole.

He continued. 'An emperor's expansion of his kingdom depends greatly on his frontline soldiers. They have to fight for every *angula* of land. Trudging in the rain and cold weather, they may even need to carry their companions and occasionally face starvation. They require complete understanding between them to execute their commanders'strategy. My endeavour will be to give you a taste of it.'

Four young heads nodded enthusiastically. Akila had given them their first lesson.

Ashoka wondered what was in store for them on this second sunset of training with Akila. Everyone had ensured they had had a quick meal of fruits before reaching class. They didn't want to starve like they had the previous sunset.

The murmuring subsided as Akila walked in.

'I trust you have all slept well,' he boomed without really expecting an answer. 'Today, we will analyse battle tactics. Why don't we start with your grandfather, the legendary Chandragupta Maurya?' he said, fixing his beady eyes on Susima and Ashoka. 'Chandragupta Maurya defeated Dhana Nanda, one of the most powerful kings at that time. Nanda's army comprised 200,000 soldiers in the *pada* division, 80,000 *turanga*, 8,000 *rathas* and 6,000 war *gajas*. Chandragupta's army was just one-fourth that size. How do you think he won?'

Susima was silent. He wanted to tell the acharya that it seemed like a miracle but he refrained from doing so. Akila didn't seem to be the kind of man who believed in miracles.

Ashoka, having heard the entire story from Subhadrangi and later studied Chanakya's notes on the war, found the question elementary. 'His strategy was to attack the weakest link in Dhana Nanda's army.'

Akila raised an eyebrow. 'Would you care to elaborate?' he said expressionlessly.

'Acharya, my grandfather was defeated not once, but several times. On all those occasions, he had made a frontal attack on Nanda's army. This was a mistake as Nanda had a far greater force than ours. After his last defeat, when Grandfather was returning home with his army, they stopped at a village to rest. He noticed a woman fussing over her young child. The child had apparently burnt his fingers while eating a hot roti. The woman explained to the child that the roti was hottest at the centre. If instead, the child would eat the corners first, it would be easier to eat. It was an epiphany for Chandragupta. In his next battle with the Nanda king, he began by chipping away at the enemy's edges which were not guarded as well as the centre. Once he had decimated those, it became easier to launch a full-scale attack on the core of Nanda's force.'

Akila nodded approvingly at Ashoka. He quickly moved on to discuss other effective battle stratagems. Just before they recessed for lunch, he held a short session on the potential security gaps inherent within the city of Pataliputra.

The water looked forbiddingly cold. Susima dipped his fingers in the water and pulled them back instantly. Devendra shivered, partly because of the cold weather, and to some extent at the alacrity with which Susima had pulled back from the water.

Mali glanced anxiously at Ashoka, wondering what was in store for them. Ashoka's face was devoid of any expression.

Every boy there awaited instructions from the acharya. Akila had not yet told them what he wanted them to do.

'Strip to your undergarments and wade into the water until it reaches your chest level.' The calmly spoken words struck a chill in their hearts. Devendra gasped in disbelief. Susima glanced sharply at his friend, quietly willing him to look strong. Ashoka still had the same stoic face he had adopted since they had reached the banks of the Ganga, after their evening lessons.

'Go on!' urged Akila. 'Or are you waiting for the sun to come out again by any chance?' he said, chuckling at his own uncharacteristic joke. No one joined him.

Susima surprised everyone by stepping first into the cold water. Devendra knew his friend was trying to make up for lost ground in the classroom. Ashoka had eclipsed all of them, including Susima, with his insightful answers on both sunsets of training. *But Susima will show that upstart when it comes to physical strength,* Devendra sniggered quietly.

Susima's breath caught in his throat as he waded further into the water. But he didn't allow his face to betray him. He knew Akila was observing him from the shore.

Ashoka watched Susima braving the cold water. His respect for his older sibling grew a notch. Succumbing to the inevitability of the situation, he grinned at Mali. 'Well, at least after this experience, we won't need to wear furs when we go for Himalayan trips.'

Mali smiled and followed Ashoka into the water. Devendra was the last to venture in, and only after he saw the gleam in Akila's eyes.

The sun had set completely by now. Akila cleared his throat. 'I have some work to attend to,' he said. 'I will be back soon. Until then, enjoy the beauty of nature.' They heard him humming a folk tune as he walked away from them, the growing darkness enveloping him completely after a while.

As the darkness gathered strength, so did the current of the flowing water. It was an ordeal just to try and stand straight without being swept away. The biting cold had given way to a certain numbness.

Ashoka noticed Mali turning a shade of blue. He nudged him, urging him to keep moving his legs to keep the circulation going. Susima was completely still and kept muttering unintelligibly under his breath. At the end of another *hora*, Mali's body started swaying. Ashoka knew it was a matter of time before his friend went under completely. He shook Mali by the shoulder, trying to rouse him from the cold-induced stupor.

'Go! Get out of the water now!' he said sharply. Mali nodded, only half comprehending what Ashoka was trying to say. He staggered to the shore, and at once collapsed to the ground. Devendra, who had been waiting for an excuse to get out, was overjoyed. 'Well, if he can leave, I don't see why I can't,' he said and waded out.

Susima glanced at Ashoka, trying to gauge if he was willing to give up too. He was met with Ashoka's resolute look. He smiled back in a brave attempt to show he wasn't bothered by the challenge either.

Akila observed all this from where he was hiding. He gave a grudging smile. *These boys might just turn into men some day,* he chuckled to himself.

Raskhita loomed over Susima who was sitting on his bed, drying his hair. 'What were you doing in the water?' she asked, masking her anger. She loved her son and wanted him to be strong. But she wasn't too happy about him being taught along with Ashoka and Mali. *One a Brahmin woman's son and the other a lowly maid's. God knows what is wrong with Bindusara – why is he allowing this?* She gnashed her teeth as she waited for Susima's answer.

'Mother, Acharya Akila had given us a test of endurance,' Susima said slowly. He could still feel the cold in his bones. 'All right,' Rakshita muttered, not wanting to say anything about Akila in front of her son. But she made a mental note to check with the acharya just how safe these tasks were.

Subhadrangi smiled fondly at Ashoka as he changed into dry clothes and got ready to settle into bed. 'Was it a difficult day?' she asked with a twinkle in her eyes.

'No, Mother, it was the usual,' replied Ashoka. 'Acharya Akila tried getting rid of us once again, but we managed to save ourselves.' He guffawed.

Subhadrangi gave him a mock-stern look. 'It was nice of him to hide there and ensure you were all safe.'

'Oh no, Mother,' Ashoka said, serious now. 'Watching over our safety was just a part of it. He wanted to see how we would acquit ourselves in his absence.'

'And did you fare well?' she asked, trying to guess his answer.

Ashoka was quiet for a moment, then he grinned. 'Well, I did have an invigorating bath in the river.' Subhadrangi smiled indulgently and was about to say something but Ashoka had already fallen sound asleep.

'Sleep, my little Mauryan. Someday, the innocence will fall away and what remains will be the real you.'

6

The acharya's class was abuzz with discussion on the tests that Akila subjected them to. The chatter died abruptly as the boys heard the unmistakable sound of Akila's feet, the impact of his sandals on the earthern floor sounding louder in the quiet *horas* of the morning.

He looked around the room, absent-mindedly brushing off an imaginary speck of dirt from his otherwise immaculate attire. Characteristically, he came straight to the point. 'You are now going to become acquainted with the forests surrounding our city. Appropriate attire has been arranged. Each of you will be given a spear, a sword and one sunset's ration of food and water.' He paused as if to assess whether his protégés were with him so far.

'What do we need to do in the forest, acharya?' Devendra asked impulsively.

'Patience will take you a long way, young man,' Akila said slowly, making Devendra squirm in his seat. Turning to the others, he continued. 'Once we are deep within the forest, you will be left on your own. It will take you about five sunsets to find your way back to the city and the palace.'

He glanced at Devendra. 'You may ask questions now.'

Devendra hesitated. He didn't want to appear foolish before the acharya yet again.

Ashoka voiced the question that was on everybody's mind. 'Acharya, if it is going to take us five sunsets to return, why are we carrying only one sunset's ration?'

'Because you will need to find your own food and water for the other four, Prince Ashoka!'

Akila's answer was met with confounded silence. For once even Ashoka did not have a suitable reply.

'Good, it is settled then. We depart within the *hora*,' Akila said purposefully. 'Your families have been informed already,' he added, almost as an afterthought.

The day had almost ended by the time the chariot carrying Akila and the boys reached the outskirts of Pataliputra and entered the deep forests. Once inside the dense jungle, whatever sunlight remained was blocked by the towering trees. Automatically, Devendra huddled closer to Susima and Mali edged towards his childhood friend. At regular intervals, Akila gave the charioteer coded instructions, and the latter changed the route accordingly.

All of a sudden, the chariot stopped. They were in a clearing – possibly the first spot in the last few *horas* of riding through the forest where the trees gave way and the moon was visible in the sky.

'This is as far as the chariot will go,' Akila declared, motioning to the boys to get off.

Mali looked at Ashoka, who shrugged. He didn't have any idea what awaited them. Susima irritably pushed Devendra away from him. He stretched his legs and gingerly got up. All of them assembled in front of the acharya for what they knew would be his final instructions for the latest task he had set them.

'You will split up into two groups,' Akila began. 'Do you have a preference or should I decide for you?'

Devendra was the first to answer. 'I will be with Susima.'

'Why am I not surprised?' Akila said mildly.

He looked pointedly at each of them. 'Remember three things. You can eat or drink only what you have been given in your packs or what you yourself find or hunt in the forest. Secondly, the only path you can take to return to the city is through the forest.' He paused before sharing the final instruction. 'Once you reach Pataliputra, you will enter through the Kshatriya gate. Any deviation from these instructions will immediately disqualify the defaulting team.'

The words were spoken softly, but there was an unmistakable warning in the tone that told the boys they couldn't take the task lightly.

Looking at their grim faces, Akila added as an afterthought, 'I wouldn't have embarked on this exercise if I had even the slightest doubt about your capabilities. Use your common sense and whatever I have taught you so far. You won't face any problem.' Akila had spent some time thinking about whether the test was apt for their age before deciding to repose faith in them.

Having said what he needed to say, he leaped into the chariot with surprising agility for a man of his age. The boys watched as the chariot was swallowed up by the ever growing darkness in the forest.

It suddenly struck them that they were all alone. Four young boys in a forest, with no idea what the wilderness had in store for them. All of them were thinking the same thing. *Nothing that Akila had taught them in the secure confines of his class and occasional outdoor forays had prepared them for what lay ahead.*

Devendra was the first to break the silence. 'I am starved,' he whined. He made to open his bag to take out the food. Susima looked at his friend exasperatedly.

Mali suppressed a giggle. 'Actually, I am rather hungry myself.'

Susima and Ashoka looked at each other, wondering what the other was thinking. 'I think we should get a fire going before it becomes completely dark,' Ashoka said with a hint of urgency in his voice. Susima nodded. It seemed the most sensible thing to do. Devendra glared at Ashoka, placing the food back in his bag.

In no time, they had gathered the necessary material and soon a blazing fire illuminated the clearing. They settled down around it to eat. The fire would serve two purposes – it would give them protection from the increasing cold and keep wild animals at bay.

Once the sparse meal was over, they sat around the fire, watching the embers flying in the wind, making dazzling patterns as they danced in the otherwise pitch-black night.

All of a sudden, they were a little more aware of their surroundings. It dawned on them that this was very different from the acharya's regular tests. This could be grievously dangerous if they made a big mistake. Every call of a wild animal took on a different meaning, every shadow at the edge of the clearing appeared more sinister than it had just a few minutes earlier.

'One of us needs to keep watch while the others sleep,' Ashoka said quietly. His words echoed in the darkness and he was conscious of Mali and Devendra shivering ever so slightly.

Susima nodded. 'I will take the first watch,' he offered. Devendra will be next,' he said without bothering to ask the latter who nodded in quiet acquiescence.

'I can be next,' Mali said tentatively. He looked at Ashoka, who smiled back.

Susima rubbed his hands together, the action giving him some warmth and serving to give him additional courage. 'I will wake you in two *horas*, Devendra,' he said quietly. 'Try and get some sleep till then.'

No more words were spoken or necessary as everyone except Susima placed their bags under their head and tried to sleep in their unusual surroundings.

As he watched the last of the three succumb to sleep, Susima felt a sudden stab of fear. Darkness had always terrified him. Sitting alone in the middle of nowhere, he felt the cold finger of fear paralyse him completely. With a surge of will power, he forced himself to focus on the fire and keep the frightening thoughts at a distance. As he did every time he was under stress, he began muttering to himself. Unintelligible to others, it was a short prayer Rakshita used to hum for him when he was much younger. It was the Ram *rakshastotra*. He repeated it over and over again until, gradually, he began to breathe normally. He sighed. There was still plenty of time before he could wake up Devendra.

'Wake up, Mali,' Ashoka whispered, shaking him roughly.

Mali woke up with a start but made no sound as he noticed Ashoka put a finger to his lips. He looked around groggily. The fire was reduced to a few dying embers. Susima and Devendra were lost to the world, it seemed.

'We are leaving…now,' Ashoka said softly. 'Susima and Devendra will awaken soon, it is safe enough to leave them now.'

Mali nodded. Ashoka was amazed at how quickly his friend was all strapped up and ready to go. They started off in a direction opposite to where the sun had arisen. That was the path to Pataliputra.

The forest was denser than it had appeared while on the chariot. Ashoka and Mali's arms were already scratched at various places. Once again, Ashoka mentally thanked Akila's foresight in providing them with body gear that afforded good protection and prevented any serious damage.

Still, it was a formidable task to march through the undergrowth. Ashoka felt he hadn't stopped chopping and swinging with his sword ever since they had left the clearing. His arms ached with the effort. Mali, although of slighter built, valiantly took up the task of hacking through the forest when he saw Ashoka was completely done in.

They walked non-stop, drinking water from their flasks on the go.

A vigilant lookout for edible-looking wild berries and fruits ensured they wouldn't go hungry for some time at least.

Dusk was rapidly approaching and they hadn't yet found a suitable place to rest for the night.

'I am tired,' said Mali half-apologetically.

'I am too,' Ashoka answered without breaking step. 'But we need to go on. We can't stop here.'

They trudged along silently for some more time. Suddenly,

Ashoka became aware that Mali was no longer with him. He looked wildly in all directions. Not finding Mali in his line of vision, he retraced his steps. In a few moments he saw him.

Uncharacteristically, Mali had stopped to play with what looked like…a bear cub.

'Stop!' Ashoka shouted a warning.

Mali looked up, startled. He wondered what had got into Ashoka who was gesticulating wildly for Mali to run. He found out the very next instant as a large, ferocious-looking adult bear dashed out of the bushes. It was headed in Mali's direction. He realized at once why Ashoka had called out a warning – Akila had taught them that the mother bear seldom left its cubs alone for too long.

Mali cursed himself mentally and began to slowly back away towards Ashoka.

The bear raised itself on its hind legs, and Ashoka estimated its height at a little more than one *danda*.

The cub sensed its parent's anger and scampered into a nearby bush. The mother bear glared at the retreating back of its cub and then turned its hostile gaze at the two trespassers.

Ashoka tried to remember what he knew about bear behaviour. Bears were normally calm creatures and it was unusual for them to attack without provocation. He wondered whether playing with the bear cub qualified as provocation. He got his answer in the loud snarl that seemed to fill up the space between them and the animal.

Ashoka scoured the area for trees they could quickly climb. There were none. He decided quickly. Signalling to Mali, he lay down in a foetal position and forced his body to be completely still. Gaping incredulously at Ashoka, Mali followed suit, albeit reluctantly.

The bear looked at them, its small brown eyes reflecting its confusion. One hundred and twenty *kashtas* passed. Nothing happened. All of a sudden, the animal bared its fangs and charged at them. Their hearts thundering within their chest,

Ashoka and Mali forced themselves to remain still. All the while the childhood story of the two friends and a bear flashed before their eyes. The bear stopped when it reached the spot where they lay. It was waiting for a movement that would betray the boys and tell her they were alive. Hearing nothing, it roared in a mix of confusion and fury. In a final attempt to confront the enemy, the bear poked Ashoka with its snout, its sharp eyes straining for any movement. There were none. In the ensuing silence, Mali thought he could hear someone's heart thumping loudly. He wasn't sure whether it was his own or Ashoka's. It didn't matter. He just hoped the bear couldn't hear it as he did.

Certain that the motionless boys posed no threat to it or the cub, the bear grunted and moved away slowly. Ashoka and Mali continued lying down until they thought enough time had lapsed for them to get up safely.

Ashoka sighed in relief. 'For a moment there, I was sure we were dead meat,' he chuckled.

'I can't imagine what you are so happy about.' Mali said ruefully. 'My legs are still wobbly.'

'We are alive, aren't we?' Ashoka grinned.

'What now?' Mali wondered aloud.

Ashoka was at once business-like. 'Now we find a tree where we can spend the night safely – away from bears and other wild beasts.'

Mali nodded. 'I wonder how Susima and Devendra are doing.'

'If I know Susima, we will soon find out.' Ashoka smiled.

'This is one task his mother can't save him from.' Mali guffawed good-naturedly.

In another part of the forest, not too far away, Susima and Devendra were battling their own demons. Susima was not in the best mood. He had been irritable right after he had got up in the morning and realized that Ashoka and Mali had got a head start on them.

Slimy bastards, Susima thought, gnashing his teeth. *I will still beat them.* After waking up Devendra with a kick aimed at his backside, Susima had set a punishing pace for them. He wanted to catch up with the other team and tell them exactly what he thought of their silent departure in the morning.

'Oh Vishnu. What is the point of all this?' Devendra whined. 'Do you believe a trek in the forest will ever be useful to us?'

Susima gave him an impatient look. 'Dev, are you really that naive or do you have a talent for pretending you are?' He looked at his cousin pointedly. 'There will be situations in the near future when we will be required to lead other men. Do you think they will respect us if we display signs of weakness?'

'What are the senapatis for?' grumbled Devendra, unconvinced.

Susima shook his head and fell silent. They walked for three *horas* before arriving at a particularly dense part of the forest. Susima tapped his spear to the ground at every step to check for the possibility of lurking snakes. He had just begun to relax somewhat when he sensed danger.

'Watch out!' he yelled at Devendra. A huge python lunged at them, its mouth open wide. Thanks to Susima's timely warning, Devendra ducked just in time.

Susima gripped his spear with all his might and struck the gargantuan snake right on its head. The python's skin was so thick that the spear barely grazed its head.

Its innate fury roused, the python lunged at them again. In a desperate attempt to save himself, Susima unsheathed his sword and swiped at the snake's head with all his strength. The snake fell down, its tail thrashing wrathfully even in the throes of death.

'That was a close call,' Susima said haltingly, his breathing ragged.

'Too close for co...com...fort,' stammered Devendra, still in a state of shock.

It was in a relatively subdued frame of mind that they resumed their journey. If anything, Susima was even more alert now. And Devendra had realized that if they had to survive the next few sunsets in the forest, he would have to do his bit too.

By dusk, their exhausted limbs refused to carry them any further. Susima found a secure-looking place and called a halt for the sunset. Their food was almost over, and they had not been able to gather more than a few wild berries on the way. The rest had seemed deadly and inedible to Susima. Although Devendra did collect some colourful fruit, Susima remembered Akila describing a poisonous fruit that sounded a lot like it. Despite Devendra's protestations, Susima had been unrelenting and had thrown all of it out of the other boy's bag.

'We will have to hunt tomorrow,' Susima said, a serious expression marring his handsome features. 'Else, at this rate, we will be dead by the time we reach Pataliputra.'

No further words were exchanged between them as they settled down for the night.

Once again, Susima opted for the first watch. *This is going to be longer than last night,* he thought wearily. Before Devendra fell asleep, he could hear Susima muttering to himself.

Ashoka and Mali were not comfortable, perched as they were on the tree. Ashoka had taken first watch. Now, it was Mali's turn. It was a struggle to stay balanced on the tree and make sure he did not go back to sleep. The other thing was that he had to keep Ashoka supported so the prince did not fall to the ground while asleep. The night passed somehow, and he heaved a sigh of relief when the first ray of light peeped through the dense trees.

He woke up Ashoka, still taking utmost care that neither of them fell to the ground inadvertently. After taking turns to perform their morning ablutions, they were soon on their way. The tiredness of the previous sunset was still palpable in their limbs, and the new day did not offer any visible solace.

'Today, we need to hunt for food,' Ashoka said tersely. 'Let us keep an eye open for animal tracks.'

Mali nodded. 'The forest is so dense, though, that it might be impossible to spot anything.'

The morning turned into noon as they trudged on, hungry and thirsty.

Ashoka stopped abruptly. 'I need to relieve myself,' he said, moving towards a clump of trees to his side.

'Whoopee!' The excited sound came from behind the trees where Ashoka had ducked into a short while back. Mali was startled by the sound, and a little bemused when he saw his friend reappear. Ashoka was doing a little jig, his tanned face shining with happiness.

'I didn't know that relieving yourself could make you so happy,' Mali said in jest. 'You must do it more often.'

Ashoka punched him playfully. 'Come here, you moron. Look what I discovered.'

Mali followed Askoka and what he saw made him dance with joy too. They had inadvertently stumbled on to a gently flowing stream of water.

Without wasting a moment, they shed their clothes and raced each other to dive headlong into the water. Ashoka relished the soothing sensation of the cool water on his parched skin. He savoured the taste of the water, drinking from the running water to quench the insatiable thirst that had plagued him for the past few *horas*. Mali couldn't decide whether he wanted to swim in the water or drink from it.

After what seemed like a long time, but was in fact less than one *hora*, Ashoka signalled that they needed to move on.

Reluctantly, they waded out and donned their clothes. Ashoka knew they were likely to find animals close to the water body, and so they began to walk along the edge of the stream. They were rewarded soon enough.

Ashoka noticed the tracks of deer. It looked like a herd. He placed a finger to his lips, signalling for Mali to be quiet. Mali watched spellbound as Ashoka gripped his spear firmly in his hands. The wait seemed interminable. All of a sudden, they spotted the deer. It was a lone one and had possibly drifted apart from the rest of the herd. Perhaps it had hoped to get its fill of water and rejoin the herd later. It didn't matter. Ashoka crouched, moving ahead silently. The spear in his hand suddenly looked like a deadly weapon – as if it had been crafted just for this moment.

Ashoka took a deep breath and held it there, as he raised his arm to strike. The deer looked around, some sixth sense warning it that there was danger beyond the bushes. Sensing more than seeing Ashoka, the deer unconsciously fluttered its ears. In one swift motion, it turned around and dug its powerful legs into the ground to make good its escape. But it had underestimated the skill and the determination of the hunter. Ashoka threw his spear. The missile raced through the air, landing in the deer's neck. The deer staggered for a while, and then suddenly dropped down, its lifeblood oozing out to soak the forest floor.

At that very moment in another part of the forest, Susima and Devendra were dragging their feet wearily. They had not eaten much the previous sunset. Exhausted, they stumbled on, one behind the other.

Devendra had never experienced tiredness such as this, and he felt a haze cloud his vision and mind. Each step was an ordeal and he walked mechanically, his eyes to the ground. It struck him that some time had lapsed since he had last heard the sound of Susima's footsteps ahead of him. He raised his head and realized with dismay that Susima had disappeared.

The darkness of the forest suddenly looked terrifying. 'This is no time for jokes,' he said, his voice trembling. 'Wh-where are you, Susima?'

A muffled sound came as he moved ahead with caution. A moment later, without warning, he was sliding down what appeared to be a deep pit. 'Ouch!' He groaned as he landed on the hard ground. Gathering his wits about him, he saw his friend's silhouette. Susima looked fine. With the exception of a few scratches, there didn't seem to be anything wrong with the prince.

'What is this?' Devendra inquired incredulously, waving his arms around him.

'It seems to be an elephant trap, you moron,' Susima replied in irritation. 'One of the tribes must be nearby.' Susima was miffed at being caught in this predicament.

'It may be sunsets before someone comes to check on us.' Devendra gulped. 'We would be bones by then.'

'Shut up and let me think,' Susima said impatiently. 'As the worst case-scenario, the city guards will start looking for us in a couple of sunsets. It's not that bad.'

As they settled in for the night, something caught Devendra's attention. He blanched in fear as he pointed towards the opening of the pit. Susima looked in the direction Devendra was pointing. Five pairs of eyes stared back from above. They spoke in a tongue that was strange to both Susima and Devendra.

It was nearing dusk when Ashoka and Mali got the fire going. Mali used his sword to carve up the deer while Ashoka sharpened the points of some wet twigs. Next, Ashoka slid the pieces of meat on to these twigs. This was held over the fire to roast the meat to a delicious-looking golden colour. There was enough meat to last them until the end of their journey.

'I didn't know you could cook so well, Ashoka.' Mali laughed. 'You can certainly look at it as a profession.'

Ashoka smiled but Mali could see his friend was pensive. He knew better than to interrupt Ashoka's thoughts at such times.

'I'd better start thinking seriously about my future,' said Ashoka after a while.

'What problem does royalty have? It's people like us who need to think about our future,' said Mali in a matter-of-fact tone.

Ashoka turned to look at the boy who had been his closest friend from as long ago as he could recall. He had a strange look on his face. 'You are like my brother. You have nothing to worry about,' he said haltingly. 'It is my own future I am uncertain about. Mother thinks I should be the emperor after father.'

He was silent for a while and Mali could see the stream of emotions behind the normally placid face. 'But Father – he prefers Susima. Besides, he is older too,' Ashoka said wistfully.

Mali grunted. 'He is barely a couple of years older. The more deserving amongst the two of you should inherit the throne. I vote for you,' he said loyally.

Ashoka flashed him a quick smile. *I wish it were that simple my friend,* he thought to himself.

The next day passed uneventfully for Ashoka and Mali. On the morning of the fourth day, Ashoka woke up with a feeling of exhilaration.

So far so good, he thought with satisfaction. *Today we need to get fresh food,* he mused. They had feasted on the deer meat for the past two sunsets, but the remainder had started to rot and Ashoka decided against eating any more of it.

'Mali, wake up! Let's go fishing,' he said, playfully kicking the younger boy in the back.

'Let me sleep,' mumbled Mali. 'You fish. I will clean and cook it. It's a deal.'

'Okay.' Ashoka shrugged. 'It might be fun, though. It will also give you an opportunity to use that spear of yours.' He laughed uproariously.

'I knew you couldn't stand the sight of me resting,' Mali grumbled. 'Back in Pataliputra, Acharya Akila doesn't let me sleep!' Still muttering under his breath, he dragged himself up and went about getting ready.

They spent the better part of the morning trying to spear fish. To their surprise, the fish were much swifter than they had bargained for.

'Come on, you little pests. I won't leave you alone. You might as well give up now,' Mali roared in mock anger.

'Look, I got a relatively big one,' Ashoka said triumphantly. 'We should be making a move, Mali. We have squandered enough time on this.'

The boys carefully wrapped their fish in leaves and put them in their bags. It was fortunate that the path they had chosen along the stream coincided with the direction of the Kshatriya gate of Pataliputra. All that was required now was to keep walking at a brisk pace and they would be in Pataliputra soon.

'Is it my imagination, or do I see smoke?' Ashoka looked incredulously at Mali.

'I see it too,' Mali said, nodding. 'We must both be imagining it. The funny thing is, I can smell a delicious aroma in the air too.' He giggled. 'I may be going crazy. Maybe our trek in the forest is proving too much for me.'

Ashoka had his thoughtful expression on. 'If I am not mistaken, Acharya Akila had once mentioned this area is inhabited by some tribes. Some of them might not be too friendly, though.' He seemed to come to a decision. 'We'd best avoid running into any of the tribes right now. We will leave the exploring bit for the night.'

Mali looked happy to comply. 'Let us camp right here in that case. Anyway, I am dying to cook the fish we caught,' he said, licking his lips in anticipation.

The thought of civilization being so close at hand filled them with cheer, though this was accompanied by a feeling of apprehension about encountering any unfriendly tribals.

Having rested for a bit, Ashoka got up. It was beginning to grow dark. He gently woke up Mali.

'It's time. Let's go and do some exploring.'

They walked stealthily in the direction of the habitation, their swords and spears held in readiness. As they got closer, they relaxed somewhat. This did not look like a hostile tribal group. In fact it looked like a peaceful tribal village. The first welcome sound they heard was the wailing of a baby. Then there were the uproarious notes of an inebriated singer. They exchanged wry looks as they listened to the drunkard lapse into a wheezing fit in the middle of a particularly loud verse.

A number of huts huddled close to each other. Each hut had a thatched roof and walls fashioned from mud. Ashoka looked closely at the long row of huts. There was one that looked grander and bigger, with painted figures in white adorning the walls. *It must be their chief's home,* Ashoka surmised.

They crouched against an adjoining wall. Making sure there was no one around, Ashoka quickly moved towards the tribal chief's abode, followed closely by Mali. Once they passed the chief's hut, there was a vast opening through which they could get across to the other side and resume their way towards Pataliputra.

As they passed the huge hutment, Ashoka stopped. He was curious to see how the chief's hut looked from the inside. Raising himself on tiptoes, he peered inside. He stared for a full minute before stepping away from the window, his face registering surprise.

'What?' Mali looked questioningly at Ashoka. Ashoka motioned towards the window. A bewildered Mali stepped up to the wall and tried peering inside. Given his shorter height, he had to haul himself up with his arms resting on the windowsill. He blinked his eyes and stared in disbelief at the scene inside.

There, in the middle of the room, Susima and Devendra lay fast asleep. The tribal leader was sleeping in the same room, in a far corner. Dirty dishes with leftovers of food lay strewn about. Everything about the room indicated that a feast had taken place here, not too long back.

Mali scrambled down and they retraced their steps in silence. Every once in a while, Mali stole a glance at Ashoka to see if he wanted to talk about what they had just witnessed in the tribal chief's hut. But Ashoka's expression was too forbidding for Mali to attempt conversation.

They were headed towards the path that ran parallel to the stream. On the way Mali spotted some hens and goats. The goats were tethered loosely and the hens were sitting quietly near a basket full of eggs, laid and collected presumably on the same day.

Mali gazed longingly at the basket. 'Let's take some eggs… and maybe some milk,' he said, pulling Ashoka back.

Ashoka glanced at him coldly. Mali was shocked to see the hard expression in his eyes. 'Do you too want to cheat your acharya?' Ashoka said softly. 'Do you!' He raised his voice suddenly, the pent-up fury finally erupting.

The sudden change in Ashoka's demeanour frightened Mali. He had not known his friend to be like this – and never so with him. 'I…I am sorry, Ashoka,' Mali stuttered, his guilt at having considered deceiving Akila bothering him even more now than Ashoka's wrath.

I deserve to be the emperor. I know that now. The man who can cheat his acharya can also cheat his subjects, Ashoka thought grimly.

It was the fifth sunset. Ashoka sensed they were very close to the city of Pataliputra. On an impulse he decided that they should take the route through the forest. He wanted to avoid the tribes and the path along the stream was bound to bring them in contact. And all tribals may not necessarily be as friendly and welcoming as the ones Susima and Devendra had encountered.

'Let us not bother with food today,' Ashoka said in a light-hearted tone. His mood had changed again and he was once more the fun-loving Ashoka that Mali had known from their childhood. 'We will have a magnificent feast once we arrive at the palace,' Ashoka continued cheerfully.

'Whatever you say,' Mali grumbled. He was still a little miffed at the way Ashoka had spoken to him the previous night, even though he knew his friend had been right.

'Trying to be dramatic, are we?' Ashoka clipped him behind his head and sidestepped as Mali tried to hit him back. Both boys fell down laughing. The previous night's tension dissipated and they were best friends once again.

By afternoon they presented a bedraggled sight. Mali, who was in the lead, stopped short when he saw a herd of wild elephants walking across. He quickly motioned to Ashoka to stop. As the two boys waited for the pachyderms to pass, one of the calves, who was lagging behind, spotted them. Ashoka, who hadn't yet forgotten the narrow escape they had had with the bear cub's mother, was in no mood to take a chance. He signalled to Mali to move away from the elephant calf and they set off briskly. A short while later,Ashoka noticed that the calf was following them.

Very unusual behaviour, Ashoka muttered to himself, knowing that elephant calves rarely left the protection the herd offered. The baby elephant ambled towards them and came to a halt close to them. 'Your mother will be waiting – go and join them, little one,' Ashoka said gently.

'We are not your brothers, dear.' Mali tittered. 'See, our noses are too small,' he said, guffawing loudly.

The calf had a prominent white patch around its left eye.

'Seems harmless.' Ashoka smiled. 'I am sure it will get tired of following us and get back to the herd soon.'

The boys turned around and resumed walking. Sure enough, when they looked back after some time, there was no sign of the calf.

Mali was famished by now. It was rare for him to go without food for so long. Spotting some wild berries, he automatically reached out to pluck them and popped them into his mouth, in one smooth action.

Another *hora* of brisk walking and the dense foliage gave way to relatively sparse woods. Soon, they were at the outskirts of Pataliputra. They looked at each other, grinning with joy.

The boys walked along the moat running all around the perimeter of the city, in the direction of the Kshatriya gate, as Akila had instructed them.

Without warning, Mali groaned loudly and doubled over with pain.

'Mali! What is it?' Ashoka asked in alarm. Mali was clutching his stomach and trying to say something. But no sound escaped his lips.

'We are almost there, Mali!' Ashoka tried to control his rising panic. Mali's face had turned a deep shade of blue. Ashoka supported his wobbling body and tried to help him walk alongside. It didn't work – Mali seemed incapable of moving at all.

Ashoka stopped and with an enormous effort hauled Mali over his shoulders. He almost buckled under the weight but steadied himself somehow. Gritting his teeth, he set off at a slow pace. Sweat dripped from his face and he blinked away the droplets that threatened to block his vision completely.

Suddenly, Ashoka heard the sound of several horses trotting behind him. Before he could react, he felt strong arms lift Mali off his shoulders. He turned to look into the kind eyes of an older soldier. There were four others with him.

'It's okay, son. Your friend will be taken care off. You can ride with me,' the soldier said in a gentle tone.

Ashoka wondered where the soldiers had materialized

from. The city gate was some distance away. He asked the soldier, but the veteran carefully refrained from saying anything. The ride to the city seemed like a blur as the horses galloped towards the Kshatriya gate.

The guards at the Kshatriya gate seemed to know the veteran and nodded to him, calling out his name. Ashoka strained to listen. Amreshwar. Ashoka made a note of the name. He owed the old soldier a lot – if Mali survived, it would be because of him. Akila had taught them enough for Ashoka to realize that his friend was showing serious symptoms of poisoning.

Amreshwar personally escorted the boys to the Lake Palace. A vaid was already waiting there. Ashoka met Amreshwar's gaze, a silent thanks conveyed.

A relieved Daya clutched her son's hand as Mali slept. He had vomited thrice after the vaid had administered the medicine. That had brought instant relief and he had soon succumbed to a deep slumber.

Subhadrangi, whose attention until now had been on Mali and Daya, finally embraced Ashoka.

'How are you, son? Tell me all about your trip,' she said, smiling.

Ashoka grinned. 'Altogether, it was fun, Mother. I managed to catch fish and cooked it too. Mali thinks I can become a good chef.' He laughed good-naturedly.

Subhadrangi made a wry face. 'Sounds like a fun hobby for a future emperor,' she joked in the spirit of the discussion. After they had chatted for a while Ashoka excused himself. He went straight to the bathing room and stripped before wading into the pool. He scrubbed a paste of *besan* all over his body and took his time in washing it off. Clean water and the aromatic *besan* were a luxury he and Mali hadn't experienced for the past five sunsets.

Gradually the warm water made him sleepy and he closed his eyes as he allowed himself to sink in deeper into the water. *I wonder whether Susima has reached Pataliputra or is still enjoying the hospitality of the tribe.* That was his last thought before he closed his eyes and let sleep overcome him.

Susima and Devendra were on their way to Pataliputra, their bags bulging with delicious meat. They knew they would have to consume it within the day as they were fast approaching Pataliputra – they couldn't risk Akila catching them with the food.

Susima had had to bribe the leader with two gold rings in exchange for the food and shelter. The potbellied leader had been only too happy to oblige, as long as he was paid right.

As they approached the city, Susima began to experience the first pangs of guilt at having deceived the acharya. But it was too late for qualms – the deed was done.

By evening, the boys reached the moat surrounding the city and walked along it until they reached the Kshatriya gate. There were at least ten guards at the gate. The bridge that was across the gate was being pulled up. Security protocol demanded that all gates to the city should be shut at dusk.

'Stop! We want to enter the city,' bellowed Susima. The gate was up by now. A guard asked him for identification.

'I am the son of Bindusara,' Susima said haughtily. 'Is that introduction sufficient?'

The guard raised his eyebrows at this and went to consult his senior who accompanied him back to the gate. 'Welcome back, Prince Susima,' the senior soldier said gently. 'Orders prevent me from allowing anyone to enter the city after the seventh *hora* of the second *muhurta* without official clearance. You are welcome to make yourself comfortable within the waiting room outside until I take permission from the senapati.' He pointed towards a sturdily built cabin adjacent to the gate, meant mainly for the soldiers to rest during their break.

Susima's face turned a deep red. 'I will remember your insolence, soldier. You are questioning the future Raja of Magadha,' he said with barely controlled fury. 'What is your name?'

'My name is Purshottam, Prince Susima,' said the senior guard in an even voice. His face betrayed no emotion at Susima's words.

After waiting for two *horas*, a rattled Susima and a subdued Devendra were escorted to the royal palace, where they were greeted by Rakshita. To Rakshita's surprise, the boys did not eat much. She had no way of knowing they were already full with the meat bought from the tribal chief.

'What will we tell Acharya Akila about our trip?' asked Devendra. His voice betrayed his concern. 'Do we tell him that we stayed for a couple of sunsets…'

'Don't you dare mention that,' growled Susima, interrupting him. But Akila's words spoken so firmly during their first session resounded in his ears: *People say I have eyes at the back of my head.*

The sun had not risen when the four boys assembled in the classroom. Akila was already there.

'How was your trip?' he asked. He was greeted with silence.

'How was the hospitality of the Kiri tribals?' he said abruptly, turning to look at Susima. 'Or did your gold rings do the trick?' he asked, sarcasm dripping from every word.

Susima was in shock. Devendra was licking his lips in nervousness. Neither of them was able to meet the acharya's eyes.

Akila was unrelenting. He continued glaring at the two of them. Finally Susima looked up from the floor. 'I apologize. It won't happen again,' he said in a subdued tone.

Akila nodded curtly, indicating that he was done with Susima and Devendra for the moment. His attention was now focused on Mali.

'Never allow your stomach to rule your head,' he said reprovingly. 'You are lucky I had the city guards tailing you.'

Mali was mortified. Ignoring Akila's instructions on forest survival tactics had almost cost him his life and certainly embarrassed him in front of the acharya.

'I am sure this experience has provided lessons for every one of you,' Akila said. 'Make the most of it.'

Ashoka looked expressionlessly at Akila. He expected some words of praise and made a conscious effort to try and not look too happy about it. The others too waited keenly to hear what acharya had to say to Ashoka – he was the only student to whom Akila had not given any feedback yet.

Akila gave them one all-encompassing look, 'I have asked Bakura to take sessions on sword fighting with you. May God be with each one of you.' That said, Akila turned around to leave.

Ashoka stared incredulously at Akila's retreating figure. He hadn't expected a barrel-full of praise from him. *But this? He could have said something at least,* Ashoka thought.

At the door, Akila turned to look at him, and Ashoka noticed the hint of a twinkle in his teacher's eyes. Ashoka understood. The acharya did not see the need to state the obvious. Ashoka's chest swelled with pride as he realized that Akila had left him to decide for himself the lessons he had picked up from the experience in the forest.

7

The *Mahapuja* was an annual event at Pataliputra. Bindusara and Rakshita were to sit at the *yagna* to participate in the prayers that would ensure the well-being of the royal family and the prosperity of the Mauryan empire. All the *amatyas* were in attendance. Rakshita looked elegant as usual, her *mekhala* made of precious stones. She had opposed Bindusara's wish to invite his 20 children from his other wives for the *puja*.

Unlike Subhadrangi and herself, the other wives were not queens. He had married them in order to forge political and economic alliances.

This was one of the biggest events in the Mauryan capital of Magadha. The 100-pillared hall and the rest of the palace had been decorated with fresh flowers gathered from all over the kingdom. A thousand Brahmins had assembled from all over the land, including large provinces like Ujjaini and Takshashila. International visitors included the famous Greek traveller and writer, Megasthenes, from the court of Seleucus Nicator. After the death of Alexander, his generals had divided his empire. The Asian region stretching from Mesopotamia across Afghanistan was under Seleucus. After losing to Chandragupta Maurya in war, Seleucus had extended a hand of friendship towards him, forging a relationship that involved trade and cultural exchange. Megasthenes was a vital link between Seleucus and the Mauryan empire.

Subhadrangi stood at the entrance of the hall. Her ornaments consisted primarily of fresh flowers arranged around her head and body. She had taken upon herself the task of washing the feet of all the Brahmins – considered the highest caste in the land – who had come for the ceremony. The hall was resounding with the soulful rendition of the veena. The Brahmins silently meditated in preparation for the *yagna* that they would soon perform in the palace gardens.

Ashoka and Susima stood behind Bindusara and Rakshita. At the auspicious *hora*, the sacred fire was lit and the prayers commenced. Bindusara and Rakshita poured ladles of pure ghee into the sacred fire. The vibrations of the chanting suffused the environment with positivity.

A sumptuous feast had been organized for the end of the day. The ministers and the other royal guests followed Bindusara and the two queens to a separate section of the garden.

Bindusara was surrounded by a visible set of six bodyguards who appeared calm but were inwardly on edge. An event like this was fraught with danger for the emperor. What no one knew apart from Akila, Radheya and Ajaya was that many covert female bodyguards were assigned duties during such events. They intermingled with the guests in disguise.

Susima and Ashoka hovered around their father as he chatted with everyone who approached him. Ashoka tried to study how his father dealt with different people. *It is a different kind of learning from what Acharya Akila teaches us, but it is equally important,* he mused.

'This is my son Susima. He will be happy to show you around the palace,' Bindusara proudly told a group of visitors from a foreign land.

'And I am Ashoka, the emperor's younger son,' Ashoka chimed in, his hands bowed in respect as he addressed the guests.

Bindusara tried to mask his irritation at the unsolicited introduction. Ashoka still looked like a boy compared to the strapping young man that Susima was.

Ashoka was only too happy when Susima walked away with the guests Bindusara had entrusted him with. *I have Father all to myself now,* he thought happily, the joy mixed with just a twinge of sadness that his effervescence was not reciprocated by his father.

The gardens were crowded and the bodyguards looked around uneasily. The Brahmins were being served first as per protocol. Ashoka watched one of the older Brahmins gorge himself on *aluka* made in tamarind gravy. Then something caught his attention and he swiftly turned his head to one side. He was just in time to see an arrow fly straight towards where the emperor stood.

The seasoned bodyguards had also seen it coming. One of them pushed Bindusara towards the side, throwing himself in front of the emperor. Because of this, the arrow only nicked

Bindusara's right ear. The other guards covered the king on all sides, creating a human shield.

Ashoka spotted a heavily built man moving away swiftly. The man had shoulder-length hair and wore a white turban. As the man turned to see if he was being pursued, Ashoka noticed he had a beard and his chest was bare. He wore a white dhoti.

There's nothing strikingly different about this person's appearance, Ashoka thought as he began to chase after the running figure. Ashoka saw the would-be assassin throw away his bow. Running for his life, he knocked down a couple of kitchen helpers who happened to come in his way. A female attendant directly blocked the man's path. Ashoka looked on in amazement as she obviously braced herself for a head-on collision. It almost seemed deliberate. But, although temporarily stunned by the impact, the man was on his feet in a few *kashtas*.

Ashoka heard rapidly gaining footsteps behind him and turned around briefly to see Senapati Ajaya following him, accompanied by a score of palace guards. Susima too had taken up the chase and Ashoka could see his older brother's chest muscles bulging with the effort of running hard.

The assassin dashed inside the palace kitchen, pursued closely by Ashoka and the others. The chefs, who weren't aware of anything amiss, were bewildered at the sudden flurry of activity in their normally placid domain. A trail of destruction followed the pursued and the pursuers. Food items and vessels lay scattered on the floor.

The man seemed to know his way well around the palace, rushing out of the kitchen and heading out to the grounds. Senapati Ajaya was now much ahead of Ashoka. Ashoka slowed down and smiled. The assassin was running towards a deadend. The high palace walls loomed in front of him. It was just a matter of a few *kashtas* before the senapati would capture him.

To his bewilderment, the assassin ran towards the wall with an increased burst of speed. Before his very eyes, the man clambered up the wall as effortlessly as a fly, as if it was the most natural thing for him to do. He flipped to the other side as Ajaya rammed into the wall, fuming, knowing he could not scale it the way the assassin had. The only trace of the man's existence lay at Ajaya's feet, crumpled. With a flick of his foot, he flung the turban high in the air and caught it deftly. Turning, he rapidly issued orders to his men who were close behind him, despatching a search party for the assassin.

Ashoka went to the bushes where he had seen the attacker throw the bow just before he had run inside the kitchen. He whistled in surprise. *This is strange,* he thought. *The assassin must have had inside help.*

The bow was no longer there.

Ashoka and Senapati Ajaya entered Bindusara's quarters at almost the same time. Susima followed close behind.

Bindusara was in an irritable mood. Sitting quietly in his room while the others chased the assassin went against his warrior nature. But Akila had been insistent. The emperor's life could not be risked under any circumstances.

Senapati Ajaya patted Ashoka on the back. 'Those were quick reflexes, son.' Akila nodded imperceptibly. He had been with some international visitors at the time of the attack. But he had heard about Ashoka's role in the chase.

'We would have caught him, father, if he had not flown up the wall,' Susima said, trying to move the discussion away from Ashoka, who he thought was getting more than his fair share of attention.

Bindusara grunted impatiently. 'So what is the plan now?' he asked, not looking at anyone in particular.

'Somehow I don't think our search team is going to be able to catch the man,' Ajaya said thoughtfully.

Akila exchanged a meaningful glance with the senapati. This was not the first attack on Bindusara. His empire had grown significantly in the past few years – it was inevitable that he would make enemies along the way.

Susima's attention was drawn to Ashoka, who was closely studying the arrow used by the assassin. Still smarting from Akila's praise of his brother, he couldn't stop himself. 'Admiring the arrow, are we, Ashoka?' he said mockingly. 'You want to keep this as a souvenir, perhaps?'

Ashoka was only half listening to him. His mind was racing.

'Acharya Akila,' he said, trying to suppress his excitement, 'this arrow is very different from the ones we use in Magadha.'

Akila extended his hand to take the arrow from Ashoka. 'Quite right,' he said softly. 'It is rather different.'

Ashoka's face lit up. 'Would it be safe to assume that different nations have their own archetypal weapons?'

Akila allowed a rare smile of appreciation to form on his face. He knew what Ashoka was suggesting. He brought the arrow close to his nose, holding it there for sometime as he breathed in the sweet-sour smell of the polished wood. Then he handed it over to Ajaya, who did the same.

Ashoka looked on expectantly as Senapati Ajaya and Akila exchanged a quick glance.

The astute Bindusara had already caught on to what was happening. 'Where is it from?' he asked dryly.

'It is from the dakshin region,' Akila said quietly.

Bindusara nodded. This was the third attempt on his life, and every time the indications were that it was from the southern tip of the vast land of Bharat. He sometimes wondered whether his enemies were actually from the dakshin region, or nearby, lulling him into a false sense of security that the enemy was far away so that they could finish him off as he grew complacent.

Nevertheless, such attempts were part of his existence now. In many cases, the investigations reached a dead-end as no country wanted a trace back to them, that had a chance of causing political instability. The assassins themselves never knew who they were working for.

He sighed. He wasn't afraid of death. It would happen when it had to. Unlike other kings who worried about questions of life and death at all times, Bindusara had no such inclination. He only desired the Mauryan kingdom to have a clear successor when he was no longer there to protect and lead his people.

As time sped along, that was a question he still did not have an answer to.

8

It was now 15 years since Bindusara had completed the successful expansion of the Mauryan empire to Mahishur. An exciting day lay ahead for the young men under Acharya Akila's training – they were going to put their physical prowess to the test in their first real contest.

The stony-faced Akila took his students to the private stadium where they had been taught various martial arts, including the art of making deadly parries with their swords and fighting barehanded. In the past, the boys had practised several times at this very place. Most of the time it had been with an opponent trained to defend or attack in a calculated manner so as not to injure them seriously. On the occasions that they had fought with each other, it had been subject to the adherence of a strict code of conduct. Today was special – it was the real thing! As real as the dangerous forest expedition seven years ago.

The four young men silently trooped into the stadium. Bakura, the acharya appointed by Akila for their physical training, was the only other person present.

Akila clapped his hands to get their attention. He spoke in a crisp voice that boomed across the stadium. 'The rules for today are…' he said, pausing for effect, 'that there are no rules.' He looked at them to assess their reactions. But, by now, the young men had learnt to keep their emotions carefully hidden away. He smiled at them.

'You will frequently face combatants who do not care about the rules of war.' He suddenly became serious. 'Under duress, even the best warriors have been known to crumble. A few will want to win at any cost.'

Susima couldn't help squirming at the latter part of Akila's statement. He remembered the incident in the forest a few years back when he had indeed succumbed to breaking the rules set by the acharya.

'Bakura will not intervene unless the situation demands it. You are on your own today.' Akila finished his brief preamble to the impending contest between the future warriors of the Mauryan kingdom.

Ashoka grinned pointedly at Susima who, despite being a much larger man, was betraying signs of unease.

As the first rays of the morning sun hit the top of the trees, Bakura blew the conch to announce the commencement of the first round. Susima and Ashoka stepped into the arena.

Ashoka reached the ring first and waited for Susima, an expression of nonchalance on his young face. Susima took a deep breath as he walked towards Ashoka. He recited the Ram *rakshastotra* under his breath and felt calmer. He knew he was bigger and stronger than the younger man. *I am going to put him in his place today,* Susima swore to himself. The thought immediately infused him with more confidence.

There had been a time, when they were much younger, when Susima would bully and publicly humiliate Ashoka. The younger boy would take it all good-naturedly. That time was long gone. Over the years, Susima's persistent jibes had managed to break through Ashoka's natural good humour. For some time now, Ashoka had become aware that Susima did not let go of any opportunity to put him down. The worst part was that Bindusara showed no concern over it. The lack of warmth from his father gave birth to a growing coldness within Ashoka's heart. Susima became his natural antagonist. It wasn't just because of his insensitive jibes – that Ashoka could have forgiven him for. What was unpardonable was the unrestrained affection he got from Bindusara – the kind of love that Ashoka now knew he would never receive.

Ashoka saw Susima flex his muscles. His face lit up with a smile of anticipation. 'Come on, baby face. Hit me.' He smirked. Spoken in a low voice, the words were inaudible to the others.

Ashoka replied equally softly, 'Let us see whether you have father's spunk in you, Susima. Or would you rather go and hide behind Mother Rakshita's veil?'

The words had the desired effect on Susima. 'You scoundrel!' he bellowed, forgetting in his rage to keep his voice down. Susima's handsome features contorted in fury as he lunged towards Ashoka and lashed out with all his might. If the blow had landed where he intended it to, Ashoka would have been knocked down instantly. However, Susima had not bargained for his younger sibling's incredible speed. Ashoka easily sidestepped the punch while the force of his own attack made Susima stagger. Susima fell face down on the ground.

Ashoka patiently waited for Susima to get up. 'All right then, I will let you really hit me now. I promise,' said Ashoka in a mock serious tone.

Susima tried to get a grip on his temper. He knew Ashoka was deliberately provoking him. Wiping the sweat off his brow, he warily circled Ashoka. He was looking for an opportunity that would allow him to hit the younger man. To his surprise, Ashoka seemed to be giving him the opening he so badly needed. Susima grabbed the chance and aimed a quick jab at Ashoka's face. This was followed by a torrent of blows all over the bruised Ashoka, who continued smiling and gesticulating that he wanted more.

Akila watched the fight expressionlessly. The growing rivalry between the two princes had not been lost on him, and over the years he had wondered where it would lead. He saw Bakura staring horrified at Ashoka's bleeding face. Bakura caught the senior acharya's attention and his eyes seemed to implore Akila to stop the insane fight. Akila hesitated for a moment. Then he shook his head, letting Bakura know that the fight should not be stopped; at least not yet.

As suddenly as it had started, Susima's attack ceased. He stood silently, panting with the effort of ceaselessly hitting Ashoka. He wanted to hurt him more but there was no strength left within him. As he stared into Ashoka's eyes, he felt an irrational fear take hold of him.

Ashoka's bloodied face seemed to mock him. 'I'm still standing,' he said in a low voice.

Devendra, who had been smiling smugly while Ashoka was being beaten up, looked confused all of a sudden. He couldn't understand why the brawny Susima wasn't hitting Ashoka anymore.

Mali stood quietly. He was perhaps the only person present who knew the depth of Ashoka's antipathy towards Susima. More to the point, he was also aware of Ashoka's deep-rooted pain at being bereft of his father's love. The storm that had raged within his friend's heart for years now looked like it was about to burst. And it would rain down on Susima with the intensity of years of suppressed fury. Even Mali had no idea what would happen in the next few *kashtas*.

Ashoka was speaking softly to Susima. 'Now here are my rules, baby face,' he said. 'The moment you stop, I'll start.'

Susima stared at Ashoka incredulously. *This is a bad dream,* he thought, panic taking hold of him in a vice-like grip. He landed a half-hearted punch at the younger man's face, but even he knew there was no strength behind the attack.

The next instant, Susima staggered back three paces as he felt the full force of Ashoka's blow on his face. He felt the fragments of a broken tooth mix with the bile that rose within him, making him want to throw up. But the pain was nothing compared to the sudden terror he felt looking at his opponent. Ashoka had a maniacal smile plastered on his face and Susima knew it wasn't even a smile. It was the expression of a man who had been pushed too far for too long.

In a moment of sheer panic, Susima looked around for a means to escape. He saw Akila observing him. The acharya's expression told him he knew what the older prince was thinking. He tried recalling the mantra Rakshita had taught him as a child – the one that never failed to calm him. But he found himself incapable of doing so. The next moment he felt another blow crack the right side of his jaw.

'Not my face,' he screamed, shielding his face with his hands.

Ashoka circled him, like an eagle toying with its prey. He took his time landing another well-aimed punch to Susima's solar plexus. Susima doubled over in pain. Anticipating this, Ashoka's knee was already at Susima's face. The sound of cartilage breaking jarred in the now deathly quiet arena. A torrent of blood poured down Susima's broken nose as he crashed to the ground. At a curt nod from Akila, Bakura rushed to intervene. But Ashoka was already walking away from where Susima lay, oblivious to the world. He bowed to Akila first, and then to Bakura who was engaged in trying to revive Susima.

'That will be all for this sunset.' Akila said in a hollow voice. 'The remainder of the contest will continue three sunsets from now.'

Akila wondered how he could have made the mistake of not perceiving the depth of animosity between Bindusara's two sons. Was it a good thing that Ashoka had found an outlet in the contest to vent years of suppressed anger? Would Susima now cease to publicly humiliate his younger brother? Or would this feud lead to an end in the future that would be more terrible and final than what they had just witnessed this sunset? Akila sighed. For once in his life, he didn't have all the answers.

Unnoticed by anyone, Mahamantri Radheya had taken in everything from where he stood, hidden behind a pillar. His expression mirrored Akila's apprehensions about the future of the two Mauryan princes.

Fifteen sunsets had gone by since the fight between the two princes. To his credit, Susima had made a superhuman effort to overcome his physical pain and return to the contest three sunsets later as Akila had stipulated. However, the psychological impact of the thrashing proved far more difficult to recover from.

Ashoka won the sword-fighting round without even working up a sweat. All tests that required hand-to-hand engagement ended disastrously for Susima. It was only in the archery round that he was finally able to beat the younger prince. That helped him regain some of his lost self-assurance.

Mali and Devendra had been pitted against each other and proved equal in measure, even though Mali was younger than the other youth.

To Mali, Ashoka appeared a lot calmer after the first sunset's bout with Susima. Whatever emotions he had allowed to surface in that brief interlude seemed either spent or once again suppressed within him.

But all of this was already in the past for the young men. Today was Deepawali, the festival of lights. Multi-hued flowers and hundreds of brightly lit diyas made the palace look even more impressive than usual. The carved woodwork had been recently polished for the occasion.

Subhadrangi's presence as the younger queen was mandatory. While she still hadn't come to terms with some of the pretentiousness that such occasions demanded, she knew Ashoka would gain invaluable learning from these experiences. It would also give him the opportunity to network with the influential people who frequented the capital of the Mauryan kingdom at such times. As usual, Mali and Daya accompanied the prince and his mother.

The *amatyas* along with their families had arrived from all over the kingdom to pay their respects to Bindusara. The main hall resounded with the tinkling laughter of young girls, attired in their best clothes and bedecked with expensive jewellery. Most of the maidens' eyes were heavily decorated with kohl which gave them a doe-eyed appearance. The reflected light of the diyas falling on their faces rendered them ethereal. The more adventurous amongst them had taken pains to tie the cloth covering their breasts provocatively low. Young men, individually and in groups, eyed the lovely women in admiration. And there were those whose admiration gave way to lustful glances that drew disapproving looks from the elders and invited disdain from the maidens.

A beautiful girl, her curvaceous body wrapped in a golden *antariya,* was the cynosure of most eyes that evening. Well aware of the devastating effect of her beauty on the men around her, she was pretending to talk animatedly with her female companions. Among the men who forgot to breathe while drinking in her beauty, there was one whose face was still bandaged. The young man was Susima and the lovely young woman was Rati, Radheya's daughter.

Susima had received a lot of sympathetic attention from the maidens present. But at the moment he had eyes only for Rati. Finally, he walked up to her, his gait betraying a hint of awkwardness, which was rare for him.

'It has been a while since you came to the palace,' he said. 'You have changed, you know.'

'In what way?' Rati asked playfully, with just a touch of coquettishness.

'Well...uh, everyone's eyes seem to be following you

around today,' he said huskily. 'And why not? You are the most beautiful girl here.'

Rati blushed at the direct compliment. Suddenly shy, she averted her eyes, trying to hide the flush that was creeping up her cheeks. Susima, who had by now regained his usual self-assurance, turned to wink at his friends, who were standing nearby.

'Let me show you my latest trophy – the hide of a tiger I hunted recently.' Susima led the eager Rati to his chambers.

Rati gasped in awe as she saw the impressive tiger skin hanging on a wall. 'You killed that!' she exclaimed. 'Weren't you scared?'

Susima smiled. 'You should know this about me. I usually get what I want, Rati.' As he held her hands in his own, she felt her pulse race. Knowing from experience that the moment was perfect, Susima bent towards her to kiss her even as Rati closed her eyes in sweet anticipation.

The romantic moment was rudely interrupted by barely suppressed laughter. Susima instinctively moved away from Rati. Ashoka and Mali stood at the entrance to his quarters. Their attempts at stifling their laughter only served to make matters worse and the two burst into uncontrollable mirth at the sight of Susima's shocked face.

'You…you killed *that* tiger?' Ashoka asked incredulously, finally gaining a semblance of control. 'The tiger that had even the most intrepid Mauryan soldiers running for cover! How did you manage it, Susima?' Ashoka's voice was dripping with sarcasm now. 'Did our best archers accompany you on the hunt or did they rush to rescue you after they saw you cowering in fear at the sight of the great beast?'

Susima stood ashen-faced. All of a sudden, it was no longer important that his wooing of Rati had been interrupted. What mattered most was that neither she nor anyone else got to know the truth about the hunting incident. At that moment, he felt a degree of loathing for Ashoka he had never experienced before.

'How dare you speak in this manner about our prince?' The voice lashed out of nowhere.

Three pair of eyes turned as one to where Rati was standing, her eyes blazing. Ashoka stared at her, his confusion apparent on his face. Mali opened and closed his mouth uncomprehendingly. Susima too looked uncertainly at her.

Rati glared at Ashoka. 'My friends in the palace have told me how you tricked Susima during the bout and broke his nose when he wasn't looking.'

'Did they now?' Ashoka smiled graciously. 'And were these friends of yours present at the contest?'

Rati had expected Ashoka to justify himself. The casual manner in which he was questioning her infuriated her further. 'I don't know why my father thinks so highly of you. I, for one, detest you.'

Susima was now openly smiling. He mentally thanked Devendra for having spread the news in the palace that Ashoka had bested him through underhanded means.

'Rati, I don't need to resort to tricks to defeat this man,' Ashoka said softly, the smile not leaving his face. Then he said light-heartedly, 'In any case, I will leave the two of you to enjoy yourselves. You seem to complement each other well.'

This last jibe proved too much for Rati. Used as she was to men fawning over her, Ashoka's subtle dismissal outraged her vanity more than anything else he could have done. She lost all control. 'How dare you sneak up on us in this manner? You are nothing but an uncouth man who will forever play second fiddle to Susima. You ugly...black crow!' she screeched, her words dripping venom. The latter was uttered more out of spite than anything, but the room suddenly went quiet. Even Susima stopped smiling, unsure of how Ashoka would react to the insult.

The smile on Ashoka's face seemed plastered. He stood unmoving, his eyes not leaving Rati who was now squirming under the power of his gaze. Then Ashoka turned around and abruptly left the room. Mali glared at Rati and Susima and quietly followed his friend. He knew the incident with Rati would have impacted Ashoka gravely.

Ashoka made his way quickly to the only place in the palace that provided him solace – the temple of Krishna in the eastern section of the palace grounds. He had told Mali he wanted to be alone for some time. Ashoka did not know why he felt a sense of peace in this place. Maybe it was the calm aura here or the manner in which nature had woven itself around the pristine white marble structure of the temple – he felt he was one with existence here in a way he never felt anywhere else. Not even at the Lake Palace where he had spent most of his childhood.

He lay down on the grass in front of the temple. After what seemed an eternity, he was jolted out of his reverie by the sound of an explosion. As he pressed his hands to the ground to hoist himself up, Ashoka's hands slipped on the mossy ground and he felt his fingers make contact with something solid. He looked closely. It looked like the tip of a handle.

The explosions were more frequent now. Ashoka knew the Deepawali celebrations had begun. The fun-loving youth in him was keen to join in the festivities. But his curiosity got the better of that instinct. He cleared the earth around the metallic object and was surprised to find that it was indeed a handle fixed on the ground. He knew intuitively that there was significance in what he had just discovered. Excitedly, he went down on all fours and started clearing the area all around it. The frenetic activity was rewarded sooner than he had anticipated. He gasped as he uncovered yet another lever similar to the first one. Both levers were embedded in a moss-covered stone slab now partially exposed.

What could this possibly mean? Ashoka wondered in bemusement. He gripped both levers and pulled with all his might. Nothing moved. He tried again, not succeeding the second time too. He was perspiring now. Ashoka took a deep breath, trying to tap into his inner reserves. He gave a loud yell and heaved, putting his entire weight behind the effort. He grinned with satisfaction as the slab of stone budged slightly.

Ashoka heaved again, with renewed enthusiasm. His face contorted with the effort, and all of a sudden he staggered backwards as the stone slab disengaged from the ground, throwing him off balance. He stayed where he had fallen, waiting for his breath to stabilize. Getting up, he slowly walked to where the slab had moved, leaving in its place a gaping hole. He peered down the cavity but it was too dark to make out anything.

He then lay down flat on his stomach at the edge of the hole. Extending his right arm into the cavity, he tried to assess how deep it was. He couldn't feel the depth but he realized that the sides of the cavity sloped downwards.

Ashoka made up his mind – Mali and he would both return the next day to explore what mysteries the cavity contained.

As he got up and dusted his grimy clothes, he was confronted with a problem of a more practical nature. He had no idea how he was going to explain to the king and to his mother the slovenly state he was in.

Ashoka wiped the perspiration off his brow. The meeting with his father had gone off rather well. Bindusara had glared at the condition he was in, but he was surrounded by too many people to question Ashoka in detail. Subhadrangi had given him an exasperated look.

Back in the midst of the celebrations, Ashoka bumped into Mali who appeared to be saying goodbye to a girl. Mali's eyes lit up as he saw his friend. 'Where were you? I have been looking for you everywhere.'

'The hell you were.' Ashoka grinned. 'Who was that girl feeding you laddoos?'

'Oh, that's Pari. She is the royal cook's daughter.'

'I see.' Ashoka smiled. 'Do you like her or is it about the benefits that she comes with – being the royal cook's daughter?' he asked slyly, aware of Mali's weakness for food.

He ducked to avoid Mali's playful punch.

Ashoka's smile broadened. 'Must be the food, in that case,' he joked as both of them burst out laughing.

'Have you been wrestling with someone?' Mali asked as he noticed Ashoka's muddy clothes.

'Uh...no. I just bumped into something,' Ashoka said evasively. Mali gave him a puzzled look.

'We will talk about it tomorrow, my friend,' Ashoka said good-humouredly. 'Right now, let's enjoy the celebrations.'

The royal vaid made his way to the Lake Palace. He had been sent for by Subhadrangi and he was concerned that she may not be well. He was a distinguished-looking man with a long beard and a thick mane of grey hair. Tall and wiry, he looked strong even though he was in his seventies.

Subhadrangi bowed and touched his feet to seek his blessings.

'You look fine, my child,' the avuncular man said in a relieved tone.

Subhadrangi's expression had a slightly lost look. 'It's not me, pranapati,' she said softly, referring to the vaid by the name of his profession.

'Is Prince Ashoka all right?' the vaid asked.

Subhadrangi hesitated. She didn't know how to explain to the vaid the discussion she had had with her son. Something had been bothering Ashoka since they had returned from the main palace, and he had urged her to call the royal vaid early the next day. After some persuasion, he had finally told her what he wanted to discuss with the physician. Nothing she said could dissuade him from the meeting.

'Is the prince well?' the vaid asked again, bringing Subhadrangi out of her reverie.

Ashoka's sudden appearance prevented Subhadrangi from saying anything. He strode confidently to the old man and bowed solemnly with folded hands.

'What can I do for you, son?' the venerable physician asked in his deep voice.

'I seem to be having trouble with my skin,' Ashoka replied, getting straight to the point. Rati's harsh words about his appearance were still vivid in his mind.

'Hmm,' the vaid murmured. 'Let me have a look.' He spent some time examining Ashoka's face from different angles.

Straightening up, he cleared his throat. 'It appears perfectly healthy to me. Why do you think there is a problem with your skin?'

'It feels rough and it...it is unusually dark,' Ashoka said quietly.

The vaid looked at him, his experienced senses attuned not just to what the prince was saying but what he hadn't expressed in words. 'Come to the vaidshala tomorrow,' he said gently. 'I will introduce you to someone who will be able to help you.'

As soon as the vaid left, Subhadrangi gave Ashoka a look that seemed to say 'I told you so'.

'Why are you so bothered about your skin, all of a sudden?' she asked.

'It's nothing,' he mumbled under his breath as he turned his face away. He had never been comfortable lying to his mother but he couldn't bring himself to tell her how badly Rati's words had stung him. Or share with her the fact that no girl had ever found him attractive for as long as he could remember.

Mali was sprawled over the sculpted stone table in the courtyard, working on a complex war tactic simulation. Engrossed as he was, he did not perceive Ashoka's presence.

Ashoka peered over Mali's shoulder. 'Working on the Garuda formation, are we?' he said, admiring the particular war tactic Mali was working on.

Mali nodded absentmindedly, his attention unwavering.

'Oh, come on now. I have something interesting to show you,' Ashoka grumbled.

Not getting a response from his friend, Ashoka grabbed the banana leaf on which the battle formation was depicted.

'Hey, give that back to me,' Mali pleaded. 'Akila will have my hide if I can't cope with his tirade of questions on strategy.'

'I don't think so. You seem to be the best amongst us on war tactics,' Ashoka said, putting his arm over Mali's shoulders and dragging him along.

He led Mali to the boathouse from where one of the boatmen took them to the shore.

'Where are we going?' demanded Mali. They rarely left the Lake Palace without good reason.

'You shall see,' Ashoka replied mysteriously.

As soon as the boat touched the shore, Ashoka set them a fast pace in the direction of the main palace. Mali's eyebrows went up involuntarily. 'Don't tell me you are missing Susima already,' he joked.

Ashoka grunted in response and kept walking. Very soon they entered the palace grounds and from there, Ashoka led Mali through a maze of twists and turns until they finally reached the temple of Krishna.

'Since when have you started visiting temples voluntarily?' Mali quipped as they stood in the centre of the temple compound.

'Well, more often since I discovered this,' Ashoka said softly, pointing to the slab of stone he had unearthed the previous night. The two levers were as he had left them, jutting out of the slab.

Ashoka looked around to ascertain they were alone. He was aware that the royal priests took a lunch break at this *hora*. They would not be disturbed for some time at least.

He pointed at the gaping hole. 'I moved that stone slab last night and found this.' He explained to Mali how he had stumbled upon the levers.

Mali whistled in amazement as he listened. Ashoka pulled out two lamps he had brought along with him. They lit up with a sizzle.

'Let's go,' he said as he clambered down cautiously, a lamp held in front of him. Mali hesitated for a brief moment before following. They were in a tunnel. The initial distance of one *danda* was cramped and they had to crouch on all fours. After that, the tunnel was high and wide enough for them to walk erect, side by side. Ashoka estimated the height of the tunnel at this stage to be about one-and-a-half *danda,* which meant that the tunnel could accommodate two large grown-up men, walking alongside each other.

Mali felt the walls on the side. They were roughly patched up with stones. The ceiling seemed to be made of the same stone. The floor had not been laid and they could feel the soft earth crumbling under their wooden sandals.

'The walls are dry and cold,' Ashoka observed thoughtfully. He glanced up to see the sky fading rapidly as they went further down. The tunnel became completely horizontal after another two *dandas*.

'The surprising thing is that this tunnel is not musty,' Ashoka murmured. 'I am sure there is a way this place is ventilated.'

The two of them soon arrived at a point where the passage forked into two different directions. Mali had become rather uncomfortable by now. 'Ashoka,' he said clutching his arm, 'these tunnels were probably built hundreds of years ago. What purpose will it solve to explore them now? We may get completely lost.'

Ashoka chuckled. 'That is the whole point,' he said excitedly. 'The tunnel appears to be endless. Yet, it is clean and ventilated. I think it is still being used. The question is who is using it and to what purpose!'

'Let's debate this once we are out of here,' Mali said, eager to get out.

Ashoka looked at him impatiently. 'Your battle tactics are not going to help in the absence of courage.' The rebuke was delivered mildly.

'All I am saying is we need to plan. I promise I will come with you till the ends of the earth if needed,' Mali said, a hurt expression on his face.

'All right! Let's return now,' Ashoka conceded. 'In any case, the priest will be back soon. We can't risk anyone seeing us. We have a break from studies in a couple of sunsets. Let's make optimal use of that.'

Mali nodded quietly, still looking deflated at Ashoka's misplaced censure.

They retraced their way out of the tunnel in silence. Once they were in the boat that would take them back to the Lake Palace, Ashoka turned to Mali. 'I did not mean to question your courage, my friend. Pardon me if my words gave you that impression. My enthusiasm occasionally makes me impatient.' Ashoka sighed. 'I know you were right in there. We need to be better prepared if we want to really explore the tunnel.'

Mali smiled for the first time since they had entered the tunnel that day.

The vaidshala was one *goruta* away from the main palace. The one-storeyed structure was large and its lush green surroundings gave it a tranquil appearance. Ashoka strode confidently into the building. The courtyard was surrounded by rooms of different sizes. A worker who did not recognize the prince pointed him in the direction of the administrative wing. Here, an attendant asked him to wait.

Ashoka wondered why the royal vaid had called him here. Moreover, he was curious to know who the old physician wanted him to meet.

The attendant returned and led Ashoka to one of the inner chambers. The sweet fragrance of sandalwood incense was overpowering yet pleasant.

Ashoka had just settled down when a young woman strode in. She seemed rushed and did not bother to look at Ashoka as she sat down and pored over some notes on her desk. Ashoka observed her closely. He noticed her doe-like eyes and the unblemished, luminous skin. Her hair was pulled back in a bun, giving the beautiful face a severe appearance.

Appears to be a deliberate attempt to look older, thought Ashoka. *She looks too young to be a physician. Must be an assistant,* he conjectured.

'Please show me your arm,' she said, hardly noticing him.

'Why?' Ashoka asked, genuinely taken aback.

She looked up then. 'Haven't you got an examination done before?' she asked a trifle impatiently.

'No...not really,' Ashoka said slowly. 'Actually, I have never really fallen ill.'

'Hmm...let me check your *nadi* before reaching any conclusion,' she said briskly.

Ashoka tentatively held out his arm.

'Please close your eyes,' she said as she felt his *nadi*.

'Exactly what is your complaint?' she questioned, looking a little confused as she finished noting down her observations.

'Well...uh, it is about my skin,' he replied hesitantly.

'What about it?' she asked.

'It is unusually dark and rough,' he said abruptly.

She came closer and examined his face intently. Ashoka was aware of a pleasant fragrance of rose water. Her examination complete, she retreated behind her desk.

'There is no indication of any infection or disease.' She pronounced her verdict quietly. 'In fact, your *nadi* examination reveals a complete balance within your system.'

'I see.' Ashoka gave her a smile. He liked her no-nonsense approach.

'Of course, there are ways to enhance the appearance by the application of certain oils,' she continued.

'There are?' Ashoka asked expectantly.

'But I don't have them here,' she said. 'I make my own formulations at home. You can collect them from my home if you wish.'

'Thank you. Uh…I don't know your name,' Ashoka said a little awkwardly.

'Revati,' she said, her attention already on the reams of notes on her desk. 'You can come to meet me at dawn tomorrow. I leave home rather early for the vaidshala. It is the second cross road from the main market. I will send someone to guide you from there.'

'Don't you want to know who I am?' Ashoka said and then mentally kicked himself for asking the question.

Revati looked up briefly. 'It isn't required. I am not writing a prescription.'

Ashoka slowly stood up, feeling like a child being dismissed by his teacher. He stole a last glance at her before walking out of the door – she was utterly absorbed in her notes.

Ashoka was up at the crack of dawn. Not wanting to attract unwanted attention, he wore a plain cotton dhoti and took off any embellishment that may betray his identity. A boat took him from the Lake Palace to the shore. The streets of Pataliputra were not yet brimming with humanity. However, as he entered the lane Revati had indicated the previous day, he saw that the marketplace was already showing signs of frenetic activity. No one gave Ashoka a second glance.

He quickly reached the spot where Revati's man was supposed to meet him. His alert eyes noticed a middle-aged man waiting there patiently. They greeted each other and Ashoka followed the man as he set off at a fast pace that belied his age.

Ashoka wondered why the man looked so sullen. He tried to strike up a conversation, 'Do you work at Revati's house?'

The man nodded without uttering a word. Ashoka shrugged. The man seemed taciturn and they walked mostly in silence, taking a path that led them away from the market to the more affluent part of Pataliputra. This was where most of the ministers resided. The Ganga river flowed parallel to this road and Ashoka marvelled at the melody of the cascading water.

They finally came to a stop where the road ended. Ashoka saw they were standing in front of a large grey-stoned house surrounded by lush gardens. To his surprise, they did not go in through the main entrance. The reticent man led him through the garden to the rear of the building. This portion of the garden overlooked the river.

Ashoka noticed that the grass here had been completely plucked out and care had been taken to make the ground entirely flat and smooth. And then he heard the most beautiful tabla beats he had ever heard. But instantly, the charm of the tabla player paled in comparison to the grace of the maiden who was dancing to the beats of the instrument. Ashoka could only see her back as she went through a series of nimble movements. *What am I doing here?* he thought, utterly puzzled. *Surely Revati did not call me here to see a dance performance!*

At that moment, the maiden turned around and he saw her face.

'Revati?' Ashoka gasped as he looked at her.

The maiden was still dancing, lost in the rhythm provided by the beats of the tabla. She seemed oblivious of his presence as she performed complex steps requiring considerable strength and agility.

The dance came to an end as she pulled her body backwards, the palms of her hands coming to a rest behind her heels.

Ashoka couldn't refrain from clapping. 'I had no idea you are so multi-faceted,' he said with undisguised appreciation.

The maiden stared back at him, a blank expression on her face.

Has she forgotten me already? he wondered.

'Yesterday at the vaidshala...you asked me to come...' Ashoka trailed off, embarrassed at having to remind her who he was.

She gave him an understanding smile and he was enthralled by how her hair fell over her eyes. At that moment, he heard rapidly approaching footsteps and a voice that made him freeze.

'There you are!' The words spoken in Revati's crisp no-nonsense manner made him turn around. He was face to face with the lady he had met the previous day! He blinked in bewilderment and looked from Revati to the other maiden whose graceful dance had captivated him just a while back. Both of them were as alike as two peas in a pod.

Revati laughed. 'I see you have already met my twin sister, Kanak.'

So that's it! Ashoka thought. *Twins!*

Kanak greeted Ashoka with a curtsy while he stared at her, wondering what it was about her that made her so different from her sister, even though they were twins.

His keen eyes spotted the subtle differences. Maybe it was the softness in Kanak's eyes, or perhaps the wisps of hair that gently brushed her glowing face. Kanak seemed in sync with time while Revati appeared permanently rushed. Mostly, it was Kanak's vulnerability that truly set her apart from Revati's brisk and matter-of-fact manner.

'I am Prince Ashoka,' he said finally, remembering his manners.

He noticed his introduction did not appear to have any visible impact on either of the sisters.

'Kanak has been learning the art of dance since she was five. She has been at it for 10 years now,' Revati said proudly, her love for and pride in Kanak clearly evident in her voice.

'It shows,' Ashoka agreed. 'She seems to have total mastery over her body. Must be all the years of hard work.'

Kanak looked thoughtful. 'You could say that,' she said softly. 'But that's not how it feels to me.' It was the first time she had spoken and Ashoka loved the lilt in her voice.

'I don't understand,' he said. 'What do you mean?'

Kanak smiled. 'I mostly dance for myself. It does not seem like hard work to me at all.'

Dance for myself. Ashoka subconsciously repeated the words to himself. Something in that struck a chord within him but he couldn't seem to place a finger on what exactly it was.

'That is an unusual thing to say.' Ashoka smiled. Then on an impulse he said, 'The annual kayak race is scheduled for the coming week. Would you care to come with me?'

Kanak looked taken aback at the sudden change in topic.

Looking at her, Ashoka felt he had been too impulsive. *Why would she want to come out with me?* he thought. *She can choose to go with any man she wants.* He braced himself for a rebuff, his face automatically creasing into a frown.

Kanak looked at the change that came over his expression and wondered whether the man standing in front of her was as simple as he appeared, or whether he was deliberately trying to hide the complexities that resided within him. *Maybe I am thinking too much,* she thought, shaking her head.

Aloud she said, 'I would love to come to the kayak race… with you.' Her eyes twinkled in amusement as she saw the smile return to Ashoka's face.

'That would be…really nice,' Ashoka replied, still unable to believe it had been so easy.

The tabla player began a new rhythm on his instrument, and Kanak was jolted back to reality. 'I need to go now,' she said softly and turned away.

'Of course,' Ashoka replied, looking at Kanak's retreating figure. 'I need to get back too,' he said as he took leave of Revati who had an inscrutable look on her face.

There was no sign of the sullen man who had escorted Ashoka to the house, and he made his way out on his own. It was only when he reached the marketplace that he slapped his forehead. He had forgotten to take the oil he had gone to collect from Revati! He gave a laugh at his own folly, wondering what Revati would make of his behaviour.

Ashoka walked towards the palace grounds deep in thought. This was the first time he had not been rebuffed by a woman.

I dance for myself. Kanak's words rang louder in his mind with every step that he took. What was it in those words that spoke to his deeper self? And then it struck him. All his life he had been driven by the urge to do things that would make his father happy. And in the process, he had been more of an observer than a participant, allowing other people's opinions to influence his emotions and leaving him vulnerable.

I dance for myself. He smiled as he mouthed the words.

9

Ashoka felt lighter today. Kanak's words reverberated in the background. *I dance for myself.* Though, in his heart, he knew it would take him a while to shed the conditionings that ran deep in his personality.

With these thoughts Ashoka walked into the palace grounds and headed straight for his morning session with Acharya Akila. The inspiring thoughts of Kanak soon faded into the background as he tuned into the realities that faced him.

Mali, Susima and Devendra were already present in the large discussion room.

'Hey, are you practising for the kayak race?' asked Ashoka,

slapping Susima hard on the back. He could not help baiting Susima. 'Father will be watching, you know,' Ashoka needled him. Susima looked at him in undisguised fury. 'I will beat you, mudface,' he snarled.

Ashoka crossed his arms, thoroughly enjoying Susima's discomfort.

'And how do you plan to do that? You won't have any assistants, you know,' said Ashoka, laughing. He knew he had touched a raw nerve.

And sure enough, Susima reacted. He grabbed the stone paperweight lying on the table and threw it at him. Ashoka deftly avoided it. With a loud crash it fell near the feet of Akila, who had just entered the room. Akila looked at all of them with cold, piercing eyes. Susima went red in the face, ashamed that the acharya had witnessed such unbecoming behaviour from him.

Akila looked at them pointedly, acutely aware of the rivalry between the two brothers. *This is not good for the Mauryan empire,* he thought for the umpteenth time. As the security adviser to the emperor, he worried incessantly that someone somewhere would take advantage of this family feud.

Distaste written all over his face, he addressed them sternly. 'Let me remind the privileged royalty of Pataliputra about a truth that my guru Chanakya pointed out. "A man is great by his deeds and not by his birth,"' Akila stated acidly. 'Don't forget that you have to earn the respect of the people of Pataliputra.' His emphasis on the word 'earn' was not lost on the princes.

Ashoka looked at Akila with a steady gaze. 'Greetings, Guruji. I couldn't agree with you more.'

Susima glowered at Ashoka and said nothing.

Akila's eyes did not miss anything. He could feel the hostile vibrations in the room. With a sigh he tried a different tactic. 'Boys, you are fast approaching a period where you will be assigned real duties related to the governance of Pataliputra.

It is a great responsibility. Let me tell you that Pataliputra has eyes everywhere. You are being watched closely,' Akila explained in a gentler voice than usual. He hoped fervently that they would realize the inappropriateness of their behaviour and make efforts to remedy it.

He launched into the lesson for the day. 'Today we will discuss the *varna* system of the society.

'As you all know, our society is divided into castes – Brahmins who are the learned ones, Kshatriyas, the warriors who protect our bounderies, Vaishyas, the traders and businessmen and finally the Sudras, who are the workers. What are your thoughts on the efficacy of this system? I am eager to know,' said Akila, relaxing in a chair.

Susima was the first to begin excitedly. 'I think the system as it exists today is perfect. It is the most efficient system that has evolved over time. This system ensures that the society functions at an optimal level. In our sacred scripture, the Bhagwad Gita, Lord Krishna has himself described the four-fold order to be perfect in accordance with the natural laws.' Susima beamed at the rest, thinking that by quoting the holy scripturehe had ensured his logic would not be questioned.

'May I?' Ashoka asked Akila for permission to speak. Akila nodded. He knew something interesting would unfold.

Ashoka spoke in a loud, clear voice. 'Yes, Lord Krishna has further described that the three *gunas* – *sattva, rajas* and *tamas* – and the law of karma are responsible for the creation of the *varnas*. *Sattvaguna* predominates in Brahmins, and they are assigned the karma of *sham, dam* and *tapas*. *Rajasguna* predominates in Kshatriyas – *sattvaguna* is secondary in them. Their karma is to be warriors and show bravery and *tejas*.'

Susima's expression did not contain the surety it had a few moments ago. He scowled, realizing afresh what a tough opponent he had in Ashoka.

'*Rajasguna* also predominates in Vaishyas – *tamasguna* is secondary. Their karma is to be farmers and traders. *Tamasguna* predominates in the Sudras – *rajasguna* is secondary. Their karma is to serve others. The emphasis is on *guna* and *karma* and not on *jaati*. The *varna* or the order to which we belong is independent of sex, birth or breeding. A *varna* is determined by temperament and vocation, not by birth or heredity.'

Akila could not help thinking that Ashoka was a rare combination of perspicaciousness and physical prowess. His logic was undeniably infallible. *All is right with you, son, except for control over your temperament,* he thought, looking at Ashoka. *I don't think our Raje sees the same spark as I do,* he considered.

Ashoka continued in the same vein, 'I ask you, why should the son of a Brahmin not have a choice to be a warrior if he has the temperament to fight? Or why should the son of a Sudra not be allowed to carry on brahmanical traditions? Or why not engage in trading, the profession of Vaishyas? He may have exceptional acumen for that.'

Ashoka paused for someone to rebut him but no one did. Satisfied that he had made his point, Ashoka concluded, 'I would like to end with the same quote that our acharya spoke of – "A man is known by his deeds and not by his birth."'

Mali gleefully started clapping while Akila could not stop a small smile from curling the corners of his mouth.

Susima felt the blood rush to his face. He knew in his heart that Ashoka had provided infallible logic to support his argument. Yet, his ego prevented him from acknowledging it. He looked at Devendra for some support. Devendra smiled weakly, torn between his desire to support his cousin and the undeniable sense that Ashoka's argument had made. Not getting what he wanted from Devendra angered Susima even more.

'Only an imbecile can talk like that.' He swore under his breath, gnashing his teeth.

Akila looked at Susima, dismayed at his immature behaviour. He stared out of the window. *It's unnaturally dark for this time of day,* he thought to himself. A gentle drizzle had started; Akila knew it would turn into a downpour by the time night had fallen. He felt the faint rumblings of an impending storm, and then something within him caused him to sharply suck in his breath. The storm he sensed was not that created by nature. It owed its origin to the growing animosity and rivalry between the two sons of Bindusara; a storm that threatened to consume all of Pataliputra in its wake.

Ashoka shoved Mali impatiently in a bid to wake him up from his nap. It was a day off from their lessons. They had already stocked their secret room with supplies for their expedition.

They reached the moss-covered slab. Ashoka heaved it open and they slid in.

'We have at least three *horas* to explore.' His excitement was palpable. Mali did not bother to answer, intent on the task that lay ahead. He opened his bag to take out the lamp. It lit up with a hissing sound.

'I am prepared with fuel for at least six *horas*,' said Mali. Ashoka knew he could depend on Mali to plan everything meticulously.

They ventured ahead tentatively. Ashoka held the lamp while Mali carried palm leaves and a dye with which he could write on them.

'Mali, you do understand that we have to record every fork and every turn of these passages. I have a hunch this information will prove to be very useful to us,' Ashoka said earnestly.

Mali bowed his head. 'Your wish is my command, O Raje,' he said in jest. Ashoka gave him a wry look. It was rare for Mali to be flippant when work was at hand. They took tentative steps forward in silence. The passage was now deep in the womb of the earth and progressed in a steady direction. They passed the fork they had encountered in the previous visit and decided to take the left. After about a *hora* they faced a wall. Undeterred, Ashoka pressed against it, gingerly at first and then with force. He then felt it all over for any secret levers. A trickle of perspiration ran down his temple.

'Nothing! Beats me,' he said, mystified. 'How can it end here?'

'Let's retrace our steps,' suggested Mali. In some time they came face to face with a fork.

'You know, Mali, we may have missed the forks as they must have been to our rear. Now how do we figure out the path that we took?' said Ashoka.

Mali let out a guffaw. 'You are going to be forever indebted to me, dear Ashoka. I used some red paste to mark our path,' said a pleased Mali.

'I am impressed. You have proven that you are fit to be my second-in-command,' said Ashoka in a mix of relief and jest. Mali did not respond, too intent on finding the way back. Ashoka knew only too well that his pragmatism in such situations was a boon.

'Well, let's rub the marks on the way back, lest someone notice.'

'But how do we get back to the temple, in that case?' Mali said worriedly.

'Oh. That's hardly a problem. I have already thought about that. We don't go back,' Ashoka stated matter-of-factly.

'Don't go back! What do you mean? We will die in here,' said Mali, alarmed.

'Mali, these tunnels are ventilated. I can tell you that. I am also certain that there are multiple places to enter and exit.'

Mali stared at Ashoka in exasperation. Ashoka knew that his friend did not like nebulous situations such as this.

'I give up. Let us get going then. I will keep marking and cover our rear while you can handle the territory ahead.' Mali tried to look brave and ignore the gnawing feeling in the pit of his stomach, knowing he did not have any other option.

They came across at least five forks which were to their rear when they were moving forward.

'Whew! These tunnels are complicated,' said Ashoka. 'We need to start from scratch.'

The tunnel followed an undulating path. After a couple of *horas* Mali and Ashoka saw that the tunnel had widened into a small room. A solitary table stood in the corner with a pot of water. Ashoka peered into it cautiously. He inhaled deeply.

'This is fresh water, my friend,' stated Ashoka in a low voice.

'That means these tunnels are in use,' said Mali, his excitement mounting.

Ashoka looked up and put a finger to his lips, bidding Mali to be quiet. They heard the soft padding of hurried footsteps. Ashoka and Mali ducked into the shadows. The footsteps paused at the room. Ashoka signalled to Mali that there were two of them. Sure enough, two men in ragged commoners' clothing emerged from the shadows.

'The quality of service seems to be slipping,' one of them grumbled to the other. 'There were always fresh fruits kept for us in the good old days. Now we have to make do with plain water.'

Ashoka peered in the darkness intently. 'I know that man from somewhere,' he thought to himself. He scoured the recesses of his mind.

Oh yes, I have seen him with Father. He is a spy. And then he had an epiphany. *These tunnels are used for spying on parts of our country and its enemies!*

'The Raje will definitely reward us for we are about to bring him important news about Takshashila,' one was saying as he wiped his chin of the water that had spilled on it.

'Have you forgotten your training?' said his companion irritatedly. 'Even walls have ears. So shut up and let us hurry.'

Ashoka and Mali stared in alarm as the men approached the tunnel opening they were hidden in. Both of them quickly flattened themselves against the wall. Time seemed to slow down for both of them as they held their breath. They got up slowly once the spies passed.

'Smelly feet hmm' smirked Ashoka. Mali grinned back at him. Without a word they resumed their exploration. About half a *hora* later one of the tunnels moved upwards. Mali and Ashoka were soon staring at a dead end.

Mali looked at it in concern. 'Now what!'

Ashoka felt the roof gingerly. 'I think there is an opening above. Right here. Let's push.'

Mali obliged, knowing that he had to trust Ashoka's instincts. The two heaved with all their might.

'I think you are wrong,' Mali said breathlessly. Worry was written all over his face.

'Oh, don't worry about yourself. Pari will feed you enough. Just keep going,' said Ashoka lightly, trying to ease the situation. His patience was rewarded. There was a slight budge in what seemed to be a stone slab. Ashoka and Mali heaved on the slab, using the force of their upper body. Mali, for all his façade of being averse to physical labour, did not flinch when the situation demanded it. The slab finally moved upwards, sending a flurry of sticky mud down at them.

'I feel something slimy on my back,' hissed Mali.

'Oh, it is a good friend from the reptilian world.' Askoka deftly caught the small snake just below the head and flicked it away. Both of them clambered up and looked around. They seemed to be in the middle of the forest.

'If my guess is right we are in the forest about half a *hora* from the Lake Palace, outside the city,' said Mali.

Ashoka nodded. He trusted his friend's judgement. Based on the sun's direction, they started walking towards the city.

After walking for some time along the formidable walls of Pataliputra, they reached the Indra gate. There was a queue of traders waiting to get in. Ashoka and Mali joined the line. 'I am relieved that we are in regular clothing,' whispered Ashoka to Mali.

'Identification please.' A young guard held his hand out.

'Look, we are not from here. I am only visiting because my uncle has sent for us,' explained Ashoka earnestly.

'Step out please. You need to go and get passes made in

that room there,' the guard said, pointing to the side, his gaze already on the next person.

Ashoka and Mali looked at each other in tacit understanding and walked to the room. A harassed official was poring over some records, frowning.

'Who is your reference in Pataliputra?' the official said without glancing up. Ashoka racked his brains to come up with a suitable answer. He did not want to divulge his identity just then. At that moment a senior marched in and the official stood up to greet him.

'Good morning, Amreshwar sir.'

The senior official waved at him to sit and continue with his work as it was a customary inspection.

'Reference?' the official growled at the boys again. 'I don't have all day.'

Ashoka was looking at the senior official. There was a flicker of recognition in the kindly old eyes – it was the same guard who had greeted them after their five-sunset field trip in the forest some years ago.

'Let them pass. I know them,' he told the official who was taken aback.

Their passes were handed over to them without a fuss. Ashoka was relieved that Amreshwar had not divulged his identity. He and Mali left quietly.

'Why didn't he acknowledge you?' asked Mali curiously.

'Oh, he was being discreet, that's all.' Ashoka mentally thanked the kindly old guard for helping him maintain his anonymity.

They headed home and fell into bed exhausted. They would need their wits about them the next day at Akila's class, which was now held only thrice a week. The boys would soon be assigned to specific departments for a taste of how things really worked in the real world of the Mauryans. Ashoka knew that the real learning would start then.

The banks of river Ganga were dotted with flags of the Mauryan dynasty bearing the traditional peacock over a saffron background. A profusion of flowers adorned the passage leading up to the kayaks. Temporary thatched-roof shelters provided seating for the *amatyas* and Emperor Bindusara, with the makeshift shelters for the rest of the public stretching for at least four *kosas*. High chairs for the referees had been placed at various vantage points along the banks. The main celebrations were planned at the palace grounds at sunset.

The Ganga was at its choppy best. The angry, foamy waters were a stark contrast to the festive banks. Navigating kayaks over such rough, furious waters would be a test of endurance and skill for the men who were competing.

Ashoka woke up early and walked along the riverbank in order to prepare himself mentally for the event. Spotting the throne set up for the emperor, he thought wistfully,

What do I do to make Father proud of me? No matter what I do, I am not able to please him. He had forgotten Kanak's words which had inspired him earlier and regressed into his old patterns of thinking.

I wonder why he favours Susima. That man is incapable of protecting the empire, he thought grimly. *And what is it about him that enamours the maidens?*

The thought of Kanak being his escort for the evening cheered him up. *She is talented and beautiful…and peaceful.* That was the quality that Ashoka was most attracted to in her – a quality that was lacking in his life.

Ah, peace peace peace…why don't I have peace of mind? Why do I always feel agitated?

As always, the answer eluded him.

Lost in his thoughts, he found himself standing at the starting point of the race. Twenty-five kayaks stood proudly, their freshly polished appearance seeming to reflect the excitement of their owners. Each kayak had a number inscribed on its side large enough for the furthest spectator to see.

Ashoka walked on, desolate. He crossed the start line. He reached the steps where the Brahmins were performing their early morning acts of purification, standing waist-deepin the water. He ascended the steps of the first temple that came his way.

With folded hands he looked at the deity being worshipped. It was Lord Shiva, the eternal destroyer of evil, his form represented through a dome-shaped stone. The stone fascinated Ashoka. It comprised two parts – one shaped like a phallus immersed into the other part, a receptacle for the former. The stone represented the union of male and female energy, and signified the infiniteness of creation.

Is he just a stone carving or does he have enough powers to fulfil my desires? thought Ashoka selfishly.

On an impulse he asked the priest, 'Why do you worship him all day?'

The priest looked stunned at the odd question and then his eyes softened when he noticed how disturbed the youth was. He understood that the question was not meant to judge. It was an inquiry coming from the heart. The priest knew that such moments of inquiry could very well lead to a twist in the understanding of divinity. He waited for Ashoka to say more and then sighed. *No, this was not that moment.*

'He fulfils everyone's desires as long as they ask with faith,' the priest offered as an explanation.

Ashoka shrugged not really getting the point. 'What is faith?' he asked unable to understand its meaning. The priest sized up Ashoka in an instant and realized that this was not the day for talk.

'Come, son. I will answer your questions another sunset. For now, chant with me the sound of the universe. Oooooommmmmm!'

Ashoka hesitated and then joined the priest in chanting the divine intonation. He felt the vibration emanating from the pit of his stomach and reaching his throat. After a few moments, to his surprise, he felt a wave of calmness engulf him. The priest smiled at him and arched his eyebrows questioningly.

'I...I feel better now. For the moment at least,' Ashoka conceded.

The priest beamed at him.

'I will take your leave now as I have matters of urgency to attend to.' Ashoka bowed and dashed off.

The priest looked thoughtfully at the retreating figure. 'The questions come from his core. But to get the answers, he needs patience. Maybe he will find it someday. But...not today,' concluded the priest aloud.

Ashoka felt a surge of energy as he walked back briskly to where the kayaks were docked. He was not sure why, but he wanted to recheck the condition of his kayak. Ashoka glanced over at Susima's kayak, which had the national emblem of the peacock dyed on the sides. He strode across the makeshift bridge across the Ganga to his kayak, number 11.

Ashoka ran his hands over every possible joint for any leaks. *No leaks. Everything seems to be fine,* he thought. He stood there uneasily, unsure of what else to do. Suddenly he noticed that the sun was much higher and the royal guards would be there any moment. He nimbly retraced the path he had come from, heading for the palace exercise stadium.

I need to be in top form today, he thought to himself grimly. He scarcely noticed the beautiful decorations at the palace.

The exercise stadium wore a deserted look except for the attendants. With single-minded dedication Ashoka started his routine. He picked up the heavy mace and swung it savagely over his shoulders, his mind focused on the kayak race. Unmindful of the perspiration dripping profusely from his body, he continued for some time.

Unnoticed by Ashoka, a couple of senior officers of the army stood on the side, observing him with interest.

'Our younger prince will definitely give a tough fight to everybody at the race,' one of them commented. He turned to his companion.

'Hey, aren't you participating too, Poulak?'

Poulak nodded cheerfully. 'I wouldn't miss it for anything.'

'So, why are you not exercising, my friend? At your age, you definitely need it,' commented the officer.

'Who says I haven't been?' replied Poulak good-naturedly. 'The prize is 100 gold coins. I intend to build a large house for Maya and myself...'

'...and live happily ever after,' his friend completed the sentence for him. They turned when they heard a loud crash. Ashoka had thrown a javelin from one end to the other where it overshot the boundaries and crashed into one of the spectator chairs.

Our prince does not know the extent of his own strength, thought Poulak wryly.

From afar the crowd on the banks of river Ganga looked like a huge army of ants huddled close together. Men, women and children from all of Magadha had come to view this spectacular annual event. The excitement in the air was palpable. It was a field day for the local vendors, who were selling all sorts of things to an enthusiastic crowd. The berry sellers and guava sellers were much in demand. The din of the crowd made it impossible to hear beyond a *danda*. Children were perched on their father's shoulders to get a better view. The women looked fresh, adorned with flowers of all kinds. They sipped cool rose sherbet to ward off the heat that is inevitable when a mass of humanity comes together.

The kayaks, lined up next to each other, presented a majestic view. The best talent from all over Mauryan empire had assembled to participate in the event. Each contestant had a loyal following in the crowd. The referees had already taken their places, perched on their high chairs. All set to watch over every move of the contestants, they looked akin to hawks. Their faces were impassive, untouched by the emotional response of the crowd. There was a small platform built up much higher so that the crowd could see it even from a great distance. That was the platform from which the race would be flagged off.

Emperor Bindusara arrived with his two queens and headed for the main dais. He was heavily protected by a team of 16 bodyguards in a double-ringed formation. This allowed them an all-round view. The event was an assassin's dream. With such a mass gathered together, an errant arrow would not be possible to trace. Akila knew this and had therefore suggested the double-ringed formation. All the bodyguards had been handpicked by him and had been psychologically trained to be human shields.

The much-loved Bindusara was greeted by a huge roar from the crowd. He smiled at them benevolently. With a flourish of his hands he bade them to subside. Subhadrangi and Rakshita sat on either side of the emperor, careful not to meet each other's eyes. Acharya Akila, Mahamantri Radheya and Senapati Ajaya also took their seats close to the emperor.

The burly man standing on the high platform bowed to the emperor, and with his permission, started announcing the names of the contestants.

'Surya Kumar…from Sanchi!' The handsome participant from Sanchi walked up across the makeshift bridge to where his kayak was docked. His supporters from Sanchi gave him an exuberant welcome. He waved at them and took his position.

'Vaibhav Udupa from Mahishur!' The crowd saw the confident man walk up with long strides and take his position. His supporters were in the far corner. Nevertheless, they managed to create quite a brouhaha when his name was called.

'Kishen Lal from Ujjaini!' roared the announcer. The stocky and proud Kishen Lal walked up to his kayak with a lopsided grin.

'Brahu Bali from Takshashila!' Bindusara looked on in surprise as the decibels rose in favour of the dark, fierce-looking Brahu Bali. He walked self-consciously towards his kayak. It was clear that his supporters loved him immensely.

The list went on and covered all the participants from different cities of the Mauryan empire. Pataliputra being the host city, the Pataliputrans were called at the end. There were four of them, including Ashoka and Susima.

'Poulak from Pataliputra!' The Pataliputran crowd was vociferous in demonstrating their loyalty to a local hero. The soldiers too bellowed their support. Poulak was known for his mettle and his amicable personality had won him many friends. He glanced back at his beloved Maya who had eyes only for him. Even in such a packed crowd their eyes locked in silent affection.

'Mandar from Pataliputra!' The soldiers looked with interest at this dark and tall man. A few remembered his contribution in the battle against Mahishur.

Bindusara could hear the tribals even though they were huddled far out. Although the tribals had contributed significantly in their war against Mahishur, memories of it were shortlived. Old prejudices seemed to have re-emerged.

This is one aspect in which I haven't been successful, thought Bindusara, rubbing his chin. The undercurrents against the tribals were still strong. These thoughts faded away as he heard a familiar name being called out.

'Our young prince Ashoka!' roared the announcer. The crowd strained to get a glimpse of this youth of medium height who walked confidently to his kayak. They acknowledged him with a weak cheer. He looked like one of them, with no resemblance to the regal bearing of Bindusara.

Subhadrangi had tears in her eyes as she watched him. She noticed that Bindusara looked impatient, as he always did in all matters relating to his younger son.

'Vijayee bhava,' she mouthed a silent blessing for him.

'And finally…our older Prince Susima!' A thunderous applause greeted him. He looked every inch the royal prince who would one day take the reins from his father. The Pataliputrans were well accustomed to the sight of Prince Susima accompanying his mother Rakshita on rounds of the city.

The soldiers of the Mauryan army seemed surprised at the vociferous reaction of the crowd. Susima had not yet earned their respect. Susima walked up to his kayak, number 10. He smirked at Ashoka, who was on the adjacent one.

A slow awareness of the drum beats swept over everyone present. Steadily the decibels and the tempo rose. In fact, it was almost deafening for the people within the first *kosa,* the drum beats synchronizing with their fast-beating hearts.

Ashoka's piercing eyes looked first at Subhadrangi and then at Mali and Daya. Mali, who was not given to showing much emotion, nodded to him. Ashoka nodded back in a silent exchange.

His eyes were still searching…for someone.

Damn her. I don't think she has come, he thought bleakly.

'Concentrate on the race, you fool,' an inner voice admonished him. He mentally tuned into the race again. He became aware of a vague sense of uneasiness but could not put a finger on it.

The beat of the drums had silenced every being present and forced them to just be with the rhythm and nothing else. Having reached a crescendo, the intensity of the beats now began to wane. Finally, the only audible sound was the water lapping against the kayaks.

Twenty-five pairs of eyes watched every movement of the announcer. Time stood still. It was as if there was no crowd – just the contestants and the man who would flag off the race. He lifted the horn that was tied to his waist to his lips and blew long and hard. That was the signal to get ready. All the participants gripped their oars and steadied themselves.

Ashoka felt his heart pound. The blood rushed to his head and his body tensed for action. To his right was Susima and on the left were Poulak and Mandar. His mouth set in a scowl as he heard the announcer blow the horn in three short bursts and simultaneously raise the green flag.

The competitors burst out like fireballs from cannons.

The crowd cheered again as the kayaks surged out, battling the choppy waters of the Ganga. One wrong move and their kayaks could overturn. The history of the annual event was dotted with incidents of kayaks capsizing and participants sustaining severe injuries.

Amidst the roar of the crowd Poulak, Brahu Bali and Ashoka took the lead, with Susima, Kishen Lal and three others a little behind. Many lost control while navigating the raging waters. This had a ripple effect on others who were behind and could not save themselves in time. The audience looked on with bated breath. Every fall of a hero was met with a sigh and every deft manoeuvre with a whoop of delight.

Ashoka, who was leading now, rowed on furiously. At that moment the kayak did not feel like a separate entity to him. It was as alive as his own body. He acutely sensed every twist and roll. And then he felt it – a sense of imbalance. Alarm bells started ringing.

What's happening to Prince Ashoka? He is struggling to maintain his balance, wondered a puzzled Poulak, who was a hair's breadth behind at this point. Ashoka's floundering was the break that Poulak needed to go past him. But then, out of the corner of his eye, he saw Ashoka plunge into the freezing water, totally out of control.

Oh Shiva! My left oar is broken, thought Ashoka a fleeting second before the momentum made him veer and completely careen. The cold water had a reviving effect on him. He understood what had happened and calmly evaluated his alternatives.

He had seen Poulak race past him and now the latter had slowed down and come back. Poulak dived into the water himself and both he and Ashoka uprighted the kayak.

'Here, Prince, take my oar and complete the race,' said Mandar who was also by their side. Ashoka hesitated for a moment before accepting the favour. Poulak and Mandar, with one oar, tried to get back into the fray. Many had crossed them, including Brahu Bali, Susima and at least six others.

'The race…I have to win it, thought Ashoka grimly, knowing that his chances were extremely weak. In fact, the misadventure had also cost the other Pataliputrans who had stopped to help him.

I can't let their efforts go in vain…I can't lose. I have to win for them. Ashoka rowed fiercely. With difficulty he overtook many contestants. Finally, he had forged ahead enough to espy Susima's broad back.

A thought flashed across his mind. *My fears were not unfounded. My oar had definitely been tampered with.*

Just then Susima looked over his shoulder. His face registered shock as he saw Ashoka right behind him. Ashoka knew then with certainty. *It was him. He was the one who tampered with my oar.*

Bindusara watched the whole episode with annoyance. *Ashoka and trouble go together,* he thought wearily. He observed that the fracas had diminished the chances of all the Pataliputran participants, except Susima of course. Susima was now dipping into his last pool of his reserve. Brahu Bali and Susima were neck to neck most of the time, but Bindusara noticed with interest that Surya Kumar was steadily catching up with the other two. He seemed calm and totally at ease even towards the end of the race.

Rakshita watched her son with bated breath. She had eyes only for him and scarcely noticed anyone else.

Ashoka was quick to close the gap. From where the surge of energy came, he did not know. Radheya's watching eyes saw Ashoka in the throes of a frenzy, desperately trying to catch up. Akila's gaze was as usual impassive. Susima and Surya Kumar were the first to cross the finishing mark followed by

Brahu Bali and surprisingly, Ashoka. This had been the most exciting race that Pataliputrans had witnessed in a long time.

The referees got off their high chairs and went into a makeshift tent, shielded from the curious eyes of the excited crowd. After a quick conference, they handed over the results to the announcer who immediately carried it over to Mahamantri Radheya whose only reaction was to raise his eyebrows. As per protocol, the results finally came to Bindusara.

By now, the crowd – especially the supporters of the final contenders – were at the edge of their seats.

Bindusara, accompanied by Mahamantri Radheya, walked up to the high platform. He smiled to the mass of people stretching as far as his eyes could see. It was amazing to see how the sea of people beyond, who could not even hear Bindusara still waited for the results to be relayed to them through word of mouth. He addressed them.

'My beloved countrymen, I will not keep you waiting. You are in the capital city of Magadha, a city we all love. No other city in the world is as fair as our Pataliputra. Everybody, no matter what their background, is provided a common platform for a test of skills. This race was a test of both skill and endurance. The winner will get a hundred gold coins. This year it goes to two people – Surya Kumar from Sanchi... and Prince Susima!' said Bindusara, smiling widely.

Already supporters of Surya Kumar had started beating drums. Both men walked proudly to the dais to receive their trophy from the hands of the emperor.

Ashoka's clothes were drenched as he stood motionless and bleak, some distance away, and watched Susima's every move.

Susima turned around and winked at him. 'The best men win, brother,' he mouthed jeeringly.

Ashoka tried his best to look calm and happy. But he was seething inside. Poulak, Mandar and Mali stood by him, sharing his dismay at losing a fair chance to win.

Poulak put his arm over Ashoka's shoulder and said. 'We know…and now all of Pataliputra has seen it.' Ashoka gave him a wan smile, not trusting himself to speak, lest his fury be displayed. Amidst all the cheering for Susima and Surya Kumar, they strained to hear what Bindusara was saying.

Bindusara continued, 'We have Prince Ashoka in second place and Brahu Bali in third.' He barely managed to complete the sentence as a storm of applause broke out at the mention of Ashoka's name. The people were shouting, clapping and stamping their feet – cheering as they had never cheered before. Bindusara looked incredulous at the reaction of the crowd.

Ashoka's comeback had not gone unnoticed. The young prince had won over the crowd with his heroic fight against the odds. Ashoka himself was stunned by the warm response. Mali slapped him on the back with whoops of delight and prodded him towards the dais. Poulak and Mandar stood on the side, grinning. With a spring in his step, he went up swiftly to receive a stiff nod of approval and a plaque from Bindusara, who had no choice but to acknowledge the hero of the moment.

They say that every misfortune brings with itself the seed of something good. The prince has not only won over the masses but also new friends, Radheya thought, smiling to himself.

Ashoka's eyes were searching. More than one nubile woman had given him a second glance. They had all witnessed his heroic comeback, and despite his plain looks he appeared to be the star of the moment. But Ashoka noticed none of them. The palace celebrations held no interest for him either.

Why isn't she here? he thought exasperated.

The effects of *madira* were already beginning to show on some of the men. Ashoka could hear merry laughter and happy voices all around. Emperor Bindusara, surrounded by

his *amatyas,* was in deep discussion. The royal help moved around efficiently, serving *madira,* lime juice and delicacies that only the royal cooks knew how to create.

Susima was, as usual, surrounded by a bevy of both young men and women. That included Rati, Mahamantri Radheya's daughter, who had agreed to be his companion for the evening. Ashoka could hear the group laughing at Susima's jokes.

'Tell us about the race all over again,' chirped Rati who was hanging on to Susima's every word.

Poulak and Mandar strode across the garden towards Ashoka. The mishap at the kayak race had several silver linings. It had resulted in the formation of instant camaraderie amongst the three of them.

'You don't look as exultant as you ought to be, Prince,' observed Poulak.

Ashoka was not given to explaining his feelings. He shrugged in reply.

'He's looking for a certain someone,' quipped Mali by way of explanation. Poulak and Mandar raised their eyebrows and looked at each other.

'There are many who desire you today. Look around, Prince,' said Mali laughing.

'And there's someone who is trying to catch your attention right behind you,' Poulak said with a wave of his hand.

Ashoka turned around nonchalantly. It was Kanak!

He gave an exaggerated bow. 'I didn't see you at the race. Didn't you think it worth your while to come?' he asked, a tad stiffly.

'Who said I wasn't there?' Kanak retorted, her eyes dancing. 'It's just that you didn't see me.'

'How did that happen? I scanned the *amatyas'* section pretty thoroughly. Weren't you sitting with your father?'

'Apparently not. Maybe I was in disguise,' she replied mysteriously, enjoying his confusion. 'Oh stop the interrogation – let's take a look around.'

Kanak pulled at his hand, urging him to come along. She glanced at the others.

'I am sorry, I am dragging him away.'

'Oh, I am sure he doesn't mind,' replied Mali dryly.

As Ashoka and Kanak passed Susima's group, Devendra nudged him. 'Your grisly brother actually has a female companion,' he sniggered.

Susima glanced furtively at them. This was the first time that he had seen his brother alone with a maiden.

'And a beautiful one at that,' replied Susima. 'I wonder who she is. Never saw her before.'

Rati turned to see who they were talking about. 'Oh, she is Amatya Sen's daughter. She hardly ever socializes. I wonder why she has come to the celebrations at all.'

'I wonder too…' Susima smoothened his hair thoughtfully.

Kanak led Ashoka to the other end of the palace gardens where young men and women were performing the Bihu folk dance.

Oh no! Can't she think of anything apart from dance? groaned Ashoka inwardly. Kanak was now tugging at his arm, coaxing him to join in as her partner. Ashoka was surprised at his own reaction at the prospect of dancing – he felt extremely ill at ease, as if a thousand eyes were watching him.

'Look, why don't you dance and I'll watch. In all probability I'll only step on your toes…' Ashoka said trying hard to avoid it.

'You won't,' asserted Kanak. 'I will guide you.'

Ashoka reluctantly followed her right to the middle of the boisterous crowd.

'Just follow me!' she said enthusiastically. Ashoka clumsily tried to follow her lead. She laughed at his valiant but ineffective efforts.

'Don't laugh at me. It may seem entertaining to you… not to me' he glared at her defensively for a moment. The continuous barbs from Susima had resulted in Ashoka being highly sensitive.

'But…I did not mean to…'

Ashoka abruptly turned around and disappeared, leaving her stranded in the middle of the dancing crowd. Rati, who had followed them, had been witness to the entire scene.

'He is a poor choice, you know,' she told Kanak scathingly.

'It's none of your business.'

'Everybody is talking about the fact that this is the first social event you chose to attend. Let me warn you, Prince Ashoka is trouble. Susima has told me a number of unflattering stories about him,' Rati whispered, grimacing.

'Like what? He seems nice enough to me,' replied Kanak.

'Well, for one thing, it's no secret that he despises Susima and will defame him on every chance he gets,' replied Rati gravely.

'The same could be said about Prince Susima,' replied Kanak in Ashoka's defence. 'Anyway, I can't fathom why we are having this inane conversation,' Kanak said dismissively.

Rati shrugged and left her to go back to Susima.

Kanak searched in vain for Ashoka. He was nowhere to be seen. She spotted Poulak, Mandar and Mali…but no Ashoka.

He's definitely touchy about his social skills, thought Kanak, trying to fathom why he had disappeared in a huff. She felt a vague sense of discomfort.

Ashoka was untraceable for the remainder of the evening. It was way past midnight. Half the *amatyas* had left with their families. The contestants too had retired to the quarters that were prepared for them. Her father was engrossed in a discussion with the other *amatyas*. In a bid to pass the time, Kanak decided to take a walk in the quieter parts of the palace.

As she reached a section adjoining the exercise stadium, she became aware of laboured breathing and looked around.

'So this is where you come to escape the world!'

Ashoka did not answer. He was busy swinging the mace over his shoulders.

'Why did you leave me stranded?' Kanak said accusingly. 'You were the one who invited me, remember?'

Ashoka continued to swing his mace, his face sullen, not meeting her eyes.

'Very well! Let me leave you to your pursuits,' Kanak said softly, walking away.

Suddenly her arm was held in a firm grip.

'Don't…I, er…overreacted. I didn't mean to behave that way. Please accept my apologies,' Ashoka replied tiredly. 'I was angry. I thought you were making fun of me.' He looked into her eyes. 'A lot of people make fun of me.'

Kanak looked at him long and hard.

'What! What are you looking at?' he asked, a little exasperated.

'Nothing,' she said hesitatingly. Then she gathered her courage. 'I was just thinking you don't look like a…'

'Don't look like what?' There was a hint of impatience in his voice.

'A victim!' she said gently.

Ashoka's face grew red as he felt his blood surge to his head. 'You can't talk to me like that,' he rasped in a broken but furious voice.

Kanak raised her hand. 'Spare me. I am leaving. I thought you were different. But you are just like the rest with your petty thoughts.'

Kanak strode out, leaving Ashoka open-mouthed. He flung the mace behind her. It hit the floor with a loud clang just a foot from her retreating figure. It was for the second time that her words had affected him greatly. Only this time they did not inspire. Rather, they pointed to a part of his personality he did not care to look at himself…because he was afraid of what he might find there.

Ashoka and Poulak embarked on a climb of the 2,000 steps to the Vishnu temple situated on Ramshila hill. It was an easy climb for fit men like them.

Looking down, Ashoka could see at least 20 carriages at the base of the hill. It was nearing sunset.

On the way, they passed a cluster of soldiers who were stationed here permanently as this temple was frequented by the *amatyas* and their families. No one recognized Ashoka as he was in the ordinary clothes of a Pataliputran. How he loved being a commoner! He could breathe the same air as all the others, enjoy the same sunshine and walk the same streets.

I hope they don't ask me for identification, he thought. These days it was mandatory for everyone to carry it. This was usually the case when a threat to the emperor's life was suspected.

The air became cooler the higher they went. They reached the top which was a large flat surface. The calm was deceptive as the large courtyard was packed with at least a hundred devotees who had come for a special *puja* of Lord Vishnu. There was silence apart from the incantations of the priests who was reciting the shlokas in Sanskrit. The *puja* was almost over.

Next to the *yagna,* two huge plates were heaped with orange laddus. They would be distributed soon after. Ashoka looked longingly at them. He sat down cross-legged in the last row, waiting expectantly. People started murmuring to their neighbours as the *puja* was declared complete by the priest. Now came the part that Ashoka had been waiting for.

Kanak entered, wearing a heavily decorated outfit for her dance performance. Ashoka gazed at her, enjoying her aura of beauty and peace.

She seemed oblivious to the audience and danced as if she was the only one present. She told a story with her performance and her eyes, her expressions and every movement of her body became the narrator. Her fluid movements were mesmerizing. Ashoka could not help thinking of water – flowing in action yet soothing in the depths. There was thunderous applause as she concluded her performance with folded hands.

This was the moment Ashoka had been waiting for. He

nodded to Poulak to guard the door of her dressing room as he followed her in. Poulak heard a loud shriek from inside.

'How dare you enter without knocking!' yelled Kanak

'It's me, Ashoka. I thought you would see through my disguise,' he said, crestfallen. Kanak looked at him wide-eyed, her alarmed expression changing to one of curiosity.

'Why are you here? she asked sternly.

'Oh, I thought I would come and see if you were any good as a dancer,' said Ashoka nonchalantly. He neatly ducked a pot aimed at him.

'I don't care about what you think of my performance anyway,' said Kanak, pursing her lips, hands on her hips.

'Actually, you dance pretty well. Not bad at all,' said a smiling Ashoka.

She glared at him, disliking his patronizing tone, her eyes blazing. The memory of their last encounter at the palace garden was still fresh.

'I have no wish for your company. Please leave.'

'I come to make peace.' He paused and then continued. 'I solemnly promise not to leave you stranded even if you laugh at me.'

Kanak looked at him, bewildered at the transformation. A smile broke out on her face. Ashoka started laughing and Kanak joined him.

'That's better. I can sleep well today knowing I have a friend in you,' he said.

Kanak did not doubt his sincerity.

'I don't have a choice, do I,' she replied with a twinkle in her eyes, the past forgotten and forgiven.

'I don't think so. You have to do as the Prince of Magadha bids you to,' replied Ashoka lightly.

There were four rapid knocks on the door. That was Poulak's signal that someone was approaching.

Ashoka was gone in a flash.

Kanak stood there, shaking her head. *What will mother and*

father think, she wondered. She drove those thoughts away and concentrated on the *pranayam* taught to her by her guruji to calm her mind after a performance. But was her state of mind influenced by the performance or something else…someone else?

10

Akila's students pored over the assignment he had given them. They dared speak very little in his formidable presence. He sometimes wondered whether that was good or bad. While the distance helped him assess them objectively, the flip side was that none of them really confided their true feelings in him. In a bid to lighten the atmosphere, he brought up a topic that was sure to interest them.

'I understand that all of you have been invited by the emperor for a hunting expedition.'

This brought out the desired effect in the form of smiles.

'Yes, sir. It is a great honour for us,' declared Susima who was adept at saying the right thing at the right time.

Devendra said excitedly, 'I hear there is a wild white tiger troubling our tribals.'

'You can be sure it will be no easy task to hunt it,' said the ever pragmatic Mali.

'Not easy, but not impossible either,' stated Ashoka dryly.

Akila left in the midst of the discussion. Ashoka looked forward to the jaunt. In the past he would have viewed it with mixed feelings. But now, it presented to him an opportunity to understand his father, irrespective of the disdain that he flung at him.

Bindusara stood impatiently in front of the full-length mirror while the palace maids tightened his iron and leather armour. One of them combed his hair with an ornate wooden comb.

They finished by sprinkling rose water all over his body. With a wave of his hand, he dismissed them. He clapped his hands.

One of the guards on duty stepped in from behind the curtains.

'See that no one enters until I say so,' said Bindusara curtly.

'Yes, O Raje,' said the guard, bowing his head and walking out respectfully.

Bindusara went to the corner of the room and pulled aside the Persian rug covering the floor. It revealed shiny grey stone slabs. He then walked to the wall where a painting of his father, Chandragupta Maurya, hung. With his index finger, he applied a little pressure on the bottom left of the painting. It swung to the right, revealing a panel of levers. There were five of them. He moved in a particular order that only he and one other person knew.

One of the grey slabs swung inwards, giving way to a gaping hole. Bindusara picked up a lamp and walked down the steps. They led to a huge room. The room was empty except for an ornate box.

Bindusara opened the lid gingerly, using both hands. The object lay there innocuously, not betraying its glorious past. With reverence, he lifted the simple yet elegant sword. A single red ruby was embedded as the eye of a peacock on the hilt. He ran his fingers lightly over the sharp blade which gleamed even in the little light that was available. The sheen of the blade had not dulled at all in all these years.

This was the sword of the mighty Chandragupta Maurya, the founder of the Mauryan empire. It had been instrumental in many victories. The sword had been passed on to him before his father foresook all that he had built and disappeared into the forest, with instructions that no one should follow him. Bindusara still remembered that day with sadness. He had felt desolate without him – to this very day, he felt the loss of his father. But his inner strength bade him to carry on…and on –

with his duties as an emperor. Bindusara touched the sword to his forehead in reverence.

He carried it up the steps, shutting the trapdoor behind him. He then sheathed his sword purposefully and strode out of his chambers.

Bindusara's face broke into a smile when he saw his favourite son Susima, who rushed to touch his feet. He took him by the shoulders and hugged him. Ashoka witnessed this display of affection with amusement and touched his father's feet too. Bindusara nodded stiffly at him, irritated by the commoner's clothes his younger son wore. The rest of the entourage, which included Mahamantri Radheya, Mali and Devendra, looked on impassively.

On Bindusara's signal the royal elephant was brought forth. The princes followed in a chariot and the rest on horses. They reached the city gate without incident. The gates were already open in anticipation of the emperor. The soldiers stood at attention and bowed deeply as the emperor passed.

Ashoka's eyes met those of Amreshwar, and both nodded in acknowledgment.

By noon, the entourage of 20 was well inside the forest. Reading the tiger's marks, a skilled tracker led them to a particularly dense part of the jungle. The chirping of birds seemed to have diminished. Sinister hissing sounds emanated from the bushes every now and then. Tense with anticipation, they were all quiet, waiting...waiting for the fearsome beast.

The guide held up his hand. That was a signal to stop. In front lay the mangled carcass of a recently killed animal. It was a gazelle with long antlers, barely recognizable now, completely destroyed by the act of violence.

Ashoka could not help thinking, *This is nature's way. It is the nature of the carnivorous beast to kill to satisfy its hunger. But killing humans is not part of nature's plan for the beast.*

The hunting party knew they had to camp here. The tiger would return at dusk to claim its kill. Some of the attendants rushed to help the emperor down from the elephant while others got busy doling out a cold lunch of curry and rice. It was not advisable to light a fire as it would scare the tiger away.

Dusk descended swiftly and, with it, gloomy shadows of beasts. It was eerie. Ashoka ate little and had his hand planted firmly on his sword. Bindusara himself was surrounded by his bodyguards in the double-ringed formation.

Ashoka was taking a sip of water when the majestic beast stealthily emerged from the shadows. Everyone froze, waiting for Bindusara to take the kill. His bodyguards shifted calculatedly, to allow Bindusara space for the kill yet not too far lest he need them. In a swift movement, Bindusara grabbed his spear and aimed at the throat. But the beast was young and agile – it moved fast and the spear struck its hind leg instead. The air resounded with growls as the enraged tiger leaped at the emperor. He grabbed the helm of his sword to strike. The beast was too quick and aimed to grab the Emperor's arm in its teeth. He missed but the sword fell from Bindusara's hands. By now everyone knew it was no longer the Raje's kill. He was now in the safety net of his bodyguards.

Ashoka gave a blood-curdling yell to attract the beast to himself. He succeeded – the tiger leaped at him, snarling. He held his sword aloft for the animal to impale itself by its own weight. But his sword broke and Ashoka had the fleeting thought, *Oh Shiva, the power of this beast must be twice that of the average one.*

Desperate to save himself he grabbed the first weapon he could lay his hands on and struck with all his might – not at the throat but at the already injured hind leg. There was a crack and the tiger fell back howling with pain. Ashoka had succeeded in breaking its leg. The next instant a spear thrown by Susima pierced the throat of the tiger. Ashoka then plunged the weapon into its heart to end the beast.

Everyone stared wordlessly at the bloodied sword still

lodged in the heart of the beast. The colour of blood trickling down from it matched the ruby that adorned it. The weapon that Ashoka had used for the kill was Emperor Chandragupta's forbidden sword.

The significance of the moment was not lost to those present. Unknowingly Ashoka had staked his claim to it.

Word travelled swiftly. The tiger killing incident was narrated by many, not only across the *amatya* community, but also the royal attendants. It was also discussed in hushed tones that Ashoka had broken tradition by using his grandfather's sacred sword for the kill.

All this irritated Bindusara to no end. He had mixed feelings. As the Emperor, he was glad that the tiger had been slain. The father in him wished Susima had been the one to do so and not Ashoka.

11

Kanak was thoroughly enjoying the late evening boat ride in one of the reservoirs built by the city architect. The cool breeze on her face felt heavenly in the heat of the sunset. She stared furtively across the boat at the youth who was rowing the boat with ease. He seemed oblivious to her, lost in his own thoughts.

'So was the tiger you killed the day before a tough kill?' asked Kanak in an attempt at conversation.

Ashoka frowned. 'I don't really like discussing anything to do with myself.'

'Why not?' asked Kanak indignantly. 'It is not as if I am asking you to divulge a state secret. Everybody has been talking about it.' She paused and then continued. 'They say the tiger was twice your size and strong enough to take on the full entourage.'

Ashoka stopped rowing and started to laugh.

'Stories do get around, don't they,' he replied with a smirk.

'So tell me what the real story is. People also say that you killed it with your grandfather's sword,' persisted Kanak.

'True…oh fair maiden, that part is true.'

Kanak loved these rare occasions when Ashoka spoke to her light-heartedly. She leaned forward.

'I did use my grandfather's sword to kill it – only because I had to. That was the weapon nearest to me. I didn't pick it up deliberately. I will wait for the sunset the sword is handed over to me by my father. The sunset he feels I am worthy of it.'

As Kanak absorbed this silently, Ashoka looked her in the eye and said, 'But that is all I am prepared to tell you about it. I am not given to narrating heroic incidents of hunting and killing.'

Kanak was unable to fathom the reason for his reticence. This was a part of his personality that she could not understand.

'But why…' she was saying when he interrupted her.

'Kanak, killing is nothing to talk about…especially with a woman,' he said firmly.

Offended at the apparent rebuff, she told him stiffly, 'I wish to go home. Please row back to the shore.'

Ashoka's expression softened somewhat and then something made him change his mind. 'As you wish,' he replied coldly.

She looked away in disgust. Amused, Ashoka stared at her. He noticed her wind-blown hair against the tense body. The boat docked with a dull thud. Ashoka leaped out and held out his hand to Kanak. She pointedly ignored him, jumped out and started to walk away. Ashoka could not help smiling as he gazed at her retreating figure. He calmly anchored the boat whistling a tune. Unnoticed by Kanak, he followed her home. The darkness only helped him from being discovered. Only when she reached the safe confines of her garden, did he leave and walk in the opposite direction. Throughout the walk back Ashoka kept wondering at the strangeness of their relationship.

Ashoka walked with a lightness in his steps. He was dressed in ordinary clothes which was his preference on most occasions. Some people did stare but soon looked away, thinking they were mistaken. He grinned to himself. Memories of the kayak race would soon be forgotten.

But at some point it will become difficult to roam the streets with aplomb, he thought wistfully. Ashoka loved Pataliputra with its colourful long and winding lanes, the open and chaotic market, the din of the shopkeepers selling their wares and the women in bright clothes walking gracefully with their heads held high.

He soon arrived at his destination, and tolled the bell, instinctively straightening his *angavastram* at the same time. The door was opened by a young girl, who looked inquiringly at him.

'Please tell Kanak I have come to see her,' he said with a pleasant smile.

'And what name shall I announce?' she asked matter-of-factly.

'Oh, please tell her it is Shoku,' said Ashoka, intending to surprise Kanak. 'I will wait for her in the garden.'

Ashoka looked around at the beautifully landscaped garden with pleasure, enjoying the peace and quiet. The stillness was interrupted by the tinkling sound of *ghungroos*.

Ashoka turned around and smiled.

'It's so good to see you.' He rushed forward to greet Kanak.

She stiffened at the display of emotion. Ashoka stepped back, surprised. He hadn't expected such a tepid response.

'Ashoka, I am in the middle of my training. Can we meet some other time?' she asked hurriedly averting her eyes.

'Sure...we can,' he said slowly, his enthusiasm dipping. 'I

was hoping to spend the day with you, though.' He looked crestfallen.

'I have to train.' Kanak shrugged nonchalantly.

Is she getting back at me for last time? the thought flashed through Ashoka's mind. He decided to clear the air.

'Look, if you really want to know about the tiger kill, I will tell you about it today.'

Kanak stared back expressionlessly. *Yes, I have been furious with you,* she thought. But, she resisted revealing the truth to Ashoka.

'Oh no, I wasn't,' she said, trying to act casual.

Her careful attempts at hiding her feelings were not lost on Ashoka. 'You are not a good liar.'

He stared at her for a response but got none. The whole charade left him with mixed feelings.

'All right! I'll leave then,' he said measuring his words carefully. 'I really don't want to keep you from your training.' His tone was tinged with sarcasm, yet there was also a trace of disappointment there that he couldn't hide.

He turned to leave. He had hardly walked a few paces when a breathless Kanak caught him by the arm.

'Stop! Yes, I was angry,' she said, her eyes flashing. 'It is because I feel there is an invisible wall around you. You share your thoughts so sparingly.' She glared at him, her tone conveying that she was furious with him, but her eyes were appealing to him to open up to her.

Ashoka was taken aback for an instant. The change in her was so sudden and he sensed anything he said right then would break the spell of the moment. They looked at each other for a while, until Kanak realized she was still holding on to his arm. She instinctively moved her hand away.

Ashoka realized he had just been granted a rare glimpse of Kanak's vulnerability. Now that the mask of carefully crafted responses had been thrown away, he did not want her to retreat into her shell again.

He smiled. 'Let's start over. Allow me to take you for a boat ride again and trust me, when I start sharing the gory details of the kill, you will ask me to stop.'

Kanak gave him a soft look. *You still don't understand, do you? It was never about the kill,* she thought. It was Ashoka's reticence in sharing his feelings that had upset her. She could not fathom why he felt the need to tread so cautiously even with her. Why could he not live with abandon? Why did he behave as if something held him back? Nevertheless, she was delighted that the wall was crumbling in places. That was enough for now.

'We'll see,' she replied cheerfully.

Ashoka glanced at her surreptitiously. It would be interesting to discover the true woman beneath the layers she chose to hide herself behind. He had an inkling that the journey of discovery would be long, with beautiful winding lanes and deep, dangerous chasms. He was not wrong. The more he met her, the more enchanted he became.

Kanak's reflection stared back at her from the still waters of the large earthen pot. The temperature soared in the bathing section which made her kohl-laden eyes appear unnaturally bright. *My lips are too thin,* she thought as she appraised herself critically. *How would it feel if someone kisses them…* She let her imagination wander.

With one swift movement she discarded her *mekhala* and skirt. She was completely naked now. Her eyes closed, she touched her face and traced her fingers slowly to her breasts, feeling the softness, and then to her smooth flat belly. She looked down at her well-toned thighs. That was one of the advantages of being a dancer – a graceful figure. The long *horas* of practice ensured that.

How would I feel if I were crushed in someone's embrace?

The question hovered in the air for a *kashta*. And then she stiffened as the terrifying visions came unbidden into her mind, the scars of childhood coming to the fore. She tried to push back the tortured thoughts to the innermost recesses of her mind so that they would never haunt her again but could not succeed.

But what about my terrible secret… Sobs wracked her body. She wept for the traumatized child she was and for the future that looked bleak and uncertain. Finally, she slumped to the floor, completely spent. Only one thought now existed in her mind.

He must never know. Never!

12

Akila sat in deep contemplation, his brow furrowed. *It's time,* he thought. *Time to make the boys' training more practical.* A minimum period of 60 sunsets in a division of the military was required for most people to gain mastery over the required skills. Yet, the emperor had given him only half that time.

'Thirty sunsets,' he muttered to himself. 'Thirty sunsets to make them proficient!' It had never been done before. Yet, Bindusara had made him achieve things in the past that at first glance had appeared impossible even to him.

Akila became aware of the boys staring at him. He straightened himself. The emperor had handed him a bunch of boys. He would return them to Bindusara as the warriors they were meant to be.

It had taken him a while to decide which division to assign to each of his students. The first division he assigned was the important as they would receive their most intensive training there. It would be their preferred mode in a battle for life. In the end, he had gone with his instincts and what he knew of each boy's strengths. He cleared his throat.

'You shall be assigned army divisions on a rotation basis with training starting tomorrow,' announced Akila. 'Your place in the division will be determined by the commander in charge and will be solely his decision. I hope, for your sake, and for your sake alone, you will remember what you have learned.'

He looked at them for a reaction but seeing none, he continued.

'Prince Susima will join *turanga,* Devendra *pada,* Prince Ashoka *ratha* and Mali the *gaja* division.'

Akila looked at them keenly, scouring their faces for some reaction. The boys' faces were still expressionless but their eyes burned with excitement.

'You will have to make the best of every droplet of experience you get as the time assigned is short,' he concluded.

As Akila left, the boys collectively exhaled. They had been unwittingly holding their breath.

Akila did not say it, but the boys knew that his eyes would follow them even there. They also knew that they could not let him down.

The majestic Kshatriya gate of Pataliputra swung open.

Ashoka looked at it with awe. *It is an engineering marvel,* he thought proudly. *If it was to fall, it would easily crush five elephants under its weight.* The gate was five *dandas* in height. The mammoth structure opened and closed effortlessly, operated by a few levers.

Ashoka stood silently, enjoying the view of the gate. It gave him the same pleasure as watching the early morning sunrise.

He had opted for a brisk early morning walk instead of taking the chariot.

Once he exited the city gate, the well-maintained road gradually gave way to a more rugged path. Rather than continue on the dusty road, Ashoka decided to cut through the woody trail on the side. After walking for about a *kosa,* he suddenly found himself in the midst of a large clearing. The frenetic activity here was in stark contrast to the otherwise serene forest surroundings.

The clearing spanned a diameter of two *kosas* and was a melee of warriors on chariots engaged in various manoeuvres. This was the training ground of the *ratha* division of the Mauryan army. Ashoka had visited the site several times in the past. This time, however, he wasn't here as a spectator. Soon, he would be training with the men he had admired so much while growing up.

Commander Akhilesh had just finished his morning meeting with his lieutenants when Ashoka was shown into his tent. On most sunsets, Akhilesh liked to engage in some friendly banter after the meeting was done. But that wouldn't be the case today. He nodded to his men who understood that he wanted a private word with the prince.

The lack of pretentiousness in the tent appealed to Ashoka. It was evidently a warrior's lodgings.

Ashoka bowed to Akhilesh with folded hands. The two men assessed each other as warriors would, dispassionately – their only yardstick was competence and commitment to the Mauryan empire. The absence of either quality in a warrior was akin to a lame man trying to walk a tightrope in order to cross an abyss. Although it was only a moment's appraisal, for both the other passed the test.

'Welcome, young prince. I am given to understand by Acharya Akila that your practical training commences from today, eh?'

'Yes, sir. I look forward to it,' replied Ashoka respectfully.

'I liked the way you fought until the end in the kayak race.' Akhilesh smiled. Then his face took on a thoughtful look. 'The real test of mettle is when you look your enemy in the eye knowing that only one of you will remain standing at the end.'

Ashoka did not say anything, his entire attention on what

the commander was saying and the intensity with which he said it.

'But you already know that,' Akhilesh said enigmatically. 'You will be assigned to Group 11,' he continued, and as if on cue, a guard walked in to escort the prince.

Ashoka knew the meeting was over.

The prince's first halt was at the uniform barracks. He felt a surge of excitement as he donned the uniform. It smelled strongly of leather and iron.

Instinctively he straightened as he buckled the last strap. *So this is what it feels like to wear the uniform of a Pataliputran warrior,* he thought with pride.

He was escorted to where a smaller group was beginning their daily morning exercises. As a warm-up, they ran five rounds of the training field.

Ashoka looked on with interest as a group of drummers beat a slow rhythmic tune. *What are they up to?* he wondered. He got the answer soon.

A pair of blindfolded warriors were brought to the centre of the field. Their job was to strike an arrow through the head of a dummy that would pop up at unpredictable intervals. A clanging sound just before the dummy popped up was intended to alert the blindfolded marksmen. However, the beat of the drums served to break their concentration, making it almost impossible for them to know when the dummy targets popped up.

'What a unique training manoeuvre!' Ashoka muttered in awe. 'No wonder our armies are the best in the world.'

The team leader caught his eye and gestured for him get ready to join the group. In training, prince or not, he would be treated like a common soldier.

He experienced an eerie feeling as soon as he was blindfolded. Gradually, his senses tuned in to the rhythmic beat of the drums. In time, he realized that when his sense of sight was no longer available, his ability to hear became much keener. The wave of panic subsided as quickly as it had erupted.

I am ready now, he thought to himself. He realized that he not only had to be alert to the dummies popping up, but also tune out the hiss of the arrows of the other trainee warriors. The complication only added to his excitement.

Before he knew it, the gong sounded.

What! Is it noon already? thought Ashoka as he felt the hot sun prickling on his back.

As the referee quickly read out the scores of the team, Ashoka realized he had barely managed an average one.

Well, well…I have a lot to learn before I can command the formidable Mauryan army, he thought wryly.

The anticipation of mastering new skills excited him.

The lunch mess was packed with a number of new recruits. Irrespective of rank, everyone dined together. Ashoka was gulping down the fresh vegetable soup when he someone tapped him on the back. His face lit up as he recognized his friend.

'Mandar! I did not know you were also with the army.'

'I wasn't. But I am now. I figured it would be more interesting to join it permanently rather than being called for specific missions,' Mandar said cryptically.

'Missions…I don't understand,' replied Ashoka, confused.

'It doesn't matter,' said Mandar, laughing. 'I am here now.' He sat down next to Ashoka and started slurping his soup hungrily.

'Which group have you been assigned to?' inquired Ashoka.

'Well, they assigned me to Group 5 and discovered that I was too good for them. I will soon shift.' Mandar grinned. 'By the way,' he whispered conspiratorially, 'I heard rumours that Prince Ashoka has joined this division.'

'Where is he? I don't see him.' Ashoka looked around in mock curiosity. Both he and Mandar burst out laughing.

Ashoka liked the feeling of anonymity. In a certain way, it made him feel more relaxed. As if he did not have to live up to a part.

It is certainly going to be interesting, he thought.

In the next few sunsets, Ashoka made rapid progress. This earned him respect amongst his team. He did not reveal his true identity but neither did he lie. He gave his name as Shoku, which was what his mother sometimes called him.

He often wondered how Susima, Mali and Devendra were progressing but did not have a clue. *I am sure Susima must have charmed the seniors by now,* he thought wryly, knowing that his brother could be very pleasant when he wanted.

It turned out that Ashoka was wrong in this case. All of Susima's efforts had failed to impress the head of the cavalry division.

This is something I am going to change when I am emperor. Royalty should not be required to go through the drill meant for common soldiers, Susima thought, peeved.

Seated on a horse waiting for his turn on the course, he fantasized about the weekly sunset off when he could do as he pleased. *Perhaps some carnal pleasures,* he thought, grinning in anticipation.

His thoughts went back to the first time he had seen bare breasts…

It happened quite by chance. Susima had been aware for some time that one of the maids in the palace had been eyeing him with intent. One late evening, she came to serve him pomegranate juice. He noticed that the cloth tied around her breasts appeared rather loose.

As she bent to pour the juice, the cloth gaped open to reveal her breasts. It seemed to Susima that she took an inordinately long time to straighten up. When she finally did, the cloth slipped down to her midriff. Susima stared openly at her breasts now. She took her time to cover them under her veil. Giving Susima a coquettish smile, she walked away.

His senses inflamed with a feeling he had not known before, Susima waited for an opportunity to meet her again. Not too many sunsets later, he chanced upon her as he was passing through a relatively isolated section of the long palace corridors. He seized her from behind. In the ensuing half-hearted struggle, he was able to untie the cloth covering her breasts. She fled into one of the dark corridors when he released her from his grip…

A tap on his shoulder jolted Susima out of his reverie. The trainer motioned for him to cross the obstacle course. Mounted on his brown equine, Susima tried to banish all lascivious thoughts and focus on the task at hand, and was able to cut through the course almost satisfactorily.

He looked at his cream-coloured *antariya* encrusted with the day's filth and winced. A hot meal and bath was what he wanted but did not dare ask for. The Mauryan army was strict about adherence to rules. Susima looked up at the sun to figure out the time and sighed. There was still plenty of time left before he could take a break.

The initial euphoria had worn off quickly enough. The dream of making his teacher and father proud of him was beginning to seem a tough task. What Susima did not realize was that like Akila, the commander too would judge him solely on ability and not his position. That whether he was the prince or not, the Mauryan army would not give him a second chance.

The Mauryan army had 15,000 elephants, more than any known army in the world. Ashoka knew this from what he had read of the writings of Megasthenes, the Greek historian. Still, nothing had prepared Ashoka for the sight that met his eyes at the *gaja* division.

The training for this division was established in a large clearing close to the dense forests surrounding Pataliputra. There were at least a thousand elephants training here, as far as he could make out. The mahouts were a busy lot, manoeuvring the elephants with great skill. The males were trained for warfare while the females were used mainly for transport and breeding.

Ashoka had asked for permission from Akhilesh to spend a sunset with the *gaja* division, observing the elephants being tamed. He scanned the place for Mali and found him awkwardly trying to maintain his balance on a beast. Ashoka sprinted up to him. They had not met for 15 sunsets. It was the longest that the inseparable pair had ever been parted.

'Amazing sight!' remarked Ashoka to Mali who had acknowledged his presence with a nod.

'Amazing, but also wasteful. These peaceful beasts are meant to roam the jungles, not captured by us to expand our empires,' Mali asserted, carefully dismounting on a wooden platform constructed for the purpose.

Ashoka gave him a sharp look. At times, these sunsets, he couldn't help but think that Mali was changing from the fun-loving boy he had been to someone Ashoka found difficult to comprehend.

'What's got be done has to be done. There is no place for such emotions in a warrior's life, Mali. I hope you understand that.' Ashoka's retort was far more curt than he had intended.

Mali was taken aback by his tone. *Ashoka always speaks in that manner whenever we have a difference in opinion. It has never bothered me much earlier. Why, then, am I feeling so let down now?* Mali wondered.

And then it struck him. They were no longer children. They were young men. Now, he looked at the world through his own viewpoint – and not Ashoka's. They say that every truth has polarities. It depends which one you choose.

'You are right,' Mali said softly, without launching into an argument. His face was expressionless. Ashoka was struck again by how much his childhood friend had changed in the short duration they had been apart.

'How's the mapping of the underground tunnels proceeding?' he asked, attempting to change the conversation.

'It's done,' replied Mali in a clipped tone.

They were interrupted when some attendants came running to the head mahout in excitement. 'Sir, a wild elephant has been captured at a distance of five *kosas* in the forest!'

The head mahout was galvanised into action. He barked orders for two subordinates to accompany him along with at least 15 attendants. Ashoka looked at him and the head mahout nodded, allowing Mali and Ashoka to accompany them to the site of the capture.

Before setting out, the band smeared themselves with elephant dung and urine. Closer to the destination they heard the trumpeting of a creature wild with rage. All of them peered into the pit. It was a half grown elephant with a white patch on the left eye.

Ashoka and Mali exchanged a look.

'Are you thinking what I am thinking?' asked Ashoka, his eyebrows raised.

'Yes,' replied Mali with a slow whistle.

This could very well be the same creature that had followed them in the jungle when they were in the midst of Akila's survival exercise.

Calm down, little one, thought Ashoka, willing his thoughts to connect with the frightened and furious creature. He did not know whether it was telepathy or that it recognized him from the encounter years earlier, but the pachyderm's wailing did reduce perceptibly.

'Calm down,' Ashoka said aloud now. He understood the trauma of being separated from the herd and being restricted to the pit was a frightening experience for the animal. Out of the corner of his eye he saw the mahouts and attendants getting the ropes ready to imprison the creature. The bullhooks lay on the side ominously, ready to be used. This was the first time it struck Ashoka that the pachyderms were subject to immense cruelty till they were broken. *But this is no time to fret over the larger picture,* Ashoka reasoned to himself. *Time enough for that later.*

Without warning he slipped into the pit. The entourage looked on in horror – the enraged pachyderm would surely trample him to death. They gaped when they saw Ashoka get up calmly and stand next to the elephant, murmuring in low, soothing tones. Their horror turned into amazement as they saw the angry young beast transform into a docile creature as Ashoka continued mumuring to the animal and stroking its trunk.

After some time Ashoka clambered up to the waiting band of onlookers.

'No one will tie up the elephant,' he instructed.

All faces turned to the head mahout for direction. He hesitated for a second or two and then said, 'Do as he says.'

The gajrani was given water and coaxed gently to follow them instead of being imprisoned in ropes.

Mali looked on pensively as he once more witnessed Ashoka steal the thunder away from him.

Kanak wrapped the veil around her shoulders. Her training had concluded for the sunset. Exhausted after the intensive *sadhana*, she was longing to get home.

'There is someone to meet you. He is waiting outside the gate,' informed an attendant.

'Who is it?' she asked. But the attendant had already left.

It was Ashoka, she saw from a distance. Trying hard to appear casual but feeling far from it, she tentatively approached him. *Why is he here?* she thought, excited and fearful at the same time. Fearful for reasons of her own. Reasons that she dare not acknowledge, even to herself.

They had not met for more than 21 sunsets, while he was training in the army. As they looked at each other, the intensity in his dark eyes made it impossible for her to hold his gaze.

'What brings you here?' she finally asked in an attempt at light-hearted banter.

He shrugged. 'Do I need a reason?' he said, folding his arms across his chest and continuing to gaze at her.

'You…don't,' Kanak fumbled, disconcerted by his intensity. 'But you couldn't have lost your way and just landed up here, right?' she said, attempting once again to be jocular to cover up her nervousness.

Her face lit up as she saw him smile, finally. However, the smile was fleeting. 'I didn't lose my way, you know,' Ashoka said softly.

'You didn't?' she felt the faint stirrings of unease as his eyes locked with hers.

Ashoka shook his head. 'No, I didn't.' He seemed to hesitate. 'I was wondering if you would like to accompany me on a ride tomorrow,' he said gently. 'I know you don't have practice.'

The seemingly harmless request weighed heavy on her. If she was to agree, then she would be alone with him. She welcomed the closeness, yet shied away from revealing her vulnerability.

'How do you know that? I don't think I mentioned this to you,' Kanak voiced incredulously. 'Do you have spies trailing me?' Her voice trembled slightly.

'Not exactly,' replied Ashoka dryly. He wondered at her edginess. He did not know that it had nothing to do with him having knowledge of her daily routine.

'Then how do you know?' she demanded. 'You have to tell me. This is frightening.' Kanak was aware of her voice becoming hysterical. She did not realize that her nervousness had nothing to do with him, but was a defence against the secret that she guarded.

Ashoka's pleasant expression changed to exasperation.

'Listen, I just came to ask you whether you could spend the sunset riding with me. That's all,' he said clearly vexed at her reaction. 'I didn't think you would react so badly to my presence.'

'So, what time do you want to start?' Kanak managed to keep her tone light, pulling herself out of her agitation with an effort.

Ashoka broke into a smile. 'All good things begin at dawn.' He gave her a penetrating look, not entirely convinced about her sudden switch, and continued, 'You may want to dress appropriately. I mean…be as covered up as you can. It can get rough at times' .

Yes, I would like to cover myself up. Cover up more than my body, she thought ironically.

Kanak gazed across the room she shared with her twin Revati. It was sometimes eerie to look at a face exactly like hers, knowing that it wasn't. There was one difference, though, between Revati and herself. A huge difference! *No one knew… apart from her sister and mother.*

He must not discover it at any cost, she reflected, with a mix of misery and anxiety. Her obsessive thoughts threatened to engulf her in their fetters if she did not make a conscious decision to come back to reality. A vortex of suppressed feelings rose up from her toes and shot up to her head, making her dizzy. Shivering, she held a pillar for support until she felt stable enough. A few deep gulps of air and she almost felt normal.

There was still some time before daybreak. No one would ask any questions as it was routine for her to get up early and leave for her training before the rest of the family woke up.

Kanak wore the female warrior's dress where the lower half of the body was wrapped up with a plain cloth and tucked between the legs for ease of movement. She covered up her breasts in a criss-cross fashion securing the cloth tightly at the waist. The *uttariya* came over it like a veil. Her teeth clean, she spit out the chewed up neem stick. An ivory tooth comb smoothened her hair to finally secure it in a severe tight bun. For the umpteenth time she looked at her reflection in the shimmering waters of the pot. *I think I look passable,* she finally acknowledged to herself. As a last touch she sprayed some rosewater over herself.

A gust of early morning air rejuvenated her senses the moment she opened the door. She took in some deep breaths and walked down the garden path. Someone was lurking at the gate.

'What! You are already here? It is still not time,' she exclaimed.

'I have been waiting for quite a while now. Woke up early,' was the laconic explanation. 'Is it so unpleasant to see me?'

Kanak regained her composure. 'Oh no!' she said hastily. 'What makes you think that? I was surprised, just for a moment.'

He accepted her explanation with a curt nod. 'Let us leave then. The horses are tethered to the tree just down the road.'

They rode together at a slow trot uphill with Kanak stealing furtive glances at Ashoka. The less frequented trail cut across a dark forest. She concentrated on manoeuvring her mount in this dense section of the forest. The path was narrow and it was impossible to ride alongside – she noticed that he kept looking back over his shoulder to check her progress.

They were soon on the banks of the Ganga.

Where are we going? she wondered.

They halted and dismounted. The horses took in deep gulps of water, grateful for the respite.

Stroking the head of her mount, Kanak turned around and found Ashoka staring intently at her. Caught in the act, he broke into a smile. She gave him an inquiring look.

'Nothing.' He shrugged.

She turned her back towards him and then jumped in shock as she felt icy cold water drench her. Before she could react, Ashoka hurled another handful of water at her.

She stood immobile for a moment, taken aback at the playfulness. But it was not long before she sprung into action. Swinging up onto her horse, she tugged at the reins to get it to move. Out of the corner of her eye, she noted the surprise on Ashoka's face. A split second later, he was in hot pursuit.

She crossed the river easily. It was one of those calm sunsets. The water reached the horse's abdomen at its deepest section. Even before they reached the other bank, he had overtaken her. But, not to be outdone so easily, she expertly guided her horse right past him.

As she did so, she fleetingly heard him laugh. *Has he let me pass in order to humour me?* she wondered, a flush creeping up her face.

He kept pace behind her with ease. The less used trail was difficult for her to see. As she struggled to ride faster, the trees increasingly took the form of a green blur. Acutely aware of Ashoka in pursuit, she slowed down deliberately. But, he did not pass her.

She now started to warm up to the game that he was playing. Or was she the one who was playing the game? It was too confusing. But then, she was always confused around him these sunsets. She sped up again, knowing he would be right behind her. It seemed like they went on like this for a long time.

Soon, they were deep in the dense forest. The trail was almost hidden by the thick foliage, the trees huddling closer as if they drawing comfort from each other. More than once Kanak felt thorns scratch her arms as she passed through.

And then it happened. Without warning, her horse reared up. Almost thrown off her horse, she somehow managed to hang on. It reared up once more. This time she slid halfway to the left,dangling precariously on the side, still holding on to the reins. She hung on obstinately.

If only I could calm down the horse! she thought desperately. But she could do that only if she could straighten herself. It seemed impossible.

Is that a boulder? She looked on in terror as she was headed for a direct collision. In a few moments her head would smash on it. Time slowed down. Aware of every *kashta,* she waited for the inevitable.

And then, her path changed. She felt a force lifting her to the light above. The light quickly faded away, giving in to a heavy darkness.

Kanak's unconsciousness lasted a few *kashtas*.

I am alive…alive, she thought incoherently as she regained consciousness. On realizing she was with Ashoka, relief flooded her being. It was a strange feeling to know how safe she felt with him.

He led them back to the path, her mount in tow. On the path, he slid off his horse. Kanak winced at his first words.

'I thought you had good equestrian skills!' he snapped.

'I thought so too,' she stammered, bewildered. 'I don't know what happened…'

Sensing her distress, his tone changed from curt to compassionate.

'It is not your fault. It could happen to anyone,' he said consolingly. 'Something must have scared our friend here. He is usually well behaved, especially around maidens.'

As he bent to examine the horse, his attention was drawn to the wound on the hind leg. He cursed.

'What is it?' she asked anxiously.

'One of our snake gods did not take kindly to the horse,' he commented, looking up at Kanak, still holding the injured leg gingerly. Relieved it was not her folly that had resulted in the mishap, she visibly calmed down. He efficiently tore off a part of his *angavastram* to bind the leg in an attempt to contain the blood circulation. All along, he patted the creature, whispering to it in soothing tones. It was so low that even Kanak, standing close to him, could not figure out what he was saying. It sounded like some bizarre language to her. But the creature seemed to understand and calm down. It was fascinating how a man, so curt and dry with people, was such a different person with animals…almost kind and gentle.

'We need to go back,' he announced presently. 'This one here needs some professional treatment. In fact, why don't we take him to Revati? I am sure she can help.'

'My sister treats humans, not animals,' snapped Kanak. 'Besides, I haven't told her I am out with you. For that matter, I haven't told anyone. My family probably thinks that I am engaged in my *sadhana*,' she blurted out.

Ashoka gave her a look she could not fathom. Kanak bit her lip. *Why did I have to say that?* she asked herself. But it was too late now. He would probably guess she had feelings for him. Feelings she did not want to have.

'Why would you not tell your family, I wonder,' Ashoka murmured thoughtfully.

His face suddenly sullen, he trudged along silently, holding the reins of the injured horse. Kanak followed on Ashoka's mount.

Surely there is nothing to be upset about? Has he guessed I have feelings for him? Is he upset about that? It can't be that he knows my secret. He can't know, thought Kanak, her heart sinking. Her confusion mounting, she shut off all thoughts that seemed to chase her of late.

'Exactly where were we headed?' asked Kanak, attempting to strike up a conversation.

'It was just some place I wanted to show you,' mumbled Ashoka, staring ahead, without looking back at her.

Unsuccessful in her attempts, Kanak pursed her lips. She wondered why they ended up like this most of the time. The conflict was that despite such squabbles, she loved being with him.

His face has changed. The three short weeks of training have made him look older – no, not older, but more mature, she concluded.

Amreshwar met them at the city gates. Their silent greeting had become a ritual now. Quick to assess the situation, he had the injured horse taken away and a new one supplied in its place.

Once they were on their own, Ashoka addressed Kanak for the first time since they had started back. 'It is best that you carry on alone. It is safe now.'

She looked at him questioningly. Usually he dropped her to the gate of her house.

'Your family does not know you are with me, remember? We will complete this trip some other sunset.'

With that, he turned and galloped away. At a slow trot, Kanak set off for home, her mind a bundle of confused emotions.

13

As usual, Queen Rakshita's attendant Kanchi chattered on, non-stop. Rakshita wondered, not for the first time, how the palace's gossip reached her ears so quickly. Sometimes Kanchi was able to tell her things before the emperor himself confided in her.

She looked at her fondly. Kanchi returned the gaze with one eye, the other a pulp of sightless grey. Kanchi had been with her ever since Rakshita had come to the palace as a newly-wed.

She looked approvingly at her own reflection in the

polished iron slab held up by her attendant. Her adornments and the styling of her lustrous long hair was exactly the way she liked it. Being particular about how she dressed, she spent a small fortune every month on new garments and ornaments.

'Why have you stopped talking, Kanchi? Where were we?' said Rakshita gaily. The stately queen behaved almost like a young girl when she was in Kanchi's company. The haughty, queenly demeanour was thrown aside when the two were bereft of company.

Kanchi hesitated.

'Why do you hesitate, dear friend?'

'I hesitate because it is about the one whom you have borne in your womb.'

Rakshita stopped patting her hair and focused her attention on Kanchi. She asked tentatively, 'What about him? I hear he is doing well at the military training.'

'Yes, I heard. It is not about that,' Kanchi said with a wave of her hand and then lowered her eyes.

Rakshita had seldom seen Kanchi look so uncertain. Concluding that it must be something of great concern, she asked more forcefully, 'Why do your lips tremble so?' She held the old woman's wrinkled hands in her own. 'Has he got into trouble regarding Ashoka...or is it vice versa. Has that wretched good-for-nothing done something to my boy?' The pitch of her voice rose dangerously.

Kanchi plucked up enough courage to continue. 'They are not boys anymore,' she said in a low voice. 'Especially not your son.'

Rakshita sensed the judgement in her tone. For the first time she felt an unfamiliar twinge of fear.

'What do you mean, Kanchi? Tell me.'

'I dare not, O Queen. I dare not,' whispered Kanchi in a tremulous voice.

Tired of coaxing her, Rakshita shook her by the shoulders and firmly demanded to know the details.

Kanchi looked up at the queen. 'If you have the heart for it, then listen. Prince Susima has on more than one occasion been indiscriminate with women.'

The queen looked at her, dismayed. How could her perfect Susima ever misbehave? This time Kanchi had erred.

She *had* to find out more details.

'But…when? How did I not know earlier?'

A part of Rakshita wanted to deny what she had heard. But she knew in her heart that Kanchi's information was seldom far from the truth.

'Oh…it's best not to get into details, my queen. I think you doubt what I say,' the maid said, wringing her hands. 'I myself did not believe it.'

'I suppose my son is growing into a man,' Rakshita offered the excuse uneasily, more to herself than Kanchi.

Kanchi looked at her with compassion. 'My queen, I know it pains you to hear of your son's misdeeds. But it is the truth. You had best accept it. Prince Susima's conduct does not befit a prince. People speak about him in hushed tones.'

The maid held Rakshita's arms tightly. She wrenched them away, her peace of mind utterly destroyed.

'Let me think, Kanchi. What should I do? I can't let the Mauryan name get tarnished. What if the emperor hears of this?'

'He might have already,' whispered Kanchi.

Kanak did not hear from Ashoka for many sunsets. The aborted riding trip came to her mind many times. She did not like the way it had ended. As if many things were unsaid.

The sharp clap of hands forced her out of her avalanche of thoughts. For the fifth time today, the dance instructor had caught her fumbling.

'Kanak! Where is your concentration today, my child. You are floundering,' he grumbled. 'You missed a step and did not even realize it.' He clapped his hands to the beat to emphasize his point.

'My apologies, Guruji. I will pay attention now,' Kanak replied earnestly.

'About time, child. You are usually perfect. What has come over you today?' He peered at her intently trying to see if he had missed something. He knew of so many brilliant dancers who had gone astray. *Would she be one of them?* He sighed. *Only time would tell.*

'Why don't you take the rest of the day off?' He dismissed her with a wave of his hand.

Kanak was only too glad for the respite. Dragging her feet, she left the academy gates with no destination in mind. At the bustling main square of Pataliputra, she stopped for a moment. Like most Pataliputrans, she loved her city. But today, it held no sheen for her. A sense of detachment engulfed her being.

Her head cast down, she trudged on aimlessly. The unrelenting heat of the sun did not affect her. But, as she sucked on her tongue, she realized her throat was parched.

'I need water,' she said to herself and looked around. Usually the market was full of vendors selling cool rose water to tired pedestrians. But she did not recognize this part of town.

Am I lost? she wondered. Unlike the wide streets and prosperous look of the main parts of Pataliputra, the lanes here looked seedy and deserted, filled with the stench of urine.

She was pulled out of her perplexity when she heard voices raised in argument. Out of the corner of her eye, she saw three burly youths emerge from an alley. At first, they did not notice her and continued hurling abuses at each other. Then one of them spotted her and nudged his friend. They fell silent, openly appraising her.

Kanak stared back, unable to comprehend their intentions. A searing pain in her foot jolted her out of her dullness. She looked down to see that her foot was covered with blood. The culprit was a sharp metal object. Strangely, the pain cleared her head.

The young men looked at her lasciviously. Grinning at her, one of them said, 'Don't be afraid. You are hurt and need help.'

Kanak looked around wildly, now acutely aware of their ill intention. Not spotting a soul on the road, she considered screaming for help. She rejected that plan, knowing her parched throat would not be able to attract attention.

Two of them started walking menacingly towards her.

Oh Shiva…no! she mouthed silently. Desperately, she tried to remove the metal object from her foot so she could make an attempt to run. The tugs only made deeper cuts through her skin. Panic welled up as she tried to think of a plan. *Wait… what is that sound?*

Horses! The hoof beats were much louder now. And then they came into view. Kanak opened her mouth to scream… in relief. They were a couple of soldiers – city guards on their rounds. She waved to them wildly. One was middle-aged and the other a fresh-faced youth no more than twenty. The middle aged one was quick to take in the scene.

'I am Amatya Sen's daughter. I have lost my way,' Kanak told them, her voice trembling.

The older one seemed to recognize Amatya Sen's name. 'You are far from where you should be.'

He looked around. The youths had taken the opportunity to disappear in the dark shadows of the alleys. He focused on her again. With a puzzled expression, he said, 'This is the only part of Pataliputra that is unsafe. You are truly lost.'

Kanak had a faraway expression. 'We all get lost sometimes, don't we?' she mumbled, more to herself than to the soldiers; her words carrying more meaning than what appeared on the surface.

'What were you thinking?' admonished Revati. 'The gash is quite deep,' she observed, expertly dressing Kanak's wound. Kanak winced as the ointment took effect.

The bandage in place, Revati looked up at her twin, concern written all over her face. 'What you were doing so far from home?'

Kanak met her twin's concerned gaze squarely. 'I wasn't lying when I said I got lost.'

'You were half a *yojana* from your dance school,' accused Revati, shaking her head.

The lack of response disconcerted her. In all her years, she had never known her twin to hide something from her. 'I thought we were as close as two eyes on a face,' she grumbled.

Kanak felt a pang of sympathy for her concerned sister. It was true that her twin was her closest friend. But how could she tell her sister what a fool she had been... 'I don't know how I ventured so far. I was preoccupied,' said Kanak, in a feeble attempt at an explanation.

'We all get preoccupied. But we don't just walk into danger.'

The timely interception of Revati's assistant saved Kanak from further inquisition. 'The patients are waiting – some soldiers as usual.'

'Start sending them in. I am almost done.' Revati looked at her twin and sighed. She knew there was more to what she had said.

Kanak limped out of the room, each step a painful reminder of how close she had been to danger yesterday. She noticed there was a long queue of at least 20 soldiers in various states of injury, waiting for treatment. Towards the end, a group of them huddled together, chortling at some private joke. The merriment subsided when they noticed her. One of them particularly locked eyes with her. She cringed, an inexplicable fear permeating her. The person who had dared to look at her so brazenly was Susima.

Thanks to Revati's healing skills, Kanak's foot felt much better the next sunset. She swung out of bed and almost decided to head to her dance school. But as she put her foot on the floor, she realized it was too soon.

'I will take up my sister's offer of helping her out at the vaidshala,' she decided.

The only thing that worried Kanak was the fact that the strong odours of certain ayurvedic preparations made her nauseous. However, the thought did not deter Kanak today, and she set out determinedly for the vaidshala. As luck would have it, Revati was enagaged in getting various formulations prepared.

'Eeeks…how do you stand it!' said Kanak, wrinkling her nose.

'And how do you stand contorting your body all day,' riposted Revati, laughing.

Knowing full well her sister's intolerance for strong smells, she put her mind at rest. 'You needn't help me here. We are expecting a huge turnout of soldiers today evening. Why don't you get involved in the preparations for that?'

Kanak was only too relieved to accept the opportunity to escape from the odours. An experienced attendant acquainted her with the task at hand. Quite soon, they were busy attending to the soldiers.

'The rate at which they turn up here is incredible. If this is the rate during peace time, I shudder to think what will happen during wartime,' remarked Revati dryly to no one in particular.

The attendant came in and announced that Prince Susima had come for changing the dressing on his arm.

Susima sauntered in casually. Kanak noticed Revati purse her lips ever so slightly. He sat down without waiting to be asked.

'Good evening, Prince.' The salutation flowed smoothly. If Revati was miffed, she did not show it. 'Let me see.' She removed the bandages herself. 'Healing well! You needn't take the trouble to see me again. I will give you some ointments that can be applied locally.'

Kanak felt a sudden onset of uneasiness. The conversation going on was harmless enough. But something bothered her. She looked up from the palm leaf parchment she was writing on. Prince Susima was staring at her flagrantly. She could not hold his gaze beyond a *kashta* and became aware of a strong desire to get away. Unaware of the tension in the air, Revati handed Kanak the prescription.

Her hands trembling slightly, Kanak busied herself under the pretext of getting the formulation down from the shelf. In her edginess, the container slipped from her hand and crashed to the floor. Embarrassed at her own clumsiness, she immediately started to clear up her mess. Her shoulder brushed against the person helping her. Kanak looked sideways and froze when she saw it was Prince Susima, his lips curling up in a lascivicious grin.

By then Revati had organised for help, to get the mess cleaned up. Kanak, her heart jumping to her throat, escaped limping, with an excuse to clean up her hands that were soiled with the sticky medicinal liquid.

Why do I feel so uneasy in Prince Susima's presence? she wondered after regaining her composure.

Not that he had said or done anything. A piece of memory buried deep within her flashed in her mind. *It was the eyes.* Prince Susima had the same eyes that had followed her when she was a little girl. Broken fragments of memory flashed past. Playing in the garden with bright yellow sunflowers for company…her fright at turning around and staring into those shifty eyes…the pain, the confusion…

It was her involvement with dance that had aided her recovery from that trauma. She had buried those disturbing thoughts deep inside and rarely encountered them again.

The bond with her sister had also gone a long way in

helping her heal and grow into the confident young woman she was now. Kanak came back to reality, unwilling to dwell on the memories that were best forgotten.

Around the same time, Revati had declared she wanted to be a vaid when she grew up so that she could take care of everyone in her family. After the incident, Revati had assumed the role of the protective sister which she continued to play with aplomb ever since.

But what Revati had failed to notice was that Susima possessed the same shifty eyes that had traumatized her sister years ago.

Kanak pirouetted expertly on one foot, her hands swaying gracefully in tandem with the rhythm. Mali had visited her, to convey Ashoka's request for her company on the banks of Ganga. She wondered, with mixed feelings, how the evening would turn out. They usually ended in a discord of sorts. Today she was determined to be amicable.

She had spent many *horas* thinking about her relationship with Ashoka. Ocean waves was how she thought of it. Sometimes angry and rough, sometimes calm and cool. The depths carrying many secrets. Just like the one that she carried…rather, dragged with herself. It had not mattered until now. Maybe because she had never become so emotionally involved with anyone before.

I do love him. However, we have no future. At best we can be friends. That was the conclusion she had come to. This way, she would never have to divulge her secret.

There were still a couple of *horas* before Revati returned home. Her mother was at the temple. She decided to set off for her meeting with Ashoka. *I shall take the long route to the river, through the woods,* she thought.

Kanak put on her leather sandals and sauntered into the forest. The woods were dark, but the trail to the riverbank was well defined and familiar to her. Admiring the flora and fauna, she strolled along, taking her time, playfully trampling the dry leaves on her path to make them crackle.

She stopped suddenly. Was that the snap of twigs under her own footsteps or was it someone else's? Maybe someone else was using this path too. She turned back to look but spotted no one. She could have sworn on Lord Shiva that she had heard something. A shiver running down her spine, she picked up her pace.

I should be out of the woods shortly, she estimated. The back of her neck felt as if an army of angry ants was crawling on it. The feeling reached a threshold and Kanak started running.

'Slow down,' said the logical part of her. 'Run!' was what her instincts instructed, completely at loggerheads with the rational part of her. In her haste Kanak did not see the overgrown root of the banyan tree, and before she knew it, she had tripped and was flat on the muddy ground.

The impact caused her breath to be knocked out completely. She took a few moments to steady herself, all the while conscious of that uncomfortable feeling. She turned around apprehensively. A pair of eyes met her gaze. They were the same pair she had encountered a few afternoons earlier. She let out a shriek, which was abruptly stifled by a calloused hand over her mouth.

'Why are you screaming?' asked Susima, who seemed genuinely puzzled. 'Breathe,' he commanded in a soft voice. He slowly released the grip on her mouth.

'W-why are you following me?' stammered Kanak, wiping the froth off her mouth. He laughed softly. 'You look different. Your face has mud streaks all over.'

He raised his hand to touch her face. She recoiled with horror, the shadows of her past surging back.

'I just want to know you better,' he whispered ominously.

Kanak looked at him – he seemed to be enjoying himself the way a beast enjoys watching its prey squirm.

'But I don't,' she replied defiantly.

The unexpected rebuff was something he was not used to. His expression changed – became blank, strange. His eyes darted left and right, not really looking at her. His expression took on a deranged quality.

'So, why here…in the middle of the woods? Why not at my house?' Kanak asked, buying time and praying that Ashoka would come looking for her.

'It's not the same. No excitement, you see,' he said slowly, smiling meaningfully.

His face was close to hers now. Feeling his breath on her face, she felt nauseated and dangerously close to losing her composure, the demons of her past threatening to take over. Kanak tried to avoid looking into his eyes. With a deep breath she scrambled up and bolted, her years of training in strength and flexibility coming in use now.

Susima, unprepared for her sudden move, roared with anger and was soon at her heels. He managed to grab her arm which she wrenched away – but not before sustaining some deep scratch marks.

As she ran, she felt her head being jerked back painfully. Kanak looked back in horror, expecting to see the demonic prince. She sighed with relief when she saw that her hair had come loose and got tangled in some overhanging branches. With trembling hands she untangled them as quickly as she could, looking frantically in all directions for her pursuer to emerge. He seemed to have abandoned the chase. Kanak walked slowly now, her legs heavy with the strain. Looking ahead she spotted Ashoka sitting on the steps leading down to the river. A powerful feeling of relief swept over her.

Ashoka looked up and saw her. He got up and was with her in a swift movement. 'What happened?' His expression was filled with alarm.

'I am all right. Have you been waiting long?' Kanak asked, trying to speak normally. What she did not realize was how dishevelled she looked.

'You…you don't look all right. Why are your clothes dirty and why do you have scratches on your arm? The flowers in your hair are half crushed,' he observed with concern. It was second nature for Ashoka to take in his surroundings with only a glance. This was a skill he had developed over years of practice. One look at Kanak was enough to make him guess someone else was responsible for her disordered state.

A sense of intuition guided her to not mention Prince Susima now. *Not now!*

'I tripped and fell,' she muttered evasively.

Ashoka gave her an exasperated look. 'At least don't treat me like a fool. If you don't want to talk to me about it, say so,' he replied curtly.

Kanak felt a certain kind of fullness, not pleasant, but the kind that one experiences when one has over eaten. Only here, it was not the food, but the inability to hold in the events of her past…and present.

A wave of intense nausea swept over her and darkness descended rapidly. She vaguely felt strong arms lift her.

Ashoka carried her home and immediately dispatched a message for Revati at the vaidshala.

Revati arrived, flustered. Her sister was the only one who could shatter her calm demeanour. She took charge immediately.

Her eyes locked with those of Ashoka's when she came out of the room after examining her sister. 'I demand an explanation!' she accused.

'I want one too. Unfortunately, the only one who can throw some light on this is resting,' replied Ashoka dryly. 'Something…or someone has frightened her. It is best not to question her today.'

It dawned upon Revati that Ashoka was not to blame for her sister's distress.

'Who could it have been?' she asked worriedly.

'By Shiva, I will get to the bottom of this,' he declared ominously.

Kanak woke up with a start. She looked around. It was dark outside her window. Her sister lay slumped on the bed across the room, deep in slumber. She had no recollection of getting back home. Yesterday's ordeal flashed before her eyes. Wincing at the memory, she wondered whether it was a nightmare or reality. Her bandaged arm dispelled any doubts of the truth. The nightmarish events of her childhood came flooding back. The eyes…the eyes! Kanak shut her own eyes, hoping that the disturbing images flashing in her mind would disappear. But the mind does not need eyes to see…

Ashoka gazed at the hollow-eyed girl in front of him. It was not lost upon him that she was desperately trying to have a light-hearted conversation. She chattered on about the dance troupe that had come down from Takshashila.

How vulnerable she looks! thought Ashoka.

'What's bothering you? Tell me,' he urged after a while, when her chatter died away.

'Nothing…nothing at all,' she mumbled.

'Something happened yesterday. I want to know what,' he said firmly, not giving up.

'Well…I don't see why you are so bothered. But if you must know, a scorpion frightened me.'

The look on his face told her the utter lie was plain to him.

Nevertheless, she continued with her charade.

'You can ask Revati. She knows I am petrified of scorpions.' She paused before continuing. 'You see, I was bitten by a poisonous scorpion when I was a child. The fear has remained since then.' Kanak bit her lip, willing herself not to think about Susima…his eyes…the eyes of the man years ago.

It pained Ashoka to see her haunted look as she tried to hide the truth. He changed his tactics.

'All right, let us start over from where we left off yesterday. Let's go for a walk on the banks of the river. Let us take the forest route.'

'Oh no!' She shrank back in alarm 'Not the forest route… not today.' Her knuckles whitened as she clenched her hands.

'Why?' probed Ashoka.

She looked at him, exasperated. 'Can't you drop the interrogation?' she said, her distress mounting. 'I am feeling tired now. I don't want to go anywhere.'

Ashoka sighed. 'All right. Go and rest,' he conceded. 'I will take your leave now. But you will have to tell me someday – without feigning fear of scorpions.'

But he felt unable to leave her without asking her, 'What stops you from telling me?' He paused. 'Are you afraid of something…or someone? Perhaps you are afraid of yourself… or is it me? You don't trust me, perhaps?' he asked uncertainly.

Kanak scoured the depths of her mind to analyse her own actions. *In a flash she understood that her past was not healed.* Afraid that a whole lot of those unwelcome, traumatic memories would jump back into her present, she resisted the truth…that she had been brutally violated when she was a young girl.

Queen Rakshita went to check on her son. She nodded to the guards as she entered his chambers. The young girls generally assigned duties to look after the personal needs of the royal family had been replaced by wiser, elderly ones. Rakshita had had no choice but to issue such orders as the gossip about him increased. This did not diminish the maternal love that swelled in her heart for her only child.

She looked at him now as he lay fast asleep on the huge bed. *How angelic he looks!* she thought fondly

It was a daily ritual. She looked in on her son sleeping and only then retired to her chambers.

But Queen Rakhita was not the only visitor to Prince Susima's chambers. Three dark shadows scaled the palace walls and entered his quarters. They seemed to know the passages well. The guards, overcome by the monotony of their duties and perceiving a secure environment, were quick to doze. The dark shadows took advantage of the lapse and entered the chambers effortlessly.

Now one became the leader and the other two subordinate to him. The moonlight revealed that with the exception of their eyes, they were covered from head to toe in black garments. A flicker of the eyelids was enough for the subordinates to understand the behest of the one leading.

All three stood over the bed, looking at Susima. The leader seemed to savour the moment. The other two waited patiently for a signal. On receiving it, each slowly took a pillow from the sides of the bed and gently placed them on Prince Susima's face.

Held in a vice like grip, Susima struggled in vain, while the leader watched in amusement. He removed the pillow and clamped Susima's mouth before he could take in a breath to cry out. His piercing brown eyes locked with the frightened ones before him. A muffled yell tried to find a way through his fingers. The leader put a finger to his lips.

'Why?' Susima whispered to them desperately, fearing for his life.

Without warning the leader struck the back of his hand hard across Susima's face. Susima tried to protect it. But his arms were held as if in chains. 'I can give you anything you want, if you stop,' he spluttered.

The leader seemed amused. 'Anything?' he rasped. He brought his face closer to Susima's, 'I don't think so.'

Another slap and they were gone as silently as they had come.

Terrorized by the episode, Susima lay still, fear and humiliation crowding his mind.

He touched his swollen face gingerly. His mind raced as he tried to figure out the identity of the intruders. He felt as though he knew, but for some reason, his subconscious was not ready to part with that vital piece of information. An unpleasant realization crept in – that his sunsets of mirth and merriment were slowly fading away. Like his father, he would now have to be on guard against assassination plots.

14

Emperor Bindusara called a meeting of his confidantes. Akila was the first to arrive. He was soon joined by the others.

'There is trouble brewing in one of our most important provinces,' Akila declared.

'Yes, you mentioned that yesterday. Why repeat it?' Bindusara replied, irked.

Knowing the emperor intimately, Akila knew the irritation was not directed at him – it was Bindusara's failing health being reflected in his moods. In a bid to pacify him, he said gently, 'I was just summarizing the situation so that we can plan our course of action, Raje.'

'Yes, carry on,' Bindusara replied tiredly.

Mahamantri Radheya and Senapati Ajaya exchanged a glance. It would be a difficult discussion today. The emperor did not seem to be in a receptive frame of mind.

The emperor's energy seems to wane by the sunset, thought Akila astutely. *Maybe it is time…* With an effort, he pushed the extraneous thoughts away and launched into the details of the situation that needed immediate attention.

'We have not had any trouble from our provinces in a long time. Takshashila, our northern province, usually runs competently following the rules set by us. The same regulations and checks have been replicated at Suvanagri in the south and

Tosali in the east. However, in the recent past, Takshashila seems to be experiencing a spurt in tax offenders.' Akila looked at Radheya whose face bore a concerned expression.

'In fact, it has been the highest ever in our history. It is like a malignant sore in an otherwise healthy body. It could spread to the rest in no time.' He paused to let that sink in. No one spoke as they brooded over the worrisome situation. The thick dark clouds hovered over Takshashila with no wind to blow them away.

The emperor broke the silence by an unexpected reaction.

'What is Huma doing? Counting his pearls?' he rasped. A niggling cough had weakened his throat.

Huma was a cousin from Queen Rakshita's side of the family. He had been appointed the governor of Takshashila at the behest of the queen. Bindusara felt the pressure on his temples rise as he thought about the trouble at Takshashila. It took very little to disturb his equanimity these sunsets. He mentally chided himself for allowing Rakshita to influence him. She could be very persuasive when she wanted. He did not look forward to her reaction when he took steps to curb the situation created by Huma. All these thoughts flashed by in a second.

In that bleak situation, Mahamantri Radheya spotted a ray of sunshine. Perhaps this was the opportunity he had been waiting for.

He smoothly interjected, 'O Raje, let this matter be tackled by one of the princes. They need to take charge now. We need to kick them off the cliff and let them grow their wings on the way. Let one of them go,' he said carefully.

Bindusara visibly sat up straighter. The princes had not been involved in any real work as yet. *Hmm, the boys have turned into men. Maybe it is time for loosening the reins*, he thought.

'That's a fine suggestion,' he finally said. 'Ajaya, who do you think we should send?'

Senapati Ajaya was caught off guard. He tread carefully,

knowing well that this was a sensitive topic. He decided to buy some time. 'Let me mull over this. Both are doing fairly well in their training, as you are aware.'

Bindusara turned to Akila. 'Any thoughts?' He raised an eyebrow at him.

Without the slightest hesitation Akila vocalized his thoughts. 'Prince Ashoka would be my choice,' he stated laconically. 'He is astute and clever. His energy and skills would be put to good use over there.'

Radheya nodded in agreement.

Bindusara sighed. 'I will wait for your judgement, Ajaya. We will take a final call on the Takshashila situation very soon.'

Bindusara tried not to feel dismayed that two out of three of his confidantes had voted for Ashoka – his younger, rebellious son. Yet, he himself had always viewed him as unpredictable.

Bindusara paced up and down the meeting room while those in attendance sat sombrely. A rattling cough struggled to find a way out. The spasmodic reaction left the emperor breathless. His brow creased with tension, he gulped the water Radheya handed him.

His other two confidantes, Akila and Senapati Ajaya, were seated facing him. Diagonally opposite him were his sons Susima and Ashoka.

'Why is your face swollen?' Bindusara asked Susima matter-of-factly.

'Oh…I fell off my horse in a manoeuvre,' Susima replied defensively. He inwardly shrank at the memory of the dark-clothed intruders. It was common for soldiers to sustain injuries. He was aware of that and thought his explanation seemed satisfactory but in an instant, he realized the rest of his appearance was at odds with his story.

His torso is devoid of bruises, thought Radheya.

Ashoka smiled at Susima, deriving sadistic pleasure at his discomfiture.

'All right, let me come to the point. Our governor in Takshashila seems to be ineffective in containing some corrupt practices. We seem to have a record number of tax offenders. Any ideas on how to tackle the situation?' asked Bindusara, looking pointedly at his sons.

His chest expanding, Susima was quick to speak before Ashoka could. 'We should at once issue orders to Huma to take action, or else face the consequences. He should be made an example of what happens when the Mauryan code of conduct is not followed.'

Susima looked at Ashoka jubilantly, confident that he had made a favourable impression. The victorious look faded away as Bindusara turned to Ashoka.

Ashoka spoke slowly, aware that his thoughts on this matter could be of crucial importance in deciding his future.

'I feel that corruption usually has long tentacles. Huma himself could be at the helm of affairs and hence desisted from taking any action. At any rate, there would be a number of people involved. I recommend that someone from here should go there on some pretext. The strategy should be to assess the depth of the wreckage before taking any drastic action that might leave the citizens confused and wary.'

Bindusara looked at Ashoka with grudging respect. He sighed. Susima's impulsive answer had disappointed him greatly.

Susima felt as if he could not breathe. He looked around his chambers. Last night's events came back in a rush.

Who could it have been and why? he had refrained from mentioning the unfortunate incident. The day had not gone well either. Sleep was a difficult proposition.

I need some distraction, he thought in desperation. *Mother has made sure I do not meet any young women,* he thought peeved.

I will have to make some other arrangements, he decided. *Devendra can help me out here. But what do I do now?*

The thought of Kanak's frightened eyes flashed into his mind. That made him smile. More so because he knew that Ashoka was fond of her.

He drifted into sleep dreaming of nubile young women. One of them, clad in flowing red clothes, walked towards him seductively. As he reached out to touch her, he discovered he had grabbed the hand of a figure in black clothes. With a jerk, he woke up, his breathing spasmodic.

Fresh flowers adorned the corridors of the palace. The sweet scent of jasmine coupled with the aroma of bitter-lime oil lent a heady fragrance to the palace apartments. Pots of coloured powder and water had been placed strategically in all corners of the gardens. It was Holi, the festival of colours. The whole of the Mauryan empire would be celebrating.

Kanak sat in the partially closed palanquin with her sister Revati facing her. Her mother was in the one behind, while Father had left early in the morning to attend to work-related matters. They were headed for the palace. It was a tradition that the senior *amatyas* along with their families would celebrate with the royal family first and then privately.

Revati and Kanak peered through the window slits to observe the surroundings as they passed. With its streets adorned with flowers, the city stood as a larger reflection of the palace. In the centre stood a huge reservoir of coloured water that would be the focal point of many a revelry.

As they neared the palace, Kanak and Revati's palanquin slowed down. Revati peered out, a look of annoyance on her face. The palace gate was crowded with numerous palanquins and chariots all awaiting entry after the security checks. Kanak bit her lower lip as the quivering threatened to give away her state of anxiousness. She was not looking forward to the sunset at all. But her sister would not hear of leaving without her. She had finally conceded, thinking it was easier to go than to argue with Revati.

Revati had promised to stay by her side as she had finally confided in her about her trepidations. She remembered her sister's words. 'Prince Susima is just a man with some imbalances in his nature.' The medical explanation of his behaviour had left both the sisters giggling. Kanak knew her sister's pragmatic outlook to life was exactly what she needed to adopt. As for her memories, they would fade away in due course – at least that was what she hoped.

The melodious notes of a sitar drifted out of the gate to where the palanquins waited. When they finally entered, the buoyant environment lifted Kanak's spirits. She mentally shook herself and resolved to enjoy the occasion. She would not be a prisoner of her past.

She spotted Mali at a distance in the sprawling garden. As she approached him, he gulped self-consciously.

'Want some?' he asked, his mouth full of jalebis.

'I can see that some people are more interested in filling their stomach rather than playing Holi,' she admonished him.

'Yes, I have my priorities right,' he replied pleasantly, unfazed by her remark.

All the while she kept a watch for Ashoka. 'Where is your friend?'

'Which one?' asked Mali mischievously.

'You know I am talking about Ashoka,' she replied, clenching her teeth in mock irritation.

'He usually does not attend Holi celebrations. Not his kind of thing,' said Mali as if it were some kind of explanation.

At that point, Revati came and pulled Kanak away. She herself was completely covered in rainbow colours. As she smeared Kanak's face with bright red and pink shades, both giggled in merriment. Revati dragged her sister to join the group near the water tank. In a few minutes Kanak was soaked to the skin, her clothes smeared with colours. The colours stung her eyes. Rubbing them only exacerbated the condition further. Revati, who never left her physician's hat, gesticulated for her to go towards the palace where she could wash off the colours in one of the guest rooms.

Almost blinded, she stumbled across the garden and entered the palace corridors. With great difficulty she managed to find a room with a pot of water and washed her face vigorously.

As the stinging sensation abated, she looked at her reflection in the pot. *I do look a sight*, she thought, noticing that her kohl had smudged completely. She stiffened as she heard voices behind her. The laughter sounded boisterous, slightly off. Kanak realized it was drunken revelry.

Before she could get away, hands grabbed her from behind, roughly smearing colour on her face. Her veil slipped off as the group rubbed colour on her neck and torso.

She turned around in anger to confront the men who surrounded her. Through the mask of colour, a pair of familiar shifty eyes greeted her. She sucked in her breath at the unexpected encounter. In an attempt at self-preservation, she tried to recollect the pragmatic explanation Revati had ascribed for the prince's deviant behaviour. However, it failed to calm her down.

'Let go of me,' she replied indignantly. 'Tell your friends to go and pick on someone else.'

The coterie was silent now, interested in the exchange.

'Ah...I just want to play Holi – have some fun,' Susima said, a tad lecherously.

Panic welled up within Kanak. Just looking into his eyes brought the floodgates of her memories dangerously close to opening up. And then she heard a familiar, comforting voice.

'Leave her alone.' The authority was unmistakable.

Everyone turned to see who it was.

'Ah, our young Prince Ashoka, is it?' Susima laughed sarcastically. 'Mind your own business.'

'I will, if you mind yours,' Ashoka stated calmly.

Usually Susima would have backed off rather than engaging in an open confrontation. But today the influence of bhang clouded his judgement.

'What is it to you? I can have a little fun with one of our subjects if I want to.'

'She *does not* want it,' snapped Ashoka. He turned to Kanak. 'Find your way out while I settle this.'

She twisted free and rushed away.

A brawny young man in the group spoke up. 'Prince Ashoka, let's end it here,' he mumbled with difficulty, as if through a fog.

'Gajendra, I suggest you and your friends leave us brothers alone to settle this.' This was less of a suggestion and more of a command.

Susima was quick to react. 'They are not going anywhere.' he said, his eyes glinting in the lamp light. 'Grab him,' he signalled to his friends.

The three of them collectively lunged at Ashoka. He dodged them easily and stepped closer to Susima now. Susima stepped back in alarm.

'Not so fast, brother. You asked for it.' Ashoka slammed his fist into Susima's left eye. He slumped to the floor.

By now Mali had arrived at Kanak's behest. Taking in the situation, he restrained Susima's coterie and then turned to his friend. 'Enough, Ashoka,' coaxed Mali.

Ashoka seemed not to hear. Bending down, he brought his face close to Susima's and whispered, 'Have you forgotten the three messengers of the dark? You couldn't have. The dark circles under your eyes betray you.'

Susima gasped. A chill ran down his spine.

'Don't try to frighten her again. I know about how you terrified her in the forest too,' Ashoka hissed. The warning was issued ruthlessly.

As he straightened up, his eyes shifted to the person standing next to Mali. It was the emperor.

'Disgraceful!' said Bindusara to the brothers. He looked at them both with a pained expression. 'I will see both of you at the first rays of dawn.'

For the first time in his life Ashoka did not care about Bindusara's reaction. It was Kanak that he was concerned about.

'Come, Radheya, today I really need your counsel, for I am grieved to see my sons competing when they should be friends.'

Radheya looked at the emperor whose brow was creased in a frown. They were alone, Bindusara watching the blazing orange hues fade away into the vast nothingness. *Time waits for none. Not even the greatest,* thought Radheya, observing the wrinkles on the emperor's skin.

Today, nothing but the truth will come out of my mouth, he decided.

He said, 'Forgive me, O Raje, but you are responsible for the rivalry between the brothers.'

Bindusara looked puzzled at the statement.

Radheya elaborated. 'You favour Prince Susima and he knows that. Your attention makes him overconfident and vain.'

Giving Radheya an accusing look, Bindusara replied, 'How is it that you never told me this before?'

'You did not want to hear it, O Raje.'

'Radheya, you speak the bitter truth today. Do not restrain yourself. Tell me more. But remember, I give you this liberty only today. So tell me, for I am listening.'

I will not let this opportunity go by, asserted Radheya to himself.

He said, 'As a single withered tree, if set aflame, causes a whole forest to burn, so does a rascal son destroy a whole family. This has been said by my late guru, Chanakya himself.'

Bindusara winced at hearing aloud what he had known for some time now. However, obessions could not be shaken off so easily. His love for Suisma was the only obsession he indulged in.

'It is not so bad, Radheya. Your words wound me,' he whispered uneasily.

'Ashoka is your son too. For reasons best not mentioned, you spurn him. You tolerate him.' Radheya paused. 'A great emperor like you is blinded by his love for his elder son.'

Bindusara raised his hand. 'Stop…stop, I cannot listen to your words any more,' he said in anguish.

Unmoved, Radheya continued. 'Today I will not stop, for you yourself have given me permission to speak.'

'Did I not give both my sons the same opportunities and the same teachers?' defended Bindusara. 'Yet, you accuse me of favouring my older son.'

Radheya sighed. 'You can convince me but can you convince yourself?'

Bindusara knew in his heart of hearts that he was partly responsible.

As he slumped over the lounge coughing, several occasions of partial conduct for Susima flashed before his eyes.

On regaining his composure, he spoke.

'So what do you suggest, O Radheya, the man who speaks the truth?' he said somewhat sarcastically.

'As my great acharya said, "Fondle a son until he is of five years of age, use the stick for another 10 years, but when he has attained his sixteenth year, treat him as a friend." It is time to treat your sons like friends…both of them.'

Ashoka entered Bindusara's chambers to find him poring over an official missive. He did not look up, although the prince's arrival had been announced by the guard. He stood uncomfortably in the middle of the large 10-pillared room, uncertain of what to do. The feeling was familiar. This was the way he usually felt around his father…uncertain.

'Pranam,' said Ashoka.

Bindusara coughed dryly and nodded.

'Son, you have to leave for Takshashila in three sunsets.

You will be briefed by Radheya, Akila and Senapati Ajaya about your assignment.'

The announcement took Ashoka by surprise.

'Are you banishing me?' he asked in anguish. 'Is…is it because of yesterday?' His tone changed to defiance, trying to cover up his hurt. 'If it is, I am not sorry for what I did. Brother deserved it,' he said coldly.

Bindusara felt a familiar irritation welling up. 'I did not ask for your opinion, son. So, don't test my patience,' he snapped.

Ashoka pursed his lips. He observed a tired man in front of him. There was more grey hair than he remembered.

With effort, Bindusara attempted to explain.

'I am not banishing you. It is an important assignment concerned with the welfare of the citizens,' he said, his voice softening.

Bindusara put his hands on Ashoka's shoulders in an attempt at some display of affection. 'I trust your capabilities and that is why I am sending you there.' He paused. 'You will need bodyguards from now onwards. Akila will take care of that.

'Good luck, son. May Shiva be with you!'

Bindusara walked out.

Ashoka did not know how to react to his father's change of heart. It was unfamiliar territory.

'So here you are! I have been searching for you everywhere.' Ashoka sauntered over to where Kanak sat by the river, a pensive expression on her face.

He gazed at her thoughtfully. 'You are not very talkative today. Is it me or in general?' he asked tentatively. She shrugged her shoulders. Ashoka wondered what was bothering her.

'Maybe it is Susima…' He decided to put her mind to rest as far as that was concerned.

'Look, I apologize on behalf of my brother. That will never happen again. He will not…chase you.'

She smiled.

'I want to talk about us today,' said Ashoka.

Kanak felt something heavy descend on her. 'What about us?' she asked hollowly.

'This is difficult for me. It is about us…'

'Stop right here. There can be no "us"' Kanak said flatly.

The confidence with which he had started faltered at her vehement reponse.

'But why…? I don't understand. Don't you like me enough?' he asked, catching hold of her hand. His tone betrayed the hurt he felt.

'No…no, it is not that.' She looked at him pleadingly.

I wish I didn't have to tell him, she thought.

She wrenched her hand away.

'Look at me.' Ashoka took her by the shoulders and turned her to face him.

She took in a deep breath. The moment that had been lurking in the shadows had come.

'I can never have children!' she said in a high-pitched voice, starting to sob.

'What?' blurted out Ashoka, shocked. He ran his hand through his hair and looked around aimlessly, unsure of what to do.

Kanak's heart sank on seeing his reaction. She turned away, wanting to escape the situation. Strong hands held her at her waist.

'Wait…where do you think you are going? We haven't finished talking yet.'

Kanak was breathless by now. 'There is nothing to say. We don't have a future! I don't have a future with anyone…' she wept.

Ashoka's face broke into a smile. 'Let me understand this. You can't have children. So what? How does it impact our relationship?'

'It will someday. You don't understand' said Kanak

frustated. Knowing the problem, Ashoka felt a shade calmer. It was not as bad as she was projecting.

'You try to see too far into the future. How do you know that it can't be medically treated?' asked Ashoka, trying to make her see a ray of hope.

Kanak felt the familiar fear rise up in her. 'Because the damage was done when I was a little girl. I don't want to talk about it,' she said, shutting her ears with her hands to block Ashoka's pleas. Kanak saw his puzzled face and felt an unreasonable impatience.

All at once, Ashoka understood. He felt nothing but compassion. He gently encircled his arms around her in an attempt to reassure her. Kanak trembled, the warmth of his embrace ineffective against the cold demons of her past.

'I came to talk to you as I am heading to Takshashila in three sunsets. Official reasons,' he explained. 'Let us leave things the way they are. Let's talk when I am back.'

'I won't be there when you are back,' whispered Kanak throatily, breaking free of his hold.

'What do you mean?' he demanded. She saw that he was furious now. The quivering nerve on his forehead gave him away. 'You are being unreasonable. If it will ease your mind, children or no children...does not matter.'

She looked at him with an expression that he found difficult to fathom. 'It will matter...one sunset,' she said in a broken voice. *One sunset when Magadha will want princes and princesses,* she thought dismally.

'For now, let's promise to discuss it when I am back,' Ashoka said, half angry, half pleading.

'I will not be there,' Kanak said firmly and started to walk away leaving Ashoka staring vacantly after her. He stood there motionless for a long time, knowing the finality of her words. A long howl escaped his lips but was drowned by the roaring of the tempestuous waters of the Ganga. There was no one to console him except for the wind brushing against his cheeks.

15

Subhadrangi was in two minds about whether to raise the alarm or not. Her beloved Ashoka had not returned to the palace last night. But he was no longer a child and she did not wield the same influence over him as she had when he was younger. She was not unaware of the fact that his affections were directed at a certain young woman.

That is inevitable. He can't be tied to me forever. But he could have at least let me know he wouldn't be coming home, she thought with concern. She gazed at the glistening morning waters of the lake that never failed to soothe her frayed nerves.

At that instant, Daya came rushing with the news she had been eagerly awaiting. 'He has just arrived!' she announced.

Subhadrangi rushed to her son's chambers. She stopped short when she saw him. Drenched from head to toe, he looked a sight. But that was not what bothered her. It was something she could not put her finger on. Something had changed about him.

'What happened?' she asked, concern writ large on her face.

'Nothing.' Ashoka shrugged. He bent down to touch her feet, his face a mask. 'I decided to swim back to the palace instead of taking the boat.'

'Where were you all night, son?'

'In the forest,' he replied simply.

'In the forest, all night with no company and provisions!' Subhadrangi exclaimed incredulously.

Ashoka gazed affectionately at her. He knew he owed it to her to tell the truth about his failed relationship with Kanak. However, he was not ready to face any inquisition at the moment. He tried to divert her attention elsewhere.

'Mother, I need a bath and then I have a meeting with Acharya Akila. I am going to Takshashila in a couple of sunsets.'

The sudden announcement caught Subhadrangi off guard. 'What! How is it that…I didn't know.'

'Mother, the decision was taken yesterday,' he replied gently, putting his arms around her. 'I will tell you all about it over breakfast.'

She stared at him pensively, not knowing how to react. This was the sunset she had been waiting for – an opportunity for her beloved to prove his worth! Yet, a deep sense of unexplained foreboding welled up inside her.

Ashoka touched Acharya Akila's feet. Akila put his hands on his shoulders and pulled him upright so that they were face to face. 'You are no longer my student. You have responsibilities now, towards your people.'

'I am and will always be…your student,' Ashoka said with difficulty. Vocalizing his emotions was always difficult for him. Akila was equally ill at ease with displays of emotion. He steered the conversation to Ashoka's impending trip to Takshashila.

'Your security is my concern now. I will have the bodyguards come in soon. But before I do that, do you want any of our officers to accompany you?'

'I would like to take Mandar and Poulak with me,' Ashoka said without hesitation. 'I can provide the details of their current assignment.'

Akila waved him off. 'Don't bother, I know.'

Ashoka raised his eyebrows.

Does Akila know everything? he reflected. He knew that he still had a lot to learn from his acharya and it was a bond that would last their days on earth.

'It is my business to know who you associate with,' laughed Akila. 'I also know that you lean towards a particular young woman.'

Other than a quiver of the nerve on his forehead, Ashoka's

expression gave nothing away. Akila looked at him quizzically but got no response.

The acharya signalled to the guard, who escorted a couple of young men into the chamber. They bowed respectfully. Ashoka looked at them curiously. One was tall and lean with hardly any musculature, while the other was of medium height and brawny. Motioning to the tall and lean one, Akila said, 'He is Angad. The other is Chitrakoot.'

Ashoka noticed that although they looked very different from each other, there existed a similarity. Racking his brains to figure out what it was, Ashoka realized it had something to do with their personalities. He looked at Akila inquiringly.

Akila understood. He signalled to the two men and they left the room to accord them some privacy.

He turned to Ashoka. 'They come from a tribe where it is customary to castrate their firstborns.' Seeing Ashoka's perplexed look, Akila explained, 'It is a proven truth that man's bewitchment with women had been responsible for many a traitor. The foremost condition of a bodyguard is that he must be immune to lust for the opposite sex.'

'But that is not entirely why they are suited as bodyguards,' continued Akila. 'Both of them are endowed with some unusual qualities. Angad is a partial clairvoyant. He is able to tune into the universal energy and see things before they manifest. Any questions?'

Ashoka had many. Restraining himself, he asked the most important one. 'How accurate is he?'

Akila sighed. 'Yes, that's a good question. Unfortunately, his vision only works sometimes.'

Ashoka folded his arms across his chest, a faraway expression on his face. 'So, how will I know when they are true?'

'When your sixth sense tells you,' replied Akila. 'It is like having some added information.' He paused. 'Don't go by his appearance, he is also extremely intelligent and resilient.'

Akila frowned. 'One more thing. His clairvoyance is largely visual.'

'What about Chitrakoot?' asked Ashoka, intrigued by his new bodyguards.

'They say he has the strength of an elephant.' Akila laughed.

'There must be something more,' persisted Ashoka.

'Memory…he has a phenomenal memory, especially with faces. This could be a very useful ability.'

'Yes, it could be,' agreed Ashoka. 'Although I would not want a dependence on them.'

'One should take all the help that one can get,' countered Akila. 'They are with you from this moment onwards. Mahamantri Radheya will apprise you of your mission in detail.'

Ashoka knew he had been dismissed for now. However, he had one last question.

'Have they guarded anyone else?' he asked hastily.

'No, you are their first assignment.'

The implication of their inexperience was not lost upon Ashoka.

Ashoka felt a strange elation at the new developments. As if a chapter of his life was nearing an end and a new one was commencing. With purposeful strides, he walked out of Akila's official chambers.

His newly appointed bodyguards were standing outside, waiting expectantly for him. They followed him, one on either side. Not used to being escorted, the experience was uncomfortable for him.

'So, are you planning to be my shadows forever?' He laughed. They nodded in unison.

'Angad, they say you are partial clairvoyant. Tell me, where are we going? You must know.'

Angad looked at him incredulously. 'It does not work

that way. My visions come to me of their own accord – if my subconscious is tuned in, that is. It takes time.'

He held up his hands helplessly. Ashoka patted him reassuringly.

He had taken an instant liking to his bodyguards. He was curious about their eunuch status however decided to broach the sensitive topic later.

The youthful trio headed towards the main market square.

'Prince, don't the citizens know you? You walk amongst them as one of them, without the ways of royalty,' observed Angad.

Ashoka chuckled. As he had assessed them, they too had observed him keenly.

'Yes, my face isn't one that they remember. I like that. It has many advantages.' He winked at them conspiratorially.

'That's a good thing as far as I am concerned,' declared Chitrakoot in a deep voice. 'It is that much easier to guard you, Prince.'

'By the way, you can stop calling me Prince. Call me by my name.'

The two looked decidedly uncomfortable at that suggestion. But Ashoka would brook no refusal.

'It's the practical thing to do,' he asserted. 'So, what say we partake of some lunch? I am famished.'

Chitrakoot nodded vigorously in assent at that and the three of them walked into a busy eatery.

'Some pigeon meat for me,' declared Ashoka.

'The same for me,' echoed Chitrakoot.

Ashoka observed the distaste on Angad's face.

'I take it you are a vegetarian.' Angad nodded. 'It shows. No muscle on you.'

'Try me, Prince. I mean, Prince Ashoka…I mean, Ashoka,' Angad said, fumbling to get the term of address right. 'It is all up here.' He tapped his head with his index finger.

Ashoka shook his head in amusement. Their food came and Chitrakoot dug into his meat dish with relish.

Ashoka mentally thanked his acharya for making the appropriate choices for bodyguards. He intuitively felt they were just right for him.

Inconsequential babble emanated from all parts of the room. The trio themselves were deep in conversation when it happened. From nowhere, an object came whizzing through the air and landed in the spicy dish on their table. The hot curry splattered all over Ashoka's face. Unable to open his eyes which were stinging with the spices, he felt around the table for the jar of water to rinse his face with. At that instant an arrow shot past him, nicking him on the ear.

I am being attacked! The realization dawned in a flash. Angad thrust Ashoka under the table in order to shield him from further injury. For the *kashta* that he was able to open his eyes, he saw there was utter chaos, with people running helter-skelter.

Chitrakoot tried to block the entrance to trap the attacker or attackers, the assumption being they were one of the crowd. Ashoka knew that in all probability the marksman would have aimed from a point outside the eatery. There was no point detaining innocent citizens. He signalled to Chitrakoot to let the people go.

Meanwhile, Angad retrieved the object from the bowl of curry. It was an innocuous pebble. Ashoka realized it had been thrown deliberately for the curry to impair his vision. He stood up impatiently, using the jug to splash water on his face. The arrow too had been retrieved by then and would hopefully provide some clues.

The pandemonium subsided as quickly as it had started.

'Let's get out of here fast,' barked Ashoka. 'But who would want to harm me?'

The question hovered ominously. It was strange that he was attacked on the very sunset he had been provided protection. This thought bothered Ashoka.

'It must be the prayers of my mother, that I still breathe,' he murmured. His cynical outlook to life never touched his relationship with Subhadrangi.

Back in his chambers in the Lake Palace, Ashoka looked at Angad.

'What happened to your visions?' he said, a trifle sardonically. 'Didn't you get any?'

'No, Prince. I did not. I told you it will take some time,' Angad said quietly. 'I apologize.'

'I know it was too much to expect from you on the first sunset of your assignment,' Ashoka conceded. 'Why would someone want to kill me, though?' The question plagued him incessantly. 'I am not the Raja…as yet.'

He started to laugh mirthlessly. 'Of course, it could be my brother Susima. He could be getting back at me,' he said aloud.

Angad and Chitrakoot exchanged a glance, clearly puzzled.

'Back at you for what, Prince?' asked Chitrakoot.

'For being born as his pesky younger half-brother, for scaring the living daylights out of him a few sunsets ago, for coveting the throne, for challenging him at every step. Do you get the drift, my friends?' asked Ashoka, continuing to laugh dourly.

Angad and Chitrakoot said nothing. It was not for them to judge. The machinations of royalty seemed strange to them.

'So, what stops you from voicing your concerns to the emperor himself?' asked Chitrakoot.

'Don't be so naïve, my friend,' chided Angad. 'Susima is his older son. Have you understood, or do I have to spell it out in black and white?'

Chitrakoot was thoughtful for a moment and then nodded in understanding.

At that moment, Mali walked in. He handed over a letter to Ashoka.

'It is from the acharya.'

'But…I just met him,' Ashoka said, unrolling the parchment.

A single line was scrawled across it as if in haste. 'Angad and Chitrakoot did well today.'

Ashoka frowned, trying to comprehend the meaning. And then realization dawned and he laughed in relief. The attack had been planned by Akila as a test.

Mali stood uncertainly, unsure of what to do. Noticing the two men, he sensed an easy camaraderie amongst all of them. He felt an unfamiliar stab of jealousy. Ashoka answered the question that he had not vocalized. 'They are my bodyguards.'

He addressed Ashoka. 'I hear you are going to Takshashila.'

Ashoka nodded in affirmative.

'I would like to come too,' he said half sulkily.

Ashoka smiled. He knew his friend intimately and understood his apprehensions.

'Who will keep an eye on Mother when I am not here?' he asked gently. 'Besides, I need someone trustworthy to communicate with here. Someone who can keep an eye on my dearest brother Susima.'

That satisfied the pragmatic Mali. 'Very well. You can enjoy the pleasures of Takshashila by yourself.'

'What pleasures are you talking about?' asked Ashoka, genuinely surprised.

'Oh, I believe the women in Takshashila are very beautiful. Especially the ones who are half Greek.'

'I have no time to fritter on such banal pleasures. I am going for a purpose, and may Shiva help me,' Ashoka said sharply. The mention of women brought to fore the memory of his parting with Kanak. He thought of her with a mix of longing, wistfulness, remorse and frustration.

For the first time Ashoka looked forward to getting away from the city of his birth. Away from the complicated relationships that inevitably engulfed him in Pataliputra.

Mandar and Poulak rode ahead of Ashoka and his bodyguards.

His mother's parting words still rang in Ashoka's ears. *'Vijayee bhava.'* He touched his forehead to feel the powdery red tilak. His mother's touch lingered. She had not flinched at all when he told her he would be gone for a while, all the way to the northern province of Takshashila, almost 115 *yojanas* away from Pataliputra. However, he worried about her. She led a solitary life with only Daya and a few servants for company. The only time he had seen her truly happy was when Bindusara visited. This too occurred seldom now.

Ashoka's exit from the city had been very low key. The Agramahisi had refused to meet him, feigning a headache when he had gone to seek her customary blessings.

As the small group rode out of Pataliputra, his hopeful eyes scanned the lanes and by-lanes for any sign of Kanak.

She meant every word...I won't see her again, he thought forlornly, his hopes of meeting her crumbling as they moved away from the heart of the city.

'Takshsashila...' he sighed ambivalently, torn between what the future would bring and the memories haunting him.

As they rode out of the city gates, Amreshwar came out and motioned for the group to stop. He walked up to Ashoka and handed him a small amulet with a black thread. 'Prince, this is for good luck. Tie it around your arm.' That was all he said and his eyes signalled for the group to continue. Ashoka locked his gaze with the veteran in a silent parting.

The distance to Takshashila would be covered in approximately 45 sunsets at a medium pace and with stops. Ashoka resolved to spend the time constructively, thinking about his future course of action. There were about 20 men to cater to odd jobs such as cooking food, washing clothes, pitching tents if they were in between villages and cities. Additionally, a battalion of 100 soldiers accompanied them for security.

They would be going through the holy city of Ujjaini,

which was not exactly en route. Ashoka had chosen the longer route deliberately as he wanted to see the different hues of the Mauryan empire. Akila had not objected to that.

The initial part of the journey was the toughest. The boredom got to most of them, including Ashoka.

At night, most of the camp slept while some soldiers guarded the royal entourage. As it was his natural tendency to be alert in unfamiliar surroundings, Ashoka kept waking up every *hora*. Angad and Chitrakoot changed guard every four *horas* at the entry of his tent.

Ashoka had issued orders to move at the crack of dawn every day so that they could make good time. The camp came to life as the darkness gave way to the various hues of orange. After sipping some fresh lime juice and honey served by his assistant Surya, Ashoka strode out of his tent. Chitrakoot, who was on guard, bowed to him.

'Where is Angad?'

'He is meditating in his tent, Prince.'

'Why is he doing that now? Doesn't he know we are moving soon?' Ashoka asked, clearly peeved.

'He got ready a couple of *horas* ago. He is particular about meditating in the mornings. Something about going inwards…'

Ashoka held up his hand. The last thing that he wanted to have now was an explanation of why Angad meditated.

Chitrakoot pursed his lips at the rebuff.

Unsatisfied with the recent inefficiency of the winding-up operations, Ashoka summoned the head of camp administration to his tent.

'We are moving almost a *nalika* later than the crack of dawn.' He raised his eyebrows at the squirming official.

The official was taken aback at his critical feedback.

His face flushed, he was quick to reply. 'This will not happen again Prince.'

'I know it won't,' Ashoka said softly. The message was unmistakable.

Wiping the perspiration off his face, the official nodded uncomfortably.

'One more thing – send the head of the battalion to me.'

At that moment, Ashoka's personal assistant walked in. 'Can I do anything for you, Prince?' he asked.

Ashoka waved him away irascibly. The young man hesitated. 'Why don't you let me do my duties, young prince?'

'What do you mean?' asked Ashoka, a trifle irritated.

'It is my duty to take care of your personal needs.'

'I don't have any.'

The young man stood stubbornly, refusing to budge. For some reason, the man's presence peeved Ashoka. In a bid to dismiss him, he said, 'Very well. Please ensure I have a clean set of garments to wear everyday. That's all.'

Bowing, the assistant left, a bounce in his step.

Chitrakoot announced the arrival of the battalion head. He walked in, looking uncertain. He had already heard about the dressing-down of the camp administration head and was not looking forward to the meeting.

Ashoka did not mince any words. 'We need to make better time, my friend. At this rate, we will reach Takshashila much later than anticipated.'

'The carts of goods are slowing us down,' the officer said lamely.

'So, devise a way to get them to move faster.'

The battalion head thought for a moment and said, 'Maybe I can check with the ironsmith. If the axle is stronger, we may be able to pull them at greater speed.'

'Why don't you attach some springs to the floor of the carts, so that they go easier on the bumps?'

'Yes, Prince. I will start working on it right away.'

He bowed and made a quick exit. It was clear to him that the young prince had to be taken seriously.

The pace was now faster than the sunset before. Ashoka rode in silence, flanked by Chitrakoot and Angad. Angad, who was not much of a talker himself, did not mind the silence. After a few futile attempts at conversation, Chitrakoot sensed his companions' lack of interest in chatter and had no option but to keep to himself.

They passed long stretches of pasture land between the villages. The grazing herds of cows, goats and sheep were a serene sight. Ashoka enjoyed the contrast between the bustling Pataliputra and the peaceful villages. It was as if a different sun shone here. It was brighter and fiercer at the same time. Curious shepherds looked up from under their straw hats at the royal entourage. Ashoka saw with satisfaction that numerous reservoirs had been created for the herds that grazed.

Post lunch they passed through a prosperous village and stopped in the main square to refill their empty containers of water. The idyllic quiet was broken by running footsteps. A young woman darted out of one of the lanes and flung herself on the ground in front of Ashoka's horse.

'Justice…I want justice!' she wailed. Two men, one older and the other younger, came through the lanes, obviously pursuing her. They stopped short when they saw the unusual sight of the royal group. Recovering from their surprise, they bowed respectfully to Ashoka.

'Salutations, O Prince. Please don't let her bother you,' the older man said, pointing to the fallen woman.

The men took an arm each and made to drag her away. The woman screamed only to be stifled by the younger man who clamped his hand on her mouth.

'Leave her!' thundered Ashoka.

The two men stopped in their tracks in surprise.

Ashoka got off his horse. Chitrakoot and Angad were quick to dismount too. He walked up to the sobbing woman, bent down and gently pulled her up.

'There is always justice in Emperor Bindusara's empire,' he said quietly.

Ashoka saw that she was quite young. Her beautiful face wore a haunted look owing to the hollow eyes surrounded by dark circles. Her thin body was less flesh and more of a framework of bones.

'Speak up and justice will be done' he said loudly enough for all around to hear. The older man started to speak, 'O Prince, as head of my family and being her father-in-law, I will take care of her troubles…'

'I asked her to speak, not you.' Ashoka's voice was a whiplash. 'If you could take care of her, she would not be in this state, begging for justice. I bid you to stay away from her until I say otherwise.'

The command was unmistakable. The father-in-law stepped away uncertainly.

Turning his gaze on the woman, Ashoka said, 'Speak, young one. Do not be afraid of your family. I assure you that justice will be done.'

She took a deep breath. 'Noble one, my husband is no more. No wife could have been as loyal to him as I was. After his death, my life did not seem worth living as I do not have any children.' Her eyes brimmed with tears and she choked with emotion. 'But now I want to marry someone else. I do not love him as I loved my husband, but I can be a good wife to him and he a good husband to me.'

'So what is the problem?' prodded Ashoka.

He observed the two men exchange a glance. Unnoticed by them, Mandar and Poulak went and stood behind them, ready to detain them if necessary.

The young woman's lips quivered with emotion as she hesitated.

'Do not be afraid,' reassured Ashoka.

'I need my dowry to start a modest life as he is poor with a large family to support.'

'So, what is the obstacle in your plans?' Ashoka asked her gently.

At that, she burst into tears and pointed at the men. 'They are not giving me what is rightfully mine.'

Having ascertained the issue, Ashoka turned to the two men. 'What do you have to say about this?' he inquired.

The older man folded his arms in defiance. 'Forgive me, O Prince, but the laws of Magadha state that if a woman leaves her husband's family for another, she has to forfeit her dowry as well as her husband's property.'

Ashoka knew the man was right as he knew the text of the *Arthashastra* like the back of his hand. However, in his heart he also knew that this was unfair to women.

I must remember to have such laws changed, he thought to himself grimly. For now, he decided to take a novel approach.

'Where is your husband-to-be?' Ashoka asked the young woman.

'He is out of the village today and will be back tomorrow.'

'And who is he?' Ashoka asked, pointing to the younger man.

'He is my brother-in-law…' she hesitated. 'He is keen to marry me.'

The younger man glared at the woman, clearly unhappy at the revelation.

Ashoka made a quick decision. 'I am here until tomorrow. I will personally have the wedding arrangements made for you – as per your choice of groom. As for your dowry, I will gift you the same amount in silver *panas* from my own account. Angad, please take care of everything. Do you have a name fair maiden?'

All present were taken aback by the decision.

The young woman felt as if her heart would burst with emotion.

'I am Gauri,' she said, suddenly shy.

Ashoka looked at the men of her family who were now looking flabbergasted. 'Will you be kind enough to give her away at the wedding?' Ashoka asked the father-in-law, his tone more a command than a request.

'I…I will, O Prince. I cannot refuse you,' he stammered.

'That you cannot,' agreed Ashoka.

He gave one last look to the overjoyed woman, satisfied he had been able to mete out justice. The pain in his heart seemed to melt away a little, as it made way for the waves of compassion that he felt at the moment.

The wedding festivities had offered a welcome break from the tedium of the journey. Afterwards, the entourage embarked yet again on the expedition to the northern province.

The wedding revelries must have worn him off, Ashoka thought as he noticed Angad's sallow appearance.

'So, tell me about your tribe,' said Ashoka, glancing sideways at Angad.

'What to say, Prince?' He shrugged.

'You look fairly civilized for a tribal.' Ashoka regretted the words the moment they spilled out of his mouth. 'I didn't mean that the way it sounded,' he said apologetically.

'That's all right, Prince. I am aware of the common perception that the civilized world has about us tribals. I know you did not have any malice in your heart.'

Ashoka was relieved to hear that from the level-headed Angad.

'Now that you have asked, let me give you some insight about us. Yes, we seem uneducated in the conventional sense. There are no formal gurukuls in our villages, but there are things that are passed down from generations that only we know. To give you an example, we are adept at using plants and shrubs found in forests for medicinal and other uses. We could probably give a few lessons to some vaids. We can hunt down any animal and survive on very little. It is a simple and pure life, Prince. It is enchanting.'

The simple words rang true to Ashoka. But he had more questions. 'Pray, what are you doing here – with me? This existence must seem repulsive to you.'

Angad smiled at that. He pointed to Chitrakoot who rode on the other side of Ashoka. 'Our tribes are fairly close and it is a myth that the firstborns are castrated. A myth we do not care to dispel.' The revelation surprised Ashoka. 'By some quirk of nature, some of us are born this way. But nature never keeps a debt. If she takes some, she gives some too.'

'You mean your gift of visions that ordinary mortals like us do not have,' said Ashoka. Angad smiled. 'Ordinary, you are not,' he said emphatically.

'Do you miss having a full life?' Ashoka continued.

'What do you mean?' Angad asked, puzzled.

'I mean, do you miss being a man?' Ashoka chose his words carefully, lest he offend him.

Angad did not seem to mind.

'One doesn't miss what one has never experienced, Prince. The answer is no. I am fine just the way the creator intended me to be,' he said firmly.

'Chitrakoot, what about you?'

'I can't think on an empty stomach, Prince! You run a tough camp. When are we camping for lunch?' Chitrakoot groaned.

Ashoka laughed at his candidness. The bodyguards felt more like friends than protectors. He felt a comfortable bond with them. Strange! When old ones were severed, new ones miraculously established themselves.

The entourage crossed a reservoir. Unusually weary, Ashoka was tempted to stop for a dip. He wondered whether he might be coming down with a fever. As far as he could remember, he had fallen ill only when he was very young. His mother had seen to it that his constitution improved dramatically with her care over his food and health.

He flung aside the cloth soaked with his perspiration. Despite his discomfort, he made sure that the pace of travel was not compromised. However, he was relieved to retire to his tent when they camped for the night.

Angad, who was on his way into Ashoka's tent, collided with Surya as he rushed out.

'Steady, man! And what are you smiling at?' he questioned, holding him by the shoulders.

'Nothing,' replied Surya, his expression turning taciturn.

Angad walked into the tent thoughtfully.

Ashoka lay on the bed looking pale, while Poulak sat next to him discussing the route.

Trying to distract himself from his throbbing headache, he changed the topic. 'So, tell me, Poulak, do you miss home?'

'Of course I do. My mother's food, Maya's playful tricks, the garden behind my house…of course I miss everything.' He beamed at the memories.

Ashoka looked thoughtful.

'What about you, Ashoka?'

'I have nothing much to miss except for my mother.' His bleak expression gave away the untruth. Poulak and Angad exchanged knowing glances, careful not to mention Kanak in front of him.

Uncharacteristically, Ashoka had to be woken up by Chitrakoot the next day. He sat up on his bed with a start, rubbing his head. It felt heavy.

Surya walked in with breakfast. He waved him away.

'Lime juice with honey for me. I don't need anything to eat.'

'I insist that you eat,' said Surya in a high-handed tone.

'You heard him. He'll eat if he wants. Get out or I'll crush your head,' Chitrakoot hissed menacingly, well aware that Ashoka found Surya highly bothersome.

'The first thing I am going to do when we reach Takshashila is replace him,' Ashoka said once Surya had left in a huff.

He caught Chitrakoot eyeing the plate of boiled rice with jaggery. 'You can finish my breakfast. As I said, I am not hungry.'

'All right,' said Chitrakoot, only too happy to oblige. Today was going to be a long day. They would not be passing any villages.

In the second half of the day, the landscape changed from fresh green to mud-streaked vegetation. This was no surprise as they caught sight of mined land. From the shade of red that tinged the land, Ashoka gauged they must be iron ore mines.

As they got closer, Ashoka noticed a large number of soldiers patrolling the area. A group of six soldiers rode out to greet the group.

'Greetings, Prince Ashoka!' said the leader. 'On behalf of the chief superintendent of mining, we welcome you. There is a sandstorm expected. It would be a good idea to camp here for the night.'

'All right,' acquiesced Ashoka who was keen to look at the mines.

The leader escorted them to the official quarters. A group of soot-covered workers returning from the mines passed them. On seeing the royal flag, they bowed sullenly.

The surroundings were a stark contrast to the cheerful villages and pastures they had encountered in the past few sunsets. A pall of gloom hung in the air. Every object had a reddish black hue to it.

A feeling of distress overcame Angad. His face betrayed his emotions transparently.

'What is it, Angad?' Ashoka asked in a low voice so that others could not hear.

'This place is full of troubled souls.' He hesitated before continuing. '*They curse your father.*'

'Why would they do that?' questioned Ashoka, startled. He could not imagine that Bindusara, who was loved by all, should be cursed by anyone, least of all his subjects.

'I don't know. Maybe you need to find out.'

'Very well.' He would get to the bottom of this soon.

When the others had left for their own rooms, Ashoka suddenly felt a wave of nausea sweeping over him. He decided to rest for a while.

When he awoke, Surya stood beside him, holding a pitcher of water. Ashoka's headache, which had dulled slightly, now flared up again. The throbbing of his head made it difficult for him to focus. The slightest movement resulted in a searing pain.

Angad's words came back to him. He could not come to terms with anyone cursing his father.

Ashoka dressed with effort and walked across towards the mines. Angad and Chitrakoot appeared out of nowhere and walked behind him like shadows. They were just in time to see the workers trooping out of the mine gates. Their faces were so blackened that it looked as though they were wearing dark masks. With their weary gait and sullen expressions, they almost bordered on the hostile.

A group walking towards them looked up and did not seem to recognize Ashoka in plain clothes.

For once Ashoka was at a loss for words. Angad opened his mouth to introduce Ashoka appropriately but he signalled for him to stop. Luckily, the soldiers had camped a little away, thought Ashoka gratefully. His identity would be no secret otherwise.

'Long day, friends,' said Ashoka finally, attempting to strike up a conversation.

They looked at him. He looked too clean and fresh for their liking.

'What is it to you, lad?' one of them replied gruffly.

'We were just passing by, and hoped to join you for your evening meal.'

'Join us for an evening meal!' another one remarked in an amused tone. 'Yes…we could do with some entertainment,' added another worker. They laughed raucously.

Chitrakoot and Angad glanced uneasily at each other, their hands stealing to their swords. An older-looking miner hushed the others. They obeyed him, stifling their sniggers.

'You can join us if you wish,' he said simply, pointing to the dining hall at the far end of the ground. 'We will wash up and be there.'

The dining hall was sparsely furnished but was probably the only thing that lent warmth to the otherwise bleak surroundings. The attendants offered *chaas* to everyone who entered.

Soon it was packed with miners. They stared curiously at the visitors. Ashoka deduced that visitors were a rare sight in this part of the country.

'Look, there they are,' said Angad, spotting the group they had met, sitting in the far corner. With their faces scrubbed, some of the gloom that had hung about them earlier seemed to have melted away. Ashoka's group joined them.

'So tell me, do you earn a good living here?' asked Ashoka.

They looked at each other. 'That's a question we don't like to be asked,' said the older one. He looked at Ashoka quizzically. 'Are you a spy?'

'Oh no, I am a humble trader. But I am close to some influential officials. I can make sure your voice is heard…in a manner of speaking.'

The miners sniggered incredulously. Their chuckles soon gave way to bitter expressions. One of them, a dark-skinned man with light eyes, spoke with hostility.

'There is a voice I would like to silence,' he whispered menacingly. The emphasis on the world 'silence' was not lost on Ashoka.

'Enough,' admonished the older miner, silencing the light-eyed one with a piercing look that commanded him to stay quiet.

Ashoka coaxed them gently to open up about their troubles. 'I mean no harm. I swear by Shiva, I am not a spy,' he said, trying to reassure them of his intentions.

'Whose voice do you want to silence and why?' He was acutely aware of Angad squirming next to him. A deep sense of foreboding overtook him.

The light-eyed one looked defiantly at the older one.

'I would like to silence the voice of the one who has condemned us to this life of…drudgery,' he said, banging his fist on the table, his expression a mix of anger, wretchedness and defiance.

'You mean you don't work here of your own accord?' Ashoka asked, surprised.

'Look around, man!' said the light-eyed one, waving his arms. 'There is ample freedom to enjoy the pleasures of life. I am blessed by my mother everyday. I take a ride on my horse in the wilderness enjoying sunrises, I eye beautiful maidens and dream of spending my life with one of them.' Almost sobbing now, he held his head in his hands.

'Yes,' he wailed. 'I would like to silence the voice of the one who had given me this wonderful life. But…that would be too easy an end. I would like to push him into a pit of snakes and see him suffer,' he said, seething with anger.

'You are talking about our great Emperor Bindusara?' Ashoka asked quietly.

The attempt to conceal the tremor in his voice was not lost upon Angad. Ashoka felt Angad's hand on his shoulder bidding him to stay calm.

'You are damn right!' exclaimed the light-eyed man, spitting on the floor in disgust.

The older one sensed that the discussion had gone too far. Afraid of the consequences of speaking deprecatingly about Bindusara, he abruptly dragged the light-eyed man away.

Ashoka felt his eyelids droop despite his attempts to keep them open. He felt the bitter bile rise up to his mouth.

In the privacy of his quarters Ashoka paced up and down the room while Angad and Chitrakoot stood uncomfortably in the corner. He licked his lips, tasting the remnants of the bitter concoction that Surya had insisted he drink.

'Can the just Bindusara sentence these poor citizens to such depths of despicable existence?' Ashoka asked dismally. The halo around Bindusara dimmed a little. A part of him felt that the Mauryan administration was like a worthless piece of stone that shone like a diamond in the sun. The moment the sun was taken away, the stone would be seen for what it was – just a piece of the earth.

The entourage stuck to their gruelling pace the next sunset. The camp administration ran efficiently now.

Angad's words had struck Ashoka like a blow. For the umpteenth time, the memory of his words came flooding back.

Angad had said, 'The emperor is cursed and hated by the mine workers, for he holds their families hostage while they toil in the mines. The men turn up here when they or their families fail to pay their taxes and subsequent penalties for the same. Some of them have committed petty crimes and have justifiably been kept here to complete their sentences. But a large majority are those who have defaulted in state-charged taxes. The understanding is that while the men lead solitary, wretched lives in the mines, their families are taken care of. The iron mines are the backbone of all weaponry needed by the huge armies of the Mauryan empire. For the condemned, it is a hard life.'

Why had Acharya Akila not mentioned this while they were reviewing the administrative policies of the Mauryan empire? Ashoka thought. *Maybe he intentionally left out certain truths for us to stumble upon – like snakes lying dormant, concealing their poisonous fangs until disturbed.*

The time would come when he would be able to do something about it. But not today. Today he was powerless to bring about changes in policy.

16

That night Ashoka dreamt of a grotesque two-faced creature with a human face in front and a dark saliva-dripping monster head at the back. Angad, who was on duty outside Ashoka's tent, thought he heard someone mumbling. He rushed in to discover that the culprit was Ashoka himself, probably in the midst of a nightmare.

He frowned. *Something is not right,* he thought.

Ashoka, who would have normally woken up at the intrusion, was still in deep slumber. On closer observation, Angad noticed the prince was bathed in perspiration. But there was something else…a sickly-sweet smell. Cautious not to disturb him, Angad took a few deep breaths to ascertain the origins of the smell. It seemed to be emanating from the prince himself. Flummoxed, he stood still for a moment. The explanation eluded him momentarily.

'That's it!' He snapped his fingers as realization dawned. He rushed out to summon Chitrakoot. It would be dawn soon. There was no time to be lost.

'Rouse Poulak and Mandar at once and meet me in Prince Ashoka's tent!' he bellowed.

'Yes,' Chitrakoot snarled. 'I am up. You don't have to act as if it is the end of the world.'

'You heard me,' Angad responded in an urgent tone. 'Rouse Poulak and Mandar *now,*' he hissed, with emphasis on the now. 'Be quick. I need you in the prince's tent.' He rushed off.

Chitrakoot grabbed his sword and went to fetch the other two. When the three reached Ashoka's tent, they saw Angad forcing a thick green paste into Ashoka's mouth.

'It's a potent emetic. He will start vomiting in a few minutes,' explained Angad, not looking up.

He closed his eyes for a moment and then turned to face Poulak and Mandar.

'You need to ride east on fast horses. He has a head start

of a few *horas*. But he is a slow rider. The prince has been poisoned…slowly and deliberately,' stated Angad.

The other three stood gaping at him, too shocked to utter a word.

'It's Surya,' he said simply. 'But it's not just him…there are others,' he said, his eyes closed as if playing a scene in his mind.

Poulak and Mandar set out on their mission on the fastest horses available.

As the emetic took effect, Ashoka dazedly began coughing up deep green phlegm. Chitrakoot ran to get a pot and placed it near the bed. Completely exhausted, Ashoka lay back when he was done.

'You were poisoned, Prince,' Angad told him simply.

'What good did you two do?' Ashoka rasped. 'You were tasting the food before I ate it,' he said, his tired voice still managing to drip sarcasm.

'Yes, we were,' reiterated Angad calmly. 'But a miniscule amount was being admistered everyday. A spoonful or two did not affect us.' He paused before continuing. 'One fine day, you would have continued sleeping…forever.'

Ashoka pondered on the implication of his words.

'You did not ask me who could have given you this poison sunset after sunset?'

A flicker of understanding crossed Ashoka's face.

'Of course! He insisted that I drink his godforsaken bitter potion every night. Who knows how much he put in the food.'

He thought for a moment. 'But why…' He trailed off.

'Exactly…why?' The words hung ominously in the air.

Chitrakoot, who had been silent all this while, jumped in front of Angad and pointed a finger at him accusingly.

'And pray, why did you not have a vision about this?' he demanded.

'I did get a vision at times. I saw him running away but did not connect it to such a disturbing occurrence.'

'Oh yes, you probably thought I was chasing the swine away,' said Chitrakoot wryly. He could not resist adding, 'Leave the thinking to me sometimes. I am not just brawn, you know.'

Angad ignored the rebuke and turned to addressed Ashoka. 'Most healthy men would not have survived this long with this particular poison in their system. It slowly weakens the blood circulation and destroys all organs…eventually.' He felt his pulse. 'You are gaining strength rapidly.'

'So have they caught Surya?' was the only question that Ashoka asked.

Angad shrugged. 'I am not sure.'

Chitrakoot threw the pot at Angad who caught it deftly. 'You're useless,' he said in mock anger.

'Yes, it was you who sniffed out the poison while I slept,' retorted Angad, albeit calmly.

'If you had told me about your vision, we would not be chasing Surya now,' retorted Chitrakoot, not to be easily put off.

Angad gave him a helpless look. 'I have got the point.'

'Good,' replied Chitrakoot, stretching the disagreement as far as he could.

Ashoka retched again but nothing except a greenish-yellow bile came out. He rinsed his mouth thoroughly, trying to get rid of the bitter aftertaste. It reminded him of his mother's karela juice, which she had force-fed him in his younger years. But this was nothing compared to the bitter truth of knowing that now he was a target for assassination.

'This time it is not a test devised by Akila – someone wants me in *mrityulok*,' he surmised.

I will get the answers, he thought to himself resolutely. The person must be very influential, to have planted an attendant so close to him. But what bothered him most was that it was an indicator of a deep rot somewhere in the system.

Surya whimpered as he was dragged into the tent by Poulak and Mandar.

The glow from the oil lamps lent a muted warmth to the austere surroundings. Ashoka was back to his former self, all apparent traces of the poison gone. He sat on a chair with his arms propped up on several small silk cushions. Angad and Chitrakoot stood on either side, inscrutable expressions on their faces.

'Here is your culprit, Prince,' said Poulak, pointing at Surya derisively.

Mandar spit on him with loathing. 'I was tempted to wring his neck but I thought the pleasure must be yours,' he said, looking at Surya disdainfully.

Howling loudly, Surya flung himself at Ashoka's feet, his whole body racked in spasms. His tattered clothes and bruised body did not invoke pity in anyone present.

'I am a poor soul, Prince. I was forced. I swear by Mother Kali, it is not my doing. I am but a puppet in their hands,' he wailed.

'Who is the puppeteer?' questioned Ashoka calmly.

Surya opened his mouth to speak and then a fearful expression crossed his face, and he visibly shrivelled up. Pursing his lips, he became very still, his eyes darting all over the tent as if some saviour would emerge and take him out of this impossible situation. The next moment, he resumed yowling and beating his hands on his chest.

'I don't know…I don't know. I was promised 100 *panas* for my family…' he trailed off, probably realizing he was only digging a deeper grave for himself.

'You can tell us what you know and be spared a harsh punishment,' said Angad, almost kindly.

No one else in the room echoed those sentiments. Chitrakoot landed a hard slap across Surya's face.

Momentarily stunned, he moaned in pain, his face swollen by the impact. 'It is not my fault…' he bawled.

Ashoka sighed. He motioned to Chitrakoot to take him away.

'Where are you taking me?' screeched Surya as he was dragged by the hair across the room. 'Mercy…mercy, Prince,' he howled.

However, mercy was an emotion Ashoka did not feel at the moment. He knew there were several effective ways of getting to the truth – methods of torture that armies used to obtain information from unwilling informants.

In the glow of the lamps, Ashoka's face appeared pallid. Mandar wondered whether it was the after-effect of the poison he had or the thought that someone was trying hard to ensure that he left this world before his time. He suspected that it was the former.

That night Ashoka, accompanied by his bodyguards, walked briskly to a nearby clearing. It was still dark. But the fading moon provided adequate light to see the ugly sight that awaited them.

His hands tied, Surya lay flattened out horizontally on the bench. A stand held an inverted pot of water that filled up a funnel. Through the funnel water dripped, one slow drop at a time, on his forehead. His hair was drenched by the continuous albeit slow trickle of the drops. Ribs stuck out of his bare torso.

Chitrakoot looked at the set-up with interest. This was the first time he had been exposed to such a simple yet sophisticated method of torture. Were it left to him, pure force would be his choice of method to break anyone.

Surya moaned in frustration and agony. His eyes travelled the fall of each innocuous drop before it landed on his forehead. His gaze steady, Ashoka was as unmoved by the sight beholding him, as a vaid who sees suffering patients everyday and yet does not get affected in any manner.

Surya now lived in a fused world of the real and imaginary. Coherent thoughts were far and few. *They* hadn't told him about the inhumane suffering he would be subjected to if caught. Actually, he himself hadn't thought getting caught was a possibility. With all his knowledge of slow reacting yet potent herbs, he was sure no one would have suspected him until he was well out of reach. He would fling the 100 *panas* on their face when he got out of this situation.

And then a crippling thought struck him.

But will I manage to get out…sane?

He looked up at the drop which grew bigger and bigger as it fell towards him – he saw this in slow motion as if time had slowed down. The drop grew in size, as big as a huge ball of a swirling angry liquid threatening to gobble him up and wipe out his miserable existence.

As the cool liquid fell repeatedly on the same spot of his forehead, bolts of searing pain ran through him, almost blinding him. He could not see clearly. It was as if a silvery white translucent curtain obstructed his vision. But he could make out the silhouette of the prince. The expression seemed to be mocking him.

He vaguely heard someone say,

'He is cracking fast. For one so slimy, he does not have the gumption to persevere. A few more *horas* and he'll be ready to talk, Prince.' It was Chitrakoot, relaying his observations to Ashoka – or was it Angad?

'I look forward to that,' he whispered in reply.

The trio left the scene, leaving the moaning and terrified Surya alone. By now, the news about the surreptitious attack on Ashoka's life had spread like wildfire. The soldiers and help alike went about their tasks with renewed vigour. It was as if they basked in the reflected glory of accompanying someone so important who was subject to an assassination attempt.

Angad pondered over the unfortunate episode. Chitrakoot was not the only one who had berated him for not mentioning the fragments of visions relating to Surya that he had seen.

His inner voice had been unrelenting in self-flagellation. He definitely needed to hone his skills on making sense of his visions. What was the point of getting these powerful visions if he could not make sense of them at the right time? On the other hand, Ashoka had not once subjected him to any kind of censure. Angad had thought Ashoka would be livid at his slip-up.

He had been unable to meditate today, his mind a flurry of thoughts. He sighed. He knew this would compromise his clairvoyance abilities. He thought of his grandfather in his village who had similar faculties and was one of the most respected there.

'Bless me, Nana, for I need my skills to perform my duties,' he said mentally to his grandfather, trying to connect with him.

He made a firm resolve to himself. *This will not happen again, Prince. If ever it does, I will not consider myself worthy of you.*

The camp stood in a circle in the clearing despite the scorching noon sun. Surya had the beginnings of a depression on his forehead, where the unrelenting water drops were falling. The writhing human was a sorry sight.

They watched quietly as he slipped in and out of conciousness. Once in a while someone would murmur to his neighbour. But overall, the mood was silent and sombre.

The punishment for trying to take a life was harsh, according to the code of conduct prescribed. Here the crime was much worse as the victim was a member of the royal family. Surya's act of treason called for the harshest of punishments followed by certain death. Ashoka could have had him sent to Pataliputra to be questioned in the terrible prisons there. However, he had chosen to handle the matter himself.

A *chandala* had been sent for from the outskirts of the nearest village. The *chandalas* were Sudras specially appointed for conducting undesirable tasks such as cremations, public flogging and other such harsh punishments.

An even deeper hush fell over the group as an official announced the prince's arrival and motioned for the crowd to part and make way for him. Under usual circumstances the questioning would have been done in privacy. But Ashoka wanted everyone to see the fate of one who turned against him.

Going close to Surya, he addressed him almost gently. 'So, tell me everything you know.'

Surya seemed not to hear and did not respond.

Surya dreamt that he was in a thick fog and someone was calling out to him in muffled tones. He seemed to be running amock with no way of knowing how to get out of the fog. He ran in the direction from where the voice seemed to be coming. Tripping, he fell face down near a pair of giant feet. He clutched the feet, hoping the owner would be his saviour. But as he scrambled up, all he saw was the taciturn face of his tormentor, the prince.

'Speak, wretched one, or we will leave you here with a couple of guards who will torture you until eternity!' bellowed Chitrakoot.

Surya tried in vain to free his hands with the last vestiges of his strength. It was a futile attempt. His muscles ached as if he had been run over by a dozen horses.

Chitrakoot motioned to one of the soldiers, who poured hot salted water into the pot above Surya's head. The unbearable sting caused him to start bawling like a child.

'Stop screaming,' ordered Chitrakoot. 'Just answer the questions and you may get the mercy you don't deserve.'

The prisoner tried to moisten his parched and cracked lips with a little saliva that he managed to gurgle out. In a quivering voice he spoke,

'T-they came to my village and asked for someone who had knowledge of herbs. I…I had no idea it was for ulterior motives. They offered 100 silver *panas* for a task.'

He paused, almost choking on his words.

'We are not interested in how much you got. Who are... *they*?' persisted Chitrakoot.

'I don't know,' wailed the prisoner. 'Do you think anyone would tell me?' he managed to say in a garbled manner. 'The person who contacted me was a wizened old man from the next village. He called himself Ami baba.'

'There has to be more...' thundered Chitrakoot.

At that point, Ashoka, who had been silent so far, held up his hand.

'I think he does not know anything other than what he has said. Let him be tied to a horse and dragged along for the rest of the journey until he is no more,' he declared.

Surya would probably not survive even a single sunset, given his present condition. This was one of the lowliest of punishments given to a person. The *chandala*'s services would not be needed after all, except for the cremation.

'I could never have imagined our young prince to be so ruthless,' one soldier whispered to another.

'Yes, I wouldn't want to cross paths with him,' the other replied.

Surya had surprisingly managed to drag his *prana* with his body for the next seven *horas* before it finally left him. When they camped for the day, his mangled body lay in a heap for everyone to see. His clothes were in tatters, his face a bloody mess. One eye seemed to have a twig stuck in it. His limbs stretched in various directions, testatment to the fact that most of the bones in his body were broken.

Everyone in the camp was in a sombre mood after having witnessed the slow, painful death of this man who had dared cross paths with the young prince. Last rites according to the Hindu custom, essential to free the soul from the body and ensure a safe passage to the afterworld, were out of the question. If Ashoka was in a merciful mood, he might allow the *chandala* to cremate the body, else it would be left rotting in the wilderness.

It turned out that Ashoka did feel merciful. The *chandala* was asked to cremate Surya without the honour of any last rites. He got to work without a word. No one envied him his livelihood. The *chandala*'s skin had a greyish pallor to it and he looked more dead than alive. His torso smeared with ashes, his bare legs had some kind of fungus growing on them.

Noticing Ashoka's dour mood, Angad commented in a quiet tone, 'You can't let some unfortunate incidents affect you too much, Prince. As for Surya, I am sure that his soul will have difficulty finding a place in the lowest realm of *patallok*.'

The black smoke from the pyre soon subsided – the fire had consumed the remains very quickly. Gazing at it, Ashoka could not help thinking, *Life and death are merely separated by a breath and no more.*

17

The heat and dust storms of the last few sunsets had rendered the journey a gruelling affair. A sunset later, they would arrive at the holy city of Ujjaini.

Mandar steered his horse to where Ashoka was riding.

'Let us camp near the Mahakaleshwar temple. The advantage being that we will be able to attend the early morning *puja* and take the blessings of Lord Shiva. God knows, we will need his help to destroy any evil that may befall us,' he said excitedly.

Ashoka smiled at him indulgently. 'Maybe our victory lies in how well prepared we are.'

Mandar's face fell at the rebuke. Ashoka's lack of reverence surprised Angad. 'Maybe the gods have some role to play,' he interjected. 'Do not take their *shakti* lightly, O Prince. Take whatever help is given to you, else it may be taken away,' he continued quietly.

'All right. Let us attend the early morning *puja* if you will. But don't sermonize,' Ashoka replied, clearly peeved.

'Your mother would definitely approve of your decision,' quipped Mandar, not backing off so easily.

The thought of his mother brought a smile to Ashoka's solemn face. 'Yes, she would.' He relented with grace.

Mandar and Angad exchanged glances as if congratulating each other on their small victory. Persuading Ashoka to do something he did not want to do was quite a feat.

Setting up camp that evening proved to be an arduous task. The dust storm made it difficult to pitch the tents. Visibility was scanty. The dust and grime found its way into many an eye. Once the task was done, almost everyone huddled in their tents except for the soldiers guarding the camp.

Covered from head to toe in grime, Poulak walked into Ashoka's tent. Angad and Chitrakoot were inside today. Ashoka was washing up from a bowl of water. He looked at the soiled water with distaste when he was finished.

'I definitely do not envy the soldiers guarding us,' Poulak remarked.

Ashoka shrugged.

'A dust storm is nothing compared to what they will need to go through when the time comes,' he said darkly.

'Lighten up, Prince. You take things too seriously at times.'

As an act of indulgence, Ashoka deliberately softened his expression.

'Yes, this is the night for hearing some stories. If you want I can tell you about the history of the Mahakaleshwar temple,' Angad offered.

Ashoka groaned. 'All right, I see there is very limited entertainment tonight. I will have to make do, then.' He sighed.

Angad smiled, knowing very well that in spite of the dry response, Ashoka was actually quite interested. He launched into the story.

There was a time when the Himalayas were young mountains and the city of Ujjaini was ruled by the pious Raja Chandrasen. He was a devotee of Lord Shiva. A boy named Shrikhar was influenced by the king and wanted to join the ruler in his prayers but was refused.

Dejected, the boy wandered to the outskirts of the city, near the river Kshipra. As Shrikhar roamed around the countryside, he overheard the neighbouring kings discuss a plot to plunder Ujjaini. He immediately began praying to Lord Shiva. The locals, who noticed him, realized the reason for his prayers. Word spread like wildfire and reached the ears of a local priest known as Vridhi. He joined the boy in praying to Lord Shiva while immersing himself in the river Kshipra.

Meanwhile, the rivals sought the help of a demon called Dushan. They were successful in plundering the city, and killed innumerable devotees of the Lord. On hearing this, Lord Shiva himself appeared and destroyed the plunderers. After pleas from his disciples, Shrikhar and Vridhi, Lord Shiva agreed to reside in the city in the form of a lingam *and guard its people from any affliction.*

The lingam *is Swayambhu, which means that it is self-created and charged with Lord Shiva and his consort Parvati's shakti.*

Listening to the tale, Ashoka drifted off to sleep while still sitting. The others left the tent on tiptoes, taking care not to disturb him.

The next morning, Chitrakoot awoke Ashoka on the fourth *hora* of the day. They had camped near the Rudra Sagar lake, and Ashoka took the opportunity to take a dip in the cool waters. A certain awareness engulfed him. Maybe it was the effect of the serene waters. He now looked forward to the *puja*.

Soon he and his aides left for the temple. Upon reaching the temple, he was surprised to find it was crowded despite the early *hora*. The compound was expansive with the five-storeyed structure in the centre. It was made of pink stone with beautiful carvings all over. The *lingam* was one of the 12 sacred *jyotir lingams* scattered all over India.

As they entered the inner chambers, a sense of stillness swept over them. The cylindrical *lingam* was made of dark black stone surrounded by a silver *yoni* representing the womb. Together they represented all creation. The huge eyes drawn on the *lingam* seemed to bore into Ashoka's very being.

The head priest, who had been informed of Ashoka's arrival, bowed to him and started the worship. Seven other priests joined him in the slow chanting. The shadows on the walls stood still as all movement ceased. The only source of light in the room emanated from an oil lamp. The vortex of vibrations from the almost guttural chanting had a calming effect on all present. It was as if nothing existed for the moment except the dance of the flame amidst the divine incantations.

As a part of the *puja* the priest offered fruits and flowers to the deity. The focus on the idol was broken when the priest at the far end passed an object with reverence to the one next to him. He passed it further down till it reached the head priest. The room was soon full of suspended grey particles that the priest had flung out of the pot and onto the idol. Someone coughed.

'What's that?' whispered Ashoka to Angad.

'That is fresh ash collected from funeral pyres,' he replied sombrely.

'Ash? Why would anyone offer a deity ash?' Ashoka asked, puzzled.

There was no immediate response as Angad had slipped into a trance, his eyes half shut.

After some time, he whispered, 'Do the ashes not remind you that time never comes back? Do the ashes not remind you that we will face death one sunset and turn to the very ashes you see now? Do the ashes not remind you of the finality of death?' His lips barely moved as he spoke. 'Do the ashes not remind you that the only fear you need to have is of *not* living to your fullest, for the wheel of time overtakes all?' It was as if some faraway voice in his head guided him.

Ashoka inhaled sharply as the impact of the *bhasmaarti* hit him. He became aware of being engulfed in a vortex of energy such as he had never experienced before. The energy seemed to lift him up higher and higher, and then swiftly subsided.

Ashoka sighed as he tuned into the surroundings again. But the realization of the truth lay in his heart. In a way, the realization of the impermanence of his life banished the fear of his death.

Yes, I too will look at death someday. But not before I fulfil my destiny and duty towards my kingdom, he resolved. His hand reached out automatically to his sheath, only to find it empty. He remembered that their weapons had been left outside the temple complex with Chitrakoot guarding them.

The *bhasmaarti* almost over, the priest took some ash and applied it to Ashoka's forehead. Impulsively, Ashoka grabbed a fistful and smeared it all over his head and hair. The stunned priest recovered quickly and blessed him along with all the others. 'May Shiva be with you,' was the sincere blessing.

As the sombre group walked out, they noticed the carvings of Shiva's wife Parvati and sons Ganesha and Kartikeya.

'You will turn to ashes some day, so what is the point of feeding your body so much food,' joked Poulak to Chitrakoot, who had been patiently waiting for them.

'What? I don't understand,' he said, a trifle puzzled.

'Chitrakoot, arrange for everyone to attend the *bhasmaarti*,' Ashoka instructed quietly, hoping that the ritual would have the same impact on everyone as it had had on him.

Sometimes, freedom lies in knowing the inevitable end, he thought.

The weary group was in good spirits as they neared the holy city of Ujjaini. Despite the beautiful hilly countryside they were now crossing, they looked forward to the halt in the city.

Ashoka glanced at Angad who looked pale.

'Angad?' Ashoka eyed him questioningly.

Angad looked up at the sky in a preoccupied manner. 'It is not possible,' he mutteredapprehensively.

'What do you see, Angad?' Ashoka asked quietly.

Chitrakoot, who was on the other side of Ashoka, caught on the thread of the conversation.

'Tell us explicitly, friend…what do you see?' he prodded.

'Prince, let's stop for a break.' Angad covered his head with his hands and continued. 'A shower of stones from the sky… but how is that possible?' he mumbled to himself.

Ashoka signalled to the entourage to stop. He indicated that a couple of temporary tents be pitched for himself and his companions. Although puzzled at the instruction that would break the pace of the journey, the tent pitchers did as they were told.

'I need to be alone for some time,' stated Angad, the troubled look still on his face. He disappeared into a tent without waiting for a response.

Pacing the length of his tent, Ashoka and the others waited for insights from Angad.

He presently entered the tent, his face still ashen. 'Sorry, Prince, I just see a shower of stones on us from the sky,' was all he could say.

Ashoka did not know what to make of it.

'Is it just us, or is it everywhere?' asked Chitrakoot.

That seemed to trigger something in Angad. 'It is just us. We are in a cramped place.'

'So, the question is, if we do encounter this unearthly shower of stones, how do we protect ourselves?' Mandar asked.

'The same way that we protect ourselves from a shower of arrows,' said Poulak.

'Good thinking!' lauded Ashoka, who had been quiet and thoughtful so far. 'We use our shields and get into a tortoise formation. Except, of course, a stone shower will be much heavier than a shower of arrows.'

'There is another aspect – a third of our group are not warriors. We need to protect them…or enable them to protect themselves,' Mandar asserted tersely.

'Your visions had better be correct,' growled Chitrakoot.

Angad gave him a long hard look. 'Believe me. I will be happy if it is otherwise,' he replied dryly.

'Cut it out, you two.'

Surprised at his harsh tone, the bodyguards turned to look at Ashoka.

'Let us talk about what we can do, instead of squabbling,' he admonished.

It was Poulak who came up with a practical suggestion. 'We have extra shields. It will take us a few *horas* to train the non-warriors. I think we can manage.'

'Right. Tell the camp administrator that we camp here for the rest of the sunset. Poulak, you handle the training.'

As everyone trooped out, Ashoka signalled to Angad to stay behind. He asked him warily, 'Do you see what happens to us after the shower…of stones?'

The question hovered ominously.

Angad replied with a steady gaze, 'I don't see it at all. Which probably means that it could go either way.'

Ashoka recalled the ashes on his forehead.

For now I want to live the beautiful illusion called life. The time for looking at the painful truth called death would inevitably come, he thought pensively.

The collective reaction of the cooks, cleaners, luggage bearers, cart drivers, horse boys and tent pitchers was one of bewilderment at the new development. The curious ones asked why they were being trained when soldiers were there to defend the group.

'Oh, this is just as a precaution. Prince Ashoka feels that knowing some basic defence tactics will be good for the whole group,' said Poulak, trying to reassure the anxious faces before him.

'But why now, in the middle of the day? He is usually so particular about our pace. So, why break the journey now?' the chief cook asked suspiciously.

Poulak chuckled. 'As they say, the moment one gets a good idea, one must execute it.'

He turned his back to the group bombarding him with questions, and grimaced at Mandar. In a mock strangulation, he clutched his throat and stuck out his tongue. Mandar guffawed at his friend's predicament. He merely sat on a rock and made no attempt to ease the situation. Poulak decided to get tough.

'All right! We needn't get into reasons for this training. We just do it. Is that understood?' he thundered.

The firmness seemed to work. They reluctantly nodded in assent. Poulak could not help thinking that at times it was force that worked rather than logic.

He did not expect much from them. If they could get into the tortoise and wall formations quickly enough and hold the impenetrable wall, that would be enough. Over the next few *horas*, they practised holding the heavy shields that would cover the person holding it as well as a part of the person standing next to him.

He hoped that Ashoka would not come to check on them. Knowing him, he would find it unacceptable that the group had been disbanded before being completely trained. But he sensed there was only so much that could be accomplished with non-warriors in one session. It would be hard to explain that to Ashoka, though, considering what a hard taskmaster he was.

Poulak and Mandar stood before Ashoka in his tent. Night had crept up stealthily, like a hunter slowly catching up with his tired prey.

'Are we done with the training?' asked Ashoka

'Yes, sort of,' replied Poulak hesitatingly

'Sort of...what does that mean?' Ashoka demanded, furrowing his eyebrows.

'Well...I have done the best I can in a sunset with such an inexperienced group,' he defended himself.

'So, do I take it that they can defend themselves if necessary?' persisted Ashoka.

'Yes, I suppose so,' Poulak replied uncertainly.

'Definitely!' interjected Mandar with confidence in his voice.

Ashoka's face was impassive, still mulling over Poulak's tepid response. He did not seem to have heard Mandar's enthusiastic reply.

'Speak your mind, Poulak. You don't seem too happy with what you have accomplished.'

It was Mandar who spoke. Pointing at Poulak's glum face, he defended his friend. 'He expects too much from them – as if they are soldiers. Fact is, they are not.'

Ashoka scratched his stubble thoughtfully.

'Yes, I suppose if they can save their lives and avoid getting seriously injured, we would have done the job.' As an afterthought he asked, 'Can they manage the wall and tortoise formations to protect their heads?'

'Yes, I have taught them those variations,' Poulak replied.

'Why so pensive then?' Ashoka asked, smiling reassuringly. 'As usual we move at the crack of dawn.'

'There is just one problem,' declared Mandar in a mock serious tone. Everyone looked at him questioningly.

'The head cook will most probably poison Poulak tonight as revenge for the gruelling training!'

The soldiers guarding the tent were surprised at the guffaws of laughter emanating from inside.

Later that evening, as they were served *khichri* around the campfire, the cook pointedly served Poulak a small portion. Ashoka, who was sitting next to him, noticed this and immediately exchanged his plate with Poulak's. The seemingly small gesture was enough for Poulak to realize that beneath the tough exterior lay a sensitive man.

18

Ashoka summoned Mandar to his tent to discuss tactics for handling the expected 'shower of stones'. Mandar did not need even a *kashta* to think. It was as if a stratagem had already been worked out, right to the smallest details. He advised Ashoka to split the entourage in two clusters, so that even if one got caught in the shower of stones, the other would be forewarned. Of course, a lookout soldier would be dispatched ahead of both the clusters to check for any suspicious events.

The discussion went well into the night before every aspect was addressed. Satisfied, Ashoka sank into the soft cushions stacked up on his divan.

'You fought with my father in the battle with Mahishur, didn't you?'

'Hmm, yes,' Mandar replied laconically. He never liked to think about that. The memory of his friend Alok's death was as fresh as if it was a recent event.

'What was it like?' Ashoka asked softly.

'Memories of bloodshed are never pleasant. Beneath the glory of victor lie the wounds of many unnamed warriors… But yes, Emperor Bindusara knows the craft of war well. It was an experience.'

Ashoka sensed his unease and did not probe further. However, he knew he could count on the older man to advise him in a measured manner. Violence would be the last resort.

As was the norm, the next day Ashoka had a soldier dispatched to scout ahead of the entourage, so that they could be warned of any danger. He kept glancing at Angad, hoping he would have clearer visions than yesterday. Angad was still pale – probably the effect of the negative visions.

Ashoka commanded Chitrakoot and Mandar to accompany the second group while he would go with the first along with few of the carts. Angad and Poulak would be with him.

Chitrakoot vehemently protested to what he thought was a convoluted plan.

'You should be in the second group. The first one is more likely to encounter the…shower of stones.'

'That's precisely why I want to be in the first group,' Ashoka replied calmly. This was a deviation from what he had discussed with Mandar – according to that plan, he was to be in the second group.

'We can't allow you to do that. It is our job to protect you and…we intend to do it, no matter what,' Chitrakoot asserted.

'You're not going to go against my orders, are you?' Ashoka asked, smiling.

Foxed at the comment, Chitrakoot did not know how to respond. Helplessly, he turned to Angad for some support.

'Prince, he is right. It would be prudent for you to accompany the second cluster,' Angad said, responding to Chitrakoot's mute plea.

'I can't knowingly put innocent people in danger, can I? Now, let us not waste time arguing and get on with it.'

Angad knew it was a lost cause and sighed. They had no choice but to follow orders.

Chitrakoot and Mandar, who were leading their cluster, were beginning to relax. There no sign of a mishap so far. The withered trees that they passed testified to the dry and hot climate, which sapped energy from men and trees alike. It was almost dusk, and soon they would catch up with the cluster that had gone ahead. In all probabilities, they would sight

Ashoka's group the moment they took the sharp bend. They stopped short as soon as they took the turn, silently taking in the scene that met their eyes.

A quarter of a *yojana* ahead were two steep hills with a narrow path winding between them. It was as if the path was squeezed between two highwalls of rocky hills. But that was not what caught their attention. A huge cloud of smoke billowed from between the hills. They could see what looked like moving tufts of grass in the distance. It appeared that the prince's cluster had indeed been attacked.

So Angad was right after all. A shower of rocks, thought Chitrakoot dismally.

Those on horses raced to the hills.

'Let us split,' said Chitrakoot under his breath to Mandar. 'While you go ahead and see what has happened, I intend to take some men up to those wretches in disguise.'

They gesticulated to the soldiers who were quick to understand. Grim-faced they sped in their respective directions.

'May Shiva be with us!' roared Chitrakoot.

His swiftness belied his bulky frame. There were at least five of the enemy that Chitrakoot could discern. Realizing they had been discovered, they were quick to react and sped off swiftly. They seemed to know the terrain well. It was rocky and uneven, with sharp mounds that would swallow them up with the onset of darkness.

Chitrakoot aimed his arrow, which found its mark on an enemy's shoulder. He fell to the ground, groaning. Chitrakoot caught up with him and jumped off his horse right on top of the man. The enemy writhed in pain as the arrow stood upright piercing the flesh of his shoulder. He twisted his neck to look at his face.

'Who are you?' he barked. 'Why did you attack the prince?'

The man seemed to be in a daze or was pretending to be so to avoid answering any questions. By now his companions had realized that one of them had fallen. The leader of the enemy group turned back and fired an arrow. Chitrakoot was alert enough to protect himself by using the wounded man as a shield. The arrow lodged itself deep into the man's neck, killing him instantly.

For a brief instant, Chitrakoot's eyes locked with those of the leader. They say that every person in the world has unique eyes. Chitrakoot knew that. Even from that distance the memory got etched deep in his subconscious. The eyes seemed to mock him and his futile efforts to catch them. The man vanished a split second later behind a mound, out of Chitrakoot's vision. The soldiers accompanying Chitrakoot had reached him now. One of them tried to revive the fallen man, but he was there only in flesh.

Flinging his sword to the rocky earth, Chitrakoot stood up in disgust. It lay there forlornly.

He hoped fervently that Ashoka and the rest were unharmed. *Or were they buried under the pile of rocks?*

Peaceful so far, thought Ashoka. *Perhaps Angad's visions were not accurate this time.*

They lumbered up a particularly steep hill. In some corner of his mind Ashoka wondered about the soldier sent ahead. He longed to have a word with him now. As they went downhill, he wondered whether the speed was too much for the sharp bend that loomed ahead. Poulak seemed relaxed. Angad still had a tight, solemn expression on his face. The well-oiled carts took the sharp bend easily. The path cut between two high rocky hills was quite narrow and constricted. It forced them to go double file instead of four at a time. Angad fell back as Ashoka and Poulak took the lead.

Ashoka decided to call for a halt as soon as they were out of this terrain, as dusk had set in swiftly. He turned around casually. And then it happened.

Ashoka did not hear it at first. Was that a faint rumble? In a flash of insight, he had perfect clarity of the situation. Ashoka looked up, and there they were – small rocks hurtling down at them at increasing speed. His eyes locked with those of Angad's in silent understanding. *But what is that amidst all the rubble?* Ashoka thought. He strained his eyes, and with a shock realized it was the mangled and bloody head of the soldier who had been sent ahead.

The rocks were streaking downhill on both sides of the path. Stifled cries rose as some of the men were hit. They would all be buried alive!

Ashoka bellowed to them to race through the narrow path between the hills but his voice barely carried across the din. It was the carts that were slowing everyone down. The horses would be able to get out before they were buried but not the carts.

'ABANDON THE CARTS!' yelled Ashoka.

In the ensuing mayhem, nobody understood what he was trying to communicate except for Poulak and Angad, who were the closest. He turned his horse around and yelled a terse instruction to Angad. In seconds the cart drivers were off their carts with only their shields and spears. The horses struggled to maintain their balance. Receiving the signal from Poulak to get into the wall formation, the non-warriors as well as warriors swung into swift action. Both Poulak and Ashoka were astonished and relieved to see how efficiently everyone worked. *Challenging situations do bring out the best in people,* the thought flashed through Ashoka's mind.

The sound of first shower of rubble as it hit the shields was deafening. The men inched ahead, taking care not to break the formation. However, since the path was narrow, at best three could be accommodated in a row.

For the non-warriors, it was an unnerving experience. It was as if the wrath of the gods had befallen them. The vibration on the shields gave the impression that they were in the midst of a massive earthquake. Most of them chanted the name of Shiva.

Ashoka touched the ash still smeared on his head. *Yes, it is true that life can end any moment,* he thought. He took a quick glance at the soldiers around him. Thanks to the rigorous training they had gone through, they appeared calm. He noticed the huge pile up happening ahead. *Would they be able to make it?*

Very edgy now, the horses started to neigh. Ashoka patted his black steed reassuringly. He realized the creatures would not be able to walk over the rocks and rubble that had piled up ahead. Some of them were likely to slip and break their legs. The only chance they had was to go around them, while trying to avoid getting hit.

Ashoka gestured to the riders to take his lead. The horse bearers followed him. The riders held their shields over their heads as protection with one hand and manoeuvred their horses with the other. Those on foot struggled to climb while not breaking the tortoise formation as far as possible. The dust clouds made it almost impossible to breathe and clouded their vision.

Hearing a loud thud, Ashoka turned to see that Poulak's horse had slipped sideways and was unable to regain its foothold. The poor creature had probably broken its leg. Poulak managed to grab Ashoka's outstretched hand before he met the same fate. Using all his strength, Ashoka pulled him up. With a final blood-curdling yell, he managed to haul him over his horse.

Despite their protective shields, many of the soldiers were being battered by the heavy rubble. For a few tense *kashtas* the scene was of chaos and terror.

Ashoka kept going, yelling instructions for whoever could hear. Finally they were out of the constricted path between the hills. Peering through grime-filled eyes, he tried to assess the casualties. All the grains and water stored in the carts was under the rubble. He looked at the bedraggled group around him, exhausted and bleeding, their faces covered with white dust. Bloodshot eyes looked back at the shadowy hills that had threatened to gobble them up.

'Poulak…'

Without waiting for Ashoka to complete his order, Poulak embarked on the task of taking stock of the damage. Men and beast alike had sustained numerous injuries in the unfortunate event.

'How could such an avalanche of stones appear out of nowhere?' Angad muttered, scouring the peaks for signs of movement. Another assassination attempt! It was eerie – there was no sign of any human activity. The assassins had probably perched on top of the hills to ambush them. But where were they now? Maybe they were demons and had vanished into the thin air.

Ashoka mentally thanked Mandar for the insight given to him for splitting the group into two clusters. He wondered whether the second one had witnessed the close shave.

But where are they? Maybe the assassins have massacred them? The questions plagued him incessantly.

He decided to wait for the second group to catch up – if they failed to appear in a *hora* he and some of the soldiers would go back to look for them. They would have to ride around the path, as the decimated carts and rubble had blocked the way.

Angad made himself busy applying a herbal preparation on some of the badly wounded soldiers. Poulak had a huge gash on his left arm.

Ashoka was deep in thought, planning his next steps, when Angad put a hand to his shoulder. A wave of relief went through him as he saw the approaching figures of Mandar, Chitrakoot and a few soldiers on horseback. They had obviously taken a roundabout route as the main path between the hills was totally blocked.

Delighted to see their friends alive, albeit dishevelled and wounded, Chitrakoot gave a whoop of delight. But Ashoka did not return the affection with the same fervour.

'Where are the rest?' he asked tersely.

'We are all right. The carts are stranded on the other side,' explained Chitrakoot.

It was then that Ashoka noticed that a body lay slung over Mandar's horse. He raised his eyebrows questioningly.

'You were attacked from up there,' Mandar explained, pointing to the peak of the hills. 'We got one of them but couldn't manage to take him alive.'

Ashoka touched his forehead to feel the ash. Instead he felt only dirt and grime sticking to his hair. *A second attempt in such a short span of time,* he thought. How many more would he survive? It can't be Susima. The meticulous planning and execution did not sound like him.

Who else would want to see me dead? he thought dispiritedly.

Mandar flung the body down at his feet. The arrow was still stuck in the body, the eyes open, staring into nothingness. Ashoka barely glanced at it. Now that he had a grip on the situation, he barked orders curtly.

'We can't let the cart drivers and a few soldiers remain behind. Too dangerous. Mandar, send a messenger for everyone to assemble here. We will abandon the carts for good. Ujjaini is close and we will replenish our supplies there. I need everyone to be alert tonight.'

'What do I do with this?' asked Chitrakoot.

'I have no use for a dead body. Let his body be dragged like Surya's.' He paused. 'Until it tears apart, piece by piece,' he finished calmly.

Long, slender ringed fingers drummed the arm of the chair very deliberately. Ghataka stared distractedly at the opulent rings with their various coloured gemstones. The red ruby in particular drew his attention.

'He seems to be like a cat with nine lives,' said the young man. He paused for a reaction. Receiving none, he continued. 'It seemed as though he was expecting us. Some of his men sneaked up on us. It was unfortunate that Birju got caught and killed.'

'You are wrong,' hissed the ring-fingered man.

The young man looked puzzled at the comment.

'You see, Birju was fortunate…I would have killed him anyway – painfully,' snarled the man in his nasal voice. 'As I will kill you if you fail yet again.'

The young man knew this was not an empty threat. Yet, he did not feel fear. He never felt fear.

'Go now, for I do not wish to see your inauspicious face. Just go,' hissed the man, pointing his ruby-adorned index finger at Ghataka accusingly. The young man clicked his heels, bowed and lost no time in getting away from the oppressive, dark chamber.

19

Ashoka had planned not to let the city governor know he would be passing through. He personally liked the advantage that anonymity lent him. But, being bereft of provisions left him with no option. He would accept the hospitality of the governor while his men restocked supplies for the rest of the journey to Takshashila.

As the entourage neared the city, they encountered unusually heavy traffic.

This is even more crowded than the bustling Pataliputra, thought Ashoka bemused. Carts full of families with members of all ages were on their way. A large proportion of the crowd consisted of ascetics and Brahmins walking towards the city.

'Ujjaini seems to be richly endowed with Brahmins. I wonder why so many are headed towards the city? They seem to be outsiders,' Ashoka observed.

Angad moved up in order to strike up a conversation with a caravan of carts just ahead. Even though the royal party was recognized on account of the emblem, they were unable to make way for the simple reason that there was hardly any room to do so. He trotted back.

'It's the Kumbh Mela, Prince. It is happening in Ujjaini after 12 years. People from all over the empire come to the event to wash off their sins, by taking a dip in the holy Kshipra river,' he explained.

'So their sins wash off after a dip, eh,' said Ashoka mockingly. 'After my cup of sins is full, I too shall come here for salvation…for I shall have many.' The dark words were spoken with light-heartedness.

'All I can think of is good food, Prince,' said Chitrakoot, licking his lips. 'The Kumbh Mela means nothing to me.'

Angad shook his head disapprovingly.

Ashoka looked down as they passed a group of ascetics. Except for a small piece of cloth between their legs, they wore no clothes and ashes were smeared all over their body. Their abstemious life sounded unappealing to Ashoka. He wondered why they chose to live such a life fraught with difficulties.

As they neared the city gates, the roads were lined with volunteers offering cool lime water to the travellers. Usually this time of the year was cold, but the heat had set in quickly this year, shortening the winter season.

A chirpy group of boys and girls, no more than six or seven years old, ran to the royal group with jugs and glasses of the refreshing liquid. A little girl offered a glass to Ashoka. He took it, smiling. 'Would you like to sit on my horse?' he asked gently. She scurried off shyly without replying.

'I like this city already,' said Ashoka. *I shall reside here someday*, he thought.

Having immensely enjoyed the bickering yet cheerful crowd, Ashoka felt almost sorry as they approached the city gates. The governor himself stood waiting for the prince. Short and squat, he looked up at Ashoka with hands folded in the traditional namaste. He had a pudgy, potbellied appearance. His nose appeared as though someone had punched it in permanently. Despite his unflattering appearance, an aura of kindness surrounded him. Ashoka took an instant liking to him.

'I am Atulya Chauhan, Prince, the governor. I welcome you to my city…to your city.' His voice was a rumble as if it struggling through an obstruction. On an impulse, Ashoka bent down to touch his feet. The gesture caught the governor by surprise. He took Ashoka by his shoulders and helped him back to his feet.

'In that case, I welcome you to your home, son. Instead of staying at the royal quarters reserved for your family, you shall stay at my place with my family,' he said, beaming.

Snapping his fingers, he called the attendant. 'Send a message home that the prince will be staying with us,' he boomed.

Chitrakoot whispered something in Ashoka's ear. Ashoka nodded. Clearing his throat, he said, 'My two bodyguards will be staying with me.'

'But of course. I wouldn't dream of separating them from you. The rest can refresh themselves in the official guesthouse.'

'That will do. Thank you,' said Ashoka.

Poulak and Mandar grinned from ear to ear. They obviously had something planned. He himself would rest today. As they whizzed past the city, he took in the sights with interest. He couldn't help comparing it to Pataliputra. Pataliputra was a bustling modern city while Ujjaini had an ancient feel to it. The striking thing was that there was a temple every 250 *dandas*.

'No wonder they call it the City of Temples,' remarked Ashoka. It was as if the main pastime of the people was to pray and appease the deities. People were either going in or coming out of the temples.

Half the road had been cleared to let the governor pass through. Onlookers stared curiously as they went by.

'It is usually not so crowded, son. Now we have pilgrims coming in from all over the nation, including Pataliputrans, to attend the Kumbh Mela.'

The mention of Pataliputra brought a twinge of pain in Ashoka's heart. He made a fist and thumped his chest unconsciously, as if to relieve himself of it.

'I heard about the accident. Some travellers informed us about the landslide. But I did not know it was your entourage that had faced the brunt of it. The mess should have been cleared up by now,' continued Atulya.

So he does not not know that it was an attempt on my life…and the life of my men, reflected Ashoka.

Atulaya Chauhan's wife was as kind and generous in her hospitality as him. Ashoka and his entourage were soon served a delicious meal.

The *aluka* in tamarind gravy reminded him of his mother's preparation which she often made for him. He hoped she was all right, considering this was the first time he had been away for so long. Making a mental note to send a message across to Mali, he put his attention back to enjoying the dish.

The next day Ashoka spoke to Atulya over breakfast.

'I wish to see the Kumbh Mela,' he told his host.

'By all means. I shall arrange for it then.'

'I don't wish to go officially. I would like to go as a regular citizen.'

It took the governor a moment to comprehend Ashoka's intentions. He weighed his words carefully.

'Your father may not like that, son,' he said quietly.

'Trust me…I do it all the time in Pataliputra.

'We are here to protect the prince,' said Angad. He then looked at Chitrakoot impatiently. 'How much are you going to stuff yourself?'

Angad turned back to Atulya. 'Sir, you see he was starved as a baby and since then feels he should keep ample reserves lest he face the same situation again.'

Atulya roared at his rustic humour while Chitrakoot glared, unamused.

'Let him be,' said Atulya's wife, her maternal instincts coming to the fore.

Grudgingly, Atulya gave his assent to Ashoka's plan. He knew that Bindusara would have his hide if anything went wrong. Apart from that, he felt protective towards the young lad. His keen eyes observed more than what people realized.

He will have his way even if I do not approve, he thought dryly.

Ashoka savoured the feeling of walking in a bustling city without the fetters of his royal attendants. The conviviality and liveliness warmed his heart and the corners of his mouth curled in a smile. His thigh muscles were sore from all the horse riding over the last few weeks. It had never felt so good before to walk on two legs with feet touching the ground.

The Kumbh Mela was largely concentrated on the banks of the river Kshipra. As they neared the venue, the streets became perceptibly crowded with the masses heading towards the religious festival. A large number of government officials and soldiers were on duty to ensure that no untoward incident took place.

Ashoka and his companions took the next turn, and lo and behold, it was a different place. Ashoka's eyes swept left and right across the banks of the river. Steep steps led to the river where the seekers of salvation bathed. In all his life, he had not seen such a large gathering of humanity in one place.

'How about a holy dip?' asked Angad enthusiastically.

'Maybe later,' replied Ashoka, his sight on a group of sadhus wrapped in blankets. At least 20 of them sat on a platform, wrapped in thick blankets. They sat stony-faced and unblinking. But there was something different about these sadhus.

'The blankets are wet,' murmured Angad. 'Dripping wet.'

'Why on earth are they sitting with wet blankets wrapped around themselves?' said Chitrakoot, flabbergasted.

Ashoka nudged a turbaned man. 'What are they doing, friend?'

The man explained, 'You are witnessing one of the competitions based on prowess in *pranayama*. The first one who can increase his body heat through the power of *pranayama* to such an extent that his blanket dries up, will be the winner.'

Ashoka understood then that they were using the technique of breathing through the right nostril – which controls the subtle energy channel, the *pinglanadi* – to increase the heat in the body.

'Interesting!' Angad seemed to be well versed with the technique as well. Many people knew that great masters of yoga could control various mechanisms of their body merely through their breath. The breath in turn controlled various subtle energy channels, which in turn controlled bodily functions such as temperature.

Mystery of the sadhus solved, Ashoka was now ready for his dip. 'Let's go,' he told the other two.

'If you can find a place. I see more people than water,' remarked Angad, turning his head pointedly in all directions. 'On second thoughts, it is not such a good idea. This is the ideal place for an assassination. Given the surge of the crowd, there would be no way to track the assassins. It would be as easy for them as plucking low-hanging fruit from a tree. In fact, we should not even be here. I had no idea about the magnitude of the mob, else I would have tried to dissuade you.'

'Are you by any chance getting any visions?' inquired Ashoka politely.

'Not yet. But, as I mentioned, my abilities are erratic. You can't go just by their efficacy,' Angad said nervously.

For once Ashoka agreed with his bodyguards. He thought of the foiled attempt at burying them alive. Maybe the assassins were close and waiting for another opportune moment.

'Let's go out tonight to explore the city. Poulak and Mandar can join us too,' he proposed as an alternative.

The bodyguards exchanged a look that said 'This is not good!'

'Not a good idea, prince,' Angad said hastily. He looked at Chitrakoot for seconding his judgement.

'Precisely. Not a great idea at all. We stay indoors.'

'Oh, come on,' coaxed Ashoka.

They hesitated, weighing the temptation of embarking on new explorations against the unnecessary danger that it exposed Ashoka to.

Finally Angad spoke.

'All right, but only on one condition. You will stay in our sight at all times. *All times*,' he said, emphasizing its importance.

'Deal!' replied Ashoka quickly before they had a chance to back out.

Angad examined his thoughts, but there were no visions today. 'All will be well,' he muttered, more to assure himself than the others.

Darkness descended swiftly, like a dark cloak. The trio were in the privacy of their simple yet comfortable chambers. Ashoka stood out on the balcony. From that height, he could see the city was still bustling with activity. The bright lights made it even more enchanting. Flooded with people, the market looked colourful and appealing. The temples would be open all night owing to the Kumbh Mela.

He decided to wait for some more time before slipping out with his companions. Atulya Chauhan would definitely not approve of their nocturnal adventures. However, they planned to be back long before dawn.

'It feels peaceful…for the moment,' sighed Ashoka.

They slipped out quietly after a while, Mandar and Poulak also joining them. All trace of weariness gone, they walked at a relaxed pace. Ashoka was in high spirits, pointing at different sights. None of the others had seen this side of Ashoka before. They knew the dark, brooding character well, but the fun-loving Ashoka seldom surfaced. They looked at him almost dubiously, finding it difficult to reconcile what they knew with what they were now experiencing.

After a barren 20 sunsets of punishing travel, the streets of Ujjaini looked alluring. The bright lights and colours were a sight for sore eyes.

They neared a temple that swarmed with people carrying earthen jars in their hands. Curious, Ashoka hailed a middle-aged man.

'May I ask which temple this is, sir?'

The man seemed to be in a rush.'You seem to be new here. I guess half the city is filled with outsiders. This is the Kaal Bhairav temple. Kaal Bhairav is one of the manifestations of Shiva,' he explained patiently.

'And what is in that earthen jar you are carrying?' asked Chitrakoot.

'Look, I am in a hurry, but there is a booth there for guiding travellers like you.' He pointed to the booth at the far end of the street. Folding his hands in an abrupt namaste, he rushed off.

The five sauntered over to the booth. A lazy-looking official sat slumped on a chair, a bored expression on his face as he fielded the questions thrown at him from the tourists.

The group waited for a lull so that they could slip in their query. Finally Angad got a chance to ask the man. 'What is in the earthen jars that everybody seems to be coming out with, from the temple?'

'*Madira*…it's *madira*. I could do with some now,' the official mumbled under his breath.

'*Madira* in a temple – that's crazy!' remarked Ashoka.

Poulak pointed to the *madira* shop a few *dandas* away. It was teeming with people almost falling on top of each other. Given his bulk, he was the obvious choice amongst them to barge into the melee. After some time, he emerged, dishevelled, with an earthen jar in his hand.

They dodged their way into the Kaal Bhairav temple, squeezing through with difficulty to the sanctum sanctorum. It was dark, only the light of a few lamps illuminating the cavernous room. In contrast to the chaos outside, this part of the temple was peaceful and orderly. The deity itself was painted in a bright orange colour with large hollows for the mouth and eyes.

They watched fascinated as the *madira* from a devotee was poured into a large thali, which was placed near the mouth of the deity as an offering. And lo and behold, the deity seemed to consume it right before their eyes! Unable to believe what he was seeing, Ashoka murmured to the others, 'A *madira*-drinking god, impossible!'

The leftover *madira* was returned to the devotee as *prasadam*. Offering their own earthen jars to the Kaal Bhairav, they saw the contents disappear again.

Trooping out, Ashoka bought five earthen jars, one for each of them. 'If God can drink, why not us,' he reasoned to his companions.

Taking swigs from their earthen jars, they merrily walked the streets. Ashoka felt his muscles relax and a deep sense of calm settle over him. It was only now that he realized how tense they were most of the time, waiting to thwart any unknown threat. In fact, he had been tense for most of his life, as far back as he could remember.

Soon, the lights appeared brighter, colours more vivid. The shopkeepers appeared to talk and act in slow motion. He felt good in a strange way. His body felt lighter, almost floating. Struggling to be alert, he tried to focus. But the delicious feeling overtook his senses. He felt as if he was an observer of all the activities around him. A part of him was keenly aware of the surroundings and the other was strangely detached from it. A woman passed him in a bright yellow *antariya*. Was it his imagination or did she look at him with keen interest? Taking a deep whiff of the sandalwood perfume she left behind, he felt intoxicated.

Angad was looking at him strangely. He noticed that his bodyguards had hardly touched their *madira*. Grabbing Angad's earthen jar, he poured the bittersweet liquid down his throat. Poulak and Mandar were down to their last drop too.

They were now at the Kumbh Mela. A large group of ascetics were dancing around a fire. The heat and light the fire radiated seemed apt for Ashoka's mood. He sat down with the others in a corner, watching the flames dance. Thoughts and visions that had lain dormant for a long time found an opportunity to surface. He smiled as he saw his mother waking him up gently from his sleep…the lotus pool where he and Mali played as children…the reprimand when he took the blame for Mali the sunset his clothes were soaked because Mali had pushed him in the pool. Strangely, the image of his father, Emperor Bindusara, who usually evoked intense emotion from him, now appeared watered down. He waited for the wearisome feeling that was usually triggered by his father's presence to come. But he felt nothing now. Bindusara almost appeared mild.

Akila suddenly appeared with his keen, piercing eyes. Even in that hallucination, the twin orbs seemed to bore into him, trying to understand, to gauge whether he was fit to be emperor. What would be their verdict? The eyes drilled through him, the face expressionless. The lips slowly curved into a smile. *Yes, he had passed the test.*

Someone handed him some roasted peanuts. He munched them heedlessly. The lady in yellow who had passed him a little while ago walked towards him now. Only, the face was a bit different. It looked familiar. As she neared, and her features came into clear view, he started as he recognized Kanak. She looked alluring, her steps a graceful dance.

Ashoka jumped up, shaking his head to clear out the wooziness. His mind had been playing tricks on him. Not ready to think about her as yet, he struggled to suppress memories of Kanak. Finally, in control, he looked up. The woman in yellow had disappeared. Poulak and Mandar were cackling at some joke between themselves.

Angad looked at him with concern. 'Are you all right, Prince?'

'Never felt better,' he said, the clamp now securely fastened on the memories that threatened to resurface.

Long, slender fingers of both hands joined together in a namaskar. The eyes were closed and the lips moved silently, uttering a prayer.

The man sat cross-legged in a white dhoti, his long and slim torso bare, praying in front of an idol of Lord Shiva. Soon the lips stopped moving and the man slipped easily into meditation. He was so still that to an onlooker he would seem to be a statue carved in stone.

After a *hora,* the still figure moved and the fingers reached out for the *vibhuti*. He took a little of the sacred ash between his ring finger and thumb, and applied it at two places on his body – middle of the eyebrows and the pit of the throat. This was done to make certain energy centres in the body receptive to divine energy. The sacred ash facilitated that function. The place between the eyebrows activated the *agna chakra* which signified knowledge. The pit of the throat signified the *vishuddhi chakra* which was responsible for power. He knew that.

His meditation over, he walked towards his chambers to get dressed. The emperor would be expecting him.

20

There was still a *hora* left before the first rays of dawn banished the darkness. Emperor Bindusara was in a deep discussion with Akila, Radheya, Ajaya and the chief priest, the rajpurohit.

The discussion centred around the assassination attempt by Surya against Prince Ashoka. Ashoka had sent a communique across to his acharya about it.

'I am appalled at this unfortunate event,' declared Bindusara. 'How is it that this vile person was appointed as my son's personal assistant?' His eyes bored into them. 'Akila, Radheya, how did this happen?' he snapped.

Akila's eyes looked even beadier today.

'I am baffled myself. He came with the highest of recommendations. But that is no excuse. I will take the blame for this mishap,' said Akila, his eyes lowered. The guilt weighed heavy on him.

'Obviously, the rot in our system is deeper than we anticipated,' said Radheya. 'We have already launched investigations.'

The emperor turned to the rajpurohit.

'Prince Ashoka is bound to have enemies given his... er...explosive nature. He listens to very few. It is his karma – something that he has to go through,' said the rajpurohit evasively.

Pacing the room, Bindusara shook his head, not satisfied with the answer.

Radheya controlled his surge of anger at this tangential explanation by the rajpurohit. But he could not utter a word against him. The rajpurohit was a chief advisor to the emperor on a wide variety of matters. He was like the emperor's conscience. Since he was not directly responsible for any governmental portfolio, he was supposed to display an independent judgement devoid of any influences.

'If it was a case of karma, then we would not be having a

discussion today,' said Radheya, ultimately unable to control himself.

The rajpurohit completely ignored him.

'We need to have a *puja* today where I will specifically perform sacrifices for the prince's well-being,' said the rajpurohit unfazed by the barb. He knew the emperor never refused any *puja* or religious ritual that he prescribed.

'You also need to welcome your 20 children who have come from Tosali to meet you,' he continued.

Bindusara coughed. He had 11 wives apart from Rakshita and Subhadrangi. The 11, whom he married to secure political alliances, were not officially designated his queens. He kept them in Tosali, away from his official queens. The queens chose to ignore them. Usually, he went to meet his other families once in a couple of years. But now due to his failing health, his children had come to pay their respects to him.

Susima sat brooding about the fact that he had a little less than two dozen half brothers and sisters. While he had heard about them, he had not met them earlier, and had never really thought about them. Mother Rakshita remained tight-lipped about them. He suspected that she was never really comfortable talking about it. He would meet them with an open mind, though. Being the eldest, he expected respect from his siblings.

He knew they were staying at the far corner of the palace grounds, away from the main palace structure. Gajendra, his friend, and Devendra, his cousin, would be here soon. He wanted to discuss his plans with them. His idea was to invite his siblings for an evening of entertainment. Susima had a whole hall dedicated for this. It included games like chess and cards. For the performance of acrobats, jugglers and storytellers, the far end housed a stage. He dare not have dancers, for fear of his mother's disapproval.

Devendra and Gajendra arrived and were only too happy to take his invitation to his brothers and sisters. They returned, giggling.

'What's so funny?' Susima asked, peeved.

'It was like entering a playground,' replied Devendra. 'Some of your half-brothers are very young. Not in their teens as yet. A number of them are, of course,' he added hastily. 'Your preparations will not go to waste.'

'You have a half-sister too. She is about 14 and...beautiful,' said Gajendra.

Susima chose to ignore the information completely.

'So, have they accepted my invitation?' he asked tentatively.

'Oh yes, except that you may need to equip your entertainment hall with some toys.' Devendra and Gajendra exchanged a look and chuckled.

'One more thing, your sister declined the offer. Perhaps it would be prudent for you to go and meet her personally. Her companions did not want to let go of her,' said Gajendra cryptically. Susima felt a surge of anger at that remark.

How dare she refuse my wishes, he thought.

Susima waited for his brothers in the hall. His mother was not pleased with the turn of events. She had tried to discourage Susima, but he was beyond listening to her except on certain things. She gave in when she realized he was adamant.

His 19 half-brothers arrived. Most of them seemed ill at ease and awkward. Susima tried to see his father's resemblance in them.

One of them stood out. He was perhaps the oldest and possibly was the most regal of them all. He was tall, almost as much as Susima. Their eyes locked. He had beady eyes like Bindusara's – and like Ashoka's. Strangely, Susima felt no animosity or jealousy.

'I am Kartik, son of Bindusara.' He spoke with a confidence almost bordering on haughtiness.

'Welcome, Brother,' greeted Susima with open arms.

Susima felt a warm connection with him and his other brothers. The feeling was alien to him as he did not feel that way about Ashoka. Ashoka was more of an adversary.

'Why didn't Sister come?' he asked.

'Her attendants are extremely protective of her,' explained Kartik.

'What harm could she have possibly incurred by meeting me?' asked Susima.

Kartik shrugged.

'I shall personally come to meet her tomorrow then,' Susima declared. Probing delicately, he asked, 'So, does Father meet you often?'

'Hardly ever. We barely know him.'

That satisfied Susima. He felt relieved to know that most of his father's time and affections were focused here, on his family at Pataliputra.

'How is it that you have never visited Pataliputra before?'

Kartik became reflective at that. 'In a subtle way, we are discouraged from coming here. Oh, we are well taken care of, but there is a tacit understanding that we need to keep a distance from Father. Our mothers are wives, not queens.'

Susima digested the information. And then a thought struck him. 'How is it that we get the pleasure of your company now?' he asked Kartik.

'The rajpurohit sent for us.'

Susima had mixed feelings about meeting his sister. He almost gave up the proposition, but then decided to go. As he walked into the guest chambers, the guards, who knew Prince Susima, did not stop him. If they were surprised to see him, they certainly did not show it.

A lady attendant in her mid-thirties emerged from the shadows.

'The prince wishes to see his sister Vedika?' she asked softly, with respect.

'Er…yes,' replied Susima awkwardly, regretting his decision to come here. But it was too late to back out now. He was ushered into an inner chamber, sparse but comfortable.

Susima drummed his fingers impatiently. He rose instinctively as a tall and thin child-woman entered the chambers. She looked older than 14 – almost a woman, a beautiful one. He suddenly felt at a loss for words.

Susima was relieved when she shyly held out a *rakhi*. At that moment he knew he would protect her as a brother all his life.

She raised her eyes to look at him. He smiled back at her and gave her a fond pat on her head.

She laughed, the ice broken between them.

'I was expecting you yesterday,' said Susima, his statement more of a question.

She hesitated.

'Your reputation precedes you, Brother,' she finally said.

Susima's face turned hard.

'What are you talking about?' he asked harshly.

She looked afraid at his change of tone. Vedika did not know how to tell him that her companions had advised her against meeting him as word had got around of his irresponsible ways with women.

She stammered, struggling to find the right words, at the same time berating herself for bringing this up.

'Please accept m-my apologies. I should not have given in to gossip.'

'What gossip?' he asked, his tone still harsh.

She shrank back, his tone frightening her. But, she could not backtrack now. 'Your reputation with women,' she whispered.

Susima felt the blood rush to his face as the impact of the words hit him. He turned away wordlessly and marched out of the chambers.

Susima rode through the streets of Pataliputra on his horse, Pavan. Despite the early *horas,* there were many who were engaged in various tasks related to their profession. The Pataliputrans were a hard working lot.

The prince tried to analyse his mental state.

What am I feeling now? he asked himself. Until now, he had never experienced this emotion. It was uncomfortable. He wanted to run away from everybody who knew him, run away from himself. He felt as if his chest would burst and his mind explode. Many thoughts clamoured for his attention.

As he rode on, away from the city and into the forest surrounding it, the turbulence in his mind subsided somewhat. Beautiful trees whizzed past. But today, he did not see their beauty. His horse trampled the colourful wild flowers as he raced on.

His mind slightly calmer now, Susima stopped to rest under a tree. With an epiphany he realized that it was embarrassment that he felt – embarrassment at his own behaviour. What had come over him to behave the way he had with women he did not know. He shrank back at the embarrassing memories. They would bother him for a long time to come. And there was something else that bothered him. In certain situations he could not control his thoughts and behaviour. It was as if some demonic tendencies overpowered his rational self.

It had taken a sister's unwitting comment to make him realize that his behaviour had been despicable.

I have to overcome this flaw in my character myself. I can't share this with anyone, he thought. He thought of his vile intentions and cringed. He would endeavour to keep his untamed self fettered from now on.

Satisfied at having come to a conclusion, he sped towards the *turanga* division.

That evening Susima went to meet his mother. She lounged on the divan against the plush silken cushions, looking every inch the regal queen.

Rakshita looked up with concerned eyes when he came in. Susima glanced at the attendants surrounding his mother. She understood and bade them to leave them alone.

Putting his arms around her, he smiled.

She looked surprised at his sudden display of emotion.

'What is it, son?'

'Nothing, Mother. Just wanted to meet you as I know I have caused you embarrassment and grief in the past.'

Rakshita was completely taken aback at Susima's candid declaration. He suddenly appeared to have grown up. The sincerity in his tone went to her heart.

'Let the past be the past, son. Will you have some of your favourite *kheer*?' she asked, tactfully changing the subject.

Susima ate it with relish and resolved to meet Vedika again soon.

A surge of unfamiliar brotherly affection swept his being when he thought of her. Her well-being would be his concern from now on, whether she liked it or not.

21

With a heavy heart, Atulya Chauhan braced himself to bid Ashoka goodbye. In the short span of time they had known each other, he had become very fond of him. He had ensured new carts were provided to the visitors, each well stocked with provisions.

Early in the morning before they were due to leave, Ashoka and his men arrived for a ritual to be presided over by a group of the most learned Brahmins, the Srotiya Brahmins. This was for the safety of the journey. Ashoka had refused the invitation at first, trying to convince Atulya and his wife that his holy dip in the Kshipra would offer him enough protection. He finally acceded to the request because of the insistence of the governor's wife who reminded him of his mother.

A group of four Brahmins entered Atulya Chauhan's garden, where the *havan* would be performed to appease the gods. Trying hard to mask his disdain, Ashoka stood upright, even as Atulya rushed forward to touch their feet in respect. Atulya's wife nudged Ashoka to do the same. His reluctance did not go unnoticed. The head Brahmin took the matter in his own hands and came forward to graciously bless Ashoka.

'Ayushyaman bhava,' he said, raising his hand, palm facing Ashoka.

Atulya tried to mask his annoyance at Ashoka's seemingly brattish behaviour. After all, Brahmins were the highest *varna* and ought to be respected. Especially the Srotiya Brahmins, who were the most learned. They knew the Vedas and presided over all rituals meant for the good of the community.

Ashoka's eyes roamed the sacred enclosure meant for the *havan*. It was an elaborate set-up with numerous offerings laid out. Half the offerings would go the Brahmins themselves. He had no use for the elaborate rituals prescribed by them and thought with disgust of the subsequent *dakshina* they demanded. Leaning towards Chitrakoot, he whispered something in his ear. Chitrakoot seemed to hesitate for a moment and then disappeared to do his bidding.

With reluctance, Ashoka went through the rituals. The chanting of mantras was done in Sanskrit. Once it was over, they handed over the *prasadam* to Ashoka who touched the pot with his hands. It was then sent for distribution amongst everyone present.

'The 20 cows you had asked for are waiting in my shed,' said Atulya respectfully to the Brahmins.

Just then, an attendant scurried up to Atulya. 'Sire, the cows…they have disappeared.'

The governor looked nonplussed. Ashoka sniggered at the dismayed expressions of the greedy Brahmins.

One of them looked at him furiously. 'How dare you. You insult us with your arrogance, Prince,' he said, gritting his teeth.

'If I had my way, the Brahmin community, as it exists now, would be wiped out from the face of this earth,' Ashoka said quietly.

There was stunned silence. This kind of brazen behaviour was unheard of, especially in the city of Ujjaini. Atulya tried to intervene.

But the head Brahmin raised his arm to stop him midway.

'This will cost you, Prince,' he said, seething, his nostrils flared in anger.

Everyone, even Ashoka's companions, were aghast at this lack of respect for the highest *varna* in the Mauryan society.

Ashoka's entourage resumed its journey. Their leave-taking was awkward owing to his behaviour during the *havan*. The only aspect that bothered Ashoka was that he had distressed Atulya and his gentle wife. He did not care whether the unflattering news reached his father.

His hatred for the Brahmin *varna* had not seeped in just like that. In fact, his own mother belonged to this community. There were important lessons of life he had learned from them. But Ashoka believed a rot had taken hold. He had seen people consumed by the undeserved powers vested in the *varna*. Like slow poison, systematically, society had become the cowering victim of the Brahmins.

His thoughts drifted back to certain events of the past.

Arindam was a trader in precious gems and stones. He sold his gemstones – diamonds, pearls, rubies, sapphires, crystals and corals, to either goldsmiths or directly to select clientele who preferred to buy the stones themselves and have them set later by their own goldsmiths. Once in two years he undertook the arduous journey all the way to the northern province of Takshashila and back, to acquire the precious stones.

This journey he hadn't been feeling well at all, and was thus especially glad to be on his way back to Pataliputra. As he sat inside his covered cart, feverish and fatigued, he took out his bag of gems. He did this every couple of horas. Just touching the stones made him feel better. He ran his fingers over a large stone, feeling the heft and hardness of the diamond. The edges felt sharp and well defined. He scratched the stone on his water vessel to assess its strength. Satisfied, he finally held it up to the sky. Passing through it, the brilliant light of the sun scattered around. Mesmerized, he looked at it until his eyes watered. The sale of this single diamond itself would compensate him for all the expenses he had undertaken for the journey.

Something made him look around suspiciously. He was the only one inside the covered cart. But the nagging feeling of being observed stayed. Arindam tied his bag securely and opened the flap at the back of the cart. Peering out, he craned his neck to look at the sides.

Satisfied that nothing was amiss, he secured the flap and went back to his task. He dutifully opened his bag again and spread a blue velvet cloth on the floor. This time he took out his pearls. There were at least a thousand of them, each handpicked by him. Perfectly round, they were smooth, lustrous and pure white. He had painfully categorized each according to size, and placed the groups in different compartments. The oval or triangular ones had all been rejected by his expert eye. Carefully taking out each pearl, he scanned it for flaws, and finding none, diligently put it back in the right compartment.

A couple of horas *later he realized he was hungry.* The other gemstones would have to be checked later, *he thought ruefully. He could miss his meals, but the cart driver needed to be fed.*

Serving out a bowl of thin rice gruel for the driver, he knocked on the front wall of the cart. The driver signalled to the others and the small group of traders travelling together stopped for their meal.

'It will be good to get back to Pataliputra at last,' remarked a trader who was bringing in a consignment of silk fabrics.

'Yes, I have not met my family for half an ayana *now,' replied*

Arindam, thinking of them longingly. He yearned to run in the fields behind his house with his son and feel the arms of his wife embracing him. He would ask his wife to take a few sunsets off from her work at the palace.

'We should be there by evening,' said the silk trader.

Arindam gave an impatient look to the cart driver who was still chewing the rice gruel. Oblivious of Arindam's irritation, he continued to do so. Finally, he went out into the fields to relieve himself. Arindam sat in the cart, his patience close to wearing out. Dragging his feet, the driver returned. Arindam sighed as the carts resumed their slow journey. Alone again in the confines of his cart, his hand reached out compulsively for his bag. His daily chore of examining his gems was still not complete. He now took out a pouch of sapphires, each delicately cut. Closing his eyes, he felt the edges of one. Perfect! He now held it up to the ray of sunlight filtering in. It was unblemished. Not a single scratch on it. After meticulously completing the examination of each stone, he slipped into a deep slumber.

He was jolted awake by the announcement of one of the drivers.

'Pataliputra gates in half a hora*!'*

A ripple of joy went up his spine. He looked at the sun. They would be able to make it in the nick of time, just before the gates were pulled up. Arindam prayed for no traffic. He abhorred being in a queue, waiting for his turn. Peering out through a hole, he saw the driver busy smoking, a faraway look in his eyes. Peeved, he felt like lashing out at him. All the drivers were too slow. The fever coupled with the sparse lunch was making Arindam's head spin. His hand automatically reached out to feel his bag. It was securely fastened to his waist.

As luck would have it, they did encounter a heavy rush of traffic. More so, because it was nearing the time the gates were to close.

He could see the gates now. His beloved wife and son were within the walls of the fortified city. The carts came to a halt. He opened the flap and got out impatiently. The rest of his group of travellers did the same. They looked in dismay at the drawbridge being pulled up before their very eyes.

A hot argument ensued between some travellers and the frontier officers.

'There is still time,' one traveller grumbled loudly.

'We've got to follow orders, understand. We are also out with you on this side of the city. So relax. You will enter first thing in the morning,' an officer said, trying to pacify the tired travellers.

'There is a clearing to your left with wood stacked for fire. Make yourselves comfortable,' said a young officer affably.

With no recourse left, the travellers dragged their feet to the clearing all the while whispering their dissent.

Arindam sighed. It promised to be a long night. He felt his head. It seemed burning hot to the touch, even to himself. His dhoti scraped against his raw skin.

Settling down, he tried to make himself as comfortable as possible around the fire. Free food in the form of potatoes in watery tomato gravy was served, along with chapatis. The food felt like dust in his mouth. He ate little.

He eventually settled down for the night. Placing his bag of gems under his head, he drifted into a disturbed sleep. He dreamed that he was playfully running in the garden after his son. He stretched his hand across and almost grabbed him. Just then he tripped and fell face down in the mud, injuring his forehead badly.

Arindam woke up with a jolt. He felt his aching forehead. He was lying face down on the ground, a small stone jutting out just where his forehead was resting.

Sitting up groggily, he tried to focus. He realized with a shock that the bag under his head was gone. The pace of his heart beat rapidly rising as his panic levels went up, he looked around wildly. It was dawn and the fire was almost out. He shook his companions awake urgently. 'My bag! Has anyone seen my bag?' he almost shrieked in hysteria.

They shook their heads, rubbing their eyes. They were quick to rouse and check their own belongings. Arindam's feverish eyes scanned the surroundings for the soldiers who had settled them last night. He could not see any trace of them. Maybe the shift had changed or they had gone back to the other side. He seemed to be the only one robbed. As the impact of his loss sank in, he felt his head and shoulders grow heavy with the burden. His vision blurred until there was nothing but blackness.

When he came to, he was in his own house. He looked into the concerned eyes of his wife who hovered over him. The other traders had brought him home after checking the address in his identification papers.

'It's a heavy loss,' he said to his wife dully. 'I put all our savings into buying new gems.'

'Hush! Don't talk right now. You need to rest. Here, drink this,' she said gently, putting a glass full of bitter liquid to his mouth. He drifted back into a slumber again.

His wife sat on the bed, looking at the face of the man she loved. It looked haggard. She pondered for a long time and came to a decision.

Two little boys played in the cowshed. A long yagna *was being conducted in the courtyard outside. The husband looked sullenly at his wife. He sat in the* yagna *largely to keep his word to her. This would ward off the evil influences of certain planets and all would be right again. Or so his wife thought.*

Arindam had been unwell for the past month. It was more to do with the depression of having lost his fortune in that unfortunate incident. To add to that, he certainly did not relish being supported by his wife. His wife worked at the palace, but that was mainly to be occupied during the long, lonely months he was away on his travels. This yagna *would strip them of whatever little savings they had left. They were required to feed 50 Brahmins. To add to Arindam's irascibility, was the fact that his wife had sold off her ornaments to fund it. Yes, that made him feel worthless.*

His wife nudged him to pour the ladle of ghee into the fire. He did that automatically, his mind a muddle a thoughts. He should never have agreed. This elaborate yagna *would cost them too much and eat into whatever little savings they had. The* yagna *over, his wife got busy serving the Brahmins an elaborate meal. The neighbouring women assisted her. He went in and now looked out through the crack in the window. He saw one of the Brahmins lick the food off his hands appreciatively. They were a greedy lot. These supposedly learned folk charged a heavy price to appease the gods.*

He went to the backyard. The sight did not please him. The backyard was scattered with humungous pots and pans, still half filled with food. Retracing his steps, he went back to the window again. His wife seemed to be having an argument with the head priest. She looked distressed. Arindam went to find out what was happening. As he approached them, she took him by the hand and dragged him off to the shed. Tears streamed down her face. In the privacy of the shed she put her head to his chest and sobbed.

'We will have to part with our cows,' she said dully

'You don't have to,' said Arindam gently.

'Yes, we do. The success of this yagna *depends on the Brahmins being happy.'*

He felt a deep rage well up in the pit of his stomach. He could feel it growing like a tumour, bigger and bigger till it gnawed at the sides of his stomach. The milk of the cow was akin to ambrosial nectar and provided vital nourishment to his family. Losing access to milk or butter would leave them bereft of an important part of their daily diet. In his heart of hearts Arindam knew that his discomfort was less to do with the cows and more to do with his loss of self-worth in seeing his wife grovel in front of the Brahmins for their cows.

Undetected by them, two little boys witnessed this conversation from under the hay. They lay stock-still, not daring to twitch a nerve. They could see Arindam's shoulders slump and the look of utter sadness on his face.

Arindam watched silently as the last of the Brahmins left their home, licking their lips, their cows in tow. He wanted to do something, but providence had endowed him with no other ability than to assess gems. He had started working with his father from the tender age of eight, and under his tutelage, become adept at distinguishing the real gems from the fake. This was the only passion he had in life, which had turned into a lucrative profession. Whatever he had earned, he put back into the trade, not bothering to save for a rainy sunset. A sunset like this one.

Arindam sat down to eat his sparse breakfast with his son, while his wife served them. She carefully roasted the chapatis stuffed with onions. There was no butter to slather them with and no curd either. These small things seemed like luxuries now. His wife served him his meal brusquely pretending not to notice the absence of butter and curd. She did however notice his hollow eyes.

Their son ate in fearful silence, watching his parents. Why were they not laughing as usual? The cheerful banter he witnessed every morning was a thing of the past. The little boy had grown up since the sunset he had witnessed his parents in the cowshed. He ate his rotis in silence, all the while watching the myriad emotions passing through his father's face.

'It has been some time now. I wonder when the salubrious effects of the yagna *will take effect?' Arindam asked his wife pointedly.*

'I will go and visit the priest for guidance,' she said in a low voice.

'I want to accompany you,' declared Arindam firmly.

'I…I don't think that is such a good idea,' she replied hesitantly.

'Why not? Why do you fear my coming with you?' he asked, knowing very well that she did not trust him to hold his tongue.

Of course, she would not admit this. 'It is just that I will see him on my way back from work.'

'I will come with you,' Arindam asserted. 'I will meet you in the main square at sunset.'

His wife sighed, knowing that it was futile to try to dissuade him.

As decided, Arindam waited for his wife in the main market square. He looked at the colourful objects on display without really seeing them. His wife presently came into view. She tried to conceal her anxiety in vain. But, he knew her too well. Beneath the calm exterior, she was worried about his behaviour. Well he couldn't help it. The priest had better have some answers for him. He tucked a wisp of stray hair behind her ears.

'Let us go,' she said, smiling, the smile not quite reaching her eyes.

'After you,' he indicated with a wave of his hand.

They walked in silence. He glanced at her a number of times. She seemed not to notice, lost in thought.

Presently they reached the priest's home. It was a double-storeyed structure with a huge garden in the front. They waited in the porch while an attendant announced them.

The Brahmin came out after some time. He stopped short, as if not recognizing them.

Then the memory must have come back in a flash. Arindam stood with his arms crossed while his wife spoke. 'We came to ask for your guidance on what to do. There has been no change in our situation.'

'Yes, I remember. The yagna was successful. You will not face the wrath of the planets any longer,' the Brahmin said impatiently.

'What about my trade?' butted in Arindam.

The Brahmin looked at him sharply. 'Everybody has to go through their karma, son. It is your past life that is catching up with you.'

The Brahmin brought his face closer to Arindam's until he could feel his breath. 'Luck does not favour you,' he rasped.

Arindam scowled and met his gaze unflinchingly. Still holding the stare, he spit on the floor and then turned around and began to walk away. The dazed Brahmin took a moment to recover and then sent a torrent of expletives after him.

Before going out of the gate, Arindam gave his wife a last look. She had shrunk into the shadows, her face full of fear of the consequences of offending a member of the highest varna of society.

Arindam left his half eaten roti and got up abruptly. His decision was made. He would swallow his pride and go to work for one of his fellow traders.

He did not pay heed as his wife called after him. Shutting the door behind him with a bang, he walked briskly to the main square. He took a left into a small by-lane less frequented by market-goers. Another left and he was facing a long row of workshops all belonging to his trading counterparts. There were workshops of goldsmiths, silversmiths and traders in gemstones.

The whole community had heard about Arindam's misfortune. Arindam walked purposefully towards the large workshop on the extreme left. It was one of the city's oldest workshops, run by one of his father's friends.

Soon, the stooped old man came shuffling into the room. He peered short-sightedly at Arindam.

'Unfortunate! What happened with you was very unfortunate, son,' he said hoarsely. 'How can I help you?' he asked, waving his hands.

'By offering me a job,' Arindam was quick to reply.

The old man looked taken aback. He stared at the floor thoughtfully and then looked up.

'Son, my hands are tied. My son runs this place now. I am just a figurehead here.' He paused. 'But if I were you I would not go asking for a job anywhere on this street. Word has got around that…' He stopped changing his mind.

'Tell me…I want to know,' said Arindam knowing that the answer would be of significance. He got up and took the old man by the shoulders.

'Luck does not favour you.' The old man paused to assess Arindam's reaction.

Arindam's face hardened. 'Who has said that?' he demanded. 'Do you believe it?'

'What difference does it make what I believe. Others on this street believe it. Oh Shiva, give this child some sense,' he muttered. He turned to the idol of Shiva in the far corner of the room to prostrate before it. When he turned back, the room was vacant.

Arindam dragged his feet back home. Was he so wretched that even his fellow traders shunned him? He thought about taking a loan. But he had nothing to offer as security except his house. He could not pledge his house. It was too risky.

He passed his courtyard, looking at the empty shed. The cows were someone else's property now. The solution eluded him. He walked around his empty house racking his brains for an implementable idea. He wondered when the virtuous effects of the yagna *would occur. As of now the* yagna *had only robbed his family of the last of their savings, not to mention the cows.*

'I will go and get the cows back,' he finally resolved. 'At least my son and wife will eat nourishing food. At least there would be plenty of butter and milk.'

He lay down on his hard bed and stared at the ceiling, a plan forming in his mind. Amidst his thoughts he heard the low rumble of the grinding machines. His house was next to a building where women got together and earned some extra income from grinding wheat. The rumble lulled him to sleep. He awoke with a start. Unable to hear the dull rumble of the grinding machines, he deduced that it was dusk. He had slept through the day. The creak of the front door woke him up; his wife and son were home.

Arindam went out and hugged his wife, smiling as he gave her a peck on her cheek. She stood stock-still, his fervour surprising her. This was probably the best mood he had been in since the robbery.

Arindam regaled his wife with funny anecdotes all evening as she prepared hot chapatis for them. She had got some leftovers from the palace to eat the chapatis with. She was fearful that the sight of the leftovers would banish his light mood. To her surprise, he scarcely noticed it.

His son saw his parents laughing again and felt better. The anxiety that had consumed him after witnessing the distress of his parents in the cowshed now disappeared. All was right again in his world.

Arindam patted him on his head and showed him a new toy cart he had brought for him from Takshashila. He had been so immersed in the repercussions of the ill-fated journey that he had forgotten to give it to his son. His son snuggled into bed with his new toy and soon drifted into a sound sleep.

Arindam went into the kitchen and dragged his wife out by the hand, paying no heed to her protests. He took her to the privacy of their bedroom and made love to her for the first time since he had got back from the trip. Sleep swept him into darkness swiftly.

He woke up past midnight. Careful not to disturb his wife, he walked across the room with soft steps. A sharp pain shot through him as he stepped on something. He held his foot up and pulled out the object that had got lodged in his flesh. It was his wife's earring. Placing it on a table, he quietly left the room and was out of the front door in seconds. The streets were quiet except for the guards patrolling the lanes far ahead.

Arindam walked briskly, passing the cheerful gambling dens and shops that had shut for the sunset. He lurked in the shadows till the coast was clear and then darted into the safety of the dark lanes again. He soon saw the silhouette of the two-storeyed structure in front of him. It was easy to scale the gate and jumped onto the other side. The garden wound around the house. Arindam knew where he had to go. With lithe steps he was at the shed in the courtyard. He opened the door and crept in. The cows sensed his presence and greeted him with grunts. He could see at least 15 of them, in the light of a lamp hanging in the courtyard. The greedy pigs! *They had probably taken them as fee from other gullible people like his wife. It was a mistake he would correct.*

He felt the horns to identify his cows.

I will take them back, *he thought with finality.*

He stepped on something soft. He stifled a yell as he realized he had stepped on someone. Probably the cowherd. He cursed under his breath. He knew he now had very little time to accomplish his goal.

A pair of hands grabbed him from behind and a shower of the choicest of expletives descended upon him. Arindam realized the cowherd would wake up the whole neighbourhood. He yanked himself free, untied his waistband and quickly tore it into a couple of strips.

Grabbing the man's head from behind to steady it, he stuffed one of the pieces of cloth into his mouth. Gagging, the man kicked him in the groin. Intent on the task at hand, Arindam scarcely noticed. He tied the cowherd's hands together and secured him to a post inside the shed.

Arindam led his cows swiftly to the door. As he walked out, he stepped on something sharp. It was just his luck that it was the same foot that was already injured with the earring. In the dark, he felt his foot and pulled out a sharp object, probably an iron nail. Standing stock-still, he tried to assess whether the fracas had woken up anyone. Satisfied, he unlatched the gate and walked out with his cows.

In the morning Arindam woke up to a worrying thought. What will I tell my wife? How had the cows mysteriously reappeared in their shed? *He would say that the Brahmin had had a change of heart and returned what was rightfully theirs. But she would never believe this, or any other story for that matter.*

'I will have to tell her the truth,' he muttered. He reflected on what to tell her as he went about his ablutions. He noticed that his foot was crusted with dried blood.

Just then his son came running to him, excited and thrilled.

'The cows are back. They are back, Baba!' he exclaimed, beaming.

Hearing this, his wife came running out of the kitchen. He met her intense gaze unflinchingly. She knew he was responsible.

At that moment, someone hammered on the door urgently.

The little boy ran to open it. He was flung aside as soldiers barged in. One of them bent to pick him up while the others pinned Arindam's arms behind him. His wife screamed in terror at the sight of the six soldiers. The cowherd stood behind them.

'He is the one! Look at his foot. It is bloodied,' he said accusingly.

'We haven't done anything,' Arindam's wife said, her voice quivering. She was clearly intimidated.

'There is nothing to be afraid of,' said Arindam quietly. 'Don't make a spectacle of yourself.'

The leader of the soldiers spoke up. 'We have received a complaint against you from the priest, his master,' he said, pointing at the cowherd.

'Did you steal some cows from his house last night?'

'I did no such thing,' Arindam said defiantly. 'They were mine in the first place.'

The leader was kind and looked at Arindam with compassion. 'I understand what must have transpired here. But once you have given away something, it is no longer yours. You must come with us. Please cooperate. My hands are tied. You have insulted one from the Brahmin varna.*'*

The words hung in the air ominously.

Arindam spat on the floor defiantly. The soldiers dragged him away while his son and wife looked on with defeated faces.

Arindam lay back on the bed exhausted. It was still early morning but he felt drained of all energy. The act of performing his daily ablutions took away whatever strength and energy he had. With his right hand cut off below the elbow, he could not perform any task with ease. Not to mention the searing pain he lived with.

When will the pain subside? *In fact, he felt as if he still had a hand. He swore he could feel it. The funny part was that he could feel the pain from the elbow down to his fingers. But when he looked, there was nothing. The vaid said he had seen such a condition before, where people felt their arms even when they were no longer part of the body. The condition was called phantom limbs. It usually affected people who used their hands for some unique skill.*

Yes, Arindam did have a unique skill, but it was a skill of the past. He would never be able to feel the smooth surface of gems and diamonds again. It was as if his right hand had possessed an intelligence of his own. A fleeting touch was usually enough to isolate the real from the fake. They had not just cut off his hand – they had taken away God's gift to him. They had taken away his ability to provide for his family ever again. They had taken away his self-respect.

Oh, how he hated it when the curry spilled on his clothes when he clumsily tried to eat his dinner. His wife had rushed to his help the first time. But he had shoved her away, ashamed of himself. She had masked her hurt and pretended not to notice his difficulties since then. He knew she was suffering as much as he was. She loved him and could not bear to see him this…helpless.

Panic gripped Arindam. He began to perspire profusely despite the cool weather. The feeling was terrifying. He swum with the feeling for a few minutes until it gradually subsided.

Mali looked exasperatedly at his cart. The wheel kept coming off. He would go to his Baba to get it fixed. Running to his parents' room, he called out to his father.

'Baba, Baba, the wheel – it keeps coming off. Please fix it,' said Mali, his gaze still on the wheel of his cart.

'Sure, son, I can definitely try,' Arindam answered in a tired voice.

Mali looked up, surprised. His Baba never spoke to him in that tone. He squirmed as the folly of his words dawned on him the very next moment. Walking out into the courtyard, he returned, silently dragging the box of tools to his parents' bedroom. His little mind rebuked himself for running to his Baba for such a thing. He was still not used to the fact that his father had only one arm now.

He tried to brush off the disturbing images of the last few weeks. Flashes of memory came back to him. His father unconscious on a stretcher…the blood-soaked stump of an arm. Running off to the cowshed, Mali had locked himself up – as if that could block out the reality that he had to face. His mother had come to comfort him then. She had not uttered a word but her compassionate touch conveyed what words could not.

Now he stood watching, a silent spectator as his father clumsily tried to fix the wheel with his left hand. He asked Mali to hold the wheel in place while he hammered at it. Mali tried to muffle his scream as the hammer went off the mark and struck his hand instead. Arindam flung aside the hammer in alarm.

'Sorry, son. I…I did not mean to hurt you,' he said, guilt written all over his face.

'It is all right, Baba. I understand,' said Mali, trying to mask his pain. He wished fervently he had not sought his father's help in the first place. Mali watched as his father left the room, his shoulders slumped – a defeated man.

Two little boys sat beside the lotus pool. They were all of seven years but looked like young adults. Instead of prancing around, they sat facing each other, talking sombrely.

'Why didn't you tell me earlier?' demanded Ashoka. 'My mother is the queen and my father the emperor. They would have taken care of your father.'

'My mother would not let me,' said Mali. 'She made me swear to not mention this. But I know I can tell you as a friend. My father's hand…his hand was cut off…as punishment for stealing from a Brahmin.'

Ashoka's eyes opened wide in shock and dismay. 'But he did not steal. The cows were yours. How can they do that…I will tell Mother right now to speak to Father,' Ashoka said with urgency in his voice.

'Don't say anything…I am not supposed to talk about this,' wailed little Mali, clutching Ashoka's hand.

Ashoka felt the blood rush to his face. His emotions were a mix of anger and frustration at not being able to help his friend despite being the emperor's son.

Arindam woke up with a jolt, the agonizing pain in his right hand the culprit. He automatically stretched his left hand to press the fingers of his right one in a bid to allay the pain. But there were no fingers to clutch. His brain was again playing tricks on him, leading him to believe the fingers still existed. But, his eyes saw a neatly bandaged stump instead.

He was alone at home. The rhythmic thump of the grinding in the nearby house was almost comforting. It was silence that was unbearable. That was the time when thoughts of his non-existent future tormented him. Pushing them away only brought them back with a vengeance. He kept thinking in circles till the feeling of panic overtook everything.

Arindam got out of bed with effort. It was noon. He took off his ring with his teeth and put it on the ledge next to the mirror where he knew his wife would find it. Taking a piece of cloth to cover his head, he walked out of their house, not bothering to bolt it. He knew it was safe. In this part of the city no one kept their doors locked.

The tempestuous waters of the Ganga comforted him somewhat. They mirrored his state of mind just then. He sat down on the steps, looking into the deep emerald waters of the river. The winding lanes of his memory took him back in time to the sunset he had married his wife. That was the happiest moment of his life. He still remembered her expression when he gifted her with a rare ruby, the size of a marble. She had worn it around her neck for a full year before depositing it for safety with the queen. He had forgotten about the ruby. It was worth enough – enough for her to take care of herself and their son Mali for some time at least.

He got up abruptly and walked slowly down the steps leading into the river. He would not be a burden on them. If he could not provide for them, then he had no right to exist. She would understand. There was a reservoir of strength in her. He knew that.

The water felt cool. The current that tugged at his feet grew stronger and stronger. It was difficult to balance without an arm. He tasted the water that came upto his lips. Aah…it was sweet. *A wave of calm engulfed him. His foot slipped and he went under.*

Oh Mother, take me into your loving fold and bless my family, *were his last thoughts.*

Ashoka stood shoulder to shoulder with Mali at his father's funeral. Arindam, who had lost all faith in his abilities to restore his trade and family's pride, had slipped into depression and had finally resorted to ending his own life. Ready to be engulfed in flames, his lifeless body lay on the pyre. Ashoka looked at Mali who held the flame in his hands, ready to set the mortal remains of his father's body on fire. His eyes were red from the tears that streaked his face.

The seeds of hatred for the Brahmins were planted in Ashoka's mind.

Queen Subhadrangi got to know about the disaster that had befallen Daya's family much later, when nothing could be done. Emperor Bindusara said that he could not interfere if the man had broken the law. She had taken Mali under her wing then, and ensured that he got the best of education along with her son Ashoka.

22

'*Pranam*, Rajpurohitji. He has done it again. He released the 20 cows given as *dakshina* for the *yagna* into the fields. He disrespects us even though his own nana is a Brahmin,' wailed the distraught Brahmin.

'This is the third incident where he has been disrespectful of us this year.' The Brahmin paused and looked at the rajpurohit for a sympathetic response. Finding none, he continued with his tirade.

'If he was not Bindusara's son, I would have lodged a complaint against him long ago.'

The rajpurohit frowned as he pacified the Brahmins, his annoyance at Ashoka's misconduct increasing with every passing moment. He had seen the signs years ago.

'It is all right, Brother. I will have this taken care of. I will personally speak to the emperor and make arrangements to rein him in before he gets out of hand. His mother is such a gentle soul herself. I wonder how such *samskaras* have passed on to our tempestuous prince?'

The rajpurohit thought for a moment. 'Destiny…it's a play of destiny,' he concluded.

After the Brahmins had left, he sat cross-legged on a

rock on the banks of the tempestuous Ganga. His house had a direct path leading to the river. A flat rock jutted over the waters flowing below. This was his favourite spot for meditating or reflecting. His spine erect, he almost looked like he was carved out of stone. A hymn from the Rig Veda came to his mind.

According to that, the metaphor of the human body is used to describe the four *varna*s. The Brahmins, the highest of them all, are the head. They decide the values to be upheld. The Kshatriyas are the arms who protect the society. The Vaishyas – the traders and landowners – are the legs who work for the prosperity of the economy. The Sudras are the feet, who serve the other three.

The rajpurohit felt disturbed that here was a lad who dared to insult the highest *varna* of the society. If the Brahmins demanded some returns for all the good work that they were doing, there was nothing wrong in it.

He thought of the emperor. A hint of disdain crept in. The emperor was supposed to follow him like a son follows a father. But no, Bindusara had other men to counsel him. Mahamantri Radheya, Acharya Akila and Senapati Ajaya.

On many occasions I am not even invited for discussions, he brooded. *I am the most learned amongst all of them. I know the ancient Vedas like the back of my hand, politics like Chanakya and the science of* yagna *like the great Raja Daksh.* He felt anger creep up his spine like a slow serpent. The tingling spread to his head. There was a time when he did not feel the slightest hint of debasing emotions like anger or hatred. But now, they seemed to overpower him at times…

He touched his index ringed finger to the *vibhuti* on his *agna chakra* as if asking his third eye for insights. He shook his head and got up abruptly, the decision made.

All is fair to protect one's country, he resolved.

The emperor lay on his bed, exhausted. The direction of the bed had been changed, and his head now pointed east rather than north. The latest malady that plagued him was of weak blood vessels. The royal physician had advised him to change the direction of the bed as the magnetic pull of the earth while facing north could cause his brain to haemorrhage. The whole situation made Bindusara immensely irritable.

Susima walked up the path leading upto the rajpurohit's home. There had been no explanation of the summons. Only a note.

Meet me at my house at sunset. Only you. No one else.

This was a request that Susima could not ignore as the rajpurohit was his father's chief personal advisor, or at least he was supposed to be. Taking Devendra and Gajendra along was out of the question. Maybe he wanted Susima to preside over certain rituals and ceremonies for the benefit of the empire.

He was ushered in by a male attendant. The rajpurohit's house looked deserted. *Where was his family?*

The attendant took Susima to the back where a lush garden awaited him with a tree-lined path running across it. The proximity to the river was obvious – he could hear the roar of the waters. The roar grew louder as they neared the bank.

Deep in meditation, the rajpurohit sat on a high rock. The attendant took his leave, and Susima waited, thinking it would be prudent not to disturb the priest.

Presently, the rajpurohit opened his eyes and motioned for Susima to sit down. Susima bowed to him with folded hands and sat cross-legged, looking at him expectantly.

The question caught him off guard.

'Why do you want to be the emperor?' the rajpurohit asked in his nasal voice.

Struggling to find the right answer, Susima stammered out a response. 'I…probably…because I want to serve my people.'

The rajpurohit threw his head back and laughed heartily. 'Are you sure?' he whispered.

Susima looked perplexed.

'Don't lie to me, boy! Look into the tiny crevices of your mind that are almost hidden away…even from you yourself, and you will get the answer.'

Susima knew then that the rajpurohit had seen through his politically correct answer.

'Prince, do you see the sun?' the rajpurohit asked, pointing to the heavens. 'It gives its light and heat to all creatures on earth equally. Ever wondered why?' He raised his eyebrows.

'Well…'

The rajpurohit raised his hand to stop him mid-sentence.

'I can see that I will have to tell you,' he sighed. 'Because it is in its nature to do so.' He paused to let that sink in. 'There are no hidden reasons, no agendas. The nature of the sun is to give its life giving force to every being on earth.'

He looked Susima straight in the eye. 'The time has come for you to look inside your being and figure out what is your nature. Who are you? Why were you born as Bindusara's son? What is your destiny?' he rasped.

Susima had no ready answers.

'Don't bother to tell me now,' said the rajpurohit haughtily. 'Go…go! Contemplate deeply, and then come back and tell me who you are and how you intend to spend your time on earth.'

The rajpurohit went back to his meditative state. Susima walked away uncertainly, an avalanche of thoughts crashing down on him.

Susima's head ached. He realized that until now he had led a sheltered life. Not a care in the world. The only bother had been the presence of that vile Ashoka. His life was largely about materialistic pleasures such as hunting and other entertainment. The only semblance of discipline was due to the fact that he was a student of the severe Akila and, now, a soldier of the Mauryan defence forces. His shoulders felt heavy as a hazy realization dawned upon him – that to be an emperor he needed to have much more than Bindusara as father. It came to him suddenly – Bindusara was unwell because running the vast Mauryan empire had taken a toll on his health.

Do I have it in me? He knew virtually nothing about the practical administration of the state other than what he had read in the *Arthashastra*. But that knowledge would come. He would be attached to some key departments of the state in due course. No…his self-doubts were due to something else that plagued him. Would he be able to lead the hard life that was the inevitable fate of powerful rulers?

He would go to the rajpurohit tomorrow, not to give him answers, but to get answers to many questions that now plagued him.

Susima walked up to the same spot that he had met the rajpurohit last time, on the ledge over the turbulent Ganga. The man seemed to be sitting exactly in the same posture. Susima wondered whether he had moved at all. Of course he would have, for he met the emperor almost every day.

The rajpurohit opened his eyes.

'I thought about what you said last time…but I seem to have more questions than answers.'

The old man smiled encouragingly. At least Susima was truthful. 'Great people spend a lifetime trying to access the inner core of their being. To tell you the truth, I did not expect you back so early. You have pleasantly surprised me.'

Susima wondered why that did not feel like a compliment. Were his frivolities so obvious?

'I think I can be a good emperor, if I try' said Susima slowly.

The pleasant expression hardened. 'Try? Try!' the rajpurohit exclaimed incredulously. 'There are no half measures here,' he snapped. 'There are great sacrifices to be made for power.

Along with power comes responsibility. Are you ready to embrace it?'

The rajpurohit's eyes narrowed. He bought his face closer to Susima's and hissed, 'While you would be surrounded by opulence, it would lose its sheen for you. While you would have the most luxurious bed to sleep on, you will probably lie awake thinking about what you have to accomplish the next sunset. While you will have many dishes prepared for your meal, you may not be able to relish a single one. While you will have the power to pass judgements where your word will be final, you will agonize over whether you did justice or not. While you will have a bevy of beauties for wives, you may not find time to establish a close rapport with any of them. While you increase your territories, your soul will slowly crumble under the pressure. I can go on about it. Do I need to explain further?'

Susima shrank back at the tirade from the rajpurohit. Such was the impact of the words that an uncertainty gripped him. Neither Bindusara nor his mother had ever tried to introduce him to these realities. The onslaught of the cold truth drained him of all energy.

'You look pale. Have I said something untoward?' the rajpurohit asked sardonically.

Susima was silent.

The rajpurohit snarled, 'So, Prince Susima, as you must have realized, the life of an emperor is not what you have lived so far. It is not about festivals and entertainment. If you wish to succeed your father, then you need guidance from someone experienced. Someone who understands politics and administration. In addition to this, he should be able to guide you on your spiritual and emotional advancement.'

He paused for a few moments, trying to decipher the expressions crossing Susima's face.

'But there is one condition without which this will not work.'

'What condition?' asked Susima hesitantly. He tried an uncertain smile.

'You are getting ahead of yourself, Prince,' the priest said condescendingly. 'First, you must decide whether you are willing to pay the price.'

The question loomed large before Susima, and he struggled to come to terms with the new realizations. The lack of reaction angered the rajpurohit.

'Go then, for I do not see that spark in you. You seem to hesitate. This tells me that either you are afraid of the responsibility or you are unwilling to pay the price for it. In either case, my efforts will be wasted.'

He paused. 'So go, Prince.'

The old man got up abruptly and walked back towards his house, leaving Susima staring bleakly into the raging waters of the Ganga. The prince stayed there for a long time, the waters mirroring his state of mind. He sat down, his legs crumpling under his weight.

It was dark before he finally jolted out of his reverie.

Yes, I will pay the price, if that is what it takes to be worthy of the great Bindusara's legacy, he thought with determination. He was sure of that now.

As he walked back to the palace, his pace quickened till he was running...running out of joy that destiny had chosen him to be the firstborn of Bindusara.

Susima walked towards the familiar spot on the ledge facing the river Ganga. This was becoming a ritual now. As usual, he found the rajpurohit deep in meditation. Knowing that he would sense his presence, Susima sat down cross-legged before him.

His eyes still shut, the rajpurohit spoke. 'Why are you here? I thought we had decided that our meeting was of no purpose.'

'You had implied that. I think differently,' replied Susima quietly.

'Why, what has changed in the last few sunsets?'

Susima knew that the question had been posed to test him. 'I am willing to submit to any condition to be worthy of following in my father's footsteps,' he said slowly.

But the priest was not convinced. 'Are you sure?' he asked in his nasal voice.

'As I said,' stated Susima simply.

The rajpurohit looked at him long and hard. The prince bore the gaze unflinchingly.

'Then the first condition is that you must submit to me… *totally*…till you are ready.'

As Susima fixed his gaze on the priest, the impact of the words seeped into him.

The rajpurohit continued, 'By submit I mean that from now on you don't have any existence of your own. You must adhere to my wishes as a son follows a father, as a slave his master. If I ask you to go to the highest dimensions of *swarglok,* you must obey. If I ask you to go to the lowest depths of *patallok,* you must obey. If I ask you to crawl like a mere rodent, you must. If I ask you to fly high like an eagle, you must. You must be like clay in my hands…mouldable.'

Susima took a step back. His confidence wavered. This was too hard a price to pay.

'What if my father's and your wishes do not converge… what then?' he asked apprehensively.

'That is the price you must pay,' the rajpurohit said quietly. 'I can assure you that if you do as I say, you will be more powerful than any ruler in India.' The purohit's eyes narrowed. 'And let us not talk about your father. He deliberately ignores my counsel on various aspects…and he suffers.'

The words jolted Susima. In all his young life, he had heard only adulation for his father. Distressed, he felt like he was joining hands with the enemy.

No…that is not so. The rajpurohit means well, he tried to convince himself. *But…total subjugation to his will…will I be able to do that?*

Unable to come to a conclusion, he folded his hands in a namaste and left.

Unperturbed, the rajpurohit smiled. *You will be back soon.*

The emperor was not feeling well. Akila, Radheya and Ajaya sat huddled together, deliberating over affairs of the state. Listening intently, the rajpurohit sat in the far corner.

Bindusara signed off a statement to abolish the salt tax for 10 villages towards the east as they had not yielded good crops that year. Radheya nodded approvingly as a tax on the farmers was justified only if they were blessed with a surplus crop. Farmers and agriculturists were given many concessions as they were the backbone of the economy.

It was Bindusara's practice to allow his confidantes to bring up for discussion any matter they wished to, before the weekly meeting concluded. This time Radheya took up the baton.

He cleared his throat. 'Your highness, we need to have some direction for…er, succession planning.'

Bindusara slumped back, the corner of his lips twitching in annoyance. This was one aspect on which he had not come to a decision – probably the only matter on which he procrastinated.

'Yes, Radheya, you have reminded me time and again about this. I will have to disappoint you yet again for I do not have any ready answers.' Bindusara plastered a fake smile on his face that told Radheya the extent of his irritation.

The usually persistent Radheya pursed his lips. Surprised at the tepid protest offered by his friend, Akila jumped in, lest the discussion meander to something else.

'What he means to say is that the crown prince is required to undergo a slightly more rigorous training. As you are aware, there are certain aspects of the administration that are not discussed in a regular educational forum.'

Bindusara took in a deep breath, knowing that he was

cornered. 'I am aware, I am aware. No matter what you think, I am still alive and will not leave any aspect concerning the nation unattended. But now that we are discussing the princes, I would like to know Susima's progress.'

Akila and Radheya exchanged a glance.

'Well, his progress in the *turanga* division seems to be average. Nothing to do with his skills. It seems to be more of an attitude problem,' explained Akila.

Bindusara sighed tiredly. 'What about Ashoka?'

'Not once, but twice attempts on Ashoka's life have been thwarted. It would seem that someone is really afraid of his progress. It is unusual for one so young to be targeted,' said Radheya.

Akila's face broke into a broad smile. It was deliberate, so as to soften the impact of Ashoka's situation.

'In a lighter vein, the governor of Ujjaini, Atulya Chauhan, could not stop raving about your son, so says the envoy who came in just yesterday.'

Bindusara raised his eyebrows. 'That's unexpected. Social skills are something I would never have given him credit for,' he remarked dryly.

A soft nasal voice spoke for the first time in this forum. 'Has anyone present here ever heard of the Chinese bamboo tree?'

Blank expressions met his stare. They had almost forgotten that the rajpurohit was present. The emperor looked perplexed at this seemingly trivial intrusion. But as it was the rajpurohit himself, he treated it with as much respect as he could muster.

'Please enlighten us,' said Ajaya to break the awkward silence.

The priest smiled. 'Let me tell you the story of a Chinese farmer.'

There was once a poor Chinese farmer. He planted some bamboo seeds. He had heard that the trees grew up to be strong and healthy. Every morning he watered the seeds and looked at the soil. After many sunsets, there was no sign of any shoot sprouting from the earth. In fact, a year went by. The farmer faithfully watered the seeds every sunset.

The whole village laughed at him behind his back. Their crops grew every year and they made enough to support their families. Another year went by. The farmer would go to his land and stare at the soil in the hope that he would see life sprouting out. Alas, that did not happen. He continued the watering, his faith in the Chinese bamboo unshakable.

After the fourth year, even his own family started doubting his abilities and pleaded with him to grow the conventional crops that others were growing. His wife cried, pointing to their little children and asking how he felt to see them almost starve. Unfazed, he asked his wife to be patient for another year.

Bindusara yawned at this long-winded story of the seemingly irrelevant Chinese bamboo tree. Unperturbed, the priest continued with the same fervour.

In the fifth year even the farmer started doubting his efforts. He trudged along to his land to water it as usual. Thoughts of his impoverished family weighed on his mind. His shoulders felt heavy with the burden of the decision of whether or not to abandon his dream.

He reached his land and stared incredulously. Small shoots were visible, struggling to get their share of sunshine. His joy knew no bounds. He ran all the way back home to call his family and show them that he was not wrong. The bamboos had indeed begun to grow. They hugged each other in happiness, tears of joy spilling down their face.

His family took turns watering the bamboos every sunset. They seemed to grow at an astonishing pace. In 42 sunsets they were 15 dandas *in height.*

Bindusara asked for some water, wondering where the rajpurohit was headed. The others sat listening, a patient look plastered on their faces.

'O Raje, you are wondering why I am rambling along with this story. It is for a pertinent cause.' He paused, looking everyone present in the eye. 'Susima is exactly like the Chinese bamboo.'

Bindusara sat up erect, his interest piqued.

'Water him with your affection, with your confidence in him. He will grow to be the greatest emperor this nation has seen.'

Akila and Radheya had nothing to say. The rajpurohit had very eloquently put across his point of view. They pursed their lips for the moment, knowing that Bindusara was already influenced by him.

Bindusara looked pleased that the rajpurohit had demonstrated so much confidence in his older son. Nevertheless, he tried to mask his emotions by striving to appear brusque and impartial. 'You may or may not be right.'

Radheya could not help thinking that the story of the Chinese bamboo tree applied more to Ashoka than to Susima.

Behind the curtains a woman had been listening to the exchange with bated breath. She now darted away, in her haste almost bumping into one of the attendants carrying lime water.

'Watch out, you one-eyed wretch,' ranted the young woman.

'I may be one-eyed but I see more than most people,' she snarled back and hurried along, not bothering to wait for a response.

'Why don't you understand, son?' cried Rakshita. 'Your wayward ways in the past have cost you. When you were a little boy, your escapades were delightful. When you became older, your pranks were still delightful. But something changed as you grew into your teens. The delightful pranks turned into wilfulness. People noticed. And rightfully so, because of your position. Your rivalry with your brother Ashoka does not help. It only makes people compare the two of you.' Rakshita paused to take a breath.

Susima had his back to her. He clenched the metal glass harder in a bid to control his frustration. The suppressed demons were resurfacing and he could do nothing but endure.

'The only one who spoke highly of you in that meeting was the rajpurohit. Even your own father faltered in his opinion of you. I would like you to meet the rajpurohit,' stated Rakshita firmly, embracing him from behind.

He stood like a rock, not yielding to her affection. How could he tell her that he would have to pay a terrible price for the allegiance? Susima looked at the setting sun. The sun sank low into the depths only to rise again in the morning. Yes, this was something he would *have* to do.

I have to bow down to one, in order to rule many, he thought grimly. He looked at the torch in the far corner, the flames mesmerizing him. If he aspired to be a beacon to many, he would have to burn.

Do I have it in me? One man believed it. He would have to as well.

Susima sat before the rajpurohit.

'Do you remember the *upanyana* ceremony that was performed when you were eleven years old? Well, I will perform it again today because today is the sunset you will be born again. The first was when you came out of your mother's womb.'

The rajpurohit chanted some mantras before putting the sacred thread over Susima's left shoulder and under his right arm. The thread comprised three strands representing one's debt to his teachers, his parents or ancestors, and the sages and scholars who had discovered the knowledge of the universe – *brahman*.

Chanting the Gayatri mantra, he asked Susima to repeat it after him. Susima knew that this verse was one of the most powerful, giving salutations to the creator of the universe.

'Now remember this mantra and internalize it. Let it become a part of you. In time you will realize the strength it will give you.'

The rajpurohit cleared his throat. He reached for the copper vessel kept next to him and poured the water down his throat.

'And for Shiva's sake, improve your posture. Do you realize how much stress you put your internal organs by slouching? And from today onwards you will not sleep on your silken sheets but on the hard floor. While you may be surrounded by opulence, do not make a habit of it. Do not give in to your hedonistic desires.'

I might as well stop living, thought Susima wryly.

The next instant, the priest changed his attitude. His eyes softened, and he said in a low voice, 'There is much that I can give you. There is much that I have. But I have not yet encountered a *shishya* worthy enough.'

He shook his head. 'Not today. I will wait for another sunset.'

23

After an arduous journey through many kinds of terrain, Ashoka arrived with his entourage at the gates of Takshashila. He had sent a message across to the governor that he did not wish to be received officially. He would enter the city as a trader. Apart from his four close aides Chitrakoot, Angad, Mandar and Poulak, the rest would enter using their real identification.

The royal emblem was taken down so that no one recognized them. Ashoka and his close aides kept their fake identification handy. This had been handed over to them in Pataliputra itself as a tool to be used when required.

The gates of Takshashila were magnificent – even more so than the capital city of Pataliputra. As the five rode through the wide roads on their horses, Ashoka could not help thinking that history was etched in every nook and corner of this city. If Pataliputra was modern and Ujjaini ancient, then this was the city where the ancient and modern merged beautifully, with its blend of Indian and Greek architecture. Alexander, the Greek invader, had reigned over this city for five years after Raja Ambhi had submitted to him. Ashoka's grandfather, the great Chandragupta Maurya, had ousted the Greeks and regained control over this city. Takshashila was of strategic importance to the Mauryan empire as it was at the junction of important trade routes from Pataliputra to other parts of the world through the Greek province of Bactria.

Walking the streets were many young men who had come from other parts of the Mauryan empire such as Tosali, Suvanagari, Ujjaini and Mathura. They were here to study. Takshashila was the seat of learning of the Mauryan empire. The streams included the Vedas, medicine, law, military training and all the arts. The great Ayurvedic practitioner Charaka too had obtained his education here. Ashoka could almost hear the verses of the *Arthashastra,* the handbook of economics, for it was here that his grandfather's teacher, Chanakya, had written it.

The world of learning was very vast in Takshashila. Students arrived from places such as Babylonia, Greece, Arabia, China and rest of the world. Of course, this also made it easier for spies of other nations to penetrate the border in the garb of students. It was not uncommon for teachers to unearth persons who were not here merely to study, but to divulge important classified information to their countries. Such cases were reported immediately.

Ashoka longed to meet the great teachers who were the hallmark of the society of Takshashila. He knew that his teacher Akila too had studied here. Teachers imparted education in their own houses. Degrees were not traditionally accorded. The knowledge imparted was considered enough. The students were known by whose tutelage they were (or had been) under. Akila had asked Ashoka to pay his respects to a revered teacher of his. He looked forward to doing that. But that would happen later. He had a mission to accomplish first.

He had refused to meet Governor Huma today. He wanted to get his bearings in place before the meeting. Ashoka noticed that the women were slender and taller than their counterparts in Pataliputra. Their skin was smooth and luminous. Some even had golden hair and light eyes with sharp features, like their Greek ancestors. Many Greeks had married locally and settled down during Alexander's time.

Just as he had liked the ancient city of Ujjaini, Takshahsila too enamoured him, but in a radically different way.

The city had an air of opulence about it. They passed some gambling houses on the way. They looked larger and far more stately than those of Pataliputra. They were owned by the local government and there were strict rules they had to adhere to. The revenue obtained from them was as accountable as any other profession. In fact, taxes were higher on gambling houses, commensurate with the large annual revenues.

After having had his fill of the city for the sunset, Ashoka looked up at the scarlet sky. He looked forward to a well-deserved rest and a bath.

They asked a local shopkeeper the way to the royal palace. The shopkeeper scrutinized the grimy travellers. 'What is your work at the palace?' he asked.

Chitrakoot started to retort but Ashoka's gaze stopped him. 'We are traders and haveto deliver some wares.'

The shopkeeper was clearly suspicious of their motives. 'Down the main road and then two rights and a left,' he said sullenly.

'Thank you,' said Ashoka politely before moving on.

The shopkeeper fixed his gaze on them until they were out of sight. Unlike Pataliputrans, the citizens of Takshashila seemed guarded in their nature. None on the streets had a friendly smile on their face. Ashoka could not help thinking that friendly people live in a friendly world, hostile people in a hostile one. But, it is the same world.

They approached the palace gates only to find them bolted. Angad went ahead to speak to the dour guards. Their demeanour changed the moment Ashoka's identity was revealed. They opened the gates and ushered them in.

A big assemblage of attendants waited silently as Ashoka and his companions approached the palace building. The head attendant, a very short man, stepped forward respectfully to greet Ashoka.

Ashoka jumped off his horse easily and stretched his legs. 'We will not need so many of them,' he said, pointing to the assemblage.

'But, my lord…they have been sent by the governor himself.'

'And who are you?'

'I am Eknath, the head keeper of the palace.'

'Well, Eknath. It's like this. I will interview them briefly tomorrow. I will discard the ones that I do not need.'

The dwarf-like Eknath looked perturbed at Ashoka's pronouncement.

The five walked in stiff-legged. That was what too much horse riding did to men. Their inner thighs were in a constant state of soreness.

A couple of young girls were waiting for Ashoka in his ostentatiously decorated chambers. With eyebrows raised, he turned towards Eknath.

'Bath preparers and shampooers,' Eknath stammered in explanation.

'I don't need any,' stated Ashoka briskly. He nodded to them.

They trooped out, eyeing the prince curiously. Eknath looked at Ashoka unsure of what to do.

'Yes? Do you wish to say something?' Ashoka asked.

'Er, no,' he said, retreating hastily.

Ashoka sighed with relief when he was alone. He could never understand how his father lived with such a lack of privacy. At that moment, Angad walked in.

'I can't understand it. I feel uncomfortable but I don't know why,' said Angad tersely.

Ashoka sighed.

'All right! Let us meet in sometime to discuss possible threats. You can also help me eliminate the staff you are not comfortable with.'

That seemed to satisfy Angad who nodded and walked out.

Ashoka ambled into the inner bath chambers. The sparkling waters of the pool looked inviting. Stripping completely, he waded in.

Ashoka grabbed a fistful of *besan* from a pot and scrubbed himself, his thoughts on what he would do the next sunset. Suddenly his gaze fell on his hands and he got a shock – they were red! 'Is it blood? Maybe I cut myself or scratched an old wound,' he said aloud.

It was then that he became conscious of a burning sensation on his entire body. For some moments, he could see nothing for his eyes were covered in *besan*. When he finally rinsed off the flour, he looked at the pool in momentary shock. It was an unpleasant mix of grime and blood.

With a flash of insight he realized what was happening. Closing his eyes, he submerged himself in the water. A few seconds later he was out, the *besan* mixture washed off. He looked at himself in the mirror. The outer layer of his skin had peeled off, exposing the raw inner layer.

That's all I needed. As if I had great skin and now this, thought Ashoka wryly. He dressed as best as he could. Every touch of cloth against his skin sent a fresh wave of pain which he tried to ignore. It wasn't the pain that bothered him as much the fact that someone was trying to get a message across.

Impatiently, he rang the bell. Eknath rushed in as if he had been waiting right outside the door.

'Please call in my companions.'

An expression of horror crossed Eknath's face as he looked at Ashoka's bloodied hand. The rest of his body had been carefully concealed by an *angavastram*.

'It's only a cut,' lied Ashoka on a hunch.

Eknath seemed to believe him. He rushed to get some balm.

Soon Angad, Chitrakoot, Poulak and Mandar trouped in. Silently, Ashoka bared his torso. Chitrakoot cursed on seeing the bloodied sight. He mentally castigated himself for leaving the prince alone.

Ashoka led the way to the crimson pool. Angad swiftly grabbed the gram paste and took a pinch between his forefinger and thumb.

'It has been contaminated by powdered glass,' he said grimly. 'Not enough to kill. But enough to impair a person seriously.'

'And you got no vision about this?' demanded Chitrakoot of Angad.

Angad shook his head, downcast. 'I was uncomfortable... but couldn't pinpoint the reason.'

'Have Eknath call in the people who have prepared the bath,' said Poulak quietly.

'There were some young girls when I came in. But I think they are innocent,' said Ashoka. 'It is too obvious.'

'That's why, that's precisely why it could be them. Sometimes we don't suspect the obvious,' stated Mandar.

'They...looked inexperienced to me,' said Ashoka, still doubtful.

'The devil does not show his face,' insisted Mandar.

'Very well! You can investigate as you wish,' conceded Ashoka knowing very well that nothing would come out of it.

Maybe someone knew about his mission. The incident was a silent warning of deafening proportions.

'They were shaking like leaves when we questioned them and I don't think they were faking it,' sighed Poulak, exasperated. He was referring to the girls who had prepared the bath. With no other leads to follow, there was no option but to wait and watch.

Ashoka had not divulged much about their mission in Takshashila. He sat now, his torso bare, covered in turmeric and honey. All eyes on him, they waited expectantly.

It was time. It was only fair to let his loyal comrades know the reason for their visit to Takshashila. His own understanding was based on the brief given by Acharya Akila and Mahamantri Radheya.

'It's a case of real turning to fake,' said Ashoka quietly.

The four stared at him, trying to decipher his cryptic statement. Ashoka tossed a silver coin to Angad who caught it deftly. He looked at it intently.

'Real or counterfeit?' asked Ashoka.

Angad looked at it from varied angles. He closed his eyes to examine it. Chitrakoot snatched it from his hands impatiently. He too scrutinized it. Ashoka waited patiently while the coin exchanged hands until it was finally in Mandar's calloused one.

'If you hadn't asked the question I would have assumed it is real,' said Angad slowly and thoughtfully.

'Exactly,' said Ashoka. 'I am given to understand that counterfeits have flooded the markets in Takshashila. It is a matter of time before it reaches other cities via trade.' He paused for a few moments to let that sink in.

'So, someone is minting the fakes and putting them into circulation,' said Poulak, more to himself than to others.

'Yes, and the person is probably a high-ranking official in the administration. No one else would be able to copy the serration on the edges and the design with such accuracy,' Ashoka stated grimly.

'So how do you tell the difference?' asked Chitrakoot, his mouth agape.

'Does anyone have a magnet?' Angad inquired. Ashoka and he exchanged a glance.

Mandar, who carried all sorts of things on his person, took out one from under the fold of his dhoti and tossed it to Angad. Keeping the counterfeit on the table, Angad took out another coin from his pocket.

'I hope this one is real,' he stated grimly. He held both at a slant and ran the magnet over them. The magnet seemed to slide slowly on one and with absolutely zero resistance on the other.

'Did you all understand what he just did?' asked Ashoka.

Blank looks met his gaze. Ashoka explained that silver was non-magnetic and hence a real coin would enable the magnet to slide off with no resistance. The fake most probably had iron underneath and hence attracted the magnet, thus slowing it down.

'Whew! This is bad,' remarked Poulak, scratching his chin.

Ashoka resumed his brief. 'Oh, this is not all. The real trouble just starts after that. Many local citizens have been put in prison or fined for paying taxes in counterfeit coins. They are innocent as they have no idea from where they acquired the fakes. It can be any transaction,' said Ashoka, waving his hands in a helpless gesture.

'There are the stirrings of unrest as the citizens feel cheated of their hard-earned money – and rightly so,' he said, thumping his fist onto the table so hard that the lamp rattled and fell off with a crash.

Scarcely anyone noticed it. The silence was broken as Eknath entered the room. Ashoka wondered whether he had been standing nearby, eavesdropping on their conversation .

'There is a celebration organized in your honour at the governor's house today evening,' he announced.

'That's wonderful. I look forward to that. Please have a message sent across to the governor that I will be delighted to attend,' said Ashoka brightly.

Eknath folded his hands in a namaste and walked out, his short legs carrying him as fast as they could.

'You hate such festivities don't you?' said Angad perceptively. Not bothering to wait for a reply, he declared, 'I hate them too. Protecting you is going to be a nightmare with all sorts of strange men and women around,' he added gloomily.

It is not the festivities I hate. It is the shallow mask of outward celebration people inevitably put on that I hate, thought Ashoka.

The governor's house had an aura of grandeur about it. It was like a miniature palace with a long winding road leading up to the portico with its intricately carved pillars. The lush green trees lining the road looked like green walls on either side. The iridescence of the lamps contrasting with the dim natural light of dusk made the house look warm and alluring. The portico was lit as though Deepawali was being celebrated.

Women adorned with ornaments held thalis of turmeric and vermilion to welcome the guests with a traditional tilak on the forehead. The governor himself stood on the steps, waiting to officially welcome Ashoka and his companions. As Ashoka got off the high chariot that had been sent for him, his eyes locked with those of the governor's. Tall and well-built for his age, the governor had curly hair, small eyes, an aquiline nose and a slit for his mouth. He welcomed his guests gaily. However, the smile did not touch his Greek green eyes.

'Welcome, Prince. It is an honour to have you with us,' he greeted Ashoka.

He nodded to Chitrakoot and Angad who tailed Ashoka

like shadows. With folded hands, Poulak and Mandar offered their greetings. Inclining their heads forward, they allowed the girls to put the tilak on their heads, enjoying the attention.

'The pleasure is all mine, Governor Huma,' Ashoka said emphatically. He too turned to the girls to finish the tilak ritual and then sauntered in, taking in the surroundings.

They trooped down a long corridor, at the end of which were stately wooden doors. Thrown open, they led to a huge room with long windows on either side. Plush chairs with silken cushions of rainbow colours dotted the room. Sandalwood incense made the air pleasantly fragrant. Coconut water, abundant in this part of the country, was being served.

The governor and Ashoka circulated around as the prince was introduced to the key officials at Takshashila. This included the treasurer, chief of mint, the coin examiners, superintendents of gambling, chief controller of entertainers, chief controller of trading, weights and measures, and many more.

As the evening progressed, the mood changed from sober to more convivial. The lamps shone brighter. *Madira* made from rice replaced the coconut water. As the *madira* took effect, the polite murmur of discussions turned raucous and merry.

Ashoka yawned. The official discussions bored him. He looked around for his companions. Angad and Chitrakoot were right by his side. It was Poulak and Mandar that he searched for.

The sound of a gong cut through his thoughts, announcing the governor's speech. His attention elsewhere, Ashoka scarcely paid attention to the well-rehearsed speech. Angad nudged him back to the present as the governor was saying, 'I offer the seat of honour to our young prince.'

Inwardly, Ashoka felt irritated at this strict adherence to protocol. Keeping a smile pasted on his face, he bowed and declared, 'I prefer to stay here amongst the people of Takshashila. I respectfully decline the seat of honour until I deserve it.'

There was silence. And then, a thunderous applause lauded the symbolic gesture. He grinned in response, pleasantly surprised at the reaction.

Relaxing in the congenial ambience, Ashoka commanded Angad and Chitrakoot to leave him alone for some time. Albeit reluctantly, they gave him the space that he desired and hovered in the background. A wave of anticipation went around the hall as acrobats entered, their lithe bodies contorting in every imaginable direction.

Ashoka stifled a yawn. He walked around a huge pillar. A young girl stood there, her back towards him.

'I see I am not the only one bored,' he remarked.

She turned around, startled. 'Oh, I am not bored. In fact, I love the entertainers.'

'Then why are you hiding behind the pillar with a poor view of the performance?'

Her dark eyes struggled for an answer.

'Oh, I think you are shy of crowds. Is that it?' he said.

She glared at him, disliking the unflattering assessment of her personality. Ashoka realized he had unintentionally touched a raw nerve. The many sunsets away from civilization had not contributed to his social skills. Trying to undo the damage, he said sincerely, 'I did not mean to offend you.'

She still looked at him suspiciously, not convinced of his motives.

At that instant a bevy of girls joined them.

'Where were you, Menaka? We looked for you everywhere.' The one who spoke fluttered her eyelids alluringly at the prince.

But he paid no heed – his entire attention was focused on the shy and slender girl, Menaka. He liked the name. He couldn't help remembering the story of the *apsara* Menaka. Legend had it that the sage Vishwamitra did such hard penance that the god of the heavens, Lord Indra, grew insecure about his throne. He sent the *apsara* Menaka to distract him with her beauty and disturb his penance. She came down to earth from the heavens reluctantly as Sage Vishwamitra was known for his hot temper. She feared that once he knew about the treachery he would curse her. But, as Indra was her lord and the king of the heavens, she did as was told. While Vishwamitra was engaged in deep meditation in the dense forest, she transformed it into a garden with beautiful flowers of every variety and started dancing in front of him. He opened his eyes and saw her – his penance was broken... and her mission accomplished.

However, this Menaka was no *apsara* – only a shy girl unwilling to wield her charms.

'I am thirsty and was looking for some lime water,' she told her friends impatiently. 'Let's go. It's too crowded here,' she added pointedly, her eyes on him.

Turning around, she walked away with her friends. He shrugged.

There were many curious glances thrown his way. It had been a long time since someone from the royal family had visited Takshashila. As far as everybody was concerned, he was here on a goodwill visit. The officials did not know about the true nature of his mission. But someone did. He fleetingly remembered the blood and grime...the warning.

Governor Huma came to him, his curls bouncing. His sharp features seemed less severe in the evening light and his mannerisms less formal.

'I hope you are enjoying yourself, Prince?'

'Oh yes. There is only one problem. I seem to have got muddled up after meeting so many people. I can't seem to remember most of them and what they do. How about personal meetings with them?' suggested Ashoka tactfully.

The governor fell for the subterfuge – or maybe it was the effect of the *madira*.

'Of course, dear Prince. It shall be arranged,' he said imperiously. Governor Huma's sallow face looked like it had a little colour now. He lumbered away, a glass of *madira* in one hand.

Ashoka turned back, only to bump into Angad and Chitrakoot. 'You won't leave me alone, will you?' He sighed resignedly.

'We think not,' said Angad nervously. 'There are too many people around.'

The three heard a loud burst of laughter coming from the other end of the hall. They turned to see Governor Huma making merry with the treasury chief and chief of mint. Ashoka had deliberately lied when he said that he was all muddled. He remembered each face and name perfectly along with their designations.

As he scanned the room, his eyes fell on Menaka again. Surrounded by her friends who were chatting animatedly, she seemed to be part of their conversation, yet aloof. But it wasn't a cold aloofness. Rather, it was an aloofness that hid something, a façade to protect. Like an old door deliberately constructed to hide the riches behind it from prying eyes.

Back at the palace, Ashoka was relieved to find that the girls employed as bath preparers and shampooers were no longer there to invade his privacy. Angad walked into the bath chamber to inspect the scrubbing powders and soaps. He returned with a satisfied look.

'No glass powder today,' he announced. He bade them goodnight as he retired to his quarters while Chitrakoot took the first watch at the door.

As the night descended, he lay in bed awake, planning his next move. Once he had decided on the course of action, he drifted into a deep slumber.

The next sunset the five of them walked on the busy streets of Takshashila.

'I sense eyes watching us,' hissed Angad. 'We are being followed.'

'We are doing nothing unusual. Just enjoying the sights,' Ashoka said, unperturbed.

Takshashila had many shops which stocked exotic goods from the Hellenic Kingdoms. They sauntered into a large establishment. An assistant came forward to offer his services. Chitrakoot and Angad were quick to spot a man disguised as a customer. He stood in the far corner, pretending to select a perfume.

An ingratiating smile on his face, the assistant bowed to them. 'May I help you gentlemen?' he asked.

'Yes, I would like to buy the best imported dates,' said Ashoka.

'All five of you want dates?' the assistant asked suspiciously.

'I would like to buy perfume,' Poulak said suavely. 'The others are just accompanying us.'

'Very well, sir,' he said and disappeared to get the wares.

They noted that the shop detective was keeping a discreet watch on them. The salesman brought the goods and they made their selection.

Ashoka whistled as he walked to the payment counter.

'That will be 10 *panas* in silver,' the clerk said

He dug into his pocket and handed over the coins. The clerk handed over the coins to an old man sitting next to him, who examined each one of them closely, turning them over and over in his calloused hands.

'We are in a hurry,' said Ashoka impatiently. 'Just hand over our things, please. I have paid you for them.'

'Not so fast, young man,' said the old man firmly. 'I have to examine the coins first. Are you new to this place? This is standard practice, you know.'

'It doesn't happen in other parts of the country,' remarked Angad.

'Yes. Those were the good old days. But now, there are

cheats. What is one to do? People come in with counterfeit coins to pay for their wares. That is why I have to establish their authenticity before accepting them.'

Satisfied, the old coin examiner nodded to the clerk who handed over the goods. The five of them trouped out of the large shop.

Once they were out of earshot, Ashoka remarked, 'A coin examiner at a shop – this is the first time I have seen such a thing! I thought coin examiners worked only in the treasury. Let us split up and check out some other large establishments. Angad and Chitrakoot will obviously not leave me in peace. You two can go independently.' He waved his hand at Mandar and Poulak.

'That's a good strategy,' said Mandar approvingly. 'We attract too much attention as a group.'

Ashoka chose to enter a gems and jewellery establishment. It was a large one with a number of items on display. A tough-looking guard stood at the door – he let them pass without comment.

'Seems to be quite a crowd here…most of them are women,' commented Chitrakoot.

It took Ashoka only moments to scan the place and the people. The attendants were mostly women too, some of them obliging customers by trying on ornaments for them to see.

'So much for being inconspicuous,' muttered Angad under his breath as the women turned to look at the three young men.

A lady attendant approached them. 'Perhaps you are here to buy something for your mother or your fiancee?' she asked.

'Yes, how perceptive of you. It is for my mother,' said Ashoka pleasantly.

Walking around, he gazed at pendants made of rubies and sapphires. A group of young women appeared from the far corner. They walked past them, chattering cheerfully.

Ashoka blocked the way of the last one. A veil partially

covered her face. Their gaze locked. Chitrakoot recognized the woman from last night's festivity.

'Trying to hide again, Menaka?' asked Ashoka, his arms crossed. 'I wonder why?'

The eyes glared now. She let the veil drop.

'If you could just let me pass through...' she said impatiently. For some reason Menaka found this young man's presence disconcerting. She remembered getting the same feeling the last time she had encountered him at the celebration in his honour. He seemed to peel away her carefully constructed layers.

Ashoka looked at her thoughtfully for a moment and finally relented, letting her pass.

Why does she avoid me? he thought, perplexed.

She crossed over like lightning before he could utter another syllable.

'You wanted to procure something for your mother,' reminded Angad who could be depended on to be focused on the task at hand.

'Oh yes. Something exotic,' he told the attendant who was hovering in the background. 'Ruby is what I really want.'

The attendant smiled at him. It was rare to encounter customers who knew their mind so well. Ashoka looked at the collection carefully, selecting what he thought was the handsomest piece.

'And how would you like to pay?' asked the attendant.

'Silver coins...will that do?' asked Ashoka innocently.

'Yes, but you will need to wait. It will take a while.'

'A while for what? I don't have that much time.' The attendant looked distressed at that. She went in and came out of the inner chambers accompanied by her supervisor, a grey-haired man

'Noble sir, we will need some time to examine your coins for...er, authenticity.'

'What do you mean? Do you think I came here to cheat you?' asked Ashoka with an injured look.

'Oh no, sir, this is standard practice. It seems you are not a frequent customer.'

'Since when is this a standard practice,' asked Angad in a quiet voice.

'For the past 30 sunsets,' sighed the supervisor apologetically.

Ashoka nodded to Chitrakoot, who took out a bag full of coins and put it on the table with a thump.

'All right. We will be back in a *hora*. That will give you ample time to check the...authenticity, as you put it,' said Ashoka acquiescingly.

They ambled over to the main market. It would be interesting to know Mandar and Poulak's experience.

It turned out that most big establishments in Takshashila had their own private coin examiners. The change obtained from them on whatever purchases they had made was tested by Angad for authenticity. It was obvious to Ashoka that they had no part to play in the counterfeit coin scam. The big question was, how were the counterfeit coins flooding the market? There were no answers as of yet, only questions.

Enjoying a dip in his private pool, Ashoka's thoughts wandered to Governor Huma. Every official was required to undergo four kinds of tests for his appointment. They were based on *dharma, artha, kama* and *bhaya*. These tests were conducted covertly through other councillors or secret agents. Depending on the post, the emphasis on the kind of tests varied. For the governor's post, ideally, there should have been acute emphasis on all the aspects. But Governor Huma had bypassed this system because he was a cousin of the Queen Mother, Rakshita. She had managed to coax Bindusara into appointing him. He had given in for the sake of avoiding discord in his marital life.

Mahamantri Radheya had categorically advised Ashoka to

be cautious in his dealings with Governor Huma. The slightest perceived insult would have dire consequences for him, if Mother Rakshita got a whiff. He would have to tread carefully at Takshashila, lest he step on any sensitive toes.

Wading out of the pool, he glanced at the mirror. His skin seemed to be healing fast.

Who could have known that I have come here for a purpose? And what temerity, to have staged a warning on the sunset of my arrival! thought Ashoka. Such an act of treachery on Bindusara's son would be dealt with dire consequences once the culprits were caught.

I will deal with them myself, in my own way, he mused, calm as the vast ocean, the storm brewing in its depths unseen to the onlooker. Ashoka was imbued with a sense of fury not because he was the target, but because it signified a deep rot in the Mauryan system of governance.

Today he would meet the treasurer of Takshashila. He was an influential man to be handling the treasury of such an important trade centre. Governor Huma had himself arranged for the meeting and insisted on being present. Ashoka had politely declined the offer. Huma's half-Greek face had fallen at that.

Ashoka recalled the information on the treasury chief. He was largely a self-made man and had joined the Mauryan administration when he was very young. He had passed the four tests of *dharma, artha, kama* and *bhaya* with flying colours. However, his rise to the post of treasurer had been slow and gradual.

The treasurer heard out the messenger impatiently. It was a bad day to meet the prince.

Aatreya Shah was not feeling well today. His tongue tasted the sourness of his mouth. Just a while ago, he had spewed some undigested food in the toilet. The acid in his stomach had resulted in a splitting headache. Just a small movement of his head caused shooting pains. Speaking required a massive effort – waves of pain darted to his temples when he spoke. He took out the balm that the vaid had provided, and for the third time since morning, profusely applied it on his temples. His impatience was palpable.

Closing the files he had been studying, he stormed out of his office. He would quickly take a round to see everything was in order. With some effort he walked across to the corner of the building. Nodding to the guard, he motioned to him to open the trapdoor. Another threw in the ladder.

Aatreya Shah gingerly climbed down to the basement, a level below. Satisfied with his inspection, he climbed up slowly. A wave of nausea engulfed him. Today was really a bad day to meet the prince. But something told him that protocol could not be ignored with this man.

Ashoka approached the brick building designated as the treasury. He approved of the fact that it was heavily guarded. He had refused any local escorts. Angad and Chitrakoot tailed him. Poulak and Mandar had been sent on errands.

The guards let them pass through without any identification check, noted Ashoka. As they entered a huge hall, an attendant offered rose water.

In a few moments, Aatreya Shah burst in. He welcomed them with profuse warmth that he did not feel. Ashoka remembered his pockmarked face clearly from the day of the welcome party. He was of medium build and average looks. He had bright, intelligent eyes which made up for the lacklustre pitted skin, probably the effect of a disease in his childhood days.

After pleasantries had been exchanged, the conversation trailed to an uncomfortable silence.

'I would love to see the *kosha,*' said Ashoka enthusiastically. 'I have heard a lot about the efficiency of administration here.'

'Really?' said Aatreya dubiously. 'Certainly. I shall personally take you there.'

They walked across the hall to the other offices. 'The chief of mint is not in today, else you could have met him too,' the treasurer told them.

Aatreya led them down the trapdoor to the first basement. This was a huge room with labelled shelves storing every variety of gems and objects made of precious metals. It was well lit and cheerful. The walls were of cool stone and a carefully constructed mechanism allowed natural ventilation. Further down, the next level of basement held coins and currency of not only the Mauryan empire, but also had a section dedicated to foreign currency.

Chitrakoot slipped in a few coins and concealed them under his *angavastram* when he thought no one was looking. Ashoka was well aware of it, though, and hoped fervently that Aatreya had not noticed. The embarrassment would be difficult to handle.

'I hear that there is problem of counterfeit coins in circulation?'

A shadow of surprise crossed Aatreya's face at Ashoka's knowledge. He concealed it quickly.

'Yes,' he said guardedly. 'I suppose there is. We are trying our best to address it.' He pursed his lips, refusing to divulge any further information.

'And what is in the next level?' asked Ashoka, pointing to the trapdoor leading further down.

'It's the coin minting machine…would you like to see that?' Aatreya asked half-heartedly.

'Oh yes. That would be very interesting,' replied Ashoka enthusiastically. All of them climbed down the last of the suspended ladder. This room was cool and bright at the same time. Their attention drawn to the noise, they turned towards the minting machine. The Pataliputrans watched, fascinated.

Aatreya held his head in his hands, the agony of his headache unbearable.

'Are you all right?' asked Ashoka.

Angad felt his pulse. 'He is unwell. Let us take him upstairs into fresher air.'

Due to Aatreya's indisposition, they had to cut short the visit. Ashoka couldn't help wondering whether the illness was brought on by natural causes or was due to his presence.

24

Menaka had loved to paint ever since she could remember. She had fond memories of her mother indulging her with every imaginable colour. They would go off to the river, hand in hand, with a picnic basket. Her mother would spread a sheet and sit by the bank while she scampered around. Amongst her toys she always found a bag of coloured dyes, and would inevitably gravitate towards them. *Horas* would fly in experimenting with them. Her gentle mother did not mind at all if her clothes got splattered by colour.

They would be back in the evening, before her father came back from work. It was important to be home before Father returned. Menaka noticed that her mother was always edgy and nervous around her father. He had a fearful temper. When she was young, she would hide under the bed when her parents got into an altercation. He loved her mother in his own way. Later, she found another way to escape the ugliness of the situation. She would race up to the storeroom on the terrace of their double-storeyed house. Her stock of dyes was always hidden under the knick-knacks. She would start painting and soon be oblivious to the *horas* that went by. Her mother knew of her haven but did not mention it. She probably thought it was best for Menaka to not witness the ugly scenes between her parents. However, inevitably Menaka grew up acutely aware of the tempestuous relationship between her parents.

The attendants had been instructed to leave the main house and stay in the kitchen when her father got into one of his moods. They obliged silently, no questions asked. Her mother paid good wages and was kind to them. That was what mattered.

Menaka sometimes wondered whether her father's behaviour was normal. He was loving one moment and demonic the next. A fight with her mother would inevitably be followed by gifts for her when he had simmered down. The fights happened for no apparent reason or, rather, for any reason. The reason could be as banal as that the house was not as clean as he expected it to be.

But, whatever the relationship with her mother, her father was affectionate towards her when she was younger. He would take her horse riding. Proudly, she would sit astride the horse in front of him. He frequently treated her to sumptuous *idlis* in the busy main market square. Menaka loved that. By nature she was a happy, contented child. It was only later that her relationship with her father gradually changed.

One sunset a cowering Menaka hid under the bed, her hands to her ears, trying to muffle out the ugly fight between her parents. This was the first time she heard her father strike her mother. It was as if she was the one who had been struck. As if lightning had struck an unsuspecting tree. As she trembled, the echo of the slap still resounding in her ears, she heard footsteps approach her room. She hoped it was the kind old woman who cleaned their house. The footsteps grew louder and the door opened with a loud crash.

'Where are you?' she heard her father say menacingly. 'You are going to grow up and turn into a replica of your mother and make someone's life miserable, as she has made mine,' her father shouted in rage.

Her mother ran in, crying. 'Why are you taking it out on her? What has she done?'

'She was born out of your womb and behaves just like you.' He paused to take a breath. 'She is a coward, running off to paint in that isolated room upstairs. I wish I had a son. Instead, I am stuck with you two.'

Her mother ran out sobbing at the declaration.

That was the first time that the realization dawned upon Menaka that her father's behaviour was dictated by the underlying anger and frustration of not having a son. Tears streamed down her face with the sting of the rejection.

When her father had left the room, she ran up to the familiar life of her colours. But, today, she was unable to paint. Her hands shook as she held the brush. Even the azure shade that she loved did not rouse any creativity in her. Menaka sighed and gave up the attempt, her mind a whirlpool of thoughts.

She walked down the stairs tentatively. Her father seemed to have left the house. She saw her mother sitting quietly on the balcony with swollen, red-rimmed eyes. Her mother's pain lay heavy on her heart. Running back to the safety of her room, she bolted the door. Yes, her father was right. She was a coward – she simply wanted to run away from it all.

The environment at home made her listless. The pattern became predictable. Inevitably, her father would burst into her room and end up yelling at her after an altercation with her mother. She served as a sort of a surrogate, to let off the pent-up frustration. A few times, Menaka summoned up enough courage to retaliate only to be subdued with threats of violence. The word 'coward'sprang up a lot.

Menaka became more and more withdrawn. She rarely took pleasure in any of the pursuits that young girls generally indulged in. From a joyous, playful child, she became a reserved young woman. Once a leader of her peers, now she had only a few close friends who stuck by her, including her best friend Zuri. Men in general started to frighten her. She believed that one sunset she would have to marry someone and be stuck in the same hell that her mother was. Her judgment was clouded by the games her mind played.

Then, one sunset, a turning point came in her life and that of her mother. Her mother had conceived after many years. She spent many *horas* visiting temples praying for a favourable outcome. God was kind and answered her prayers. After a difficult labour, she was rewarded by a healthy male child. Her father's happiness knew no bounds. He became loving and attentive to her mother after that. As impossible as it seemed, but she soon put the past behind her and basked in the attention showered on her.

Menaka was relieved the worst was over and they could look forward to a better life. But she felt like a spectator. Her wounds never healed properly. Like frayed ends of a cloth, her family relationships would never resume its newness. The scars remained. She watched as the three of them formed a close bond while she stayed on the fringes.

Now that there was some distance from the past, she suspected that her father regretted his actions. She caught him looking at her quizzically a number of times. But he was a man of few words when it came to emotions. He could not seem to break the barrier that had come between them. An air of formality hung in the air in their interactions.

The world of colours still enticed Menaka and she delved deeper and deeper into it. But an integral part of her appeared to have wilted much before time.

Menaka was in familiar territory, her room full of paintings, when the attendant came up to tell her that her father had arrived home early from work.

How strange, she thought. Her father, a workaholic, rarely came home early. Her mother and brother were away visiting some relatives. Most of the attendants were on leave today.

She felt the stirrings of uneasiness in the pit of her stomach. Not relishing the prospect of the sole company of her father, she tried to refocus to her artwork. Usually when her mother was away, she would have an early dinner and closet herself in her room, staying out of her father's way. It was fine when her mother and brother were around. As her father had eyes solely for his son, she was content to remain on the sidelines.

Menaka continued painting the serene eyes of a Buddhist monk she had seen on the streets yesterday. She wished she could attain that serenity someday. It would be so nice to not swim against the current of her thoughts.

Finally, she reluctantly put the brush down, and looked around at her small but tastefully decorated room. Her mother had converted the small store to a cheerful haven for her. Bright colourful rugs were strewn on the floor with low tables set around.

She went down the stairs, hoping her father would be asleep or would have eaten his dinner. But luck was not on her side. In fact, he was waiting for her. She furtively glanced at his rash ridden face. It looked fierce against the background of his pitted skin. She sat at the table silently while the attendant served them.

'Why do you remain closeted in your room all day?' he snapped.

'Because everything bores me,' Menaka replied defiantly.

'How dare you speak to me like that!' said an enraged Aatreya Shah. Menaka pushed her plate aside, her appetite gone. She stormed out of the room, tears spilling down her cheeks.

She heard Aatreya call out behind her, 'You are no good. Where are you always running off to?'

Menaka slammed the door shut. Blowing out the lamp, she lay down on her bed, willing sleep to overtake her and take her into nothingness. But that was the thing with sleep. The more you called out to it, the further it ran. She shut her eyelids tightly and lay still for an *hora*. Sleep still eluded her.

She could hear a rhythmic sound coming from somewhere nearby. It was the same sound that she heard sometimes at night. Tired of the effort of trying to sleep, Menaka got out of bed, her throat parched. She walked out of her room quietly and tiptoed down the stairs to the kitchen. She thought the sound seemed to get slightly louder. But she was too intent on rushing back, lest she encounter her father again.

He has his beloved son now. Why is he still mean to me? she thought miserably. Her thoughts went back to the altercation. *Yes, that's what I am, a no-good.*

She would cancel the exhibition of her paintings that was earmarked for seven sunsets later. She had been excited about it. But now she had lost her enthusiasm. Listless, she sat on her windowsill, staring at the deserted street in front ofher house.

It was now early morning. As she lit the lamp, her face came into focus on the shiny stone slab on the wall. Her eyes were swollen to almost twice their size. Frustrated, she lay back on the bed, staring into the mesmerizing flames of the lamp. Mercifully, sleep stealthily overtook her.

She woke up feeling woozy. An uneasy feeling washed over her being as she remembered the events of last night. Gazing at the sun, she gauged that it was time for her mother to be back. She would not tell her anything.

Menaka decided to go to her friend's place for the day. Zuri would be sure to make her forget her troubles. She washed quickly and dressed in fresh clothes. A generous dose of sandalwood perfume and she was walking down the stairs, just as her mother walked in with her brother. They were laughing over something. Menaka rushed down and hugged her mother.

Visibly surprised at this overt display of affection, her mother asked, 'Are you all right, child?'

'Yes, Mother. I am going to Zuri's house for the day.'

'Zuri...' Menaka knew her mother did not approve of Zuri's spirited and casual attitude towards everything. But Menaka loved her like a sister.

'Mother, can I stay the night at her place?' she asked hopefully, dreading the prospect of facing her father again today.

'Well...all right. But be back tomorrow, a couple of *horas* after sunrise.'

Menaka dashed back to her room to pack, eager to get away from the suffocation that she felt in her home.

Menaka burst into Zuri's house unannounced. Zuri's family did not mind it – they understood. Zuri's mother greeted her warmly and then got busy putting things in order before she left for the sunset. A senior physician, she had been working for many years in the government-run vaidshala.

It was a blissful home. The moment Menaka entered Zuri's house, she felt her tensions ebb.

Zuri came running from the inner chambers, a bound text of palms in one hand. She was an avid reader. Zuri's mother had wanted her to pursue the science of Ayurveda just like she herself had. But Zuri had other plans. She never attended the lectures, instead preferring to immerse herself in reading in the city library. A harried teacher had spoken to her mother one sunset and admonished her for forcing her daughter into something she had no interest in.

Since then, the free-spirited Zuri was allowed to do what she wished. She had been relieved to know she would not have to put up a charade just to please her ambitious mother. Fortunately Takshashila offered almost 60 to 70 different specializations to students from all over the world. Zuri chose to study Sanskrit, the sacred language of the Vedas, and Mandarin. As there were trade links with the rest of the world, including China, this would be a useful skill to have.

Menaka herself had chosen fine arts and the science of making medicines from herbs. The subjects were at complete loggerheads with each other. But Menaka was equally at ease with both. The hands that could make soft strokes on a canvas could also brew some potent medicines.

She had discovered her affinity for herbs by accident. When Menaka was a little girl, her mother suffered from bouts of splitting headaches which would go away only after *horas* of lying still. On one such occasion, Menaka heard an old lady who worked at their house telling another servant that she could easily cure such a headache. Little Menaka consulted the wizened old woman who gave her the recipe and took her to a place where she could procure the herbs.

Menaka's small hands went to work. The herbs were cleaned and brewed into a potent combination.

The recovery was miraculous. In a *hora,* her mother was her usual self, all traces of headache gone. Since then, at the onset of an attack, her mother would ask Menaka to brew the 'magic potion' as she called it. It worked every time. Over time, Menaka realized that she loved poring over texts on herbs and their properties. Her father would take her along when they visited their family physician. He would allow her to pore over some of his palm leaf bound texts. But the full-fledged science of being a physician was not her calling. The sight of blood made her queasy.

She was thankful that her father considered the specialization of making medicines a worthwhile pursuit. He arranged for her to have the best of teachers. Not many students were taken in at the same time as this knowledge was highly classified. It not only involved the brewing of life-giving combinations, but also poisonous ones that were taken for treating very specific conditions. Apart from this, this science was also used by the defence forces for creating lethal combinations to poison enemy troops.

Zuri now dragged Menaka inside to show her the new attire for her Kathak performance. It was a lovely shade of deep blue with a delicately embroidered gold border. Zuri put on the dress, draping a semi-transparent gold *uttariya* over her shoulders. She broke into slow graceful steps, pirouetting several times. The cloth swirled around her sensually. Zuri's steps increased in frenzy until the naked eye could not discern the discrete moments of her footwork. Finally, she did a few fast pirouettes and bowed deeply. As she straightened up, her *uttariya* fell from her shoulders, revealing her barely covered breasts.

'That was intentional,' she told her friend with a twinkle in her eye. 'Just in case my dance doesn't impress the judges, the final act will.'

Menaka burst out laughing. 'You can't be serious, Zuri!'

'Oh I am,' Zuri replied nonchalantly

'Your dance is so perfect…why do you think you will need to resort to such a strategy?'

'You see, there is a Chinese friend of mine whom I want to entice,' Zuri replied, fluttering her eyelashes.

'Oh well. Your choice in men is strange.'

'And your choice in men is…non-existent. They are harmless creatures, you know,' coaxed Zuri who was well aware of Menaka's inhibitions.

Listening to her voice, Menaka sunk into the cushions contentedly, feeling a deep sense of belonging in this home away from home.

25

The rajpurohit stood waist deep in the tumultuous Ganga, his palms cupping some water. He stood facing east, offering his obeisance to the rising sun. With him, stood the tall, lithe figure of Susima doing the same.

'Offer your gratitude to this universe, Susima,' said the rajpurohit to his attentive student. 'Offer it to the sun without which we would not exist. The millions of creatures and plants in this universe owe their existence to the sun. Remember that if the sun can give life, it can kill too. After every couple of *yugas* great wars of destruction and famines occur when the radiations of the sun intensify. Remember that we are intimately linked to the cycles of the sun.'

The two poured the water cupped in their hands into the river.

'Offer gratitude to not only the sun, but the supreme force which gives energy to the various suns of the universe. Acknowledge the planets and stars whose harmonious vibrations marked your destiny at birth. Offer thanks to the moon whose lunar cycle governs us in mysterious ways,' said the rajpurohit, pointing to the sky.

He continued. 'Express your gratitude for your mother, from whose womb you emerged. To your father too, for you have come from his seed. Offer thanks to every person that you have come in contact with, for they have influenced you in some manner.'

The rajpurohit locked his gaze with Susima before uttering his next words. 'Last of all, offer your gratitude to your brother Ashoka,' he said quietly.

Susima stiffened at the mention of his nemesis.

'Yes, you heard me right, son. He too has made a significant contribution in shaping your destiny. Were it not for him, you would not covet the throne as much. Were it not for him, you would have probably not made efforts to earn it. His shadow behind you makes you walk faster, lest the shadow overtake you. And it can. He only needs favourable conditions like the sun behind him, and no force in the world can change that.'

Susima was lost in the various connotations of that last sentence.

Yes, Guruji is right. Favourable or unfavourable situations can occur at any time. However, one can always turn to face the sun and the shadow will be forced to tag behind, thought Susima.

Aah, Ashoka…I almost miss having you around, he thought wryly.

He looked at the reflection of the sun in the water absent-mindedly. He realized with a start that his guruji was now wading towards the bank. He immediately followed suit.

Following him was becoming second nature to Susima now. He was strongly drawn to the rajpurohit for he illuminated a path for him to follow. In a strange way, he felt glad about it. *In the subjugation there lay the promise of freedom*

Ashoka opened his eyes and lay in bed, planning his day. He would not engage in any official activity today – that would mislead the spies tailing him. He wondered at Governor

Huma's audacity in engaging in such a practice. If the spies were caught, they would probably pretend they were guarding him from harm.

Ashoka swung himself off the bed and headed for the pool, rubbing his palms vigorously. Fingers had many nerves which connected to the rest of the body. Rubbing them jolted him awake.

This pool is the best part of the palace, he thought. He waded into the pool and started scrubbing hard, his senses alert for any burning sensation. The only sensations that he felt was the cool tingling of *besan* mixed with rose water. He would be alert for any odd sensation for a long time to come. His senses recorded every experience like a manuscript written with permanent ink. The welcome to Takshashila would not be forgotten in haste. He sighed and scrubbed harder.

But what could he do about the wave-like emotions that rose time and again from the deepest corners of his mind? They would peak and then recede to merge with the vast ocean. He wondered about Kanak. The laughter, the arguments, the fights…and the end. All those moments were memories now.

'Learning is a process of becoming,' Akila had once told Ashoka. 'If you learn archery, then you must become a warrior for that time. If you learn about economy, then you must think and become an economist…you must become it to know it.' His words came to Ashoka's mind as he got ready to visit the greatest university of the world. Today he would keep aside the purpose he had come for – solving the mystery of the counterfeit coins – and spend time at the university of Takshashila, which had produced the most formidable minds in all the sciences and the arts.

Ashoka refused the use of the official chariot. He along with his bodyguards would ride their horses. Poulak and Mandar had been instructed to roam the streets of Takshashila aimlessly – a ploy to confuse the spies tailing them.

As the three of them neared their destination, the streets

became quieter and cleaner. The foliage of trees overhung the paths, shielding them from the sun. A large section of Takshashila comprised the homes of teachers, large, simple houses painted with bright colours. In order to accommodate the thousands of students from all over the world, they had huge courtyards and rooms where they frequently taught their students.

They reached a sort of crossroad where they saw signs for the state owned buildings offered free to the teachers for their use. The teachers could book them whenever required. Later Ashoka learnt that teachers could place requisitions for any special or exotic material that was needed by them for their classes.

Students of various nationalities walked about the streets. The culture of this part of the town was markedly different from the rest of Takshashila. Unlike the dour citizens, the students seemed quite friendly. When asked the way to the home of Acharya Kichaka, a group of blonde-haired foreign students readily gave directions to the strangers without the air of suspicion typical of other parts of the city. To Ashoka and his companions, it was a welcome change similar to home.

'You can follow us if you wish,' said one of the students with a heavy accent. 'But I see that you are on horses and would prefer to ride.'

The riders presently reached a large house which was plain but neatly planned. The Mauryan flag flew at the centre of the courtyard. The flag was at half-mast. That usually happened when there was a mourning of some sort.

Has there been a death in the family? No, that would not justify the lowering the Mauryan flag, mused Ashoka. Similar thoughts had obviously occurred to Angad and Chitrakoot, for they were looking at him with quizzical expressions.

The gates of the house were thrown wide open and students walked in with easy familiarity. They gave curious glances to the horse-backed riders.

The riders dismounted and trooped inside with a bunch of students, following them to a large hall. The hall was large enough to accomodate at least 150 people. Approximately a hundred students were present today, sitting cross-legged on the floor. No one spoke. It seemed to be a tacit understanding. None of the students questioned the Pataliputrans.

Angad and Chitrakoot looked at Ashoka for directions. He nodded to them to indicate that they would take their place amongst the students. They chose to sit in the second last row. Small tables were placed in front of each student for the ease of taking notes.

Not a single woman…interesting! mused Ashoka.

As the acharya strode into the hall, the students got up to greet him. Kichaka was a huge man with a shock of thick white hair. His long beard matched the colour of his hair. The hair and beard were a stark contrast to his youthful countenance.

He sat down cross-legged on the platform meant for him. Closing his eyes, he muttered a prayer. Then, without looking up, he started speaking.

'I see new faces today. They seem to have lost their way, for I have not admitted them to my gurukul.' He paused before continuing. 'Would they care to stand up and explain their presence?' The voice was soft but there was an underlying firmness that censured their impudence at walking in uninvited.

The three stood up sheepishly. All eyes bored into them. Except for Kichaka's, who busied himself with some parchments.

'We are from Pataliputra, Guruji,' Ashoka said calmly.

'That does not tell me much,' prodded Kichaka.

Ashoka folded his hands in a namaste. 'We apologize for barging in like this. We are not students. It is an honour to meet you, Guruji. My acharya, Akila, sends you his greetings.'

At the mention of Akila, Kichaka looked up, his grey eyes flickering.

'We will wait outside until you are free to meet us.'

Ashoka and his companions left the hall deferentially.

They waited at the gate of the acharya's residence. Presently, a student walked up to them with a message.

'We are taking a break for lunch. Guruji has invited you in.'

Chitrakoot exhaled with relief – as usual, he was starving.

'This way…' said the student, beckoning them to the dining hall.

Kichaka sat in the far corner surrounded by students engaged in animated conversation. Some of the students had volunteered to serve the others. The visitors ate their fill of a hearty meal of dal, rice and vegetables.

After lunch, they were ushered into the inner rooms of the house. Entering a large study, they saw Kichika seated cross-legged on the floor, a low table in front of him. He was busy writing something. Ashoka raised his hand, a signal to Angad and Chitrakoot to wait outside for him.

He went around the table and touched Kichaka's feet in the traditional mark of respect.

'Allow me to give my full introduction. I am Ashoka, the Prince of Pataliputra, son of Queen Subhadrangi by birth, a student of the revered Akila and a Mauryan Kshatriya by deeds.' Ashoka was facing Kichaka now. He settled down across the table, directly opposite the venerable teacher.

Kichaka smiled, revealing a set of perfect teeth. He spoke softly. 'About time someone from Pataliputra took the trouble to come here,' he said with a hint of sarcasm.

Sensing an underlying grievance in Kichaka's comment, Ashoka prodded, 'Guruji, do not hold back.'

Kichaka gazed at him expressionlessly.

'While being a Mauryan Kshatriya is like a second skin, I am simply a student of your student. Let my being a Kshatriya not stop you from telling me the truth…the way it is,' coaxed Ashoka.

Chewing on Ashoka's words and trying to assess him at the same time, the acharya was quiet for a few moments.

'I am in mourning, son,' he said softly.

Ashoka stared at him, puzzled. Kichaka was clearly not a man given to loquaciousness.

'I...I don't understand.'

'Do you know what I teach?' quizzed Kichaka.

Ashoka shook his head slowly, his eyes not leaving Kichaka's face for a moment.

'Law...I teach law. Now, do you understand why I am in mourning?'

Ashoka thought for a moment, and then said, 'A teacher of law can be in mourning only if the law that he upholds so deeply is either not applied requisitely or is disregarded.'

'What would you say when innocent people are put in prison for no fault of theirs?' Kichaka said accusingly. The only thing betraying his emotions was a flush behind his ears. 'Innocent people who are trying to earn a livelihood are put in prison just because they have unwittingly broken the law of the great Mauryans. Laws are meant to protect people, not make victims out of them,' he said angrily.

'Are you here on a goodwill visit or can you do something about it?'

Ashoka paled.

'You asked for the truth, then here it is. Counterfeit coins, son. That's what I am talking about,' Kichaka hissed. 'Counterfeit coins find their way into the hands of common people. Once they pay their taxes, the counterfeits are detected at the *kosha* and the innocents are punished if their tax submissions had fake coins.'

'I am sure Governor Huma knows about this. What has he done?' asked Ashoka, his eyebrows furrowed.

'You are asking me?' Kichaka said incredulously. 'Pataliputrans should be in control of what is happening here. If not, there is definitely a failure in your administration. Tell Akila that I expected more from him,' he snapped.

Ashoka folded his hands.

'I beg you to not insult my revered teacher. I understand the problem and I will not hide the fact that I have been sent here to address it. I know I can trust you with my secret,' said Ashoka, trying to pacify the agitated Kichaka.

Kichaka had regained his composure by then. 'You asked me about Governor Huma…he has done nothing. He chooses to look away when atrocities are being committed in his own province.'

'Why is that?' Ashoka asked sharply.

Kichaka shook his head silently. 'Alas, I am just a teacher of law. I do not have the answers with me now, Prince.'

'Then I ask this teacher to work with me in ameliorating the situation at hand' said Ashoka staring unblinkingly at Kichaka. His intention was perfectly clear to Kichaka.

'Do not set such small goals, Prince. I will work with you only if you swear to uproot this canker by its roots. We need to cut the roots, else the plant will grow again,' said Kichaka passionately. He smoothed back his mass of white hair.

'It will be done, acharya,' whispered Ashoka. 'And one more request, Guruji. Please do not hoist the Mauryan flag at half mast. It pains me,' said Ashoka with emotion.

Kichaka smiled. Someone cared at last.

It was a grim trio who walked out of Kichaka's home. Ashoka looked at the flag. His hands itched to go and hoist it up. The true place of the Mauryan flag was up there amidst the vastness of the sky. But he thought better of it.

The intensity of his emotions surprised him. Maybe his mother's recounting of the stories of his grandfather, the great Chandragupta Maurya, had instilled in him a sense of pride for his heritage. Clenching his fist, he forced himself to look away. Ashoka ruminated over the discussion with Kichaka.

Kichaka must be a very respected teacher to have gotten away with his blatant disrespect for the Mauryan flag. This behaviour would have cost him dearly if this had been Pataliputra. Ashoka's thoughts drifted to his father. He did not seem larger than life now. The time and distance away from him had done him good. *They say that to see a mountain for what it is, you need to stand some distance away*, he mused.

They reached a crossroads. Many young students hung about. It was close to dusk and they were possibly going home, or in the case of foreign students, to their paying guest accommodations.

Chitrakoot and Ashoka noticed a couple of young women at the same time. The three of them bowed.

It was Menaka with her friend Zuri. She greeted him half-heartedly. 'Greetings, Prince. It is strange to find you in this part of the city.'

'Why would you say that?' asked Ashoka, unable to decipher her statement.

Menaka bit her lip. Why did she have to say that? 'Oh, I only meant that your stature begets that you would be involved in more important matters of the state,' she replied vaguely.

Ashoka waved away his so-called stature. 'In fact, it is I who envy the fact that you have the opportunity to learn under such great masters. Pray, what skills do you acquire here?'

Menaka hesitated.

'Menaka is pursuing fine arts and the subtle art of brewing potent herbs,' Zuri spoke up quickly.

'That's…unusual for a woman,' said Ashoka, his interest piqued.

Angad looked visibly interested. 'Brewing herbs – this skill would have various applications. Some not very pleasant.' He looked at her, hoping she would elaborate.

'For that very reason, I can tell you no more than what has already been said. We are not allowed to discuss the subject while we are still students,' explained Menaka hastily.

'There would be no breach of security if you told me anything as…er, I am part of the government,' said Ashoka, uncharacteristically inarticulate.

Menaka laughed at the feeble attempt at humour. 'That's a nice way of putting it,' she said. 'But we have to get back home.'

Ashoka pretended not to notice the snub.

Trying to take the edge off her friend's curtness, Zuri spoke to them cheerfully, inviting them for a cultural festival where she was to perform.

Later as they were walking home, Zuri questioned Menaka. 'There was no hurry to get back, so why the false excuse?' she said, exasperated at her friend's aloof behaviour.

'Honestly, I don't know,' replied Menaka, telling the truth.

'We haven't come here to attend cultural festivals, you know,' muttered Angad, decidedly uncomfortable at the idea.

'Look, it is a good idea to mingle with the youth here. The youth are fearless. They tend to be vocal about current issues. We might get some information that may come in handy,' explained Ashoka patiently.

'I think he has a point,' conceded Chitrakoot.

'Oh really? I think you are just looking forward to free snacks there and nothing else,' retorted Angad.

Chitrakoot dug into the bag hanging from his saddle, grabbed the first thing he found and threw it at Angad. He ducked effortlessly. The apple flew past him and was caught deftly by Ashoka.

'Sometimes I wonder whether I have bodyguards or clowns,' he said, making a droll face.

He thought about the festival. He was interested in attending for reasons of his own.

Ashoka and his four comrades made their way to the university the next sunset. Drum beats guided them to the cultural centre located amidst the other state-owned buildings of the university.

Ashoka had not expected an event on such a massive scale.

It is true that Takshashila is one of the greatest cultural hubs of the world, he thought with a sense of pride. There were various stalls on display not only depicting Indian arts and sciences, but also flavours of China, Arabia and Greece.

Chitrakoot nudged Ashoka and signalled to a stall where Chinese delicacies were being served.

He gave his bodyguard a look of mock exasperation. 'All right…let's go,' he conceded.

Enjoying the vegetables in pungent sauces, he shot a look of appreciation at the tiny Chinese girl serving him. She blushed at the not so covert display of admiration.

Moving around, he took in the sights – exquisite Greek pottery, Quranic verses on carpets and many more.

He saw Zuri talking animatedly to a Chinese fellow student. She looked up and gave him a quick smile.

'Namaskar! Good to see you here. I did not think you would come,' she said gaily but soon rushed off to prepare for her performance.

Ashoka sent the others to mingle with the students while he continued to admire the works of art. He came across a brightly lit section full of Buddhist paintings. Captivated, he found himself staring into the serene eyes of a Buddhist monk.

And then he saw her – a lithe figure in a red dress. He unconsciously stood straighter and taller. Menaka gave him the hint of a smile.

There was an awkward silence before he pointed at one of the paintings with a monk sitting on a lotus flower. 'These paintings…the artist has done an amazing job.'

Menaka brightened. 'Really, you think so?' she asked tentatively.

'I wonder why the Buddhist monk is sitting on a lotus flower, though,' pondered Ashoka, scratching his chin.

Menaka gave him a dubious look. 'Well, it signifies various things. Most obviously, that the person has to rise above the world of vices and attachment and achieve enlightenment…'

Ashoka laughed derisively, cutting her off.

'What's so funny?' she asked sharply.

'For one thing, no, it's not obvious…to me at least. And what is enlightenment? I don't understand it at all. It seems like a lot of mumbo-jumbo to me.'

Menaka gave him a frosty look.

He realized what he had done. 'I think I have offended you again.' He paused and looked at her exasperatedly. 'But I am free to express my views, right?'

She did not answer.

'I am sorry. I think I interrupted your explanation. Please accept my apologies,' he said hastily. 'But I do feel that you are overreacting to an innocuous comment from me. I don't think the artist would have minded as much as you have.'

He saw her face flush with embarrassment.

'Wait…you are the artist?' he asked, waving his hand at the twenty-odd paintings.

'Does it matter?' Menaka replied off-handedly.

He looked at her pointedly. 'It does.'

Their conversation was interrupted by the increased rhythmic beat of the drums. Those engaged in animated conversation stopped of their own accord as if magnetically pulled towards the music as the beats became louder and the pace quickened. Ashoka felt the vibrations coursing through his body, as if the beat of his heart had decided to synchronize itself with the reverberations produced by the drums. Soon, the sound of drums was interspersed with the mellifluous tinkle of a bell.

The group of thirty-odd drummers relentlessly striking the huge drums strapped around their shoulders seemed to be in a world of their own where nothing existed except for the rhythm of existence. The crowd watched mesmerized until they reached a crescendo. And then suddenly there was dead silence.

A huge roar of applause emanated from the excited crowd. The programme had begun.

Ashoka realized that Menaka had disappeared. He sighed and decided to focus on the show.

The next *hora* was mesmerizing for the Pataliputrans as they witnessed one stellar performance after another. But Ashoka was distracted. He kept stealing glances at the corner where the Buddhist paintings were exhibited. It looked deserted. He looked back towards the stage, frowning, trying to concentrate on the performances.

'Bravo, bravo!' yelled an animated section of the crowd.

He felt strangely detached from the excitement, and wondered why.

26

'We have checked all large establishments and shops in Takshashila. All of them have their own coin examiners. They are careful to neither take counterfeit coins, nor submit them in taxes to treasury,' Poulak reported.

Ashoka was seated with his five lieutenants in the middle of the courtyard where no walls with ears could be privy to their conversation. Ashoka frowned, the beginnings of an idea germinating in his mind. 'What about the gambling halls?' he inquired.

Mandar and Poulak exchanged a look.

'Well…no, we haven't checked those as of yet,' muttered Mandar.

'Why?' asked Ashoka with a hint of irritation.

'For one thing, they open only at night. We did not venture out at that time,' said Poulak defensively.

Ashoka's eyes hardened. He could not take complacency even from his closest aides. He seethed inside but to all present appeared calm. It was perhaps only Angad who sensed his rising anger.

'We will cover them tonight,' said Mandar quickly, before Ashoka had a chance to interrogate them further on this subject.

'We will all go,' Ashoka declared grimly. 'We meet outside the back gate at midnight. Make sure Eknath knows nothing about our nocturnal activities,' he ordered curtly.

Ashoka sipped cool lemon water in his favourite thinking place, the pool. The cool water soothed him every time.

I am sure the gambling halls will have their own coin examiners, he reflected. Being a state-owned establishment that was expected. But lots of money exchanged hands there.

Hopefully, I will stumble upon something. And even if I don't, it will be an experience, he thought with anticipation. Back home in Pataliputra, his mother Subhadrangi would not allow him such past times. Usually he was content to go along with what his mother prescribed. But, in the short time away from her, he felt grown-up. The Ashoka of Pataliputra seemed like a child to him now.

He closed his eyes, planning his strategy, and soon drifted off into a nap.

He woke up with a start, and realized he was still in the pool. He wondered how long he had been sitting there. Wading out, he went to the window to gaze at the moon.

A little more time and I must leave, he thought. He put on the clothes of a commoner and carefully put away the royal peacock emblem.

In a few moments he had swung off his balcony with the ease of a trapeze artist. On reaching the back gate, he was pleased to find everyone waiting for him.

'Did Eknath see any of you?' asked Ashoka tersely.

Everyone shook their heads.

'Why the smile, Chitrakoot?' queried Ashoka

'Angad made sure he wouldn't be able to hang around corridors until late tomorrow morning at least.'

Ashoka raised an eyebrow at that.

'I gave him a potent mixture of some somnolent herbs,' said Angad, shrugging nonchalantly, making the others smile.

They did not take their horses as the noise would have woken up the stable hands. The streets of Takshashila looked deserted. They passed houses with barred windows and doors.

'People actually bolt their doors in this part of the country,' remarked Poulak thoughtfully.

The group reached the main market square. A few guards looked at them lazily. They did not budge from their places as it was common to have people out late in this part of town. This section of the city was well-known for gambling halls and brothels, and hence attracted all types of nocturnal visitors.

Taking the first left, they saw a large, brightly lit building just down the road. The huge pillars of the porch clearly demonstrated Greek influence. A steady stream of people walked in and out of the building.

As they approached, a short potbellied man came up to greet them. He walked up to them with arms outstretched, as if he knew them intimately.

'My friends, what a pleasure to see you here,' he gushed.

The five instinctively metamorphosed their personas to reflect his. From grim men, they changed to laughing and boisterous men, slapping each other on their backs.

'You look new to this place. I definitely haven't seen you here,' he said, giving Mandar a tight hug. Mandar made a face over the man's shoulders at the rest, who were thoroughly enjoying the situation. But they were not to be spared either. The potbellied man exchanged embraces with all of them, while a tall bald man stood some distance away, watching them discreetly. Ashoka guessed that their new friend was of some significance and the big bald man was probably his bodyguard.

'Are you from Takshashila?' asked the potbellied man.

'Traders…we are traders,' said Ashoka quickly.

The potbellied man looked intently at them, trying to assess the veracity of Ashoka's statement.

'Would you be so kind to offer me an introduction?' asserted Ashoka firmly.

'I am the gambling master,' the man said, winking at them. 'All of Takshahila knows me. Or at least the gamblers do.' He roared at his own insipid joke, his stomach jiggling.

The group guffawed with him in camaraderie.

His laughter subsided as abruptly as it had started. 'Identification please,' he asked, his outstretched hand revealing thick pudgy fingers.

The five of them calmly handed over their fake identification documents.

'I love traders,' the man said, rubbing his hands together gleefully. 'They are men with a heart. They are generous souls who gamble to the hilt.' The gambling master burst into merry laughter again. This time the laughter did not come out but rolled somewhere inside his cavernous tummy as if he were enjoying a private joke. Lowering his voice, he leaned his head conspiratorily towards Chitrakoot – probably because he was bulkier than the rest and appeared to be a well-fed trader.

'I hope you and your friends are generous with their *panas*,' he whispered.

'By Shiva's grace, last year was good for us. We work very hard, you see, and want to relax now.'

'By all means. Welcome, welcome!' he said, waving his hand to the burly bodyguard to let them in.

The bodyguard beckoned to them to follow him. He led them to a frisking booth manned by a couple of guards who looked exactly like him. They could have been brothers, with their similar bodies and facial expressions conveying a sense of surly inhospitality.

'What is his name?' asked Ashoka as he was being frisked, pointing to the gambling master who was doing a repeat performance with another customer who had walked up the steps. He could see the man through some airholes in the frisking booth.

The frisker remained tight-lipped.

'You have a tongue, don't you, or do you keep it in safe

custody? People here seem very…closed,' finished Ashoka for want of a better word.

'Aksadevana,' the man said finally through clenched teeth.

'Ah…this literally means gambling in Sanskrit. Very apt,' remarked Ashoka.

He stepped out of the booth, looking at the boisterous gambling master in amusement. *He must be one of a kind in Takshashila. I wonder whether he is trained to behave that way or it is his natural proclivity?*

Finally they were escorted to an enormous wooden carved door. The doorman pressed a secret lever in the wall and it swung open. A blast of cool perfumed air hit them as they walked into a corridor. A lone man sat in a booth.

'This is wonderful!' exclaimed Angad who had a penchant for perfumes.

'What's this now?' remarked Mandar, who found the ways of the cities amusing. The concept of gambling was alien to him, and he was bemused by the set-up confronting him now. Being of tribal origin and inquisitive by nature, the pastimes indulged by the so-called-civilized population never failed to arouse his curiosity. He usually hovered in the background, his keen observation soaking in every new experience. Much to his chagrin, on this trip he had had to rely on Poulak to educate him as staying in the background was not possible.

Ashoka grinned at him reading his thoughts. Mandar returned the smile sheepishly.

'The entrance fee will be 20 *panas*,' the man in the booth informed them without looking up from his records on which he was scribbling something with his silver lined quill.

'Per person or for all five of us?' asked Angad innocently.

The man stopped scribbling and looked up. He stared hard at them. 'You seem to be novices.' He paused. 'It will be 20 *panas* for each person, please,' he said brusquely.

Ashoka wished they had done some homework before landing up here. They were unnecessarily drawing attention to themselves. Angad held out 100 *panas*. The pleasant faced man indicated a silver plate on which it had to be deposited.

'You can go in while we check the authenticity of your currency.'

The five strode to the end of the long corridor and pushed open a huge wooden door. A slight pressure was all that it needed to swing open. They were greeted with an even headier whiff of scented air.

They walked into along, spacious hall dotted with small submerged box like alcoves. Some of them even had curtains to be drawn around them for privacy. Plush divans were arranged to face each other, with large low tables offering ample space to spread the gambling paraphernalia. The mellifluous notes of a sitar lent a pleasant touch to the milieu.

A smiling attendant came forward. 'Will you be expecting more to join you, sirs?'

'It's just us,' said Ashoka quickly.

'This should do then,' the man said, indicating an alcove in the middle of the room.

'Perfect,' Ashoka assured him. A place in the centre would give them a good view to observe the happenings around them. As of now, the hall was sparsely populated with only a few alcoves filled with some early gamblers. One of the alcoves had men who were obviously not seasoned gamblers. They seemed to be observing the others.

Guards, Ashoka deduced, smiling to himself. At least they were not copies of the large bald men on the outside.

The attendant rushed away in order to greet a large group waddling in.

Very soon, some lemon water was served to them.

'Some *madira*?' the server asked pleasantly.

'In a while,' said Ashoka, returning the smile.

Each table had a huge lamp dangling over it, lending a warm glow to all around.

'So, we've turned gamblers,' laughed Poulak.

'So, this is what they call a gambling hall,' commented Mandar. His gaze travelled the hall curiously.

'Yes, my country bumpkin, it is,' said Poulak, laughing.

Mandar grimaced.

'Would you like some equipment?' asked a soft voice. They turned to see a tall slender woman dressed in sensuous flowing silk robes. She took their silence as assent and set the equipment on the table. It comprised dice, cowries, ivory rollers and leather cups.

The inexperienced gamblers made a pretence of shuffling around the equipment.

'You will find the rules in the drawer of the table,' she whispered to them, smiling.

'Do we look so unaccustomed to this?' Ashoka hissed under his breath when she had departed.

'Every gambler was once an innocent man,' said Angad. 'It's not such a big deal.' He opened the drawer and took out a parchment. As he strained to read the small writing, the others looked around, admiring the silk-robed attendant girls scattered all over the hall.

Having finished reading the rules, Angad looked up.

'Yes, we are all ears,' said Ashoka.

Angad rapidly explained the game with all the little nuances mentioned, including the fact that five percent of the winnings would go to the gambling establishment. He pointed to the large glass box at the centre of the hall. 'The revenue from the sunset's gambling will be put in there for all to see.' He scratched his chin. 'Why would they want to display the money?'

'For one thing, it is indicative of the winnings of the sunset. The more it fills up, the more motivated the gamblers would be to try their luck. Plain psychology,' explained Ashoka.

A couple of middle-aged gentlemen sat on either side of the glass box. Their table was scattered with an ensemble of devices such as cutters and magnifying glasses.

'Those are coin examiners. The state will not take a chance with its revenue,' Ashoka explained.

'So what are we waiting for? Let us begin,' he said, giving an appreciative glance to the young woman serving them *madira*. He took a swig. The others followed suit except for Chitrakoot and Angad. They made a pretence of it, though.

Soon the hall was packed. By now, the Pataliputrans were thoroughly enjoying the game themselves. The winnings box rapidly filled up. The coin examiners did not have a moment's reprieve. What started as low mumbles now turned to boisterous laughter.

As the salubrious effect of the *madira* took effect, Ashoka relaxed inwardly. A part of him was still alert for any unusual happenings. His patience was rewarded when the tenor in the hall changed unmistakably. People grew quieter and craned their necks. A person of importance had arrived.

Governor Huma entered the hall. Walking in with stately elegance, he was accompanied by three men who appeared to be friends of his. Aksadevana seemed to be almost running on his short legs, trying to keep pace with the long strides of Governor Huma. The display of welcome was overt, obsequious. A couple of the large bald-headed men followed them. They were characteristically poker-faced.

'It's good that we are seated in the centre with a crowd around us. I prefer to be anonymous at the moment,' remarked Ashoka.

Governor Huma's black curls shone in the iridescence of the lamps. He shook them back imperiously before disappearing into one of the curtained booths.

'That must have been reserved for him,' guessed Ashoka, taking a sip of *madira*.

Mandar looked a trifle settled now. He threw the dice with a flourish.

'Hey tribal, you're not bad at this,' joked Poulak.

Ashoka stole glances at Governor Huma's booth every now and then. Much to his chagrin, the curtains stayed drawn.

Presently, Aatreya Shah appeared at the doorway. He appeared preoccupied. There was no pomp and ceremony accorded to Aatreya Shah, the respected treasurer of Pataliputra. No one came running to greet him. All the respect and awe was reserved for Governor Huma.

'He obviously keeps a low profile,' observed Ashoka.

Aatreya walked straight to Huma's alcove and disappeared behind the curtains.

'Maybe they are gambling partners,' Ashoka murmured. *No, Aatreya Shah looked too hassled to take part in some pleasant gambling,* he thought.

A booming voice interrupted his thoughts. Aksadevana was making an announcement. He stood next to the coin examiners. The five of them strained to get a good view of him through the crowd.

'What generosity…generosity indeed. We are blessed to have a governor like Huma,' he said, putting his hand on his heart. Ashoka inadvertently looked at his jiggling belly. The potbellied gambling master held up a silver plate piled up with gold coins for everyone to see.

'Our kind governor is donating all his winnings.' With a flourish the gambling master swept the coins into the glass box. Putting his arm into the box, he jiggled the coins to mix them well. There was resounding applause from the players. With a low bow, Eksadevana walked away, beaming at everyone he made eye contact with.

Angad and Ashoka locked eyes with each other. A second later it struck the rest too.

'By Shiva! This cannot be,' muttered Poulak.

Mandar struck his fist to the table, making the cowries jump.

'The governor's coins are not subject to any screening!' exclaimed Chitrakoot a trifle loudly for Ashoka's comfort.

'Yes, it does seem like it,' sighed Ashoka.

The five lay sprawled on the lush green lawns, the events of last night fresh in their minds.

As they had got up to leave, one of the silk-clad girls had whispered in Ashoka's ear.

'You have to deposit 100 *panas* in copper at the winner's box.'

With a start Ashoka realized that these seemingly guileless women had been keeping a discreet eye on their game all along. The coins were subjected to scrutiny before being deposited in the box. They were not allowed to leave before that.

'The gambling halls are run like well-oiled establishments and obviously rake in huge sums of money for the state,' he said aloud.

There were a few moments of silence before Poulak spoke. 'The plain truth is that Huma's money is not checked for counterfeits. But it's a little more complex than that. Wouldn't Huma know that he was the only one accorded this privilege and hence put himself at the risk of being detected? Finally, the revenue would be subject to scrutiny before entering the halls of the treasury,' reasoned Poulak.

'That is a very pertinent point,' agreed Ashoka. 'But it could also be that the collections from the gambling halls are not verified again. Since they are state-owned establishments, the assumption would be that the coins have already been checked carefully.'

'It could also be that the coin examiners work for Huma and let selective counterfeits enter the treasury,' said Angad quietly.

'That is unlikely. He would be putting himself in grave danger by doing that. The punishment meted out for such a severe offence would be commensurate.'

Ashoka made a decision. 'We need to get hold of a large sample of coins from the gambling hall, on a sunset that Huma contributes. This sample needs to be scrutinized by us or someone trusted by us. That is the only way to implicate him...'

'Or to free him from our tentacles of suspicion,' finished Chitrakoot.

Ashoka smiled. 'Yes,' he said simply. 'The question is, how can we do that without arousing any suspicion?'

'We keep going to the gambling hall until we get a chance. One never knows what might come up,' suggested Angad.

'We might become inveterate gamblers, if we were to take that route,' retorted Chitrakoot.

'Do you have a better plan?' Ashoka asked him calmly.

Chitrakoot shook his head slowly, his ears turning red.

'Then we do as Angad has suggested.' Out of the corner of his eye Ashoka saw Eknath peering through the balcony. He was too far away to hear their conversation unless he was skilled in lip-reading.

Once more Ashoka swung off the balcony, to meet his companions at the back gate. They walked the now familiar streets. Angad slipped behind and gesticulated to the rest that he would catch up with them. In a few minutes he was beside them again, a worried expression on his face.

'We are being definitely followed.'

'How many?' was Ashoka's calm response.

'At the most, three.'

Ashoka barked out his orders without delay.

'Split up to confuse them and wander the streets for a couple of *horas*. Poulak and Mandar will head back home while the rest of us will hopefully shake them off our trail and carry on to the gambling hall.'

Luck favoured them. They were approaching a road with by-lanes in all directions.

'Now,' Ashoka said.

The cluster of five rapidly fragmented into separate individuals and darted into the obscure by-lanes. Ashoka smiled to himself, thinking of the plight of the men following them.

Having shaken off the men on his tail, Ashoka reached the gambling hall, hoping to be the first. But Angad was already skulking in the shadows, waiting for him.

'Chitrakoot is yet to arrive,' he offered by way of explanation before he was asked. Sometime later, they spotted the bulky figure of Chitrakoot approaching.

'Here,' hissed Angad, drawing his attention.

As they walked up the steps, Aksadevana, the garrulous and potbellied gambling master, greeted them in the same intimate manner as before. Walking towards them, his arms outstretched, he said merrily,

'Welcome! Welcome, my young friends. It is lonely without you. I was hoping you would grace us with your presence today.' His jelly of a tummy had a huge gold waistband around it, probably to keep his dhoti in place.

Aksadevana lunged at Ashoka, holding him in a tight embrace for a second. He was about to kiss him on the cheek when Ashoka pushed him away reflexively. Aksadevana gave him a hurt look.

'I…I have a contagious infection,' explained Ashoka lamely. 'I don't want you to catch it.'

'Of course, of course. How thoughtful of you,' he said smoothly, regaining his composure. 'I can't afford to catch a cold.'

Ashoka watched amused as he meted out the same effusive treatment to Angad and Chitrakoot, who went along with it for the sake of appearance. Now that the trio knew the drill, they went through the expected motions smoothly.

This time they were late. The hall teemed with gamblers. The quiet of the streets was a complete contrast to the boisterous milieu inside.

They joined a group of four at a large table towards the far corner. The four were young men and did not look like hardened gamblers.

'Are you from here?' asked Angad politely.

'Here...what do you mean?' one of them replied suspiciously.

Ashoka smiled. It would take more than polite conversation to get something out of the surly locals.

'He means Takshashila. You see, we are traders from Pataliputra,' he explained evenly.

'Oh.' That was all the response that was forthcoming.

Ashoka smiled as he started the game. The men knew their game well and so Pataliputrans concentrated, lest they be labelled amateurs.

Golden *madira* was served, matching the colour of the silk robes of the girls.

The colour of sunset, thought Ashoka as he relaxed into the cushions.

They were engrossed in the game when an uproar somewhere in the centre of the hall broke their concentration. All at once, the guards ran from all directions to the epicentre of the mayhem.

Ashoka frowned, unable to comprehend the reason for the ruckus. He sat calmly at the table with Angad, while the rest darted ahead to find out the cause.

A guard was pushing a young lad head down on a table. Several others pinned his arms behind his back. The lad's face was contorted in pain. The guards did not allow anyone to get up close.

Aksadevana ran to the scene as fast as his short legs could take him.

'Please head back to your tables. The situation is in my control,' he coaxed the gamblers who had surrounded him. His chubby arms looked almost comical as he waved the crowd back to their seats.

He nodded to the guards who dragged the dishevelled young man off the table. Blood oozed from his mouth and dripped all the way down his torso to his white dhoti. His struggle was put to an end with a smash on his head.

'Look at him. Look at him,' said Aksadevana, clutching the lad's head by his hair. 'He has dared to defy the prescribed rules. Look at him closely.'

The guards held up the unconscious man like a rag doll, for all to see.

'Can you see that he has four limbs? Well, in seven sunsets, he will have only three, for his right arm will be cut off as punishment for cheating. He tried to cheat us of 20 whole *panas*.'

Aksadevana nodded to his men to take him away. Hoots and howls followed them. Aksadevana held up his hands to pacify the crowd.

'For those of you who play an honest man's game, I am your servant.' He bowed theatrically.

Ashoka crossed his arms, his thoughtful expression masking his distaste for the cheap histrionics displayed by the gambling master. His thoughts drifted to Mali's father.

Is this the great Bindusara's justice, to cut off a man's arm for trying to steal a mere 20 panas? thought Ashoka, dismayed. This would not only sever the man's arm but also his dreams. His thoughts drifted to Mali's father again. That injustice had cost a man his life, taken a husband away from his wife, a son away from the protective arms of his father. *The degree of punishment was disproportionately harsh for the crime,* thought Ashoka, acid rising up his throat.

No. I can't let this happen. I need to do whatever I can to save this man from the fate of a lifelong cripple, he thought with a sense of urgency. He motioned to his bodyguards to call off the game.

The local players merely shrugged at their hurry to get out.

'Looks like mother has called her cubs back home,' one of them sniggered. His companions slapped his back and roared with laughter at his joke. Paying no heed to their insinuations, the trio walked out briskly. There were no winnings to declare. That was just as well.

Once out in the cloak of darkness, Ashoka finally addressed

his bodyguards. 'We need to free that man before fate deals him a cruel hand.'

Angad and Chitrakoot looked at Ashoka in surprise.

'That would be inviting unnecessary trouble,' objected Angad.

'We will try to do this without revealing our identities. Shiva will be with us,' Ashoka replied simply.

'What do you have in mind?' Chitrakoot asked nervously, looking over his shoulder. The three lurked in the shadows not far from the gambling hall.

'Here's my plan,' said Ashoka. 'Pay attention as I won't repeat it.' The rebuke was directed at Chitrakoot who looked distracted.

'They will definitely bring out our man soon, to take him to the state prison. We need to ambush them on the way. If he reaches the prison, he will be beyond reach,' explained Ashoka tersely.

Chitrakoot gulped. Being a body guard was one thing. But, ambushing a platoon of men was something that made him timorous.

Angad looked at him, amused.

'What is it, fatso? No appetite for adventure?'

Chitrakoot bore the barb sportingly.

'I will do whatever our prince tells us to do without any qualms,' he said, steeling himself.

Angad nodded in agreement.

'All right then,' Ashoka said impatiently. 'We need to jam the wheels of the wagon that they take their prisoner in. Any ideas?'

'A simple thing, actually,' said Angad. 'All we need is a strong stick and use it as a stopper.'

'And then?' said Chitrakoot. He brightened up suddenly as an idea struck him. 'I have some chilli flakes that we can use to blind them.'

'I like your ideas. Keep your tools ready,' said Ashoka

pragmatically. He knew they would have to make do with what was available.

Angad scoured the area for a stick strong enough to be used for the task. Finally, their implements at the ready, the three lay in wait in the shadows. They expected a wagon to emerge any moment. It had crossed Ashoka's mind that Chitrakoot could have got Poulak and Mandar for help. However, he could not afford to take the chance of confronting the men with just two of them.

More than a *hora* later, a cart came into view. The wheels clattered noisily on the stone-paved path.

I hope the offender is in this wagon, Ashoka thought. The windowless wagon offered no clue. *We will have to take a chance,* he thought decisively.

'How many inside, do you think?' muttered Chitrakoot.

'My guess is at least three,' replied Angad.

The Pataliputrans covered their mouths with their scarves and braced themselves for action. Out of the corner of his eye, Ashoka saw Angad taking deep long breaths. Angad, who had been flexing his fingers all along, now took a firm grip on the stick. With grace and ease he flipped it powerfully across the road. It somersaulted and then firmly entangled itself in the spokes of the wheel. The impact almost broke the stick in two, but not before it served its purpose. The horses reared their front legs in alarm as they jerked to a halt.

Chitrakoot surprised his companions by taking out a catapult. He took aim and a large pebble hit the driver in the left eye. The man yowled in agony and let go of the reins.

In the chaos that ensued, the three darted out of the shadows to the wagon and yanked the door open. The offender was sitting on the floor, completely conscious now. The guards were quick to unsheathe their swords.

I hope this works, Ashoka thought worriedly. For a warrior, being weaponless was akin to being unclothed.

Chitrakoot scooped out chilli flakes from somewhere in his

dhoti and signalled to his companions to stand back. He shook the packet so that a huge amount disseminated in the air. He slammed the door of the cart shut for a few moments for the effect to take place.

Cries of pain and the sound of chaos emanated from the interior of the wagon. Chitrakoot now yanked the door open with such force that it came off its hinges. The three guards and the captive alike were writhing in agony, rubbing their eyes. Chitrakoot quickly lifted the young man by his shoulders, while Angad took the legs. One of the guards tried to trip them and was rewarded with a broken shin bone thanks to Ashoka.

As the Pataliputrans fled, a knife came hurtling through the darkness and lodged itself on Ashoka's shoulder blade. Cursing, he twisted himself to wrench out the knife, even as motioned to his companions to keep moving. Blood gushed out in rivulets, and he tried to stem the flood with a scarf.

The young man, who did not have a clue as to what was happening, thrashed his arms wildly.

'Calm down,' hissed Chitrakoot. 'We are rescuing you. All this is for your benefit, you idiot.'

He grew quiet, his eyes still burning.

Angad looked over his shoulder to make sure that Ashoka was following them. He looked steady.

'We need to hurry. They will come after us soon,'snarled Ashoka.

The group darted in and out of dark lanes in a bid to shake off anyone following them. They crossed a house that had an earthen pot sitting on its verandah. Angad scooped it up and offered it to the young man who seemed to be in a daze.

'Wash your eyes,' he said kindly. He poured the water into the lad's hands.

'Yes, we are getting tired of carrying you like a baby,' said Chitrakoot gruffly.

The man tried to open his swollen, red-rimmed eyes. 'I…I can walk.' He took a few shaky steps.

'Move on,' commanded Ashoka.

Angad and Chitrakoot did as he instructed, dragging the poor man behind them. He half walked and was half dragged. Finally they reached the vicinity of the palace.

'Have Poulak open the door. I can't hoist myself up,' rasped Ashoka. Only when they were in Ashoka's chambers, did everyone realize that the prince was near collapse. He flung himself on the bed, lying on his stomach.

Angad untied the scarf and stared at the gaping wound. He examined the wound quickly. The cut was deep enough to show bone. Thankfully, the bone had not cracked.

'The blood loss is of dangerous proportions,' said Angad in a low voice to his companions. 'We need to take him to an *arogyashala* right now.' He sounded very worried.

'I can't go…to an…*arogyashala*,' protested Ashoka although he was almost comatose by now.

'He's right,' said Mandar. 'They will ask too many questions to which we would rather not give any answers.'

'Take me to…Kichaka.' Ashoka just about managed to complete the sentence before slipping into unconsciousness.

All this while, no one had bothered to take notice of the bewildered and frightened figure in the corner. Poulak took the matter in his hands. He leaned his face close to that of the young lad, who was the reason behind the trouble.

'Look, boy. You'd better keep your mouth shut. In any case you don't have a choice. We are the only friends you have got. You have committed a crime for which the guards will be looking for you. That kind-hearted soul on the bed there,' he said, pointing to Ashoka, 'is in that condition because of you.'

He paused to let that sink in. 'Now, do you have friends with whom you can hide for a month or so until this blows over?'

The frightened man nodded his head vigorously.

'You know nothing about us,' growled Chitrakoot. His words held an underlying threat.

Mandar said urgently, 'I will escort him to safety while you take our prince to Kichaka. Let us make haste.'

The bed on which Ashoka lay was an ominous shade of scarlet.

Ashoka was swimming up to the surface from deep within the ocean. The sounds reaching him were muffled. His movements were slow and laboured. He peered up at the bright light. It seemed further than he had initially thought and the effort was wearing him out.

Maybe I will have no breath left in me to reach the top? He struggled to find reserves of strength to carry on.

Never mind if I can't make it. The ocean was beginning to grow on him. The sensation was soothing in an odd sort of way. It felt like home. Only a little different.

'Don't give up,' said a voice. *Was it his own mind goading him to persevere with his efforts?* That was a voice he usually listened to. Flapping his arms vigorously, he struggled to fight against gravity and move to the bright light that was his destination.

'Almost there,' the voice sighed in satisfaction.

Ashoka opened his eyes to find his face on a clean white pillow. He was on his stomach. He tried to turn over but the effort was too exhausting.

'It's all right. Keep lying down in this position,' said a soft voice.

Ashoka racked his brains to put a face to the voice. He almost had it, but it slipped away into the recesses of his mind.

'There has been a lot of blood loss. That is why you may be feeling fatigued. It will go,' said the voice.

Soothed by the calm voice, he slipped back into a state of deep rest.

Menaka looked at the prince lying in deep slumber and recalled the events from early that morning.

The moment she had arrived to attend her classes, she was intercepted by a messenger waiting for her near the gates of her acharya's residence.

'Pranam. *Acharya Kichaka asks you to meet him.'*

'Very well! Tell him that I will meet him after my classes,' replied Menaka, wondering at the reason for the request.

'You are requested to come right now,' insisted the messenger.

Menaka suppressed her annoyance and replied in an even voice, 'What could be so urgent? I have important lessons today.'

'You will get all your answers once you meet him. But I can't leave without you,' persevered the messenger.

Acharya Kichaka was related to Menaka from her maternal side of the family. She had great respect for him.

'All right,' she sighed. 'Let's go.'

The moment she arrived at Kichaka's house, she was ushered into the inner chambers. She balked as she entered the room. Many men were crowded around a bed which was soaked in the blood of a man sprawled on his stomach. The sickening-sweet smell coupled with the sight repulsed her. Recognizing Angad as he came forward, she felt a sense of foreboding steal over her.

'I have stitched the wound. But I have no medicines to apply to it. It will turn septic soon,' he informed her.

Menaka felt her energy sap – it was as though a gate had been opened accidently and all the life-giving water was flowing out. Seeing Ashoka in a sea of scarlet, almost lifeless, she realized for the first time why she was drawn to him. It was his sense of vitality that really attracted her. The irony was that the same aura of vitality disturbed her as well. It brought to the fore her own lack of it. It was something difficult for her to face and hence perturbed her greatly.

She couldn't bear to see Ashoka lying so still floating in the sea of blood. She felt dizzy. Perspiration trickled from her temples.

Kichaka emerged from the next room.

'Daughter, we can't take him to the arogyashala *for reasons best left unknown to you. I know I can trust you to do the best,' he said simply. 'There has been a huge delay already.'*

Menaka went to work with a vengeance. She asked for ghee and some special herbs and created an antiseptic mixture. The ghee would speed up the process of healing by adding impetus to the natural healing properties of the body.

When Menaka applied the mixture, she recoiled in shock. 'He is running a high fever,' she said in dismay.

Turning to Angad, she said, 'I need some more herbs.' She rattled off some names that were familiar to him.

The urgency in her voice was not lost on Angad. He rummaged in Kichaka's well-stocked cabinet and quickly located them.

Menaka hurriedly prepared the bitter concoction, put it to Ashoka's lips and followed it up with some cooling ghee.

'Don't give up,' she whispered in his ear.

He seemed to understand and took in the bitter medication without any fuss. Soon he slipped into a deep slumber.

A few *horas* had passed since she had administered the medicine and Menaka now felt his pulse. Elated, she went to tell the rest that he was recovering. She had felt a similar joy when she had cured her mother of her debilitating migraines.

The men gathered around her. Angad came forward and bowed to her in gratitude. The rest followed.

Menaka wished that they would not make such a big deal about it. The attention made her uncomfortable.

'You have a gift from the almighty,' said Angad. 'It was the blood loss that really complicated the whole thing, otherwise a knife wound is something that would not bother him too much.'

The limelight on herself disconcerted her. 'I didn't do anything at all. The healing happened by itself. Must be someone's prayers and will power.'

The men felt amused at her shyness. Feeling overwhelmed by the excess attention from all the men in the chamber, she quickly bade them goodbye after giving them instructions for his care.

'Don't forget to give him the medicine every *hora* for the next four *horas* and then twice each sunset for the next seven sunsets.'

'You can count on us,' said Poulak gravely.

She hurried to Kichaka's study. He was engrossed in scribbling some notes. 'I am leaving, Uncle.'

'All right. Give my regards to your mother,' said Kichaka, hardly glancing up from his work. 'And thank you, Daughter.'

After Menaka left, it struck Poulak precipitously that Eknath would be wondering about Ashoka and them. He might even have alerted Governor Huma.

'We were out on hunting trip' Poulak reflected. 'That's what they would have to say. Yes, that would explain the wound too.'

Back at the palace in his comfortable chambers, Angad gave Ashoka some tepid water mixed with a herbal concoction. He grimaced.

'Drink without any fuss, Prince. It will increase the blood in you,' insisted Angad.

Ashoka gulped it down and lay back exhausted.

'You are worse than my mother,' he remarked. 'What happened to the poor man we released from the clutches of the gambling master?'

'Must be all right. He won't open his mouth,' said Mandar dryly. He had just walked in.

'These bandages…I can do without them,' said Ashoka hoarsely. He winced at the effort of rotating his arm.

'A Kshatriya cannot live with such restrictions.' He said irked.

Eknath walked in, scowling. 'You have a visitor, Prince.'

'Tell them to come some other time,' snapped Ashoka. 'Do I look as though I want visitors?'

Eknath turned away and started to walk out of the

chambers, muttering to himself all the while. 'First no one tells me about the hunting trip and now I have to turn away visitors.'

'Wait, who is it?' asked Poulak.

'It's a young lady who calls herself Menaka.'

'I will go and receive her myself,' said Poulak. 'I'll explain later,' he said to Ashoka over his shoulder as he strode out of the room.

Ashoka visibly straightened up at the mention of Menaka.

'Why is she here?' he asked Angad, perplexed.

'Let's just say she had something to do with your recovery,' Angad replied cryptically.

'I don't understand,' said Ashoka, totally muddled. He looked at Chitrakoot for an explanation.

Chitrakoot was lazily chewing on a piece of straw sitting by the window. He winked at Angad.

'The medicine that you love so much is her prescription,' he said, enjoying the uncharacteristic disconcerted look on Ashoka's face.

At that moment Poulak walked in with Menaka in tow. Ashoka smoothed his hair and smiled. He would question his companions later.

'Pranam,' she said pleasantly to everyone.

The men bowed to her respectfully. Ashoka noticed that they seemed to have a strange familiarity with her. As if they were in on a secret.

He smiled at her. 'They haven't told me much,' he said, pointing to his companions.

She met his gaze.

'There is nothing much to it really,' Menaka said modestly. 'You needed some immediate medical attention and I happened to come across and provide it.'

Ashoka looked at her thoughtfully.

'I came here to check on your progress,' she said quickly in order to fill the awkward silence.

Ashoka was enjoying the change in her usual grim countenance. Usually it was as if some force weighed her down.

'I am planning to rip off the bandages by evening and start my exercises,' he informed her.

She looked horrified. 'It's too early. It's just been a couple of sunsets!'

'What is it with women? Maybe mothering comes naturally to them,' Ashoka said exasperatedly. 'All right, tomorrow morning then,' he gave in grudgingly.

They smiled at each other, an easy camaraderie replacing the stiffness of the conversations they had had earlier. This time Menaka felt no wish to run away from him.

27

Ghataka walked into the dark, cavernous room. It was a stark contrast to the rest of the house which was bright and sunny, with open windows welcoming the breeze from the sacred Ganga. This room did not have a single window open. In fact, the room did not have any windows.

Slender fingers gripped a quill firmly, scribbling notes on a palm leaf. The only light came from a lamp on the low table, at which the man sat. The huge ruby on his finger glistened in the light of the lamp.

Ghataka bowed in obeisance.

'He's hurt,' he said matter-of-factly. 'I didn't do it.'

'How could you? I didn't tell you to.' The hypnotic eyes met Ghataka's gaze steadily.

Ghataka lowered his gaze.

'True.' Ghataka waited for direction.

'All in good time,' was all that was said.

The meeting over, Ghataka bowed and left.

The rajpurohit looked around the musty room. No windows. That was exactly how he had had this room designed. This was a place where he neither wanted the sun to come in nor the cool winds from the Ganga.

His own family was forbidden to enter it. It was as if this one place existed on earth where he could shut out the universe – from knowing about his dark plots...and judging him for it. But he knew that nature never judged. It only followed some laws. The bitter neem seed would never yield anything sweet but a bitter neem tree. The bitterness would be there in the stem, the leaves and in its every pore. But the bitter neem had its uses and cleared the blood of toxins. Just as he would – in Pataliputra, the seat of the Mauryan empire. However, he would have to embrace the bitter consequences of his misdeeds someday.

But I am ready for that. I have always known there will be consequences. I will be ready to face them when the day comes, he thought grimly.

That is the sunset that I will burn this room down. For its purpose will be served. The rajpurohit smiled in anticipation.

Ashoka wiped the perspiration off his face. He swung the heavy mace around his shoulder. His recuperation had been rapid. He had been religiously gulping the prescribed medicine every day. And he was being careful with his left shoulder – too much pressure and the wound would reopen.

Later in the day, Ashoka rode the streets of Takshashila flanked by his bodyguards. Digging his heels into the horse's flanks, he urged it to gallop faster. Chitrakoot glanced at him quizzically, wondering at the reason for the haste. Ashoka seemed to be smiling to himself. But he could not be sure as dusk was setting in and it was getting difficult to see.

The bodyguards struggled to keep pace. Finally, they slowed down in the busy market square.

'Where is he?' bellowed Chitrakoot. 'He's disappeared!'

'I don't know,' said Angad, puzzled. The two stopped. Infuriated yells followed.

'Move on, you two. You don't own the streets,' barked a man, waving his fist.

'Neither do you,' retorted Chitrakoot, turning beetroot-red.

Angad gave him a meaningful glance. 'Let's not draw attention.'

He looked around, reflecting on the possibilities.

He has deliberately thrown us off his trail. Why? thought Angad.

'Let us systematically comb the by-lanes,' he told Chitrakoot. Deep down he knew their search would prove futile.

Ashoka was not far away, his mount taking him to the university of Takshashila. He felt a great sense of freedom. Even though his bodyguards were his friends, there were some things he preferred to do alone.

He reached the main square and stopped at an eatery. Walking to the far corner, he ordered some sprouted horsegram salad. The attendant scowled as he took Ashoka's order.

Ashoka frowned. He would never get used to the unfriendly ways of the citizens of Takshashila.

Maybe I should thrash a few of them to put them in their place, he thought sadistically.

The place where he sat offered a full view of the market square. He laughed inwardly at Angad and Chitrakoot's plight. They must be searching for him frantically. But he knew it was only a matter of time before they found him.

The surly attendant came with his plate of horsegram and found him chuckling away. He glared at him.

'Something funny, pal?'

'Doesn't concern you, does it?' retorted Ashoka. Waving the server away, he started to eat his horsegram sprouts, one seed at a time.

After an uneventful *hora*, Ashoka put the last sprout in his mouth and slowly chewed on it. It was dark now. The owner of the eatery had looked on him twice to see whether he was done.

'There you are!' Ashoka heard a triumphant shout from Chitrakoot. The two bodyguards strode into the eatery.

'Watch it,' snarled the attendant. In their haste Chitrkoot had banged his shoulder against his. Paying no attention, Chitrakoot went and plonked himself next to Ashoka. The attendant glared at him.

'I apologize on his behalf,' Angad said, trying to assuage the man's fury.

'Prince…Prince, what do we do with you?' wailed Chitrakoot.

'Shut up and stop drawing attention to us,' snapped Ashoka. 'Let's go.' He got up and walked out with the two in tow.

Having incurred his displeasure, the bodyguards didn't dare speak to him till they were more than halfway home.

'Why didn't you want us with you?' Angad asked tentatively as they galloped home.

'Sometimes I like my own company,' Ashoka replied sullenly.

They had to be satisfied with the meagre explanation. Angad realized there were many facets to their prince's personality that they were unacquainted with.

The next evening, the five were exercising their horses when Ashoka galloped away without warning again. The rest started to follow when Angad held up his hand, bidding the others to stop.

'He wants to be by himself,' he stated matter-of-factly.

'But we need to be by his side at all times,' argued Chitrakoot, unwilling to relent so easily. Poulak and Mandar appeared vexed too.

'He is a human, after all. He craves privacy at the moment. Let us give him some time at least,' coaxed Angad. 'We know where to find him.'

'He seems to be in an unpredictable mood these sunsets,' muttered Poulak.

'While we are out, why don't we eat?' suggested Chitrakoot, trying to lighten the mood.

They were near a tiny shop in a rundown part of the city. Mandar looked hungrily at the delicacies on offer.

'Looks like our tribal yearns for city's street-food,' remarked Poulak humorously. Mandar grinned at them sportingly.

The four placed their order and were soon enjoying a potato dish served with tamarind chutney. Satiated, Poulak offered the man two silver *panas*.

The man looked at the money in exasperation.

'I don't have any change to give, sir. I've been waiting for the change to arrive all morning.'

Just then a man walked in with a bag. 'Change,' he said gruffly as he plonked the bag on the table, the coins tinkling. The harried shopkeeper took some silver coins in lower denominations and handed the change to Poulak.

'Is this a free service?' asked Poulak curiously.

'Yes. They don't charge me anything. What a relief that he has finally arrived. In fact, a lot of other shops in this area also use this service.'

The Pataliputrans marvelled at the efficiency of the economy of Takshashila.

'Let's catch up with Ashoka now,' suggested Mandar. They all nodded vigorously – clearly, he had expressed what was on everyone's mind.

'Lead the way friend,' he said, waving his hand at Angad.

'If anything happens to Ashoka, it will be the emperor's axe and our heads,' muttered Chitrakoot, glaring accusingly at Angad.

The four arrived at the university and headed for the market square. The square was flooded with small eateries catering to world cuisines. Delicacies from around the world were available to cater to the needs of the varied student population. Some eateries opened only in the evening and were run by foreign students after their study *horas*. This was done in partnership with the local shopkeepers as permits were not given directly to students.

The four marched into the eatery where they had found Ashoka last time. He was nowhere to be seen.

Poulak and Mandar looked at the bodyguards accusingly. 'You said you knew where to find him.'

'Yes, he should be somewhere around,' Angad replied with a concerned look.

Chitrakoot had already started to scan the area systematically. He located Ashoka sitting in an eatery in the far corner, sipping a glass of *chaas*.

They walked over to him and he grinned at them.

'So soon. Can't live without me, I see,' he said half mockingly.

'Good view,' replied Chitrakoot, plonking himself next to him.

'Are we so lack lustre that you need to be away from us?' Mandar asked tentatively.

'So, what did you guys eat?' asked Ashoka, evading the question. Chitrakoot belched in reply.

Ashoka's companions realized nothing would make him share his secrets unless he wanted to.

'So you actually went to check on him?' Zuri remarked, disbelief written all over her face.

'Yes, I wanted to know how my herbs were faring,' Menaka replied simply.

'But this is so unlike you. I would have thought you would stay *yojanas* away from the prince and his unpolished Pataliputrans.'

'They are fine people, and why would I want to stay away from the prince?' Menaka replied, smiling.

'I got that impression the last time we interacted with them,' Zuri said dubiously.

'Oh, Zuri. It's complicated. How do I explain?' Menaka said, taking Zuri's hands in her own. They were in the privacy of Zuri's room.

'Tell me,' coaxed Zuri.

'I don't understand it myself. In any case, I don't think anything of consequence will happen. I don't even know whether I will meet them again.'

Zuri looked at her thoughtfully. This was the first time Menaka was actually discussing a man.

Menaka sighed as she took out a jar of medicinal syrup. She took a gulp and lay back on the bed. She had been unwell and had not gone to the university for a few sunsets. The funny thing was that the herbal concoctions that she made for herself did not work as well as they did for others. It was very much like the skill of an astrologer. While an astrologer could predict the future of many with accuracy, even the best faltered when it came to themselves.

'You don't go for your classes and you make me miss mine too,' grumbled Zuri.

'It's not the classes you are grumbling about. It's the trip to China,' said Menaka dryly.

'Yes. I will visit China with my China man someday,' said Zuri dreamily.

Menaka knew the infatuation would pass, like many that had come and gone. Zuri flitted from one flower to another like a butterfly.

'I'd better be going, Zuri,' said Menaka as she got up from the bed with effort. 'We have guests coming today. I need to be home.'

Lately her father had become very particular about everyone being present at home to welcome the guests.

'Who are they?' queried Zuri.

Menaka shrugged. 'I don't care really. Must be one of father's friends.'

Menaka always marvelled at the fact that her father managed to come across as a jolly, convivial man to his friends. His demeanour would change the moment they had guests at home. From a surly, bad-tempered man, he would transform to a cheerful person with a keen sense of humour. Inevitably, her brother would be called to show his skill in the narration of difficult *shlokas* or display his proficiency with numbers. While her whole family and the guests would be in splits over some joke, Menaka would feel like a bystander. Tired of putting on fake smiles that made her jaw ache, she would finally excuse herself. It was the façade of it all that she could not tolerate.

Menaka felt drained by the time she reached home. The attendant let her in. She was surprised to find the house abuzz with activity. The attendants were busy dusting the hall while her mother seemed to be fretting over the flower arrangements. For once her brother was not prancing around.

'Who is coming, Mother? Is it someone important?'

'Someone important…yes, you could say that,' her mother replied distractedly. 'A very good friend of your father's. The whole family will be here.'

Not really interested, Menaka turned to go to her room.

'Wait…what are you doing?'

'Mother, I am still not feeling too well. Can I be excused?' Menaka asked, hoping to spend the evening in the sanctuary of her room. There was an interesting text on rare herbs found only in the east that she wanted to pore over.

'Oh no! I thought that you would have recovered by now. Nevertheless, you have to be present. It would be disrespectful to the guests. The whole family will be there, as I said. It is only fair that we reciprocate,' her mother was quick to object. 'Your father would want you to be there too.'

Menaka trudged up to her room slowly. If Father wanted her to be present, then she would have to be there. It was like the emperor's command. *Defy at your own peril*, she thought.

She flung herself on the bed and lay there staring at the

ceiling, her mind blank. After some time she looked out of the window dolefully. It was dark now.

Time to get dressed, she thought wearily. Her lack of enthusiasm was partly because of her health and partly because of the prospect of another evening where she would have to smile until her jaw ached.

Menaka opened her cupboard and stared at her clothes. None of her clothes appealed to her. They were all old and worn out.

When was the last time I went shopping for clothes? she thought.

She chose a blue coloured *antariya* and a silver threaded *uttariya* to match. Her eyes looked puffy and she splashed some water on them, and then lined them with kohl.

'I think I look all right. Who cares anyway?' she muttered to herself. She walked out, ready to endure the evening.

She almost bumped into her mother who was walking up the stairs to call her.

'Where were you, child? Your father has been asking about you.'

That was enough to nettle Menaka. Why the sudden interest in her? All these years she had been relegated to the sidelines.

As she entered the hall, she was greeted effusively by her father.

That's the façade he puts on when people are around, thought Menaka, peeved.

'Come, daughter. Meet my friend, his wife and his son.'

Menaka was startled to see a handsome youth lurking in the corner of the room. He bowed deeply to her.

'Namaste,' said Menaka to everyone. It was as if she was the centre of attention. She felt unnerved.

'This is Chandravapus. He is a bright lad, studying to be an architect. In fact, he is already working with his father.'

Chandravapus grinned at her. 'A flattering introduction. I don't think I deserve it,' he said unpretentiously. 'Father does all the work. I just add a few touches here and there.'

'How about some *madira*, son?' asked Aatreya Shah.

'Yes sir, a small glass will do.'

The three men sat sipping *madira* in the far corner while the women huddled in the other. Chandravapus' mother seemed to be assessing Menaka quite openly.

'Come and sit by me, child,' she said, patting the seat next to her.

Menaka went over and sat down tentatively, not knowing what to expect. The woman took Menaka's face by her chin and peered at her closely.

'Looks like you don't take care of yourself too much,' she murmured.

Menaka was taken aback at the scrutiny. Her mother seemed to be completely oblivious to her plight and excused herself for organizing some delicacies.

'So, what do you do all day, child?'

Menaka looked around helplessly, wishing that some distraction would appear and save her from the inquisition. Where was her brother? She would be happy to clap at his antics. Anything to get away.

'I study fine arts and…about herbs and medicines,' replied Menaka vaguely.

'What about keeping the house? Cooking and other work,' the lady persisted.

Menaka took a few moments to respond to that. As she looked around exasperated, she caught Chandarvapus' eye. He was looking at her openly over his glass of *madira*.

He sauntered over to them.

'I would love to see your home. It looks very well kept.'

Menaka jumped at the opportunity to escape from the interrogation. 'Oh, sure,' she said brightly.

His mother frowned at her son. He patted her cheek smoothly and escorted Menaka out of the room.

'I apologize. My mother can be very…persistent,' he said when they were out of earshot.

'I am eternally grateful to you for rescuing me.' Menaka sighed with relief. 'I don't suppose you really want to see the house?'

'Actually, I do. I am an architect, remember,' he said, smiling.

Menaka smiled back. He seemed to be very easy-going and it was refreshing for Menaka. She dabbed her eyes with her handkerchief. They seemed to be watering slightly.

'You are not well,' he observed. 'Why don't you rest? I will find a way to explain your absence.'

She looked at him gratefully. 'I owe you...'

He held up his hand. 'It's all right.' With that he bowed and left.

What a charming man! she thought as she walked up the stairs.

Menaka woke up late the next morning. The medication she had taken at night had been highly soporific. Walking groggily to the bathroom, she looked at herself in the pot of water. Her eyes were still swollen but thankfully not watering.

The events of last night flashed before her eyes like a play. Her thoughts lingered on Chandravapus.

He seems to be a noble man. Understanding and subtle in his mannerisms, she thought appreciatively.

She bathed quickly and grabbed her quills. As she walked down the stairs, her mother called out to her. 'Chandravapus has sent something for you, daughter.'

Menaka walked slowly to the ornate box that lay in the centre of the room. It was still sealed. She opened it tentatively, not knowing what to expect. In the box lay a container which contained a viscous golden-brown liquid. Next to it was a palm leaf with something scribbled on it.

> *Bees travel five times around the earth to make one drona of honey. Will you at least travel one yojana with me?*
>
> *I would like to show you something. I will meet you*

at the university a couple of horas before sunset. In case you are wondering, I have already taken your parents' permission.

Chandravapus

Menaka did not know what to make of it. He seemed to have thought of everything. She looked up at her mother.

'It's all right, child. Go ahead. He took your father's permission last night,' her mother said, smiling.

Just then, her brother came scampering into the room and wrapped his arms around Menaka's thighs affectionately.

'Where were you last night?' Menaka asked him, patting him on the head.

'I heard there was a party. I wasn't allowed to come,' he said, pouting.

That surprised Menaka. He was usually the centre of attention at these gatherings.

'Next time, I will come get you. Dare anyone stop you,' Menaka said to him.

Reassured, he went off with a happy expression on his face.

Grabbing a pear, Menaka walked out briskly. It was a good day with plenty of sunshine. She looked forward to meeting the suave Chandravapus again.

Last night was a disaster. I must have come across as reclusive, she thought guiltily. *He did save me…from an uncomfortable situation, after all. I will definitely make up for that today,* she resolved.

As she passed Acharya Kichaka's house, the memories of the sunset she saw Ashoka lying comatose came flooding back. Menaka felt a flurry of emotions assault her unexpectedly. She felt a strange heaviness in her heart.

He must be totally fine by now. I don't have any excuse to meet him anymore, she thought with a twinge of disappointment. She frowned. *In a way that's good,* she reasoned to herself, *I don't want to feel unsettled for no reason.*

But Menaka felt drawn towards him like a moth to fire, and once she started thinking about Ashoka, she couldn't stop.

Oh, stop it, she admonished her wandering mind. She searched the recesses of her mind to focus on something else. *Yes, it will be a pleasant evening with Chandravapus.*

Menaka walked towards the main market square after a hard day's work at the university. Today she had attended a class on the preservation of rare herbs. The quantity supplied for demonstration had been minimal.

Her timing was perfect. Chandravapus emerged just as she reached the market square. Riding his mount, his lustrous locks flew behind him. She was amused to see that he made quite a few female heads turn. Stopping near her, he jumped off his horse gracefully and gallantly bowed to her.

'Punctuality seems to be one of your many virtues,' she said pleasantly.

'You look much better today,' he remarked ignoring the compliment. 'We have a fair distance to go. Would you like to sit on Agni? I can keep the pace with a brisk walk,' he said, pointing to the mount.

'Oh no! I prefer to walk,' replied Menaka hastily. 'Unless of course, you feel that it would delay us inordinately.'

Chandravapus looked baffled at her refusal. Riding a horse was the swiftest way to travel.

'I must admit, I am confounded by your outright denial to oblige this gentle one here,' he said, patting the stallion. 'Any particular reason for your refusal?'

'I can ride if necessary. It's just that I don't prefer it.'

'Why?' he persisted.

Menaka was thoughtful for some time. 'Actually, I never thought why I prefer to walk or take a chariot. But as we speak, I realize that it has something to do with being so intimate with them. Being so close to a living creature…sensing their breath going in and out…I don't know whether I am able to explain it.'

'Sort of,' said Chandravapus. 'I take it that you are not such a fantastic equestrian. I mean, you have to be one with the animal to make it obey your commands…' He trailed off, looking at her to assess whether he had offended her. She did not seem to mind.

They were now strolling away from the university.

'You know there is an old saying, "Show me your horse and I will tell you who you are,"' said Chandravapus pensively.

'They also say, "Show me your tongue and I will tell you who you are,"' Menaka retorted, smiling.

He was contemplative and did not reply.

'So, what is our destination?' Menaka asked, trying to change the topic.

'This stallion here,' he said, patting it affectionately, 'is actually a war horse which I acquired through a friend in the ranks.'

Menaka looked at the stallion. It seemed to be a tall one.

'He measures 16 hands,' said Chandravapus proudly. He looked up and squinted at the sun. 'We need to make haste or we won't reach on time.'

He seemed to make a sudden decision. He looked at her. 'May I…' He indicated whether she would oblige him by riding the horse.

She nodded, knowing it would be futile as well as rude to refuse. All at once she felt herself being hoisted onto the tall stallion. Her legs felt the steady pulse of the living creature as they made contact with its sides. Menaka tried not to grimace.

Chandravapus stifled a smile. Menaka felt embarrassed at her inept ways with the creature. He gripped the reins and walked on briskly, saying no more.

They reached a lesser developed part of the city and swiftly crossed that too. There were no houses or habitation of any kind now. They followed a narrow track where a single carriage could ply at a time.

'Would it be all right if I rode with you?' Chandravapus asked, vexed at the slow pace.

'Yes, I suppose so,' Menaka replied tentatively.

Immediately, he hoisted himself up and they were riding at a speed that was inconceivable to Menaka. Chandravapus relaxed and seemed to have excellent rapport with the stallion. Trees whizzed past. Menaka clenched her eyes shut.

'Almost there,' he said soothingly.

And sure enough, soon they arrived at a large clearing. It was obvious that the clearing was man-made. It was a construction site of some sort. Trees and bushes had been uprooted to reveal the whitish soil. The whole expanse was in the process of being tilled.

Why am I here? Menaka thought, confounded.

Chandravapus helped her off the stallion. She was only too glad to feel the steady earth under her feet.

'You are probably wondering why you are here in the middle of nowhere.'

She looked at him silently, her eyes waiting for the answer.

'This is the first construction that I am going to handle independently.' He paused. 'But that's not why I brought you here. We will come to that. I want you to see this first.'

He led her to the centre of the clearing. Menaka saw a single stone-layered boundary enclosing a small, whitish patch of land.

Chandravapus stepped gingerly into the inner edges and kneeled down, looking at the earth closely. Menaka did the same, perplexed at his actions. He pointed to the centre. She peered hard and spotted a small bright green shoot.

'I see the shoot of a plant there...' Menaka trailed off, knowing implicitly that it had some significance.

'I am now sure the *devasthanam* that I build here will please the devas,' he said, slapping his thigh triumphantly.

He looked at her puzzled expression and laughed. 'I suppose you haven't had any close association with architects before?'

Menaka shook her head mutely, now eager to know the importance of that little shoot.

'It's a well-known secret in our community that before starting the construction of a temple, the land is tilled well and a seed is planted in the centre. If the seed grows into a healthy plant, then the site is fit for building the sacred structure,' he explained patiently.

'So, if the seed does not sprout, you would abandon the site?' Menaka asked incredulously.

'Yes, at least for the time being. The land would have to be imbued with the purity of *yagna*s and mantras, and tilled again.'

He looked at her intently. 'You know, I came here yesterday and there was nothing.' He paused. 'Your presence is propitious for me.'

Menaka looked away, embarrassed at the undeserved compliment.

'I haven't done anything to deserve your compliment. Even if I hadn't come, the outcome would have been the same.'

Chandravapus sensed her awkwardness.

'I have brought you here for something else.' He pointed to the far end of the clearing where there was a small gate.

They walked towards it and to the other side. Menaka gasped. It was a large botanical garden filled with numerous herbs and shrubs. It was being tended by three gardeners. Her eyes darted in all directions as she recognized common as well as rare herbs.

'This is wonderful,' she murmured, unable to take her eyes off the profusion of greenery.

Chandravapus enjoyed the elated look on her face. This was the first time that he had seen her so animated. 'And you are welcome here any time. It won't be open to people until the *devasthanam* is fully constructed. The *devasthanam* is being built for the Brahmins.'

Menaka barely heard him. She walked the paths admiring the life-giving powerhouses. After some time, she turned to Chandravapus, who had been vicariously enjoying her enthusiasm.

'It's too far out. How will I come here?' The practical difficulty of reaching this place brought a frown to her forehead.

'I will arrange for you to be transported…in a carriage,' he added with a twinkle in his eyes.

Menaka looked at him gratefully. Darkness had descended quickly she now realized.

'Let's get back. It's beginning to get eerie,' Menaka said, looking at the dark shadows.

Ashoka pushed away the plate of sprouted grams. It felt like coarse sand in his mouth. Eating it daily for the past week had rendered it almost inedible. The surly attendant had begun to smile at him now. Even without his asking, he had brought the plate and slammed it down on the table.

Poulak, Mandar and the bodyguards appeared in a few minutes. They had been hanging around out of sight for some time, keeping a sharp lookout for any suspicious activities. Now, they sauntered over to where Ashoka sat, grim-faced. He gave them a hostile look.

'Your eyes search for someone. I think we know who. But we can't do anything unless you tell us to,' said Poulak, his mouth full of the apple he was chewing. He exchanged meaningful glances with the others.

Ashoka looked at them, his expression contemplative.

'Find out about her then. Make sure there is no intrusion on anyone's privacy,' he barked.

Angad spoke now. 'I took the liberty of doing some initial investigations.' He paused to assess Ashoka's reaction. 'She is the treasurer Aatreya Shah's daughter.'

When Ashoka didn't react, he continued. 'She likes to visit a far-off botanical garden. She leaves the university early. Frequently, a young man accompanies her there. A family friend. He is an architect who is building a *devasthanam* for the Brahmins.'

'A *devasthanam* for the Brahmins!' exclaimed Ashoka, momentarily distracted by his loathing for this section of Mauryan society. 'As if they don't have enough privileges.'

'Interesting,' was all he said after that, refusing to discuss the matter further.

Ashoka sat in his usual place at the eatery in the university market square. He refused the food, preferring to sip some cool *chaas* instead.

Presently, two young women emerged from around the corner, talking animatedly. The suave Chandravapus lounged lazily some distance away, the hint of a smile on his face. As Menaka spotted him, she half skipped, half ran to meet him. He said something to her that made her wave her arms excitedly in joy. They waved goodbye to Zuri and set off on their own.

Ashoka gulped the remaining *chaas* in one go, thumped the glass down on the table and stormed out.

Chandravapus had been able to coax Menaka to ride on his horse today. The last ten sunsets he had arranged a chariot for her. He timed his visits to the site of the *devasthanam* to coincide with Menaka's trips to the botanical garden. He would busy himself with the workers while she would be engrossed in tending to her herbs. They had developed an easy friendship.

Chandravapus wrapped up his work for the sunset and walked towards the gate of the botanical garden. He stared at Menaka, enjoying watching her at work. She was engrossed in cutting some leaves and carefully placing them in a bag strapped around her shoulder.

He took slow deliberate steps to where she squatted on the ground, peering at some herbs. Sensing his presence, she looked up. It was close to dusk and the shadows made it difficult to see.

'All right. I am almost through,' she said apologetically. 'Are we late?' she asked closing the flap of her bag and standing up simultaneously.

'Take your time,' Chandarvapus said. He caught a strand of her hair that had come loose from her knot and tucked it behind her ear.

Menaka took a step back awkwardly, the intimacy making her uncomfortable.

'Relax,' he said. 'Why are you so tense?' he asked soothingly. He took a step towards her and caught hold of her hands. Menaka froze.

'I can understand that you are uncomfortable with horses. But I am not one,' he teased.

Menaka took another step back, baffled at his intimate tone. Chandravapus threw his head back and laughed at her bewilderment. She gazed at him, hurt written all over her face.

Chandravapus realized he had offended her. He came nearer, not laughing anymore, and brought his face close to hers.

Stepping back, she stumbled on a loose piece of rock. Chandravapus caught her flailing hands in the nick of time and steadied her. 'What's the matter?' he asked, concerned. 'You are almost behaving as if you don't want my company anymore?'

The tears in Menaka's eyes confounded him. He turned his back to her. 'Have I done anything I wasn't supposed to?' he asked in a low voice.

'What was that all about?' Menaka demanded in a quivering voice.

'What was *what* all about?' he asked incredulously turning to face her. 'I was doing what any man who has blood running through his veins would have done.' He paused. 'Are you unhappy?' he asked suddenly. The question confused her.

'I thought you were happy with the alliance,' he said dryly.

'What alliance?' asked Menaka, wiping her tears with the back of her hand.

He looked at her, baffled. 'I can't believe this!' Chandravapus exclaimed. He looked up at the sky. 'We are to be wedded in four lunar cycles and she asks what am I talking about,' he said, shaking his head in amazement at an imaginary figure up in the skies.

'I…I know nothing about this,' whispered Menaka.

Chandravapus turned to look at her, an expression of utter disbelief on his face. 'You mean you had no idea why I came to your house?' he asked with a frown.

'No. Why did you?' Menaka asked with trepidation.

Chandravapus was scowling now. 'Why do families meet? Obviously the whole point was a marital alliance,' he said impatiently. 'It's hard for me to digest that you were not informed about something so important. If you must know, I set eyes on you for the first time at the event organized to welcome the young prince. I liked you in that very instant. I asked Father to propose the alliance, if you were agreeable.'

He looked at her, his eyes blazing now, 'You seemed to be happy enough with my company earlier. Or so I thought,' he added, unsure as he watched the changing expressions on her face.

Menaka felt like a spider caught in its own web.

How unfair of my parents, to keep me in the dark, she thought, anger welling up in her.

Looking at Chandravapus' silhouette in the gathering darkness, she felt his intent eyes on her. His arms were crossed over his chest.

Menaka knew she owed Chandravapus an explanation. 'I…I like your company…'

Chandravapus held up his hand to stop her. 'Save the explanations for later. Let me take you home now,' he said with an air of false nonchalance.

Neither spoke a word on the ride home. When they reached Menaka's residence, he jumped off easily and held up his hand to help her down from the stallion. His expression unreadable, he bowed and in one fluid movement was back on his mount.

Menaka looked at his retreating figure, wishing they had not parted like that.

Menaka lay on her bed, staring blankly at the ceiling. It was stuffy today or maybe her state of mind made her feel it was. She was apprehensive about demanding an explanation from her father. Seething with fury, she had confronted her mother the moment she had reached home. Thankfully, her father had still not come home from work. Her mother had helplessly wrung her hands in response.

'You are so reserved that your father thought it best to keep you in the dark. If we had told you about the alliance, you would have never entertained it, child. It was for your own good,' she had said. 'What will I tell your father now? Have you said something to Chandravapus that you shouldn't have?' her mother had wailed, more concerned about the wrath of her father than her feelings.

Menaka said no more. She had walked up the stairs, utterly drained, and bolted the door to her room.

It was again one of those nights when sleep eluded her. She knew by now that forcing her eyes shut would have no effect at all. It would in fact drive sleep further away.

'Oh no, not the awful rhythmic thudding sound again.' She had always wondered from where it originated. Swinging off her bed, she sat on the windowsill, her legs crossed. As she stared at the streets beyond the garden, she drifted into a half-asleep state. The events of the evening played back in her mind again, as they had numerous times earlier.

Looking up at Chandravapus...his attempts to get close... her surprise at his disclosure...his annoyance and frustration... It always ended with her looking at his silhouette. But this time there was a difference. It wasn't his silhouette she saw – it was someone else's. This time she felt herself drawn to that person and walked towards him slowly. As she inched closer, he turned sideways and she noticed a scar on his shoulder.

She snapped out of her dream-like state, her eyes wide open now. Waves of confusing emotions overwhelmed her as she clutched at her throat. It felt like being on a hill slope full of flowers. She wanted the one that was too high for her to reach.

'She does not seem to meet Chandravapus anymore,' Poulak informed Ashoka.

Ashoka swung the mace around his shoulders gracefully. His wound had healed completely by now.

'Chandravapus who?' Ashoka asked with fake nonchalance.

Poulak smiled, amused.

'Very funny. In case you are interested, there seems to have been a falling-out of some sort.'

Ashoka smiled, deriving a perverse satisfaction at the news. The next moment he flung down the mace and walked out of the exercise arena.

'Do me a favour and don't follow me,' he called behind his shoulder.

He rode swiftly to the university. He dismounted and went into the familiar eatery. The attendant looked surprised at his uncharacteristic smile.

'What can I get you?' he asked gruffly.

'Today, my friend, you can get me anything you want.'

'Anything?'

'That's what I said, isn't it,' replied Ashoka evenly.

The attendant rubbed his hands together in glee. He came back presently and slapped a plate down on the table. It contained some sort of porridge.

'This will make you strong. I eat it all the time,' he said. Ashoka nodded in appreciation. The attendant grunted in acknowledgement and left.

Ashoka soon spotted what he had come for. Gobbling down the last spoonful, he dashed out after throwing some coins on the table. Menaka was crossing the square with her books tucked under her arm. Ashoka pulled the reins of his stallion in order to intercept her.

'What a surprise!' exclaimed Ashoka.

His sudden appearance made her nervous. She bit her lip.

'The scar on your shoulder has healed,' she commented in an attempt at conversation.

'Oh yes. I never got a chance to thank you properly for that,' said Ashoka effusively. The greetings over, an awkward silence ensued, characteristic of two people who did not speak much.

'Why don't I drop you to your house,' offered Ashoka. He held out his hand. She took it and he hoisted her up in front of him. The stallion cantered along the path.

'You know, this is going to be a problem. Neither of us talks too much and I want to know you better,' stated Ashoka simply.

Menaka threw back her head and laughed aloud as if it were the most natural thing in the world.

'How do you know the way to my home?' she asked.

'Actually I don't. I was taking this path on a hunch. Am I off course?' lied Ashoka.

'You are on the right path,' she said cheerfully.

28

Bindusara held a handkerchief to his mouth and coughed out phlegm. He threw the soiled cloth in the pile next to his bed. His body seemed to produce phlegm every few *kashtas*. The pile next to his bed was taken away after every *hora*.

The royal vaid carefully attached leeches to the emperor's thighs. His blood had turned impure – that was what the vaid had told him. The leeches did the trick temporarily by sucking out the poison. He did feel energized for some time. But weariness eventually set in again. Bindusara thought nostalgically about his younger days when he was strong and felt that no force in the world could bring him down. He felt a pinch as the leeches sucked at his blood hungrily.

The vaid had arranged for a steam bath after the leeches were satiated. 'The excess toxins will be released by the perspiration,' he explained to Bindusara.

Bindusara walked into the chamber especially built for the purpose. The small room was made up of heated stone slabs with openings on the top through which water was poured in. This resulted in immense steam being released. He sat on the slabs, enjoying the trickle of perspiration from the pores of his body.

Bindusara emerged after some time from the hot chamber, his grey hair plastered onto his head.

After a bath, as the attendants dressed him, Bindusara reflected on the future.

Maybe it is time now for me to forsake all luxuries and undertake vanaprastha. Life is giving me signals to move on. A spartan forest life may do me good, he thought.

His thoughts wandered to Subhadrangi and Rakshita. *Subhadrangi will gladly accompany me,* he thought. He wasn't too sure about Rakshita.

I should not entertain such thoughts until the throne of the Mauryan empire is secure, he chastised himself. Right now, his top officials awaited him at a meeting to discuss some incidents of trouble on the borders with Kalinga, a neighbouring kingdom known for its fiercely independent people.

Bindusara marched into the discussion hall purposefully. The rajpurohit, Radheya, Akila and Ajaya stood up to welcome him.

Radheya cleared his throat. 'Raje, there is trouble on our borders with Kalinga. As of now, it is not of great magnitude. But the spark can turn into a raging fire if not controlled at the right time.'

Radheya had very skilfully set the tone. Bindusara nodded impatiently, his impatience directed not at Radheya, but at yet another situation on the borders. He was growing tired of it all.

'What insight does our intelligence bring forth?'

Akila was quick to respond. 'The trouble is largely created by our own soldiers. They are inciting the soldiers of Kalinga. Small petty brawls have turned into battalions fighting each other.'

Akila looked at Bindusara worriedly. 'It is a sad situation when our army starts having a mind of its own.'

'What do you suggest, Ajaya?' Bindusara focused his attention on him.

'I can go there myself. The endeavour will be to get the situation in control without another drop of blood being spilt.'

The nasal voice of the rajpurohit broke smoothly into the discussion. 'The magnitude or the lack of it does not warrant the senapati taking the trouble.'

All eyes bored into the rajpurohit. He smoothed his hair and took his time to utter the next sentence. Bindusara waited patiently. Tradition demanded that he listen to the rajpurohit who was entrusted with the task of offering an unbiased view of any situation, as a *margdarshak* would.

'Prince Susima could be entrusted with this task,' the rajpurohit said simply.

No one spoke, for everyone was busy reflecting on the suggestion. It was no secret that Susima had been spending a considerable time with the rajpurohit lately. Bindusara sat up straighter, as he always did when his firstborn was discussed.

'Raje, it is time for the eagle to be coaxed out of the nest. You cannot stop it. It is nature's way,' said the rajpurohit.

Bindusara stared at his aides, trying to assess their verdict.

'Akila, Radheya…what do you think?'

Akila scratched his chin thoughtfully. 'Actually, this could turn out to be a good experience for the prince…as well as us. It will be a test of diplomacy and possibly war skills.'

Ajaya and Radheya nodded in assent, knowing they did not have any compelling argument against the suggestion.

'Have him called then,' Bindusara said with the hint of a smile on his face.

Susima strode into the hall purposefully. He had not been far away since he was expecting the summons. His guru had warned him. Bowing to each senior individually, he then looked at his father for direction.

Akila observed some subtle changes in his former student. There was an air of assurance about him. He appeared calmer, relaxed, more watchful and less impulsive. It was a marked change from his demeanour earlier, where he would be hovering around Bindusara for his approval.

Something told Akila that where he had failed as an acharya to Susima, the rajpurohit had succeeded.

'Sit down, son. You don't have to stand,' Bindusara told him. 'Are you aware that there is trouble on our borders with Kalinga?'

'Yes, Father.'

'How do you propose that we address it?'

'I need access to our intelligence reports in order to assess the situation. While we could take the situation as an excuse to wage war and usurp parts of Kalinga, my feeling is that Kalinga needs to be tackled like a hot dish: Carefully, without burning our hands.' The Susima of yore would have chosen the path of force. But not any longer.

'You shall have access to all the reports you need, son. I appoint you to create a task force to address the Kalinga situation with immediate effect. Akila will offer his strategic guidance in the matter.'

Akila nodded his assent to Bindusara, but his gaze was fixed on his former pupil. He was still trying to fathom this new Susima.

Later that night, Bindusara and the rajpurohit were the only ones in the emperor's private chambers. Bindusara lay supine on the large four-poster bed, weary with the efforts of the sunset.

'Do you think I did right by trusting my firstborn to handle the Kalinga issue?' Bindusara knew it was a redundant question as it was the rajpurohit himself who had proposed Susima's name in the first place. The rajpurohit sensed that Bindusara derived vicarious pleasure from the praise of his son Susima.

'Let me tell you a story, Raje. This one was told to me by our friend Megasthenes.'

Bindusara closed his eyes and settled down for another one of the rajpurohit's tales.

There was once a Greek sculptor, Pygmalion. Life's experiences were such that he became disillusioned by women in general. He vowed to create his perfect woman, albeit in stone. He worked relentlessly for many months on the smallest of details to carve out the woman of his dreams. When the statue was complete, she looked so beautiful that he fell madly in love with his own creation. He named her Galatea. He fervently wished her to be alive and prayed to the Goddess of Love, Aphrodite, to breathe life into her. Seeing his fervour, Aphrodite had no option but to infuse breath into the lifeless statue, creating a living person. Pygmalion could not believe that what he had worked so hard for and prayed for had come true. Galatea was a living woman…the woman of his dreams. They wed and lived a happy life thereafter.

The rajpurohit, who was himself absorbed in the narration, paused and looked dreamily outside the window. A passing bird fluttered noisily and broke his reverie.

'Such is the power of expectations, Raje. It turns into a self-fulfilling prophecy for the person.' He paused to let that sink in.

'Trust him without an iota of doubt,' continued the rajpurohit, enjoying himself now. 'Even cow's milk has the same effect as mothers milk to us as we call her *Gomata*. Nature has to bow down to fulfil our heartfelt expectations.'

The rajpurohit looked at Bindusara whose eyes were closed

now. He got up to leave, knowing full well that the emperor had heard every word uttered by him.

On his way out, he nodded to the double layer of guards. The *antahpura* was designed in such a manner that Bindusara occupied a double chamber. A chamber within a chamber. The inner guards would not allow visitors to enter unless the ones on the outside said it was fine to do so. The protocol was reversed for visitors moving out.

The rajpurohit smiled sardonically to himself.

'It is Susima who needs guarding now, old Bindusara. His time has come,' he whispered to himself.

It was a tacit understanding between Menaka and Ashoka that they would meet everyday at the university square. They would ride around on his stallion or go to markets and parks. Acutely aware of each other, to them the surroundings did not matter at all. The attraction was palpable. However, Ashoka by ingrained habit took in every detail wherever he went.

He made sure his bodyguards were at a safe distance, and that he would be able to lose them if and when necessary.

'So, why are you here?' Menaka inquired casually one sunset. Ashoka raised his eyebrows, unable to comprehend the question. 'I mean, you are the prince. I am sure you are not here to while away your time sightseeing.'

They were seated on the steps of an old temple, their backs resting against the pillars.

'I am not whiling away my time,' said Ashoka quietly. *This is possibly the best time of my life,* he thought. His hands were crossed over his chest and his eyes were half closed. The warm sun made him feel drowsy.

'Oh, wake up,' said Menaka impatiently, throwing a marigold at his face.

He did not twitch a muscle. 'Was that supposed to wake me up?' he asked guilelessly.

Menaka threw a whole bunch forcefully at him in exasperation.

'Nice. Very fresh. I like the fragrance. I think I can have a pleasant nap now,' he said, sliding off the pillar and lying down.

'All right, sleep all you want. You may be a relative of Kumbhakaran for all I care. I am going,' Menaka snapped, standing up.

The temple was deserted. Even the priest had left. Ashoka made no attempt to stop her, knowing they were a fair distance away from habitation.

I must be slipping, thought Ashoka. He had actually dozed off in the last few minutes. The sun was halfway down on its journey to illuminate another part of the earth. Menaka was nowhere to be seen.

He jumped up swiftly and strode around to the front of the temple. It looked deserted.

'Menaka!' he shouted. No answer. *Where could she be?* he thought, uncertainty taking a firm hold on him.

Maybe I need to tell her that someone wants me killed and she could be the unwitting victim of a plot. That disturbing thought flashed across Ashoka's mind – the first time such a thought had struck him.

The temple was surrounded by a thick forest. The luxuriantly green shrubs now began to look ominous as the shadows grew longer. His gaze scanned the forests swiftly for any movement. An uneasiness gripped him. This was no longer a game.

'Menaka, if you are hiding somewhere, please show yourself!' he shouted in an attempt to draw her out of hiding.

The only sound he heard was the chirping of the crickets in the bushes. Anticipating danger, Ashoka gripped the handle of his sword firmly and started forward.

'Surprise!' shouted Menaka as she jumped in front of him from behind a pillar.

Ashoka exhaled in relief. 'Don't...ever do that again, Menaka,' he said slowly, emphasizing each word.

She looked at him, surprised at his tone. Was it her imagination or did she see a shadow cross his face? Maybe it *was* her imagination for he was smiling crookedly now, all traces of worry gone from his face.

'You will pay for this, Menaka,' he said, lunging at her playfully.

She was surprisingly agile and dodged him, running off towards the forest. The tip of Ashoka's sword snagged an object in the air which he deftly caught in his hands and put in the pocket of his dhoti as he started to pursue her.

Menaka flew across the temple premises and was into the forest now, laughing at Ashoka's vain attempts to catch up with her. She was so intent on looking back at her pursuer that she did not see a patch of slippery moss ahead. Before she knew it, she had slipped and fallen face down. A clump of nettles scraped her knees and elbows.

She sat up, half wincing, half laughing. Ashoka had caught up with her by then. A comical sight awaited him. Tears streaming down her face as she half laughed and half cried at her own predicament.

'I must be quite a sight,' she said, getting up gingerly.

Ashoka held out his arm to support her.

'Now I don't have to do anything. Nature has settled the score for us,' he said in jest.

She limped slowly, holding on to his arm. 'Do you want me to carry you?' he asked gallantly. Menaka shook her head vehemently.

'You have to get back home on time. It's dark.'

That was enough for Menaka. She nodded her assent. He hoisted her on his back and headed back to the temple premises where his stallion was tethered.

Their voices carried across to the other end of the ground where Ashoka's bodyguards stood well hidden in the trees.

Later that night, Ashoka carefully wrapped in a handkerchief the object he had picked up from the tip of his sword, and hid it under his clothes in his cupboard. It was Menaka's anklet.

The secluded temple became a favourite haunt of Menaka and Ashoka. They would have many long discussions on seemingly inane topics. Ashoka was usually in an amiable frame of mind and indulged her with tales of many escapades of his younger days.

Today Menaka sensed a difference. Ashoka seemed ill at ease for some reason.

'You must learn some form of self-defence,' he asserted.

'Why do I need that? I am not a warrior,' argued Menaka.

'Exactly! That's why you must learn. It is simply self-defence, Menaka. I am not suggesting you train in archery or the sword. Just learn how to wield a small weapon such as this.' He showed her a small knife. 'A dagger, at least,' he coaxed.

Menaka screwed up her face in disgust. Weapons meant violence and violence meant blood. The very thought of blood was revolting to her. She got up to leave.

He caught her wrist and pulled her back.

'Not so fast. I am still talking to you.' He looked her straight in the eye. 'I would not be discussing this if it were not of great importance to me.'

Menaka wrenched her wrist free. 'But I can't. This is just not my thing,' she snapped.

'It does not need to be…your thing. Just shut your mind and learn this skill.' Ashoka made a conscious attempt to keep his temper in check.

Menaka did not budge from her stance.

'Nothing has ever happened to me in all these years. I have never been caught in a situation where I have had to defend myself,' she argued.

'Situations can change overnight. You did not know me

earlier either…and now you do,' Ashoka said, his impatience visible now.

'Just because you are the prince and a Kshatriya does not mean that I too have to be like you,' Menaka continued, refusing to bow down to his demand.

Ashoka looked at her, his eyes blazing.

You don't have a choice. The choice was taken away the sunset a Kshatriya fell in love with you, he thought. *If anything were to happen to you…* Ashoka shook his head, refusing to consider that possibility.

However, he remained silent now, knowing that the discussion was futile and best left for another moment. Lying down on the steps, he closed his eyes.

Menaka was already walking away on the pretext of gathering some flowers. He looked at her through the slits of his eyes.

She shies away from any kind of confrontation, he reflected sighing deeply.

'I will have to find a way to coax her into it.'

Not the sweet smell of flowers, not even the fragrance of sandal, tagara or jasmine blows against the wind. But the fragrance of the virtuous blows against the wind. Truly the virtuous man pervades all directions with the fragrance of his virtue.

Dhammapada

Ashoka read the text of Menaka's painting and burst out laughing.

'What's so funny?' Menaka asked, miffed at his reaction.

'Do you really want to know?' Ashoka asked, smirking.

'Yes,' she answered simply, holding up her brush in mid-air.

'Whoever has said this has his head in *swargaloka*. What does being virtuous mean anyway? Don't you think it is the sweet fragrance of power that spreads in all directions?' Ashoka said with emphasis on the word 'power'. He frowned. 'The so-called virtuous in our society use it as a garb to hide their lust for money and wealth. I am talking about the Brahmin *varna*. I will wipe them off the face of the earth one day,' he whispered, gnashing his teeth.

Menaka looked at Ashoka suddenly afraid at what she saw. It was as if violence lay buried in the depths of his being – it only needed a spark to erupt like a volcano. She took a few steps back. This was not the Ashoka she loved – this was a stranger. She peered at his face. It looked different. She wanted to run away, back to the old one.

Menaka ran, not knowing where she was going.

He looked at her back, surprised. It took him a few seconds to realize what was happening. He raced behind her and overtook her easily. Catching hold of her arm, he pulled her to a stop.

'Where…are you going…and why?' he asked confounded at her extreme reaction.

Menaka took some deep breaths and looked into the familiar concerned eyes of the Ashoka she knew. He was back.

'I don't know…you acted so strangely. You looked different…almost spitting wrath. It's frightening.'

'By Shiva…please forget what I said. I wasn't thinking,' Ashoka said, distressed.

Poulak smiled at his bright student. She had picked up the nuances very quickly. He recalled the first sunset when he had asked her to take a few swings. Being the novice that she was, she had swung the dagger in an arc to attack.

'Attack in a straight thrust for maximum damage. It's a thrusting weapon. You need to point it in a straight line,' he had instructed matter-of-factly. She looked horrified and almost quit the notion of learning how to use the weapon.

Poulak had been reluctant to teach her at first as she had requested him to keep her training a secret from Ashoka. But he had given in to her persuasion.

Mandar, who had been watching from the galley the first sunset, had shaken his head at Poulak, indicating it would prove to be a futile exercise. But Poulak was a gentleman and could not disappoint Menaka.

'Not bad,' he had lied about her clumsy initial attempts to encourage her.

He taught her the 16 basic positions, covering high, low, left and right, with the dagger held forward or in a reverse hand. Initially, they progressed at a snail's pace. But after a week, he could not believe the change in her skill level. What she lacked in strength, she made up for in nimbleness of foot and accuracy of attack. But her strength was defence and not attack. *Just as well*, he thought.

'Ashoka will be surprised,' he told her, smiling, after a few sessions.

'That's what I want,' Menaka said mischievously.

The surprise for Ashoka came sooner than intended. When they were on one of their jaunts together, an object fell out of the folds of Menaka's attire as he helped her down her mount.

'What is this?' said Ashoka, picking it up. 'A dagger! You know you have to learn how to use it. Just keeping it on your person is no good,' he said vehemently, shaking his head.

Menaka glared at him, exasperated that Ashoka had spotted the dagger before she was ready to disclose her secret. In one swift movement, the dagger zipped past her ear and firmly lodged itself in a tree trunk behind her.

Marvelling at his precision, she walked to where it was wedged and pulled it out with difficulty. On an impulse, she threw it back. It stuck in the earth at Ashoka's feet.

He looked at her, astonished.

'How did you do that? Not bad for someone who does not know how to wield a weapon. Shows your potential,' he said encouragingly. 'But no. You have closed your mind to learning this skill,' he sighed.

'Try me,' Menaka challenged him.

Ashoka laughed at the invitation.

'I don't fight women. Especially ones who can't stand the sight of blood!'

Menaka responded by hurling another dagger that lodged itself in the basket of fruits they were carrying.

'All right. If you insist.' Ashoka handed one of the daggers back to Menaka and himself gripped the other. He walked towards her.

She felt her palms grow sweaty. The idea did not seem to be such a good one now. She shifted the dagger to the other hand, rubbing the free hand against her clothes to wipe off her perspiration.

Menaka glanced at him to get a clue of his line of attack. But he seemed to be carved out of stone.

'Help me, Shiva,' prayed Menaka, mentally kicking herself for creating this difficult situation for herself. What was she thinking? But now there was no turning back.

Ashoka was close to her now. 'We can abandon the exercise if you wish,' he said suddenly, sensing her unease.

'I don't think so,' retorted Menaka with a new resolve.

Ashoka shrugged. 'Have it your way then.'

He launched a sudden attack on her left shoulder. Menaka stepped back on her right foot and blocked it with ease. Ashoka smiled, surprised at her expert move.

'Not bad at all. When did you learn…' He did not have a chance to finish the sentence. In a flash Menaka thrust her dagger at his unprotected solar plexus. He blocked it just in time.

She shifted the dagger, alternating between her right and left hands, to confuse him. He then launched a series of quick attacks which she evaded by nimbly stepping away each time. By now she was drenched in perspiration – a stark contrast to Ashoka, who looked cool and composed.

With a fresh burst of energy Menaka held the dagger in a reverse grip and attempted to attack his right shoulder. The second he blocked it, she came out with a surprise weapon that she had concealed until now. The deadly curved dagger. Noticing his momentary distraction, she swung an arm to his thigh. He was ready for it and jumped up easily to avoid it.

Menaka now yelled in frustration and launched attack after attack which he blocked easily. Interlocking her foot against his, she tried to trip him. He wouldn't budge. He now went on the offensive which she tried to dodge by stepping back. Stumbling against a rock, she fell to the ground. He swung his dagger at her, and Menaka covered her eyes as a reflex, knowing that she was near defeat. The next moment she felt his hand prying hers away. He pulled her up.

'Did you for a second think I would spill even a single drop of your blood?' He threw the daggers away and kissed her hands. 'Who taught you?'

'Poulak.'

'I must thank him. But why did you not learn from me?' Ashoka asked, sounding a trifle disgruntled.

'I wanted to surprise you.'

'You have succeeded,' he said, pulling her close.

'I don't want to go,' wailed Menaka to Zuri, who had come to spend the sunset with her.

Zuri grinned at her. 'Stop sulking and get dressed,' she told her firmly.

'Now I know why Father insists I attend these silly official functions. He hopes someone will catch my attention or vice versa. He wants to wash his hands of me by marrying me off,' Menaka ranted. She was sitting cross-legged on the bed.

'So, what's wrong in that?' retorted Zuri. 'That is what is good for you. A chance to move out of here. Besides, you have already found someone. He will be there too,' she coaxed.

She carefully laid out some garments on the bed.

'I like meeting him alone. I am sure Governor Huma will drag him off. You too are not going. I will be all alone and bored,' Menaka continued her tirade. 'Besides, Ashoka does not want too many people to know that we are…friends. Something to do with my security.'

Zuri pursed her lips, knowing very well it was useless to continue talking. She walked up to Menaka, and amidst vehement protests, pulled her clothes off.

Grumbling all the while, she put on the sea green *antariya* and wrapped it around her waist. A dull gold band covered her breasts with a silken *uttariya* flung casually over it. Zuri applied kohl generously to her eyes. A little colour to the lips and she was ready.

Aatreya Shah did not say much on the journey to Governor Huma's house. He was probably tight-lipped as he did not approve of Zuri. Menaka's mother looked nervous, probably fearing that her husband might say something to offend her.

Menaka and Zuri spoke in low voices and giggled. Menaka's initial trepidation had given way to excitement and anticipation of the evening ahead. Her mother looked at her curiously, unable to comprehend the change in her daughter.

They dropped Zuri off and continued. Aatreya belched, the acid rising up his throat. It was a chronic disease now.

On an impulse, Menaka put her hand in her pouch and took out a fragrant smelling powder.

'Here Father, take this. It will help you,' she said, handing over the powder to him. He hesitated for a second and then poured the powder down his throat and took a sip of water. Menaka had never dared to offer her concoctions to her father before.

'I feel better,' he said after a while, a grudging smile curling the edges of his lips.

As they approached Huma's house, Aatreya commented to no one in particular, 'He sure puts on a good show doesn't he?'

The colour green dominated the decorations. Green lamps, plants and artefacts all adhered to this colour scheme. Menaka looked down at her green clothes in dismay – why, of all the colours, did she have to wear this?

Governor Huma stood at the porch, waiting to welcome all the guests. He himself wore a green *angavastram*. As they got off the carriage, Huma gave a cursory nod to Menaka's father. They were after all colleagues and met each other at least once in seven sunsets.

As Aatreya and his family walked in, he shook his head in disdain. This blatant show of wealth annoyed him.

They were escorted to the huge, ostentatiously decorated hall at the far end of the corridor. This was only the second time that Menaka was here.

'Today, I will enjoy every moment,' she resolved with mounting excitement.

The green lamps lent an eerie glow to the hall. An attendant came up to them with a drink that echoed the colour of the day.

'What is this?' asked Aatreya, grimacing.

'Khus syrup, sir' said the attendant deferentially. Everyone in the hall knew him.

Menaka scanned the room but could not spot Ashoka anywhere. She sighed and helped herself to a drink. Hearing some giggles, she craned her neck to see a group of girls behind the pillar. She recognized them.

I might as well join them, she thought.

Soon, the party was in full swing, the *madira* flowing freely. Aatreya, Huma and another official huddled together in the corner.

'How are you, Menaka?' whispered someone in Menaka's ear. She turned to face the speaker and exhaled sharply. It was Chandravapus. His head tilted, he was staring at her, a glass of *madira* in his hands. From the looks of it, he had already partaken of a lot of the stimulant.

'Oh,' was all she said, completely at a loss for words. She had not expected to see him here.

'I see that you are doing well. You look happy.'

'I am,' said Menaka, looking sideways for an excuse to leave.

As if sensing her intention, he put his arm across the pillar, making it impossible for her to walk away.

'I thought we would be happy together,' said Chandravapus, his eyes boring deep into hers.

She stared back embarrassed and at a loss for words.

'Is there someone else? Is that why you refused to marry me?' he asked in a low voice.

Menaka froze. He looked at her face and knew his arrow had found its mark.

'There was no one when we were friends,' Menaka defended herself.

'I don't believe that! You with your innocent doe eyes had me fooled. But not any longer,' he said angrily.

'Look, I think this conversation is inappropriate and you have had too much to drink. Now, if you will, I have to go somewhere,' said Menaka, trying to push him away.

He did not budge.

'She is saying she would rather be somewhere else,' said a calm voice.

Chandravapus turned around and glared at the intruder. His hostile expression changed to a confused one as he recognized the young prince. He bowed to him but stood his ground.

'With all due respect, this is between me and her, Prince. I am no stranger to her and was going to marry her,' explained Chandravapus patiently.

'Well, she does not seem agreeable to the proposition now,' Ashoka continued to speak evenly. He noticed Menaka putting her hand to her head, dismayed at the mounting tension.

Chandravapus held his ground. He saw the two of them exchange a glance, and realization dawned upon him.

'So, it's the prince,' he said incredulously, waving his arms in agitation. 'I don't stand a chance, do I? I still want to talk to you…in private, Menaka,' he said, grabbing her arm.

It did not go unnoticed by Ashoka that Menaka looked terrified. Glancing sideways, he signalled to his companions to intervene. In a flash, Poulak and Mandar emerged from behind the pillars. They pinned Chandravapus' arms behind his back.

'Don't create a scene,' whispered Poulak in his ear. He gestured to Ashoka. 'It won't go down well with him. Trust me.'

Chandravapus knew a struggle was futile. He had no option but to witness Ashoka escorting Menaka away. Ashoka shot a glance back at Chandravapus – anger and hatred were written all over his face.

'I can explain,' Menaka said nervously to Ashoka.

'It's all right,' said Ashoka. 'I know about him.'

'You do?' she asked incredulously. 'How…when…' she trailed off.

'It's not important,' Ashoka said, brushing off her queries.

She stared at him, confounded that he knew about Chandravapus.

'It's really not important, Menaka. Let us enjoy ourselves while we are here. I promise he won't trouble you anymore.'

Chitrakoot and Angad trailed Ashoka and Menaka, keeping a safe distance. Angad was edgy as the hall was too crowded for his comfort.

Chitrakoot's gaze wandered across the room and settled on Governor Huma and his coterie. Aatreya Shah, who was one of them, gulped the last of his *madira*. A man emerged from behind and whispered something in Huma's ear. Huma looked up at him, obviously peeved at the unwelcome intrusion. He issued some orders rapidly, to which the man bowed and then left.

Chitrakoot, who was watching the exchange, suddenly caught hold of Angad's arm.

'Get away, fatso,' Angad said, jerking his arm free.

'That's it! That's it!' said Chitrakoot, jubilantly slapping his thighs.

'What's that matter? Did you see a plateful of meat or something?' asked Angad, smirking.

'From this sunset onwards, you are going to respect me, Angad. I know you don't think too highly of my brains. But you will change your opinion soon,' said Chitrakoot, upbeat. 'I need to speak to the prince right now.'

He began to stride towards Ashoka.

'I wouldn't try to catch his attention now,' Angad cautioned, looking in Ashoka's direction. He seemed to be in a deep conversation with Menaka. Chitrakoot stemmed his excitement and reluctantly came back to where Angad sat.

'Want to tell me why you refuse to sit still?' coaxed Angad.

'Admit it. You are not the only one who has brains…' Chitrakoot crowed.

'Admit what? You haven't told me anything as yet. I am all ears,' Angad retorted.

Chitrakoot scratched his chin and grinned. 'Did you see that man who was speaking to Governor Huma? The one who seemed to be taking some instructions from him and then disappeared…'

'Yes, I did,' said Angad. 'So?'

'So, he is the one who supplied change to the shopkeepers.'

Angad frowned, trying to recollect.

'Remember, we ate at a place when Ashoka rode away on his own. Well, he's the one. Trust me. I never forget a face,' explained Chitrakoot.

Angad's eyes sparkled as he made the connection. The two looked impatiently in Ashoka's direction. Nevertheless, they kept a rein on their excitement, waiting for an opportune moment.

Later that night Ashoka and his companions huddled together across the table in his chambers.

'So, that's how the market is flooded with counterfeit coins. It's ingenious. Simply supply the small shops with change. They don't have any coin examiners to sift out the real from the fake.' Ashoka paused, smoothing his hair thoughtfully.

'How come it did not strike you the first time you saw the man dumping change?' he asked Chitrakoot. 'In fact, all of you were there...' accused Ashoka, looking hard at each one.

There was silence as they hung their heads in shame. Each knew it was best to avoid any excuses, for Ashoka did not take kindly to that at all.

'Here is the plan.' He looked at Poulak and Mandar. 'Both of you seem to have hit a wall as far the gambling hall is concerned. You have been going there everyday with no luck at getting a sample of Huma's coins. Tomorrow is your last chance. Get a sample of Huma's gambling money.'

They looked down, ashamed.

Ashoka moved on to Angad and Chitrakoot. 'You will kidnap Huma's man who supplies change to the small shops and get him here. We will keep him in the basement...without Eknath's knowledge. It's your job to plan this to perfection.'

The instructions were issued tersely. Everyone present instinctively knew it was the only chance Ashoka would give them.

Chandravapus rode swiftly to the site of the *devasthanam*. He had resolved to immerse himself in work. That was the only way to stay sane.

'You are a fool of the highest order,' a voice inside his head chided him.

'It was the *madira*,' he pleaded his case.

'It's a lame excuse. You made a fool of yourself for a mere woman. Did you even know her some time back? The prince's men humiliated you,' the voice in his head said, unheeding of his pleas.

'It won't happen again,' he told his voice of judgement.

Chandravapus reached the site of the *devasthanam*. It was noon and the sun was at its hottest. He slumped off his horse when he saw the scene before him.

The workers sat on their haunches, staring at their work site and talking excitedly amongst themselves. Their leader ran towards Chandravapus as he saw him approach.

'Sir…I can't understand what has happened!'

Chandravapus was oblivious to the frantic cries of the man. He stared at the *devasthanam*…now reduced to rubble and ashes. Frantically, his eyes scanned the scene for any hope. But, it was not meant to be. Every inch of vegetation was burnt to the roots. A telltale haze of smoke hung in the air. The hot ashes scalded his feet even through his sandals. The clean slabs of the half constructed temple now lay broken into small pieces piled haphazardly. He clambered onto the pile, hoping he would find at least one intact slab. His legs gave away and he slumped on the pile of rubble and rolled to the ground. A spurt of blood gushed out of his forehead, pierced by the sharp edge of a rock. But Chandravapus scarcely noticed.

Standing up with effort, he walked unsteadily to the far corner where the gate to the botanical garden lay. The garden was alive and cheerful in the sunlight.

This is no accident, thought Chandravapus grimly. *Someone has wrecked my creation on purpose. Who could it be?* he thought scratching his chin. The thought momentarily distracted him from his state of distress.

I have no enemies, he emphatically told himself. *Wait…unless it was the prince. Didn't those thugs of his tell me yesterday that he would not take kindly to my behaviour? But a prince would never destroy a temple. The Kshatriyas worship the gods, for it is by their grace that they win battles against all odds.* Chandravapus shook his head violently as these thoughts passed through. Still, an element of doubt remained.

I shall make this temple again from scratch. I will till the earth myself and plant the first sacred seed, he resolved.

He felt a new energy surge through his veins. In a strange way, he felt exhilarated. It was as if the new goal had renewed his sense of purpose in life.

He looked up at the sky with folded hands. 'Thank you, Shiva. Thank you. Strange are your ways of jolting us awake.'

He walked purposefully towards the workers.

'Clear the whole land and start tilling it again. Give me a shovel too. We have work to do. I will call our *kulbrahmin* to consecrate this place tomorrow.'

The workers stared at Chandravapus, unable to comprehend his excitement amidst the destruction. He had already begun tilling the land.

29

Susima walked into the court, taking long strides towards the throne where his father sat. He had arrived from Kalinga a little while ago. Still attired in his armour, he had not bothered to wash up. Strangely, the dust on his clothes and the perspiration on his face added to his stately persona.

He bowed deeply to Bindusara. The court was silent.

'What news do you bring from our borders with Kalinga?' asked Bindusara.

'Kalinga sends you a gift.' He nodded to the aide standing behind him.

The aide held a cushion in both his hands on which lay a brightly painted box. At Susima's behest, the aide walked up to Bindusara who took the box in his hands and opened it. The single emerald reflected a beam of green light to the carved ceiling of the hall for all to see. The emperor held up the ring.

A cheer went up from the ministers present. This meant that the formidable Kalinga had extended a hand of friendship towards Magadha.

Bindusara wore the ring and looked at the royal scribe who was sitting on his left. The scribe rose. He was equivalent in rank to the councillors and received a handsome salary of 48,000 *panas* a year. His job was to officially document all communication from the emperor to the rest of the world.

'Please send a befitting message to my friend at Kalinga that I gladly accept his token of friendship.'

He then returned his gaze to Susima. 'I am curious to know how you managed to turn the situation around.'

'Actually, there were some misunderstandings which I resolved.'

'Was there bloodshed?'

'Not a drop,' declared Susima with aplomb.

Bindusara relaxed back on the cushions. Susima had fared better than he had expected.

'Go, commander. Go and rest for now. Tomorrow the court will be interested in a detailed account of how you handled the potentially explosive situation at Kalinga. It must have been an exercise in diplomacy.'

Susima bowed and strode out of the court.

'Well done, my son,' Bindusara murmured under his breath.

Poulak and Mandar looked at the man tied to the bench, lying on his back. The single lamp created gloomy shadows in the windowless basement.

'He is coming around,' remarked Mandar who was quick to notice some movement in the man's toes. It was evident that the man was in pain given the contortion of his features. There was a convulsive movement followed by a fountain of green bile from his mouth. As he was tied to the bench, the spew landed back on him, soiling his face and chest.

The two made no attempt to help the man. In a way it was good. The putrid smell of vomit was sometimes more difficult to bear than pain. This might save them from the bother of torturing the man.

'I hope he doesn't suffocate,' Poulak remarked. 'We don't want him to die before we get the information we need.'

'Forget the information – Ashoka would kill us for carelessness,' Mandar said nervously.

'Yes, for carelessness, he would.'

The two awaited the arrival of the prince. It had been easy to track down the captive. A day lounging around the small shops was all it required. He had emerged with his sack full of change. They had followed him and accosted him in a deserted by-lane.

Ashoka emerged from the low doorway. He straightened up, his eyes taking a moment to adjust to the dim surroundings. Followed closely by his bodyguards, he walked slowly up to the bound man. Something told him that it would be an eventful sunset. He looked down at the man's face. He was a picture of disarray.

'Too much hair. I can't see through his beard and hair. Shave him.'

The command was adhered to swiftly. Mandar took it upon himself to complete the distasteful task.

'I am a man of many talents,' he jested with the rest. 'There!' Mandar sighed with satisfaction.

Poulak finished off the job by throwing a bucket of icy cold water on the half-conscious man. The man jolted into consciousness. He looked different now. There was an ugly bruise on his jaw that was turning blue. Unusually fair, he had a square face with a perfectly round scalp. A long scar marked the face, starting out from the side of his jaw upwards, winding around his left ear – a feature that had been hidden under the beard.

'Beautiful!' remarked Ashoka. 'Where did you get that?'

The dazed man opened his eyes wide as he recognized the prince.

'I don't understand,' he murmured weakly.

'Of course you do. If you don't, then you'd better soon,' said Ashoka gravely.

'He is known to lack patience,' explained Chitrakoot. 'Especially with people like you,' he added.

Ashoka turned to Poulak and Mandar. 'You know what we want.'

They nodded in understanding.

Ashoka strode out as swiftly as he had come in, Angad and Chitrakoot close at his heels.

Many secrets will unravel soon, he thought.

That night Ashoka drifted into a deep sleep through the howls of pain which almost seemed like a lullaby to him. He knew he was closer to the culmination of his mission than ever before. The answers would be revealed to him in the morning.

Early the next morning Ashoka entered the basement and took in the scene quickly. The captive did not have any marks of torture on his body.

'Pulling out a couple of toe nails was enough to make him talk,' Mandar informed him.

Ashoka raised his eyebrows questioningly, eager to know the answers.

Poulak said quietly, 'The culprit seems to be the treasurer… Aatreya Shah.' He pointed to the man who was in agonizing pain. 'Officially, he works for Huma, unofficially for Aatreya.'

Ashoka closed his eyes. The revelation shocked him. It was as if the blood running though his veins was now racing, the confines of the body too stifling.

Why him? Anybody but him, he thought with a flash of dismay. Menaka's father as the culprit was too close for comfort.

'Are you sure about the treasurer?' Ashoka asked Poulak, trying to conceal any signs of distress.

'Yes. I am. He is telling the truth. We also have a sample of Huma's coins,' he said somberly. Despite the breakthrough, there was no sense of jubilation in any of them.

'How did you manage that?' Ashoka asked curiously.

'I bumped into Huma at the gambling hall yesterday. I suppose some old skills die hard,' Mandar said with a wan smile.

'I will test those,' Angad offered.

'What does he say about Huma?' asked Ashoka.

'Huma, for all his ostentatious display of wealth, does not seem to be a part of this murky plan. He lives well, that's all,' said Poulak.

'Where does Aatreya mint the counterfeit coins?' Ashoka asked, trying to fit all the pieces together.

'You will never guess,' Poulak stated gravely. 'In his own house.'

The temerity of Aatreya's actions shook Ashoka. *Why?* he asked himself again. *He is the treasurer of Takshashila with immense respect and power, not to mention a handsome salary of 48,000* panas, he thought, trying to understand the motive behind the man's betrayal to the Mauryan Empire. Unable to comprehend, he made some quick decisions.

'Contact our battalion from Pataliputra. Recall them to the palace. The grounds are big enough for them to camp here. I also intend to take control of the local forces stationed here by tomorrow. Angad, please set up a meeting with Huma.'

All present nodded gravely at Ashoka's terse commands. The grave complication this would have on his personal life was not lost upon them.

Ashoka looked at the sky. The sun's heat was harsh and unrelenting. It was noon.

They were stationed outside Aatreya's house. Instructions had been issued to bar the local population from frequenting this path on the pretext of construction work. Aatreya had not gone to work today owing to his ill health.

The prince gave the signal to his men to advance. He

had taken the necessary precautions to avoid unnecessary pain and embarrassment to Aatreya's immediate family – Menaka's family. A message had been delivered to his wife that a relative was unwell and requested her presence. She had left some time ago, taking their son with her.

And Menaka is safe in the university, Ashoka thought. He shut his mind to the imminent truth Menaka would have to face regarding her father. She would not only have to face the fact that her father was a traitor, but also come to terms with the reality that it was Ashoka who had issued the orders to put him in prison. The thought of her reaction made him feel almost dead with pain.

Will our relationship change? he thought dismally. *Will she still love me? Will she understand that I am bound to do what I have to?* The questions plagued him relentlessly, the answers to which only time would tell.

Poulak led a group of eight men into Aatreya's house. The treasurer looked unruffled as he came out of his house. Force had been unnecessary.

To Ashoka, watching from afar, he seemed almost nonchalant. He felt rage well up within his being. Rage, not only because the man had dared to dupe the Mauryan empire, but also because he was Menaka's father. Unable to contain his emotions, he abruptly left the scene.

I will not speak to him outside Menaka's house, thought Ashoka as he rode away followed by Angad and Chitrakoot.

There was no jubilation at the rapid advances made in his mission. Instead, a deep sense of foreboding dominated his being.

I will have to tell her myself, he thought, greatly perturbed.

Ashoka was waiting for Menaka much before she arrived at the university square. She started to run as soon as she spotted him, and playfully jumped onto his horse.

'Anything the matter?' she asked him, who was left holding the reins.

'Er…no. Why do you say that?' he asked quickly, trying to put on a mask of easy camaraderie.

'You seem a little lost today. Somebody hasn't obeyed your orders, is it?' she joked.

He took in a deep breath and turned to her, smiling. 'Let's go our favourite temple,' he proposed.

'Sure, any place is fine with me as long as I am home by dusk. Father has been cantankerous of late.'

'All right,' Ashoka spoke slowly, jumping up on the horse behind her.

Once they were there, Menaka ran up the steps and prostrated herself before Lord Shiva. Ashoka did not follow her in. He could see her mouthing prayers, her eyes tightly closed. As usual there was no one around except for the priest. He acknowledged Menaka as she held out her cupped hands for some holy water. Gulping it down, she ran down the steps of the temple.

Not finding Ashoka there, she followed the walls to the backyard. He was sitting with his back towards her, staring vacantly at the ground. He did not seem to hear her approach.

As she moved closer, he became aware of her presence. He pulled her in a tight embrace.

'Is everything all right?' Menaka asked, surprised at his uncharacteristic display of emotion.

'I…can't live without you,' Ashoka said, not releasing her.

'That makes two of us. Neither can I,' she said brightly.

'What if I was in some way responsible for some unfavourable event in your life?' he whispered in her ear.

Menaka's mood changed from exuberant to sombre. A sixth sense warned her of some catastrophe that lay ahead. She pulled herself free and looked into his eyes, her heart thumping.

'Tell me – now. I know something has happened,' she said apprehensively.

He stared into her anxious eyes and for the hundredth time wondered why Shiva had played such a trick on him. Everything had been fine a few sunsets ago. And now, it was as if all was out of control. As if a huge rock bursting out of a catapult had found its mark.

Why did Menaka have to be Aatreya's daughter?

Why do I have to be the person to inflict this pain on her? he thought, the agony in his heart cutting through like a knife.

He felt Menaka tugging at his arm. Taking a deep breath, he took the plunge. 'You have asked me several times why I am here at Takshashila. And I always deflected your query. The sunset has come for me to share some painful truths. I am here on a mission.' He paused. 'Do you remember the sunset you bought jewellery?'

'Yes.'

'Your coins were checked before acceptance, weren't they?

'Yes,' Menaka replied, her voice quivering.

'That's because the market is infiltrated with counterfeit coins. From where do they come? Who mints them? Who is the mastermind behind this despicable operation? Those are the questions that led me to the streets of Takshashila.'

'Have you found the answers?' Menaka asked tentatively, gripping his hand tightly.

'Yes.'

Intuitively she knew that the answer would bring grief. She turned to walk away. 'Let us go from this place. I am not feeling too good.'

Ashoka folded his arms and stayed where he was. 'Don't you want to know who the mastermind is?'

'No!' she said, her voice trembling. 'Let's go.'

But Ashoka did not back off now. 'It's the treasurer,' he whispered. The softness had gone from his voice.

She looked into his eyes with a pained expression. His eyes were hard and his face was carved out of stone.

'It can't be!' she shrieked. 'He has not been an ideal father to me. But he is not a dishonest man. He is a man of principles. I don't believe it. You must not have the whole truth.' Menaka was vehement in her denial. He stared at the dark forest steadily, as if by not looking into her eyes, he could spare her the pain.

'He has been arrested,' he said in a flat tone.

Menaka felt her legs grow weak. Unable to support herself, she slumped onto the ground.

Menaka walked as if in a dream to the outhouse. It was funny to see guards in their backyard. They stood guard outside a dilapidated door.

It was way past midnight and sleep had eluded her. Her head pounded as if someone was beating the insides with a mace.

Her mother had put on a brave front on learning the facts about her father's deceit. Menaka knew that she secretly went off to cry in the privacy of her room. However, her brother's presence served as a panacea for her mother. She busied herself with his affairs and spent the evening fussing over him. Menaka was left to cope with her feelings on her own.

She did not remember much of how she had got home from the outing with Ashoka. Just that Ashoka had dropped her home safely.

As Menaka approached the outhouse, she recognized Mandar standing amidst the guards. He looked at her with compassion.

'I want to see the mint,' she stated simply.

'I am sorry, that can't be allowed,' one of the guards said firmly.

'It's okay. I will escort her down myself,' said Mandar.

The leader reluctantly agreed. Menaka followed Mandar into the outhouse. The sacks of mud had been thrown aside to reveal a trapdoor. Mandar opened it and led the way, a lamp in his hand. At the end of the stairs, they entered a large room that probably extended all the way below their house. She sucked in her breath. The evidence was in front of her. She walked in tentatively, lightly touching the machines.

'Yes, they are real. It is not a dream.'

Her hand accidently pressed a lever that activated the machine with a clang. It set off in motion, in harmony with the rhythmic pounding of her head.

'All these years, the thumping sounds at night…they were right beneath my house.'

Menaka clutched her head with both her hands.

'It's too loud. I can't bear it,' she said in agony.

Mandar looked at her in alarm. 'Let's get out of here,' he said, taking her arm. He escorted her back to her house silently.

'Who gave the orders to arrest my father?' she asked, her gaze on Mandar.

He flinched.

'It was Ashoka.'

Aatreya Shah sat silently in the solitary confines of his prison cell. They had kept him away from the regular prison cells for some reason. He stared at the iron bars that let in some of the moonlight.

So my time is up, he thought calmly. *It was rewarding while it lasted*. He laughed mirthlessly and the cavernous room echoed his laughter, mocking him. That was before the pangs of guilt started emanating.

For the last four *ayanas*, he had nursed the plan of flooding the market with counterfeit coins. He had minted them regularly. Initially, he had put out some meagre amounts so that they had been largely undetected. It was only recently that he started to put them out in the market in a big way.

It was foolhardy of me, he thought now. His basic nature was that of calm decision-making. He had given in to impulsive action only recently.

Why? he thought, trying to analyse his own actions. *Why did I commit such suicidal actions recently?* The moment the shops hired coin examiners, he should have heeded the signals and curled like a centipede. Instead, what he had done was akin to a suicide mission. He had flooded the market with counterfeit coins at a steady pace. It had been an enjoyable exercise.

An open challenge to catch me…if you can, he thought wryly. *Maybe I wanted to be caught. Maybe I wanted to abort the whole game that was commenced by me. Maybe I am tired.* All of it was true.

I should have guessed why the prince was here. But such a young man! Who would have thought? he thought, bemused.

Aatreya ambled to the corner of the cell and poured himself a glass of water from the pot. It was cool and refreshing. Made of thick stone, the solitary cell allowed no external sound to seep through. But his thoughts – there was no barrier to stop them. He hardly ever recalled the time when he had been an idealistic young man in the Mauryan administration. That was an old Aatreya – an Aatreya he did not recognize anymore. But today he had all the time. He reminisced about the young man who had once been handsome, despite his pockmarked face.

Aatreya vied to perform his tasks better than anyone else and hoped to be the governor one day. He had passed all the tests that were required for him to be the governor of the city. He knew all the aspects of trade and commerce, as well as the civil aspects of the well-being of the citizens.

That morning his mother had applied turmeric on his forehead and given her blessings. On reaching the official quarters, the first thing he read was the welcome message put up outside: 'Takshashila welcomes Huma as the new governor.'

His jaw dropped.

'That oaf! He knows nothing about how to run the city.' Jealousy wound its tentacles around him firmly.

He has got the post due to his proximity to the chief queen, *thought Aatreya grimly. He felt immensely betrayed. The kind of betrayal a lover experiences when the partner turns to someone else, breaking all promises.*

He felt empty and hollow.

I gave you everything I had, *he thought, hurt and furious at the same time, thinking of the long sunsets and nights he had spent working tirelessly for Takshashila.*

'And this is the reward I get.'

He bent down and picked up a fistful of earth. The tighter he held, the more it slipped through his hand. He spoke to the leftover earth as if talking to a living entity, because that was what Takshashila was for him. That was how he thought of her, with her beautiful winding lanes, adorned with cultures of the world. He spat out the bitter bile that rose up his throat.

'So, blood wins over merit.'

Slowly, he walked to his desk. His hand reached out for the quill and ink. He calmly penned down an application for leave of 30 sunsets. That would give him enough time to gather his thoughts and think of his next steps. The next sunset, he embarked on a journey to Pataliputra to talk to the amatyas in charge of appointments. He rode day and night, paying no heed to the calls of his body to eat and sleep.

The reception was neutral, if not cold. They regretted to inform him that Huma was the choice of the emperor himself and to openly challenge that would be suicidal. He would report to Huma as of now.

Perhaps the long journey back to Takshashila gave him enough time to think about his situation as his anger had abated somewhat. Humour was his closest ally in bearing it. He was rewarded a few years later when the post of the Treasurer of Takshashila was offered to him. The reward came too late. By then Aatreya's values and notions of idealism for his country had changed. A plan to avenge the betrayal had already germinated.

Aatreya shook his head as if clearing out the old thoughts that had found a way into his consciousness after a long time.

He looked around in the confines of his prison cell. It was bare except for a bed, a pot of water and a small attached room for his daily ablutions.

Now what? he asked himself. The game was up and his choices were limited.

Now, I am tired of my own creation, he thought wryly. Maybe the innocents who had been put in prison for unwittingly submitting the counterfeits in taxes had brought about the change of heart. This unwitting outcome was never intended.

He thought of his gentle wife and son, and the daughter he had never learnt to love, and was suddenly filled with remorse.

I must resolve this, before they pay for my deeds, he thought with a twinge of guilt.

I must resolve this somehow.

30

Susima walked across the garden to the familiar ledge overlooking the sacred Ganga.

He touched the feet of the rajpurohit. '*Pranam,* Guruji,' he said respectfully.

The rajpurohit blessed him with both hands on his head. 'May you lead us to many more victories.'

Susima sat cross-legged facing the rajpurohit. This was their first meeting after the success of Kalinga.

'Ashoka has to die.'

Susima was taken aback. He stared at his mentor with astonishment in his eyes. Had he heard him correctly?

'Yes, you heard me correctly,' said the rajpurohit as if reading his thoughts.

I wished Ashoka to be dead a countless times. But now I don't like what I hear, thought Susima in a flash. For some inexplicable reason he felt uneasy with the suggestion. It was one thing to be a part of machinations against his younger half-brother. It was a different matter to discuss his death.

Susima covered up his dismay as quickly as it came. But the fleeting uneasiness had not gone unnoticed by the astute rajpurohit. Susima's hesitation angered him.

'You have become too conscientious, Prince. It may be an unintended side effect of my tutoring,' the rajpurohit said dryly. 'Let us not be swayed by useless emotions, losing sight of what we set out to do in the first place.' The rajpurohit's gaze bored into Susima's. 'You want the throne…and I want to see you on the throne. It is as simple as that,' he whispered.

Susima struggled to keep his face impassive. Something told him he must not reveal his innermost feelings. Yet, he could not accept this suggestion wholeheartedly.

'Maybe…maybe I am worthy of the throne even with Ashoka alive,' he said, making an attempt to dissuade the rajpurohit from his misintentions.

The rajpurohit seemed to be absorbed in his own thoughts and paid no heed to Susima's tepid protest. Deep down, Susima felt a sense of betrayal. Did his guruji not see him worthy of the throne, if Ashoka challenged it? Feeling a myriad of emotions, he felt let down by his mentor. A sense of morality that had crept into his subconscious, prevented him from being party to plots of assassinating his brother.

'Two foiled attempts,' muttered the rajpurohit seemingly to himself.

Did I hear him correctly? Susima pursed his lips, knowing his opposition had no credence at the moment. Despite that, he tried one last time.

'If Ashoka is killed, the blame will inevitably fall on us. The emperor only has to think of who will benfit the most by his death,' said Susima in an even tone.

'Don't worry. I have a scapegoat who will take the blame for it.'

The rajpurohit threw his head back and laughed raucously. Susima felt a shiver going down his spine.

The commander at Takshashila did not bat an eyelid when he was informed that Prince Ashoka would be taking charge. Ashoka's reputation preceded him. For one so young, he showed immense promise – this was what a colleague had told him. It would be interesting to see how he would manage the show.

Ashoka addressed the army at Takshashila. One-third of the Mauryan army was stationed here as this was close to the volatile borders of the Greek provinces. Even though there was an amicable agreement with the Greeks, Bindusara had taken the necessary precautions to protect his country.

All the four divisions were present. There was absolute silence. Many in the crowd had fought alongside Bindusara. It was a pleasing sight to see his son standing before them today.

'Today, I don't stand before you to lead you. I stand before you to salute you.' Ashoka bowed deeply before continuing. The crowd cheered loudly. 'I know that many amongst you have fought numerous battles for our country. I thank you for that. I thank you for protecting our borders from invaders. I thank you for supporting my father.' His eyes clouded as he continued. 'But sometimes the enemy is within. Within our own borders, our own countrymen, who choose to poison the very body that is their own. They may not have weapons but may be armed with something more dangerous – their deceitful intentions, eventually leading to rot and corruption.'

Ashoka looked around. All eyes were on him. He met their gaze steadily.

'Let us take an oath, that as Kshatriyas we will fight this enemy too – this foe that does not wield the weapons we are familiar with.'

In unison they shouted, 'WE TAKE THE OATH!'

Ashoka lounged in the plush divan in Huma's study, at his palatial home. Four guards stood outside the door, while

Angad and Chitrakoot stood behind the prince, their hands folded across their chests.

Huma wiped the perspiration off his forehead. He was sitting at his table in a high-backed chair. The tension within him was apparent to everyone present. The curls on his head that usually bobbed up and down were plastered to his forehead owing to profuse perspiration.

'So, what you are saying is that you knew nothing about what the treasurer was up to?' Ashoka asked.

'Not ex-xactly,'stammered Huma.

'You will have to be exact today,' Ashoka replied, smiling. 'In fact, this could be your last opportunity to be exact.'

He frowned as he looked at the painting of Buddha behind Huma's desk. The serene half closed eyes disconcerted him for some reason.

'Look, the easiest route for you is to be honest. This is all going where it rightfully belongs,' continued Ashoka, his eyes assessing the wealth on display. 'If you choose to withhold information, there will be consequences which may be uncomfortable for you to bear.' The threat in his voice was unmistakable.

'Well, I knew that Aatreya did have something to do with the coin…fraud. But I was not sure,' Huma said fearfully.

Outwardly, Ashoka appeared composed to Huma. It was only Angad and Chitrakoot who noticed the vein standing out on his forehead.

'Did you attempt to find out what it was?' Ashoka asked in an even voice.

Huma said nothing.

'Did you?' persisted Ashoka. It was important for him to ascertain whether Huma had or hadn't attempted any action. Huma pursed his lips in a stoic silence. Ashoka finally nodded to Angad and Chitrakoot. Chitrakoot walked up to the shelf on which a hand painted Chinese vase was kept. He picked it up and dropped it to the floor where it shattered into smithereens.

A rattled Huma looked at them.

'And so...this whole palace of wealth that you have accumulated will be destroyed piece by piece if you do not cooperate. And after that, it will be your turn,' Ashoka informed him.

'You dare not touch me, Prince. The emperor will not tolerate that.' Huma spat the words out.

Ashoka threw his head back and laughed. 'Do you see anyone here who will inform the emperor?' Ashoka leaned forward. 'And even if someone does, do you think I would restrain myself on that account?' whispered Ashoka.

The soft menace in his voice was chillingly apparent to Huma now.

'Do you think I would let anything...*anything* come in the way of finding out the truth?' Ashoka asked, his eyes blazing with emotion.

With one heave, Chitrakoot overturned a whole shelf.

Huma looked at him with fury. 'That was my souvenier collection!' he shrieked.

'You are right. It was...' said Chitrakoot, smiling at his own work of art. Shards of glass and pieces of metal and wood were strewn all over.

Ashoka sighed. 'I thought you would cooperate.'

He turned to Chitrakoot. 'I have to talk to the troops and will be back soon. You know what to do.'

Angad and Ashoka got up to leave. The last glimpse before Angad closed the door shut was of Chitrakoot rubbing his palms together in glee.

A scene of destruction awaited Ashoka when he got back. Every piece of furniture and object lay broken except for the chair that Huma sat on. Huma himself was whimpering, clutching his bloodied nose.

He looked at Ashoka through pain-filled eyes. 'I was not sure,' he wailed.

'Why didn't you try to find out?' Ashoka asked calmly.

'He was important to me. He…he did most of the work which left me with free time for my hobbies.'

'Hobbies…you mean gambling and collecting wealth?' Ashoka asked sarcastically. 'You disgust me, Huma. You deliberately chose to turn your face away. You have cost many people their honour and lives, just so that you could live, undisturbed, in your illusory world of wealth. As with all illusions, this too shall disintegrate and reveal the true face of reality,' Ashoka said quietly.

'As of now, I claim all the property you own. It now belongs to the Mauryan Empire. You are hereby removed from the post of governor for negligence of your duties. You will be taken to an undisclosed location, until I decide what to do with you.'

Poulak and Mandar, who were behind Ashoka, now went up to the disgraced governor and took him by both arms.

He shook himself free in defiance. 'You can't do this. When the emperor hears of this, you will be sorry,' ranted Huma.

Ashoka sighed. *How people overestimate the power of relationships. People hold on to them like they will exist forever. Barring a few, the rest are like a fistful of sand. They slowly slip out of your hand,* he thought. Even Bindusara would not spare Huma once he knew the depth of his negligence. Ashoka was sure of that.

Of course, Agramahisi Rakshita, would never forgive him as Huma was her cousin by blood. *She hates me anyway. Nothing will change as far as she is concerned,* thought Ashoka coldly.

Huma did not have a family. At least there was no burden on his mind as far as that aspect was concerned.

'Take him away. This is the last time I wish to set my eyes on him,' he told Poulak. Angad watched as a struggling and screaming Huma was dragged away mercilessly.

Ashoka walked up to the window. The palace grounds were surrounded by soldiers who were now under his command. He heard the commander walk in. Without turning back, he issued a quick order.

'Free all the prisoners held for cheating the treasury for submitting counterfeit coins.'

Ashoka waited for Menaka to come down the stairs. His concern for her had brought him to her house first thing in the morning.

Angad and Chitrakoot waited outside with the rest of the guards. The garden swarmed with soldiers guarding the mint, the place that symbolized Aatreya's treachery.

Menaka walked down tentatively.

Ashoka touched her cheeks lightly, noting the tell-tale dark circles under her eyes. 'Are you all right?'

'Yes,' was her monosyllabic reply. She forced a smile.

He noticed she was carrying her bag. 'Where are you going?' he asked.

'To the university. I have classes,' she replied evenly.

'Wouldn't it be prudent to rest for a couple of sunsets considering…' Ashoka was at a loss for words. He clenched his fist in frustration. He hated to see her this way. He realized she wished to engage herself in her usual routine. It probably offered a distraction from the morbid reality.

'Let me escort you,' he offered, anxious to prolong his moments with her. She nodded, a distant look on her face. They rode in uncomfortable silence.

He glanced at her face numerous times to get some clue about how she felt. For all his astuteness, he was at a loss as far as she was concerned. Her expressionless face did not betray anything. Desperately wanting to reach out to her, he thought of a hundred different ways to strike up a conversation, but she seemed to have formed a wall around herself.

Just before he was about to leave, she turned to him and said, 'I understand you had to do what you did.'

'You do? I am so glad to hear that,' Ashoka said in a relieved voice. 'I was worried that…'

'That I will blame you,' she finished the sentence for him. 'No. I don't blame you at all.' She paused. 'It's just that...I don't know,' she finished lamely. 'I don't feel too good about anything at the moment.'

He tried to understand her feelings. His prime concern now was for her well-being. He finally spoke. 'All right. Perhaps you need to be by yourself for some time. Maybe you should get back to your world of colours. Perhaps you need time... away from me,' he said with great difficulty.

With that Ashoka bowed deeply and hoisted himself up on his horse. Taking one last look at her, he said, 'Remember, I am only a summons away.'

Aatreya sat cross-legged in his cell, staring at the opening up on the wall. The gleaming rays of the sun filtered through, creating a patch of golden glow. He himself sat in the shadows, reflecting. His wife had come to visit but he had refused to see her.

His life seemed like a horse race to him now. He had almost won but midway realized this was not as rewarding as he had expected it to be and abandoned it.

I have done my duty as husband. I have provided well for my wife. He thought of the huge sums of money stashed away across the borders. It seemed like a preposterous plan to him now.

She will be fine with our son for company. Heartbroken but fine, he thought, knowing that she loved him more than he loved her. *But Menaka...*he scratched his chin as he thought of her.

It's too late to bridge the gap with her now. I am tired. Really tired, he thought, closing his eyes and lying still. Presently, he felt the steady slow hum of his blood flowing through his veins. It was peaceful to listen to his body instead of his mind for a change.

I need a new start, he thought.

Aatreya watched the small opening that sufficed as a window, to see the dusk set in. A small creature crept in through the opening, barely the length of his thumb. His interest piqued, he struggled to get up. He was fatigued as he was starving himself – he had been throwing his food in the small toilet. Walking unsteadily, he went closer to the tiny creature. It seemed to be the only thing alive in the cell at the moment. Aatreya frowned with the effort of focussing his gaze.

'Aha…a red scorpion!' he muttered, recognizing one of the deadliest creatures in this part of the world. The four pairs of legs moved nimbly across the floor. It was probably after some prey of its own. It ignored Aatreya.

Aatreya took off his gold chain and waved it in front of the deadly predator. It took the bait and held onto it by its pincers. The next moment he jubilantly wore the necklace back around his neck with the creature still hanging on. Before the scorpion could release its grip, Aatreya pressed it hard to his chest. In moments, he went into a world of peace and Nirvana. Perceiving the pressing to chest as a hostile act, the scorpion had dug its venomous sting into his chest. That was exactly the outcome that Aatreya desired. He released the creature and lay back on the mattress…waiting. Waiting in anticipation for the final moment of release. It would come soon. The poisonous sting was close to his heart and lungs.

Ashoka took the news of Aatreya's death with ambivalence. In a way, it saved him from making harsh decisions about the man. He had been procrastinating on what to do with him.

'Have the body returned to his family with respect.' Ashoka issued his orders in clipped tones.

Almost everyone present heard that statement with disbelief. A traitor to the country was denied the last rites so that his soul would not receive a place in the afterworld. It was unlike the ruthless Ashoka that they knew. Only his four close aides understood. It was Menaka he was thinking about. Even Ashoka was prepared to bend the rules in order to assuage her grief.

31

Ghataka walked the streets of Takshashila. The city enchanted him as it did other visitors. But he was here on work.

He took his work very seriously, and strove to do it with perfection. It was very much like a physician's work – exacting and detailed. Except that he was no physician. He was a trained assassin who accepted money for his services, a mercenary. He was not employed by the secret service of the administration of Pataliputra as rules and regulation stifled him. He himself had very few rules about his work: Getting his payment on time and not killing women. It was strange to have scruples in his line of work. But everyone was eccentric in some way.

I will break my own rule for the first time today, he thought apprehensively. *I have to execute a woman.* He had seen her from afar. Her youth and innocence made the task even more difficult for him. He had accepted the assignment to kill only one man. His lack of success in this weighed heavily on his mind. He had accepted the additional work purely to compensate for the failure – akin to how a shopkeeper throws in some free goods when the main item is defective.

I will do it at night, he decided. He had been instructed to make it look like suicide.

As he walked the streets, the posters of a circus caught his eye. *I can use the distraction,* he thought. He decided to go and attend it.

Ghataka enjoyed every moment of it and laughed as loudly as the children when the funny man fell on his buttocks. He even bought sweet laddus for children. They thought he was one of the kindest man they had ever met.

When the show was over, reality came flooding back. Steeling himself, he went over his meticulous plan.

Menaka stared vacantly at the scenery outside the window. She seemed to see it, yet not see anything. The funeral of her father was over. She had never really been outwardly fond of him. Yet, his death had made her feel hollow inside. Maybe it had to do with the dubious manner in which he died.

Ashoka was with her. He had called out to her a couple of times but she seemed oblivious to him.

'Are you all right?' he asked in a louder tone, his voice full of concern. On still receiving no response, he continued, 'I understand the death of a family member can be devastating.'

She faced him now. 'Do you…understand?' she asked mockingly.

Ashoka did not know what to make of that statement. He closed the gap between them in a swift motion and held her tightly. She stood limp, unresponding. It did not matter to Ashoka that she did not reciprocate. All he wanted to do was to comfort her as best as he could. He did not release her. She finally shook herself free.

'Was it necessary?' she asked.

'I don't understand,' Ashoka replied, stupefied.

'Was it necessary to kill him?' she repeated.

It then dawned upon Ashoka that she was referring to her father. He stood rooted to the spot, the accusation sinking in slowly.

'It was an accident. He was bitten by a red scorpion. I did not meet him even once after the arrest,' he said slowly, in his own defence.

'Yes, they say it was an accident,' Menaka mocked under her breath.

'I didn't do it,' Ashoka said in utter despair. His chest felt heavy, as if it bore a load on it.

'Maybe you didn't. Maybe you asked someone else to do the job. I understand that he was guilty. But did you have to kill him?' Menaka asked, a tear trickling down her face.

'How can you believe such a preposterous thing?' Ashoka asked, his voice quivering. But, it was as if his apparent involvement in the whole episode was etched on a rock.

'I think you should leave now,' Menaka said, her back to him.

'I won't leave until you say you believe I am innocent,' Ashoka protested desperately. 'I won't leave until...until you stop thinking such morbid thoughts. I am worried about you.'

'I still think you should leave,' she said in a tormented voice.

He stood stock-still, distraught at her behaviour. 'All right. Maybe you need some more time away from me. Maybe the distance will enable you to see the situation in more objectivity. But I did not do it.' In desperation, he asserted his innocence one last time before leaving the place. But it seemed to be a lost cause.

The next afternoon, Menaka espied Ashoka waiting for her at their usual spot at the university. He hadn't seen her as yet. Instinctively, she darted into one of the lanes.

Why is he here? I don't want to meet him. Not yet, thought Menaka wearily.

She peered through some bushes and saw him gazing in her direction.

Has he seen me? she thought, her heart thumping. She skulked in the shadows for a reasonable period of time before peering through the bushes again. He was nowhere to be seen.

But Ashoka had seen her dart away into the lane. The rejection cast a fresh pall of gloom over him.

She still blames me for her father's death, he thought bleakly. Raising his eyes to the heavens, he cried, 'Oh Aatreya, what a quandary you have put me in! Neither your life nor your death is acceptable to me.'

He skulked in a corner, making sure he was not visible. In due course, he followed Menaka home, unseen by her. Only when she was safely within the boundary of her house, did he leave.

Ashoka strode into his chambers after the morning drill, feeling hot and dehydrated. Pouring a glass full of water from the earthen vessel kept in the corner of his room, he gulped down the liquid thirstily

From the window, he gazed at the palace grounds which teemed with soldiers. It had virtually turned into an exercise stadium. Most of them were headed to the grounds at the back where huge cauldrons of porridge simmered, giving out an aromatic smoke.

A dip was what he needed. The water felt cool and soothing against his skin. He sat back with his eyes closed, trying to sort out his plan for the day. The only way he could stop thinking about Menaka was to immerse himself in tasks.

Ashoka scratched his thigh which was itchy. Instead of subsiding, the itchiness spread out further to his torso.

Am I being poisoned again? The fleeting thought crossed Ashoka's mind. *No, the same technique can't have been used twice. Angad always checks the water in the morning.*

A sense of uneasiness swept over him. He got out hurriedly and appraised his body critically.

'Yes, there is an outbreak,' he thought, looking at the angry red rashes. He yanked a rope that was connected to a bell outside his room.

In a fraction of a *kashta,* Chitrakoot and Angad dashed in.

'It seems to happening again.' Ashoka gave a mirthless laugh, pointing to his torso.

Angad inched close for a better look.

'No. It is not the same thing. This seems to be an internal reaction to something you have eaten. Like an allergy. I will have Menaka called right away.'

'No, stop! Don't call her. This does not warrant her coming down all the way. I feel fine apart from the itching and rashes.'

Angad was taken aback at the quick refusal.

'All right, I will apply some sandal paste for you to cool off,' he said.

Ashoka sat gulping his porridge along with some of his men. He felt like an observer to the boisterous conversation around him. The hardiness of the soldiers was obvious. They had seen many upheavals.

Wiping off a small bite that had mistakenly fallen on his chin, he tried to concentrate on the conversation.

I am getting clumsy, he thought.

He looked around at the melee. Most of the men had been in service for a long time and were old hands. His gaze travelled to his bowl of porridge and up his hand.

He suddenly noticed that his fingers were trembling, and almost instantly became aware of a mild numbness. Rising abruptly, he walked towards his chambers, Angad and Chitrakoot behind him. He held up his arm that was visibly shaking.

Losing no time, Angad felt his pulse. 'It's fine. Lie down for some time, Prince. It can't be poison for we are all eating the same food.'

'Thank you for ruling that out,' Ashoka replied with a hint of irritation. Inwardly, he felt relieved it was not a case of poisoning.

'Please have the division in-charge called up to my chambers for a discussion,' Ashoka said, determined to stick to his schedule for the day. The work would keep his mind off the distrurbing symptoms and, more importantly, from thoughts of Menaka.

Angad watched as Ashoka and some of the men hunched over the table, engaged in a discussion. A couple of *horas* had passed and the discussion showed no sign of abating. Angad noticed a trickle of perspiration flowing down Ashoka's back.

He handed over a piece of rough cloth to Ashoka who took it brusquely, barely looking up at him.

'You're welcome,' Angad muttered to himself.

It was only when everyone had departed that Ashoka stood up.

'You are perspiring profusely,' Angad remarked.

Chitrakoot poured a cupful of water and handed it over to Ashoka.

'It's boiling hot,' Ashoka muttered under his breath.

Angad and Chitrakoot exchanged a glance. The water from the earthen pot was cool and fresh. Angad took a small sip. Puzzled, he handed the cup over to Chitrakoot.

'It tastes like an astringent,' Chitrakoot said thoughtfully after taking a sip.

'Exactly! If it is what I suspect, then the prince needs an antidote quickly,' hissed Angad. He rushed to his room.

Ashoka held his hand out for the water that Chitrakoot had poured from a jug fetched from his own room. As Ashoka reached out to hold the cup, his fingers froze straight, unable to get a good grip.

I am losing my sense of coordination, thought Ashoka, as a sense of dread gripped him.

Chitrakoot felt Ashoka's head. He was burning up.

By now, Angad returned with a piece of tree bark. He ground the bark into a powder and added some honey and ghee to it.

'Here, Prince. Your fate and poison seem to be intricately linked,' he said, pouring a spoonful down his throat. 'Some more time and you would have been beyond recall.'

'Don't tell…anyone…' were Ashoka's last words as he slipped into nothingness.

For the next few *horas* Angad and Chitrakoot kept a close watch on him. Thankfully, his recovery was as rapid as his plunge towards death.

'I wonder how the water was poisoned with this Himalayan herb, *vatsanabha*,' Angad said aloud.

'The security here is less than perfect. The place is teeming with soldiers and help. It would have been an easy task for anyone,' declared Chitrakoot.

'So, what were the chances if you hadn't caught on?' asked Chitrakoot.

Angad gave him a grave look. 'It starts with loss of coordination. The next stages would have progressed to deformation, frothing, wasting of body and ultimately death.' The word 'death' hung ominously in the air.

'Whew…that was a close call,' Chitrakoot said finally.

Ashoka had recovered by the next morning. He thought little of the attempt on his life, his thoughts more preoccupied with Menaka. The unspoken outcome of the latest attempt was that the security was ramped up to a greater extent.

Poulak strode in to apprise Ashoka of some latest developments regarding the coins fraud. A shiny object, half covered by the rug on the floor, caught his eye. He reached for it and held it up for Ashoka to see.

'This may be the key to the mystery. Looks like the intruder was careless and left us a clue,' stated Poulak.

Ashoka put out his hand for the object. A thoughtful expression on his face, he went to his cupboard and dug out something from under his clothes.

An exact match! So, you were here, Menaka. Why? The answer to the question eluded him. Why didn't she meet him if she was here? The image of her darting into the lane flashed in front of his eyes. He stood staring at the anklets, a bleak expression on his face. Nothing made sense.

Poulak's shrewed mind understood the quandary that Ashoka was in. But he had seen unbelievable things happen in the past. Humans did behave in the most bizarre ways.

But I can't say this to Ashoka, he thought. *The suggestion of Menaka's involvement in the attempt on his life would kill him. But it is still my duty to tell him,* he decided.

Poulak took a deep breath. 'It could be…her,' he said haltingly.

Ashoka looked at him with hollow, red-rimmed eyes.

'How dare you propose such a ludicrous thing?' Ashoka said through clenched teeth. 'Get out of my sight!' he said, seething in fury.

Poulak closed his eyes for a brief second, taking in Ashoka's wrath towards him. He walked out of the room, head bowed, aware that he had hurt Ashoka deeply.

Ashoka looked at Angad, hoping he would deny Menaka's involvement. Angad had nothing to say. Nothing to comfort his prince.

'Strange are the mysteries of life,' was all he said. He knew that *vatsanabha* was commonly used in a number of Ayurvedic preparations after purification through cow's urine. The herb would be easily available to Menaka. But he decided not to tell Ashoka that.

Ghataka walked out of the gate. No one stopped him as he was dressed as a soldier and there were many around. He walked briskly for a *hora* until he reached a secluded farm. It was only when he entered the empty stable that he collapsed on the hay. His hands and legs shook violently in a reaction alien to him until now.

I should not have killed her. It will haunt me forever, he told himself, anguished. It was one thing to kill men for money and it was quite another to kill a woman.

Ashoka looked at Menaka's serene face as she lay on the bed in her room. It was as if she was in deep slumber, lost to the world…and him.

The house was silent except for the quiet sobbing of Menaka's mother who was downstairs in the hall. Ashoka was alone in the room with Menaka's lifeless body. His bodyguards had chosen to stay out, respecting that he would want to be alone with her.

He stood stock-still for a long time, unable to comprehend the truth that she was no more. Sometimes, the mind prefers to block things out. Especially when insanity seems just a fence across. Time stood still for him.

He walked tentatively towards her and shook her arm, softly at first and then violently, trying to shake her awake. But, Shiva had deserted him today.

Shiva, is this justice? He looked up beseechingly at the skies. But even the skies did not grant him their presence – he was left staring at the ceiling of the room.

The pure love he had found after many tribulations in life had been taken away from him even before he had begun to savour it. She had left him alone, without even a goodbye.

'How could you do this to me, Menaka? How could you leave me?' Anguish filled every pore of his being.

'They say you took your life. But I don't believe it for one *kashta*.' Ashoka took her hand in his and wept for the first time in his life. The life force seemed to drain out of him. He slumped to the floor sitting on his knees still holding her hand. It was cold to his touch.

He sat motionless for a long time. Angad came in a couple of *horas* later. Something told him that he must not intrude right now. He retreated, only to enter the room at dusk. Ashoka sat on a chair, his eyes vacant.

'We will have to take her…for the last rites,' Angad said haltingly.

Ashoka seemed more in control now. 'Yes…make arrangements. Before that, do your investigations. I am sure her life was taken and…' He seemed to struggle with the words. 'It has something to do with me. That's the price she has paid.'

Angad nodded and set to work. The poison seemed to have been shoved down her throat. Some of it had soiled her clothes. He examined her nails closely. There was someone's skin and blood there. Just a minute trace. There must have been a struggle.

Ashoka dragged himself out of the room, unable to watch someone he loved now reduced to a corpse being examined like an object.

He passed the hall where Menaka's mother sat with a little boy, a bewildered expression on his face. He locked his gaze with her and they had a silent exchange of understanding. He gesticulated to the little boy to come to him. The boy turned to his mother for permission. She nodded.

He walked hesitatingly towards Ashoka.

'What is your name, little one?' Ashoka asked kindly.

'Vikrama,' he said clearly.

'Would you like to come with me,' Ashoka asked gently.

'My mother needs me,' he said gravely.

'In time then!' Ashoka patted his head and strode out.

As the flames licked the skies, Ashoka's bodyguards looked around, waiting for him to appear at any moment. But he did not attend Menaka's funeral.

Immediately after the cremation he went away on his own, leaving his bodyguards in a quandary. If anything were to happen to him, they would face a death sentence. However, it was futile to try to follow him. They waited anxiously for him to return.

He emerged from his self-imposed exile after seven sunsets. To Angad, he appeared different. It wasn't just his outward appearance. Something seemed to have changed inside, in his soul.

He looks much older now, thought Chitrakoot, taking in the dirty stubble.

Poulak gave him a tight hug. 'I hope I am forgiven,' he whispered in his ear.

'Of course! It's of no consequence now,' Ashoka replied calmly.

Angad waved a greeting to him from afar. *He has accepted the facts,* he thought.

'Who will laugh at this tribal's goof-ups if you slink away like this,' Mandar chided him.

'I could do with a bath,' Ashoka said.

'Yes,' they all agreed, crinkling their noses. 'You smell awful,' declared Chitrakoot.

Ashoka smiled wanly. He had retreated to the forest for a week, preferring to sort out his raging emotions in the privacy that it accorded.

Poulak stood impatiently on the side while Ashoka finished sparring with a skilled veteran of the Mauryan army. The prince looked at him, miffed.

'Can't it wait?' he asked.

'No, it can't,' insisted Poulak. He glanced at the veteran soldier.

The soldier graciously bowed and left.

'There is a man who insists on an audience with you. He says that...he knows who killed Menaka,' Poulak said tremulously.

Ashoka's sword fell from his hand as it went limp. A few *kashtas* later he was in his chambers. He looked at the earthen pot in the corner but decided against having any water. It could wait. Chitrakoot and Angad stood behind him, their hands close to their swords.

Poulak and Mandar escorted a large, well-built man into Ashoka's chambers. It took a split *kashta* for Chitrakoot to recognize him. It was him all right – the one who had led the assault of the 'shower of stones'. Chitrakoot had only seen his eyes but that was enough. They were light brown like many. But, it was as if he could decipher nature's design within the eye balls.

Instinctively, Chitrakoot unsheathed his sword. The cue was enough for the others to be on alert too. Only Angad stayed unperturbed.

'Who are you and why are you here?' Ashoka asked coldly, steeling himself for the response.

'I have a confession to make,' Ghataka said. 'Oh…and you can be assured I will not harm anyone present. They can sheathe their weapons.'

'How should we know, murderer?' hissed Chitrakoot. 'You tried to bury us alive.' Chitrakoot turned to Ashoka. 'Prince, he is the one responsible for the shower of stones.'

Ashoka stiffened.

'Yes, I did try…but not today.' Ghataka looked into Ashoka's eyes unflinchingly.

Ashoka stared at him coldly. A sixth sense told him that what he was about to hear would impact him greatly.

'Get on with the confession, man,' Angad prodded him.

Ghataka sighed. 'I am a trained assassin. There are many like me who work for riches and wealth and not for loyalty to the country or glory. I am not a part of the famed secret band of spies. I have no mother or father. No sister or wife. There are no bonds. For bonds make one weak. That is how we are trained. I don't know where I was born or from where I originated. I live life like a nomad. But I kill for riches promised to me. Half of it goes to my teacher and I keep the rest. Sometimes kings employ us, not even daring to trust their own men in certain conditions.'

Ashoka's mind was in a whirlwind. This was an education to him.

'I was the one who led the assault of rocks down the hill to bury you alive. It was I who poisoned your drinking water with *vatsanabha*. But destiny protects you.'

Ashoka held up his hand as his men drew their weapons at the revelation. 'Who hired you?' he asked impatiently, seeing only the instrument in front of him – the hand who wielded it was still unknown.

'The rajpurohit from Pataliputra.'

Why did the revelation not surprise him? His only reaction was the twitch of a nerve on his head.

'Why?'

'I never ask why,' the man replied candidly.

There was an awkward silence.

'But that is not my confession,' he continued.

Ashoka felt a deep foreboding. A part of him wanted this man standing in front of him to stop…right now. He steeled himself. 'Continue.'

Ghataka's steady gaze belied the rest of his appearance. Ashoka noticed that his hands quivered with tension.

'I…killed the young woman,' he mumbled with difficulty, 'and made it look like she took her own life. I have never killed a woman before and never will again.'

Ashoka's four aides immediately grabbed Ghataka from all sides and pinned him to the floor. He did not resist. He seemed to welcome the pain inflicted on him.

Ashoka sat frozen in shock at the revelation. It was as if a thousand thunderstorms raged in his mind all at once.

'Take him away – this instant,' he snarled, afraid of what he might do to the man if he remained in his line of sight.

'It was a mistake,' Ghataka pleaded as they dragged him away. His cries were unheard.

32

'He has appointed Kichaka the new governor. It is as if he is running his own country in Takshashila. Did he even take your opinion, Raje? He has completely overruled you,' spat the rajpurohit.

'He has got to the bottom of the coin fraud, hasn't he? The mission we sent him on is accomplished,' stated Radheya quietly.

'He has gone beyond the mission, O Raje. He has freed the prisoners too,' the rajpurohit ranted, unfazed by Radheya's protests.

'And rightly so,' said Akila loyally.

'And what about Huma? Where has he disposed of him? Not a thought for the queen.'

Bindusara clenched his teeth. He was rattled with Ashoka for his disdain towards diplomacy and procedures.

'He still needs taming…he is like a tiger run amok.' The rajpurohit continued his tirade.

Akila locked his eyes with Radheya. Ashoka had completed his mission with flying colors but such disregard for the emperor would cost him.

Bindusara took a deep breath and said hoarsely, 'Mahamantri Radheya, I expect a list of candidates for the posts vacated in Takshashsila within one sunset. The people that I decide will be appointed as soon as possible.'

Bindusara paced the room. 'Send a message to Ashoka congratulating him on the success of his mission. Tell him he is to return to Pataliputra with immediate effect. Tell him…that his mother awaits his return,' said Bindusara, knowing that Ashoka would return from the other end of the earth for her.

In the last few sunsets Ashoka had made several visits to Ghataka, and each time, he came away with a haunted look. No one said anything but all wondered what transpired between them.

On one such visit, as Ashoka walked into the heavily guarded cell that housed Ghataka, he had resolved, *I will be merciful. After all, he surrendered and confessed to the crime himself.*

But now, as he faced the assassin yet again, a deep voice resonated through his entire being, 'But he murdered your beloved and she can never be with you now.'

'But that is what mercy is,' another voice said. 'To be able to forgive someone even if they have committed grave atrocities against you.'

'Ah…but Menaka died a cruel death…because of this demon,' the deep voice persisted with his side of the story.

'But who is the demon? Ghataka is just an instrument that was used by evil incarnate, the rajpurohit.'

The factions within himself battled incessantly.

Ghataka was chained up, his arms spread wide.

'I will be merciful,' decided Ashoka and turned away.

As with many nights in the past, that night too, the demons did not let Ashoka sleep. Like umbriferous trees, providing shade in winter months, the ogre like thoughts hovered over him, unwanted. He was ready before dawn the next day. It was apt, for the day brought about sweeping changes.

The messenger from Pataliputra read out a command to him signed by Bindusara himself. It was all in official langauge except the end that mentioned his mother – that was the only flicker of warmth.

He dismissed the messenger, asking him to refresh himself. His close companions waited silently for his commands.

'Make arrangements for my battalion to head back to Pataliputra. The march will be led by Poulak and Mandar.'

Poulak looked at him, startled.'What about you?'

'I will head back alone on a faster route with my bodyguards…and no one else.'

Mandar and Poulak nodded numbly. They were at a loss to understand him. They looked at his sunken eyes and strained face – he had aged even more in the last few sunsets.

'I will go to the prison one last time today,' Ashoka said grimly.

'I am not sure that is such a good idea,' said Angad. He knew, though, that the prince would do what he wanted.

Ashoka was ready to leave Takshashila.

I will never return to this city if I can help it, he thought. He galloped with his two bodyguards, preoccupied with his thoughts. The city that was usually so appealing now smelled of death and decay.

They rode to the prison that housed Ghataka. Ashoka held up his hand to signal that he wanted his bodyguards to accompany him no further.

Ghataka still hung to the wall in heavy iron chains. He opened his eyes with difficulty.

'O prince, ask your men to release me from the chains. I can't feel my arms anymore. Give me death if you wish. A clean death.'

'I will be merciful and keep you alive,' stated Ashoka without emotion.

Ghataka looked at Ashoka with unmasked hatred. 'I saw life ebb out of her bit by bit…as I strangled her,' he whispered.

Ashoka gulped. He felt as if he was there and it was him that Ghataka was strangulating. Taking several deep breaths, he tried to calm himself. But the *prana* refused to soothe him, and he felt dangerously close to losing his senses.

Angad, who was standing just outside the cell, was close enough to witness the exchange. He saw Ashoka grab the hilt of his sword for the final vengence. The assassin saw the colour of Ashoka's eyes change and laughed a raucous last laugh, knowing his release was close. He welcomed it with open arms.

Angad saw Ashoka lift his arm to deliver the final strike.

Just as well, he thought, knowing how the demons plagued Ashoka every night. They would hopefully die with the death of the assassin.

But instead of cutting off Ghataka's arms, Ashoka slowly put the sword back into the sheath.

'You will live, my friend, for you deserve no mercy. I shall spare your life. But you will live until your last sunsets in this cell, cut off from the sun and civilization. Your chained arms will ache to the point that if released, you will readily kill yourself. For now…you will live.'

Ashoka turned abruptly and left – never to return.

A shepherd sighted three young men riding like the wind, leaving a trail of dust behind them.

'I wonder where they are headed,' he said.

The wizened old man sitting under the tree, who seemed to know the secrets of nature, laughed. 'One amongst them will influence the destiny of many.'

Epilogue

Ashoka stood in the shadows of the magnificent 100-pillared hall. The pillars themselves were placed on an elevated timber platform. Despite the predominantly wooden architecture, each pillar held a torch, lending a seductive glow to the surroundings. The golden vines on the pillars came to life as the flames danced upon them. Megasthenes had been awed by the beauty of the architecture which surpassed even the palace of Ekbatana in Iran.

With vacant eyes, Ashoka watched Bindusara hand over the ancestral peacock-hilted sword of his grandfather to Susima. The veena played in the background.

A loud cheer emanated from the crowd for this symbolized Susima being declared the successor to the throne. A seat next to the throne lay vacant – it was where Ashoka was required to be seated as per protocol. However, he preferred the shadows. Darkness connected more with his inner being now. In a strange way, it masked the ugliness of his life, or whatever was left of it.

The silver birds on the golden vines of the pillars seemed to mock him, joining in the victory of his nemesis. All his life he had coveted the throne. And now, he felt nothing. Menaka's death had taken away something from him. The *prana* in him was slowly ebbing away as he himself walked on the torturous path towards death.

Someone whispered in his ear, 'It is not about death. It is about how alive you are before death.'

Author's Note

Some factual aspects of the Mauryan history have been modernized keeping in mind the current readership. For instance, the attire worn by the women was mainly the *antariya* and *uttariya*. The *antariya* was a strip of cloth attached to the *kayabandh* (sash) and tied around the waist in various styles. The *uttariya* was like a scarf usually taken over the shoulders or used to cover the head. Sometimes a *patka* – a decorative piece of cloth – was worn by tucking it into the *kayabandh*. The materials used were mainly cotton, silk, linen, wool and muslin.

The shields used by the Mauryan warriors were not large in size. However, *The Mauryan* uses larger ones in a war scene.

Very little is known about the methodology of minting coins, i.e. manually or through the use of machines. We have taken the liberty of depicting the usage of machines to aid storytelling.

Glossary

acharya	learned person
agramahisi	Chief Queen
aluka	yam
amatyas	ministers/councilors
angavastram	long rectangular piece of cloth meant to cover the torso
angula	finger
antahpura	royal residence
antariya	cloth used to cover the lower half of the body in various styles. This was secured by a sash called *kamarbandh*
aratnis	18 inches
arogyashala	hospital
artha	knowledge of the science of money and economics
astra	weapon
ayana	half a year
ayushyamaan bhava	May you have a long life
bhasmaarti	ash ritual
bhaya	fear
bherigosha	war drums
chaas	buttermilk
chakra	energy centre
dakshin	south
dakshina	donation
danda	six feet
devasthanam	temple
dharma	values
dwitiya	second

gaja	elephant
garuda	eagle
goruta	3.75 km
gurukul	school
havan	sacred fire
hora	hour
kama	temptation by flesh
kantha	short necklace
kashta	approx. 1.2 seconds
kosha	treasury
kshira	dish of boiled milk, rice and sugar
kulbrahmin	family priest
lingam	idol representing Lord Shiva
madhuparka	drink made my mixing honey, curd, ghee, milk and sugar
madira	alcohol
mahamantri	Chief Minister
mahapuja	a worship ritual that allows many devotees to simultaneously participate
margdarshak	who shows the way
mekhala	stringed hip belt
nadi	pulse
nalika	24 minutes
nayaka	chief constable
pada	infantry
patallok	hell
pinglanadi	subtle energy channel
prahar	approximately 2.5 to 3.5 hours long – the day and night have four *prahars* each
prana	breath
pranapati	doctor

pranayama	breathing techniques
prathma	first
rajpurohit	chief priest
rakhi	a thread that a sister ties to her brother's wrist as a symbol of their bond
ratha	chariot
sangwan	teak wood
samskaras	values
senapati	chief of defence
shakti	power
shishya	student
srotiya	the most learned
swarglok	heaven
thali	plate
tritiya	third
turanga	cavalry
upanyana	traditional ceremony where a guru accepts a person as his student
uttara	North
uttariya	An unstitched piece of cloth that can be worn in various ways – casually draped across the shoulders, as a turban, wound around the arms and draped across the back
vaidshala	hospital
vanaprastha	the last stage of life
vataka	fried rounds of fermented or ground pulses
vibhuti	sacred ash
yagna	ritual done in front of a sacred fire along with mantras
yuga	five years (in our story)

Acknowledgements

To all the bright flowers in my family who light up my life – Bhoomi, Arya and Leo.

Special thanks to Vikas Shahdadpuri, who promptly took time out from his hectic schedule for this project.

A warm thanks to the Hachette team, especially Prerna Vohra and Poulomi Chatterjee, for their patient editing and support.